TERENMORO

Terenmoro

Wolfcat
Rising Sun

Sam Ritchie

To Connor, my wolf brother who encouraged me to fight and made this whole world possible.

Prologue

"Wolves!"

Hasefi's head jerked up at the sudden cry and she quickly forgot her fatigue from trudging through the snow for so long. The other lynxes around her halted, their gazes peering through helmets and under hoods as they scanned the space around them. Hasefi saw that the tribe had come to a small, flat clearing surrounded by a short incline, but she knew this easier terrain wasn't what caught their attention.

The other lynxes were too big for Hasefi to look over so she tried crouching instead to peer between their legs and glimpsed something that made her fur spike with fear.

Large black shapes were appearing on the ridge ahead, staring down with fiery yellow eyes. They looked as if they were three times bigger than an adult lynx and their figures were complete shadows despite the bright sun sparkling off the snow.

Those are wolves? Hasefi wondered.

"Those aren't normal wolves!" a voice gasped and Hasefi turned her head to a lynx in heavy silver armor with a helmet that hid all but her green eyes. "Their fur is black!"

"Why are they all the way up here?" another questioned, this one wearing soft purple armor almost dark enough to be black.

"We're surrounded!" a third voice called. Sure enough, Hasefi saw that the terrifying figures were lined along the entirety of the ridges surrounding the lynxes. Her legs shook as the horrible wolven gazes burned down towards them. *What's happening?* she thought desperately. *Are they going to hurt us?* A bone-chilling howl rose into the air and the black shapes flowed down toward the lynxes at a speed that sent icy terror through Hasefi's entire body.

"Protect the Highchief!" a voice beside her commanded immediately. "Hykalof, hold the frontlines with my knight. Kilarsa, watch their backs. Tenarli and Dahsefer, fall to the middle with me and make sure nothing touches the Highchief!" Panic whirled through Hasefi as voices rose, melding into one indistinct sound as lynxes in various armors circled around her and the lynx who had spoken.

"Sefonis?" Hasefi squeaked, her heart racing. The lynx at her side lowered his head to hers, flipping open the silver and black helmet he wore so she could see his sandy brown face.

"I'm here, Hasefi," he told her gently. "Do not be afraid. Remember, it is our duty to protect you. We'll have these wolves fleeing with their tails between their legs before long."

Hasefi wanted to be comforted by her uncle's words, but she could see in his pale yellow eyes he was afraid.

More blood-chilling howls cut the air and Sefonis lowered his helmet over his face again. "Stay close to me," he told Hasefi. She immediately ducked under his legs and pressed against him until the spikes on her armor clanked against his plated chest.

"Mersaka!" a voice called. "We will summon a barrier to break their charge! Tribe, brace yourself!"

Sefonis crouched, forcing Hasefi to do the same. For a moment, she was lost in awe as the snow around the lynxes began to rise into the air and swirl around them. It went faster and faster, roaring with a wind that did not touch the lynxes.

However, she could hear the surprised and pained grunts and barks outside the barrier as the wolves were stopped.

"We're not strong enough to fight them," a lynx near Hasefi murmured. She was wearing tough brown armor and had wide, scared eyes.

"Aye, we are" Sefonis told her. "We've been caught off-guard, but that doesn't make us helpless. They're creatures, just like us. We just need to push them back and gain some ground." Sefonis raised his head and called out. "Guardians, expand the barrier and give us ground to work with!" There was no verbal response to Sefonis's words, but the barrier slowly began to move outwards. A ring of lynxes followed it, expanding the circle around Hasefi and Sefonis.

"Look out!" a lynx hissed.

Hasefi gasped as a long black muzzle appeared from the whirling snow, flashing giant fangs and piercing yellow eyes as it snapped at one of her tribemates. *They're so big,* Hasefi thought as she tucked further underneath her uncle. Her terror seemed to ripple through the other lynxes as screams rang in the air.

"They're getting through!"

"How is that possible?"

"Claw anything that breaks through the barrier!" Sefonis cried, his voice rising above the rest. "These wolves may be big, but even they can't fight the snow!" Screams turned to snarls as the lynxes met the wolves trying to push through the barrier. Claws and teeth flashed and the giant creatures were sent back into the blizzard with agonized howls. One wolf managed to get through fully, but the lynx in brown armor shouldered it back into the blizzard before it could find its balance.

"Don't worry, Highchief," the lynx gasped as her eyes met Hasefi's. "I won't let any of these funny-looking mutts touch a hair on your pelt."

"Kilarsa!" a scream tore its way to Hasefi's ears and she saw the blizzard waver. The thick smell of blood entered the air and she gagged.

"The barrier is weakening! I can't hold this alone!"

"My healer can lend you strength!" A lynx in white raced past and the blizzard thickened again. Despite their effort, Hasefi watched lynxes get pushed back as several wolves made it through the whirling snow. Snarls and shrieks rang painfully in her ears as full battle broke out within the circle.

A yowl nearby made Hasefi jump. Terror raked through her as she watched the brown-armored lynx get pushed into the ground, her throat crushed by a set of giant jaws. Hasefi wanted to scream, but she froze when the weight over her vanished. She watched as Sefonis sailed through the air and landed on the wolf's back. It let go of the other lynx to try and snap at him, but its teeth only banged against his armor as he shredded the wolf's back. The wolf let out a frustrated snarl and shook him off, but Hasefi's uncle twisted in the air and kicked out with his hind legs, sending the wolf howling helplessly into the barrier.

The moment Sefonis got up, he went to the injured lynx's side. Hasefi remained crouched where she was, staring in horror as hot blood melted the snow. The brown-armored lynx made a choking sound and jerked before going suddenly still. Her face was half buried in the snow, but one of her eyes stared blankly towards Hasefi.

Cold claws dug into Hasefi as realization swept over her. *She's dead. It killed her. She's dead.*

"Hasefi." Her uncle came to her, blocking her view of her dead tribemate, and nudged Hasefi, but she was rooted to the snow with shock. "Hasefi, look at me. Don't let fear take you. Hasefi!" Sefonis flipped open his helmet and Hasefi flinched, meeting his gaze.

"I don't want to die," she whispered.

"I won't let that happen," he growled. Another terrible cry sounded and Hasefi pressed her face against her uncle's chest, not wanting to listen to the anguished screams of her tribe any longer. "Be strong, Hasefi. Please."

"I can't," she whispered.

"They're getting in! There's too many! We—" the frantic warning ended in a shriek that clawed through Hasefi and the blizzard wavered again.

"Stars help us," Hasefi heard Sefonis whisper. She let out a whimper, which turned into a terrified squeal as Sefonis suddenly raced away. Hasefi was about to run toward him, but stopped when she realized he was charging towards a wolf with blood dripping from its jaws.

Her uncle rammed into its chest, sending it sprawling backwards. Then he leaped onto its flank and clawed into it, the armor on his claws gleaming dark with blood. The wolf thrashed, managing to get its hind legs under Sefonis and kick him off. Hasefi gasped as Sefonis hit the ground with a thud. When he didn't get up, she let out a wail, unable to bear the thought of him being dead, too.

A lynx clad in full armor as black as the wolves' fur darted into view. Like a shadow, the lynx swept underneath the wolf as it got up, clawing its stomach and kicking its front legs out. Spikes on the lynx's armor caught parts of the wolf and more blood melted the snow. The wolf stumbled forward and whipped its head around, but the lynx retaliated by smacking its cheek with armor-clad claws. The wolf shook its head and the lynx closed in, raking the wolf's throat open so a stream of dark blood spilled forth. The wolf slumped forward and, to Hasefi's relief, the blood-stained lynx went to Sefonis and helped him up.

"Thank you, Hykalof," Hasefi's uncle gasped.

"We cannot win," Hykalof said with a low growl.

"We have to try," Sefonis returned. "We need—"

"*You* need to take the Highchief and escape. Return to the Tribe."

"No, I won't—"

"You do not have a choice!" Hykalof hissed urgently. "We are beaten here. But if you leave now, we may be able to cover your escape. The Highchief must survive." Sefonis started to protest again, but another lynx came over, her eyes glowing beneath her dark hood.

"Sefonis, I can open up a path and have the blizzard follow you," she said quickly.

"Kilarsa, please—"

"I'm sorry, Sefonis," she cut him off, her voice strained. "But you know there's nothing else we can do here. This is our only option if we want any hope of saving the prophesized daughter." Hasefi crept up to her uncle's side, not understanding what they were saying.

"Sefonis, what's going to happen? What do they mean?" she squeaked. Sefonis looked down at her, but he was silent. Hasefi caught a glimpse of the fear in his eyes and it only made her more upset.

"Highchief." Kilarsa crouched in front of her and held Hasefi's gaze with her glowing one. "You and your uncle must go on. I will protect you."

"But, what about everyone else?" Hasefi protested weakly. She wanted to look around, but the screams and howls frightened her too badly.

"Just worry about you, tuft. That's all you need to do."

"We shouldn't have been beaten so easily!" Sefonis hissed suddenly. "We've fought their kind before. Why have the stars doomed us?"

"What's done is done, Emperor," Hykalof said firmly. "There is no time for anger and blame."

Kilarsa nodded in agreement, then straightened and held her face up to the sky. "I won't be able to hold this long, so you need to go. Now!"

Hasefi watched as the barrier before them opened up, revealing the ridge ahead. A heartbeat that felt like an eternity passed before Sefonis responded.

"I will not forget this," he whispered, his voice strained. Then Hasefi's uncle straightened and looked to her. "Stay close to me!" He bounded towards the opening and she followed, pumping her legs to keep close to his heels. As they passed through the opening, the blizzard remained at their backs, following them as they ran towards the steep ridge. "We need to climb," her uncle told her urgently. "I'll give you my shoulder." Without hesitation, Hasefi darted past and used his shoulder to scramble up the rocky ridge. She hesitated at the top, but Sefonis quickly urged her onwards. She took one last glance back just as a terrible shriek split the air and the blizzard fell away. Her insides flipped as she caught sight of Kilarsa being torn between two wolves. Hasefi opened her mouth to scream, but Sefonis shoved her forwards.

"Don't let them hear you," he told her as he ushered her through the snow. The terrible image remained in front of Hasefi's eyes even after she turned away, joined by the brown-clad lynx's dead stare. Shrieks of agony and terror ripped the air. The smell of blood clogged her nose. Hasefi felt nauseous and couldn't move her legs. But her uncle pushed her onwards as her mind raced.

Why is this happening to my tribe? They're dying. What do I do? I don't want to die!

"Look! On the ridge!" The strangely accented voice broke through Hasefi's trance and sent ice through her, but Sefonis continued to push her.

"Run, Hasefi," he hissed urgently. "Don't look back. You see the crack between those rocks? You can squeeze in and hide."

"But what about you?" she whimpered, terror making her voice tremble.

"Don't worry about me—just focus on you. Run!" He gave her a final shove and Hasefi raced through the snow, her gaze locked on the spot her uncle had pointed out. It didn't seem to get any closer with each leap and the screams of her tribe raged louder and louder in her head until they were deafening. The thought of the wolves closing in behind her kept her from looking back and she pushed harder towards safety.

Finally she ducked between the rocks, her armor scraping stone. She slumped to the ground, trying to catch her breath.

"Sefonis, I made it. We—" her words were cut off by a vicious yowl. Hasefi got into a crouch and peered out of the hole to where she watched her uncle barrel into a wolf. He raked his armored claws deep into its flank. It let out an agonized howl and thrashed, spattering the snow with dark blood.

A second wolf appeared over the ridge, but Sefonis used his hind legs to send it rolling back down. Hasefi began to hope that maybe her uncle could beat the terrifying monsters that were attacking them.

A third wolf, bigger than the others, stalked over the ridge. Sefonis swiped at it, but the wolf was quick. Her uncle started to lunge at its throat, then veered to the wolf's side, clawing its flank. The wolf made little reaction to the blow, turning to face her uncle and clamp its jaws in his shoulder. Even from where she hid, Hasefi could hear teeth crunching through the heavy armor. Sefonis let out a cry, jerking the wolf's head in an attempt to free himself. But the wolf was stronger and lifted Sefonis off the ground. Then it whipped its head side to side, shaking Sefonis until he went limp.

Hasefi wanted to shriek, but her uncle's warning went through her mind. Instead, she covered her face and ears, trying desperately to block out Sefonis's screams as the wolf tore him apart. *The wolves are killing everyone,* she thought. *I'm going to die, too.* She saw herself suffering the same fate as the other lynxes she watched die and she shivered fiercely. *I don't want to die!*

It felt like moons until silence had descended upon the clearing. Hasefi waited, trembling violently, for the wolves to find her and drag her out of her hiding spot.

"There was a pup," a deep voice sounded and Hasefi flinched, wrapping her paws tighter around her face. "Find it."

"It's just a pup," a second voice argued. "It won't survive long in these mountains."

"I don't care!" the first snapped and Hasefi clenched her jaws against a whimper. "Find it and kill it! No survivors!"

Hasefi shivered harder, feeling as if her fur would fall out with the force of it. Snow crunched as paws moved and she knew it would be mere heartbeats before they found her. She tried to push farther into her cramped hiding spot, but her tail was already pressed against stone. One thought echoed in her mind and it was all she could cling to as she waited helplessly for one of the wolves to figure out where she was.

I don't want to die.

Chapter One

Hasefi cried out and shot to her paws, expecting to see fiery yellow eyes and huge gleaming teeth at the entrance to her cave. When she was met with only bright light reflecting off the snow outside, she let out a relieved gasp and slumped against the rocky wall, waiting for her pounding heart to settle.

A nightmare, she thought. *Just another nightmare.* A shudder passed through her as the last memory of her tribe raged through her head, bringing with it a wave of grief and terror as she saw images of blood and darkness.

A darkness that still hunted her.

They're obsessed with finding me, she thought despairingly. *They won't rest. I don't know why.*

Hasefi looked again to the entrance of the cave she was sheltering in, knowing it was time to leave. But first, she had to clear her mind, otherwise she'd be as good as fresh meat for anything that got to her while she was distracted.

Closing her eyes, Hasefi forced the horrible memories in her head to change until all she saw were the faces of her tribemates. She began thinking of their names, a ritual she had started when she had begun to forget some of them since they had been lost about four moons ago. And the process usually helped her calm down after a difficult night.

"Sefonis," she whispered, seeing her uncle's sandy brown face and yellow eyes. A pang of despair threatened to spill a wave of emotion over her, so she quickly moved to the next name. "Kilarsa." The hooded lynx took his place. Hasefi flinched when the gifted lynx's image changed briefly to the one she had last seen of her. But she quickly forced the memory aside until she was able to see the lynx's kind green eyes smiling down at her.

"Hykalof," she continued, remembering the swift assassin. He had been quiet towards most of the tribe, but she remembered his friendliness towards her. She smiled until she saw him ripping through a wolf until it slumped lifeless in the snow.

"Dahsefer." A white clad lynx, gifted like Kilarsa, but with an expertise in healing instead of combat. "Mersaka." Another gifted. Hasefi couldn't entirely remember the ranks of her tribemates, but she recalled that this one was under Kilarsa's command. "Gelinaf." Hasefi frowned, trying to remember his face, but all she could see was dark armor. "Farsalim...." Her memory grew clouded. She couldn't see any more faces and couldn't remember any other names even though she knew there were others. She tried desperately to remember, but she knew she had little time to give.

I'm remembering less and less. I knew more names before...but I'm still forgetting them. Why is it so hard to remember? Hasefi opened her eyes and let out a defeated sigh. *I have to go.* Despite feeling almost worse than before she started her ritual, Hasefi prepared to leave.

She looked around the small cave she had taken shelter in for the past couple days. It had two entrances, the one she peered out being hardly big enough to fit even her, while the other was hidden among some fallen rocks she guessed were the result of an avalanche. She crept slowly to the first entrance of the cave, but stopped before she could peer out of it.

Taste the air. The words came as a whisper that barely tickled the tufts of her ears and she opened her mouth to take in a deep breath. *Be wary of predators and be ready for prey.* A face came to mind as more words floated to her ears, but she was unable to put a name to it. She pushed the thought aside and returned her attention out-wards. Taking a deep breath, she tasted the scents that floated into the cave, analyzing them until she determined the most threatening thing she could detect was stale hare.

Nevertheless, Hasefi double-checked the scents before she dared to peer out and glance around. *Spot everything you've scented,* the faint whispering continued. *Know where the breeze blows so you aren't caught off-guard by hidden smells. Watch the shadows.* There was a narrow clearing of snow surrounded by sheer rock-faces that threw half of it into shadow. The other half shone brightly with cold sun-light from above, forcing Hasefi to narrow her eyes. She spotted the tracks of the hare she scented which were already half-filled with snow, moving towards the right where the sun was rising. A very faint breeze blew in the same direction. Her attention went to the shadows in the closed area, trying to detect even the faintest hint of movement. She dared not move until the shadows had stretched a couple claw-widths across the snow.

Finally, Hasefi let her head leave the cover of her cave and she looked up. No warning words were whispered to her now. Instead, frantic images of strange, curved claws and large, fierce eyes entered her mind. As Hasefi scanned for danger, all she discovered was a bright blue sky with hardly a cloud in sight. Again, she remained still as she watched it, waiting for any sign of movement.

There was none.

With a deep breath, Hasefi carefully left her shelter and slunk into the shadows along the rocky wall. Her ears were pricked for any sudden sounds, especially voices. *At least the wolves are easy to avoid if I hear them in time,* she thought. *They're always complaining about having to hunt me. It's almost like they have minds of their own.* Hasefi didn't know why lynxes were different than the other creatures she had encountered, but she was still unsure how the minds of wolves were compared to her own. However, she wasn't curious enough to try and get close to learn more about them.

They had managed to get close to her, though, on many occasions and she'd overheard some of their words. She'd learnt that the wolves seemed to have a leader whom they called Sal and, as Hasefi continued to flee her hunters, she grew more confident that this 'Sal' was the same wolf that had killed her uncle. It was he who twisted her dreams along with the devastating images of her broken tribemates.

I have to keep following the rising sun, she quickly told herself, eager to push aside the horrible memories.

The terrain was often difficult, which helped slow down her hunters, but also forced her to take detours along her path towards where her tribe had been heading. Despite her difficulty in remembering her time before her tribe's end, once in a while she would experience a flood of memory. Through this, she recalled about a moon ago in a dream that her tribe had been following the rising sun. Whatever lay at the end of the path was supposed to be their home.

Hasefi wasn't sure if this was supposed to be a 'new' home or if her tribe's destination was the place they had originally come from. All she could dredge up from the scattered pieces of her memories was that her tribe had been on an important mission from the stars and it involved getting to the end of the rising sun's path.

And that was all that mattered now.

Hasefi forced aside any lingering thoughts and memories so she could ensure each step she took wouldn't be her last. Her eyes darted around warily, waiting for movement, and her mouth was parted so no scent went undetected. She became so focused on survival she almost forgot she was supposed to keep the sun in front of her. When it was midday and she didn't know if she was still following the right direction, Hasefi stopped at a twisted, gray bush hiding a split in a large boulder. It was enough to keep her hidden so she could rest her legs and wait for the sun to move into an ideal position.

Rubbing warmth back into her paws, Hasefi allowed thought into her mind again and studied the plant that was keeping her hidden from hungry eyes. *Sefonis once told me plants could be beautiful. How could this scraggly old thing ever be beautiful?* She snorted bitterly. *He said there were places in the world where it was warm, too. But I must have travelled the whole world by now. Maybe he was just telling me a story to hush me.* She started to push the thought aside, but her mind was beginning to sink into the memory of that night. She wanted to fight it so she wouldn't be distracted, but she couldn't help but welcome it into her empty heart. Giving in, she closed her eyes.

Hasefi opened her eyes and looked out of the large hole at the front of the cave her tribe was staying in. She'd barely closed her eyes for a heartbeat, but she knew she wouldn't be falling asleep anytime soon with the way the cold was making her shiver. Frustrated, she turned so she was facing her uncle who was curled around her. "Why is snow cold?" she asked him, trying to appear inquisitive even though she just wanted a solution to rid herself of the numbness in her paws and the snow clumps in her fur. Sefonis lifted his head and Hasefi saw the sympathy in his kind eyes.

"Because it is part of what makes snow, snow," he responded gently. Hasefi tried not to twist her face up at his strange answer, but she knew she'd failed when Sefonis chuckled.

"Is it everywhere?" she tried. He gave her a sympathetic purr and his armor began folding into itself until all that remained was his helmet. Then he took it off and curled tighter around her, his pale brown fur brushing her armor. "Wait, it's too cold to take your armor off," she protested even though she could already feel herself warming up.

"I'll be alright, wee lass," he assured her. After a moment of hesitation, Hasefi let herself relax into him. "And to your question, no. There are places where the ground is green with life and the sun warms the surface of any stone it touches." Hasefi's whiskers quivered the way they always did when her uncle was being silly. Only, she realized it wasn't humor sparkling in his eyes, but something she couldn't comprehend. She sat up so she could look directly at him.

"Really?" she asked with disbelief, unable to imagine the kind of place he described.

"The few plants we see up here are nothing compared to the trees and shrubs that layer some of the land," he told her.

Hasefi twitched her ears with confusion and frowned at her uncle, wondering if he was talking nonsense.

He laughed softly, his voice warm as he continued. "You will see one day, wee lass," he promised her. "There will be a day when your fur is warmed by the light of the sun."

Despite being unsure about his words, Hasefi curled up again, trying really hard to imagine the place he told her of. But she couldn't.

Hasefi kept her eyes closed for a few more heartbeats as she tried again to imagine this place, only to fail once more. With a defeated sigh, she opened her eyes and looked unhappily through the twisted branches to the snow outside.

It doesn't matter, she told herself before despair tried to drag her down. *Even if Sefonis's words were just a story, I have to finish my tribe's mission to find home. I need to follow the rising sun.*

Hasefi got up and, after checking that all was clear, continued her journey with the sun behind her. She came to a long, shallow rise that wound up the side of a peak before it broke off where a piece of the mountain had collapsed. There was a jump that she easily made onto wider ground, but it was covered in snow that brushed the fur on her belly, forcing her to slow down lest she slip off and plummet to the ground below.

No one would be here to help me if I got hurt, she thought not for the first time. A darkness crept into her at the thought, but she pushed it aside with practiced ease, knowing that even just acknowledging it could be as deadly as the jaws of a wolf.

Her path eventually began to slant down until she was in a narrow ravine between two steep rock-faces. A ledge above her kept her wary of predators that could stalk her from above, but also allowed her to take cover from others that didn't use ground to hunt.

I need to keep an eye out for lynxes, too, she reminded herself. *It wouldn't do me any good to pass right by this 'home' we were trying to find.*

The ravine widened out into a path that slowly rose back towards the sky. It opened out into a flat clearing that Hasefi hesitated to enter until she had ensured there were no threats awaiting her there.

However, the moment she stepped out, a small shadow passed over the ground and she leapt under the safety of a jagged boulder providing cover from the sky above.

Hasefi's gaze was glued to the ground and her ears were pricked, but there were no other signs of danger.

She poked her head out into the open and, with an eye on the sky, proceeded through the clearing, keeping her pace quick until she could jump onto a narrow ledge. It snaked along a sheer rock-face, the surface slippery and slanted. Hasefi flexed her claws, letting them scrape the ice beneath her paws in order to keep herself from slipping.

The path slowly straightened out and brought her to a summit where she could gaze across the countless other snowy summits that rose around her until clouds blocked her view or they blurred into gray and white on the distant horizon. The sight was discouraging, but, being used to it by now, she turned her gaze away from it and followed the summit she stood on along its top, hopping onto rocks when she could to keep her paws out of the cold snow and to prevent predators from using her tracks to find her.

When she began to descend down the shallow slope of the mountain, she came across a small hollow in the rock rising ahead of her. She debated staying for a few heartbeats to rest again, but a faint scent entered her mouth as a breeze rolled up the slope. It was a scent she hadn't caught in a few days and, instead of urging her to take cover in the hollow, it made her mouth water and her whiskers twitch with anticipation.

Prey.

Hasefi identified the direction it came from and crept down the slope. She kept herself wary in case she wasn't the only one to notice the enticing scent.

It's mountain goat, she thought. *I've only ever eaten goat when the hunters provided food for me. I haven't hunted them myself.* A prick of uncertainty made her hesitate. *I've gotten bigger these last few moons,* she thought. *And stronger. I might not have my armor anymore, but I'm faster and stealthier without it.*

She continued to move towards where the scent was coming from. It led her past the hollow and up an incline until she came across sets of hoofprints in the snow. *I can't remember when I ate last,* she thought, licking her lips. *I can't afford to ignore this. I can't outrun wolves if I'm weak with hunger.* Her belly tightened, reminding her how intensely painful hunger could be when sorely neglected.

I have to try.

Hasefi moved away from the hoofprints so she wouldn't accidentally stumble upon the prey and startle it. She used rocks jutting out of the ground and snow mounds as cover, taking advantage of how her gray and white fur blended with the environment.

The rise she climbed grew steeper until she had to hop from rocks and ledges to reach the top. The ground immediately flattened out, dipping slightly ahead to where Hasefi caught sight of white fur.

Hasefi pressed herself against the rock she was balancing on, flattening her ears to keep herself as invisible as possible.

There was a group of five goats surrounding a meager bush that was pushing its way into the air between two rocks. Feeling a little discouraged, Hasefi tasted the air, trying to find a scent that would give her hope. *Maybe there's an elder?* she hoped. *One that won't be able to keep up when they're on the move again?* Despite her thoughts, Hasefi knew that most—if not all—creatures didn't make it to old age.

One scent did catch her attention and she breathed in deeply, trying to determine what it was. To her surprise, the scent brought faint memories of her mother, even though Hasefi had no idea who she was.

One of them has kittens, she realized, straightening slightly so she could see a little more. *Where?* Her gaze landed on light fluffy fur within the herd and she felt another claw of disappointment.

Fallen stars, she thought with dismay, preparing herself to slink silently off the ledge. A sudden bleat caught her attention before she could move and she went rigid as two slightly older kittens came bounding out of the herd. Hasefi bunched her muscles to run, but realized the goat-kits were just chasing each other around. She watched as they bounded closer and closer to the opposite ledge, as if seeing which was braver than the other.

They're still bigger than me, she thought. *But if I could catch one off-guard, I might be able to kill it.* Her thoughts battled against each other, weighing the risks of attempting a catch and not. *Sure, they'll be stronger, even if they are lean. And I can't risk getting hurt, but I can't risk going hungry, either.* Her gaze slid to a boulder near where the goats were circling. *If I can get there, I could get close enough to pounce.* She looked towards where the herd was still crunching on the helpless bush. *I'll have to be quick.*

Hasefi waited until the goat-kits were farthest away from her, then she darted over the edge she was hiding behind and bounded silently towards the boulder. She tucked herself close to it, so focused she hardly noticed as the rock sucked the heat from her pelt.

She realized that, though the two goats were much smaller than the fully grown ones just a few paces away, they were bigger than she had initially thought. But she was becoming overwhelmed by the hunger twisting her belly and was already lost within her hunting instincts.

The goat-kits came together not far from where she hid, butting heads, their tiny horns clacking lightly every time they hit. One of the kits was getting pushed back towards her as it proved unable to hold off the other goat's attacks. Hasefi's claws flexed eagerly.

A grunt sounded from the herd and Hasefi nearly jumped out of her pelt. She watched the older goats warily as they shifted, waiting for them to turn and spot her. Their narrow hooves and sharp horns made her uneasy, but she was still determined to end the day with a kill.

Today has been pretty good, she pointed out to herself as the goats settled again. *Maybe it'll stay that way.* She quickly pushed aside her hope, reminding herself how dangerous it was to be distracted when she was hunting prey as lethal as some of the predators she hid from.

Hooves scraping on rock brought her attention back to the goat-kits and she watched with dismay and annoyance as one of them suddenly turned while the other followed. *Did it see me?* she wondered. *I shouldn't have let my fear distract me.*

Her thoughts were quickly brushed aside as the lead goat veered back towards the boulder, tossing its head as it ran in her direction. Hasefi tensed, her eyes widening with excitement as the goats grew nearer.

Come on, she thought. *Come play by this harmless boulder. Don't be shy....*

The goat turned just as it reached her cover, but it had come into her pouncing range and she was already in the air. She landed square on its shoulders and dug her claws and teeth into its neck. The goat jerked once, trying to get her off, but the motion caused it to slip onto its side. Hasefi put all of her weight on the goat's throat, keeping it pinned as it struggled.

Hasefi saw the second goat rear up in the corner of her eye, sending a wave of dread through her as she waited for it to crush her spine. But the goat-kit twisted at the last second, bleating fearfully as it ran towards the herd that was already turning at the distressed sounds of their young.

Before any of them could take a step towards her, Hasefi released her prey and jumped onto the boulder, facing the herd as it came to circle her kill. One of them charged ahead of the others, but stopped as soon as it reached the twitching goat-kit. Hasefi waited silently as the others joined, some of them throwing warning grunts at her while others nosed the goat mournfully as its movements weakened until they were no more.

One of the goats, the one that had charged, let out a loud cry and Hasefi tensed, prepared to leap off the boulder and run to safety. But the herd began moving away, leaving her and the dead goat-kit as they fled the dangerous area.

They don't want to face the scarier things that will be drawn in by the scent of blood, she thought. *And neither do I.*

The herd moved off towards the opposite ledge and followed a narrow path down. Hasefi waited until they were out of sight, then leapt down beside her kill and began devouring it.

Hasefi ate until her instincts screamed at her to leave the area. She was forced to follow the same path the goats had taken lest she run into something that was tracking her from the way she had come. However, she didn't have to go far before the rock widened and broke off in another direction.

The goats had followed the path farther down the mountain-side, but Hasefi followed the part that slanted in towards the rock-face, making the snow deeper on one side. She trudged through it, not wanting to risk herself on the slanted side that glistened with slippery ice.

Fortunately, it soon flattened out, leading her up a small peak. She scanned its rocky side for any signs of shelter and let out a relieved breath when she spotted a round tunnel.

Hasefi ensured there were no signs of other creatures within and quickly scouted through it to see if there were any other ways to get in. When she found it narrowed out to the point even she couldn't fit, she declared it a dead end and returned to the entrance where she began washing the evidence of her hunt from her fur.

A flicker of pride went through her and she couldn't help but dwell on it. *This is the biggest prey I've killed,* she thought. *And I got away practically unscathed.* She noticed a small wound on her shoulder where she guessed her struggling prey had gotten her with its hoof, but the bleeding had stopped before she was aware of it.

I did it, Sefonis, she thought without really meaning to. She smirked to herself, but her amusement faded when she could almost feel her uncle's presence with her. *Could you really be here?* she wondered, not for the first time, while pulling white fur from her claws. *I know you're with our ancestors now and I know the gifted sometimes talked to them and that they told us to follow the rising sun. And I know something has been helping me survive. But could it actually be you?* She waited for a moment, hoping she might get an answer. But she was met with silence. *I'm being foolish,* she told herself with a snort. *I can't dwell here any longer. Something might have picked up the scent of my blood.*

After ensuring her pelt was clean, Hasefi left the shelter of the tunnel to find somewhere safer to stay the night. The sun was dipping close to the mountain tops and she wondered if she should remain in the tunnel, but she decided it was too risky and she had already been daring enough that day.

Fortunately, it seemed the day had more fortune to offer and she came across a small cave entrance half buried in snow. She clawed at the snow until she could squeeze in, then replaced some of the snow that had fallen into the tunnel so she couldn't be easily followed. Then she turned to face the darkness that loomed just a few steps away.

The shadows will protect you. The words echoed in her mind, but she wasn't sure if they were from memories or from the strange voices that had been guiding her. *But they will protect others, too. They are as much your enemy as they are your ally.*

Is this place safe? she asked silently, moving through the narrow tunnel with her whiskers brushing the sides. *I can feel a breeze and the air is still fresh. Am I alone here?*

She soon found herself padding back into light as the tunnel opened up, revealing a wide cavern with an opening where the wall had collapsed across from her, leading out onto a thin ledge. Climbing onto it, Hasefi found she was surrounded by a sheer cliff, making it impossible for any creatures to get in, but also eliminating it as a safe way to get out. Back in the cavern, a small tunnel opened up to the right of the ledge. A quick investigation revealed an end within several paces of entering.

I only have one entrance, Hasefi thought as she returned to the cavern. *And snow is the only defense I have. It's too late to find anything else, so I'll just have to pray nothing traps me in here.*

Hasefi gave herself another quick wash, lapping up the water from the snow melting in her fur to sate her thirst. Then she sat where she could watch the fading light as the colder touch of the moon fell onto the mountains. In between a snowy rise and a jagged incline, she could spot several stars looking in towards her. *Could they be my tribe?* she wondered. *Or just some other ancestors watching over me?* Hasefi curled up tightly as she tried to retain some warmth.

No longer using every bit of her focus to survive, Hasefi's mind began to wander, letting in thoughts of her tribe. *How did we find places big enough to stay for the night?* she wondered. *This is one of the biggest caverns I've seen and we still wouldn't have fit in here, at least not comfortably. And food? How did we manage to find enough to keep going?*

With a defeated sigh, Hasefi let the thoughts melt away, knowing there would be no answer to them. She rubbed her paws and tucked them deep into her belly fur to savor the little heat she managed.

I don't think I remember what it's like to feel my paws, she half joked to herself. *If only I were gifted. Then I'd be able to make warmth like Dahsefer did.* She let herself imagine he was with her, using his magic to bring back feeling into her toes and ear-tips.

If I were gifted, her thoughts continued, *maybe finding this home the ancestors are leading me to would be easier.* Hasefi couldn't remember much about the gifted, but she did know she had been envious every time one of them used their abilities. *Maybe they aren't so great,* she thought with a sudden, strong stab of despondency. *It wasn't enough to keep us safe from wolves.* She tried to brush aside the thought, but without the necessity of being alert to her surroundings, her mind sank into the despair that followed her more closely than her own shadow.

How much longer do I have to keep going? I've been moving for longer than a moon. What if I missed it? What if I need to go back? What if something happened? There has to be other lynxes out there, right? I must have a mother and father somewhere. But where are they? Why weren't they with me?

Hasefi wrapped her paws around her head, the questions as painful as if some creature was yowling them directly into her ears.

I just have to keep moving, she tried to tell herself, but her despair was as relentless as it always was. *I'll just sleep. I'll feel better once I get some rest. Today was an eventful day.* Hasefi squeezed her eyes shut, willing her body to relax against the cold so she could sink away from the thoughts racking her mind. Fortunately, it wasn't long before her thoughts faded and she was able to escape into sleep.

Chapter Two

"I'm so tired...."

"I know, wee lass. But we have to keep moving."

Hasefi gave Sefonis a pleading look. "Can't we just rest for a little while?" she tried, wishing she were still small enough for him to carry her with ease through the snow. "Why don't we just stay in one of the caves we find?"

"Because they are not home," he told her, looking at her with sympathy.

"Then what is home?"

Sefonis looked ahead before responding. "I don't know," he admitted. "But that's where we're going. And the only way we'll get there is if we keep moving."

Hasefi frowned down at the snow as she broke through it. "How much longer?" she asked.

Sefonis let out an amused purr. "If you have the energy to pester me with questions, then you certainly have the energy to keep moving," he chuckled, giving her a gentle nudge.

Hasefi gave the muzzle of his helmet a playful swat before bounding ahead a couple paces. She wasn't satisfied with his responses, but she trusted him nonetheless. If he believed it, then it must be true.

It wasn't long before a new idea popped into her mind. She gave her uncle a side glance, wondering how to ask him another question without seeming like she was pestering.

"Sefonis?" she said nonchalantly.

"Yes, Hasefi?" he responded, giving her a knowing look.

"Why am I the only kitten?"

Sefonis didn't answer right away, instead looking ahead again to where the ground began to slope down. "Because you are special, wee lass."

"Special?" she asked excitedly. "Like...gifted?"

Sefonis gave her ear a gentle swipe. "No, silly. If you were gifted you would have a star on your chest."

"Then how am I special?" she pressed.

"Because the ancestors chose you for an important destiny."

"Really?" Hasefi bounced forward a few steps so she could stop and ponder her uncle's words. I'm chosen? By the ancestors? "What am I going to do?"

"Only the ancestors know that," he told her.

"Then how can it be my destiny? Don't I have to know, too?" she pointed out to her uncle, pawing the tuft of fur sticking out underneath his helmet as he walked by.

"I am just a knight, wee lass. The magic in the stars is beyond me."

Hasefi realized her uncle was looking tired—maybe even annoyed—so she decided to cheer him up a little.

"What if I get powers?" she began, catching up to his side again. "If I do, I'll give myself bigger paws like you have so I don't sink in the snow so much." To her delight, Sefonis chuckled.

"You'd be tripping over yourself if you had paws like these." He stopped to lift one paw and shake the snow off of it.

Hasefi squeaked as her face was spattered with half-melted snow. "Hey!" she laughed, running up ahead again. Another question came to her mind and she waited for Sefonis to catch up. "How do you know I was chosen by the ancestors?" she asked carefully, hoping she wouldn't make him upset again. "Did they tell you?"

"No, wee lass," Sefonis told her, giving her cheek an affectionate nuzzle. "They told your mother."

"My mother?" Hasefi frowned as Sefonis's warm breath on her fur suddenly vanished. She lifted her head to find out where he had gone, only to remember she was in a cave her uncle had never set paw in.

Depressed, she lowered her head back onto her paws and closed her eyes, trying to recall the dream-memory so she could return to her uncle's side. She had begun to doze off when something tickled the tufts of fur on her ears and she jerked her head up, staring towards the tunnel leading out of the cavern.

Hasefi waited, trying to figure out what the sound had been. She was still for what felt like days until she began to wonder if it had been a dream-sound. Getting to her paws, she caught more faint sounds, but she still couldn't identify what they were—if anything. Her tail twitched restlessly as she waited again. Finally, she dismissed the sound as the wind whistling through the mountains.

The sound came again and she quickly realized it wasn't the wind's voice she heard. The words were indiscernible, but Hasefi could recognize the smooth accent of wolven speech in a heartbeat.

Wolves! Hasefi tried to control the panic that was building up within her. *I haven't seen any signs of them for almost a quarter moon! How have they suddenly appeared?* She drew in a quick breath, then followed it with another longer one. *They could be a long way away,* she reasoned, her fur flattening somewhat. *Sounds carry far on the wind.* She peeked towards the entrance, but quickly drew her head back. *I can't take any chances.*

Hasefi hurried over to the part of the wall that had caved in. It was still dark, but the first rays of sunlight were beginning to pierce the sky. She climbed out onto the ledge outside and looked at the ground below. It was covered in soft snow, but the drop was at least twenty full-grown lynxes down.

Injury can mean death in a place as harsh as this. The warning was one she'd heard often from the helpful whispers, but instead of shying away from the risk she was considering, she clawed the rock apprehensively.

The wolves will find me if I leave through the other way. My scent, my prints—something will lead them right here! It's why they're even out there in the first place! She hesitated. *Right?*

Going against all of her instincts, Hasefi moved back into the cave, her ears perked. The voices were still faint, but she was beginning to make out words. After a few heartbeats, she could hear their conversation.

"…blood. She's been here recently." Hasefi flinched and looked to her shoulder. It hadn't started bleeding again, but she figured wolves' noses were keener than she thought. *Broken stars!*

"If we finally catch this lynx-pup, it'll feel like the weight of a mountain slipping off my shoulders," a second voice added with a groan. *There's two of them,* she thought. *I could try sneaking around them, but I don't know how far away they are.*

"I sure hope we catch her," the first wolf responded. "If we return empty-pawed after picking up her trail again, Sal will have our tails."

"We don't have to tell him we found her trail," the second pointed out.

"He'll smell her on us. I swear by the shadows he could pick up her scent anywhere. But does *he* hunt her? No."

"If you two would stop whining like a pair of pups, then maybe we'll actually have a chance of finding her." A third voice, deep with age and seething with menace, caused a chill to run down Hasefi's spine. *Okay, I don't want to risk being seen.* Hasefi returned to the ledge and stared fearfully down. *I have to jump.* She shuffled nervously, unable to urge her paws to step off. *Come on, I don't have much time! Don't let fear take you.*

"Hey, I think I see prints!" The wolf's voice echoed down the tunnel and Hasefi's fear of being caught overpowered her fear of injuring herself. She dropped off the ledge and aimed her paws at the ground, clenching her jaw so she didn't yowl.

The snow was deep, softening Hasefi's fall. Relief flooded through her as she felt nothing more than a little winded. When she recovered, she fought her way through the snow, thankful for her wide paws that kept her from sinking further and getting stuck in the deep snow, until she could pull herself onto a tumble of rocks and scurry off in the opposite direction of the wolves.

Hasefi fled, following twisting trails to confuse her hunters and trying to stay aware of her surroundings in case a new danger presented itself. When her legs throbbed and her chest ached from gasping, she found a crevice to squeeze into so she could recover. Her senses remained alert in case the wolves still managed to track her down.

All they would have to do is dig their way into the cave, she thought. *Then they'd see that I jumped out. I can't stay here.* Her breaths still labored, Hasefi started to leave the crevice. A shadow darted across the ground and she bit down a frustrated hiss. Glancing up, she narrowed her eyes against the sun and saw a small black dot circling above her.

Broken stars! she snapped silently. *I hate monster-birds. If I had wings, I'd be hunting* them!

Hasefi backed into the crevice again, watching the ground as the shadow danced across it every few heartbeats. Eventually, the shadow stopped appearing, but she continued to wait until she was sure the bird had given up to find easier prey.

She hurried out of her crevice, expecting to hear wolven voices or their vicious howls at any moment. But only the cold breeze hummed past her ears and she resumed putting distance between her and her hunters.

I'm going away from the sun, she permitted herself to think when she was satisfied she had gained some ground on the wolves. *But I can't risk getting caught. Then I'll never finish my tribe's mission.* For a brief moment, helplessness lurked dangerously at the edge of her mind, but she quickly brushed it aside, focusing again on her surroundings so she didn't accidentally walk into the waiting jaws of some predator.

Hasefi quickly came to a halt as a piercing cry cut the air. Her head snapped up and she caught a glimpse of a shape diving through the sky above her, disappearing behind a narrow peak to her right.

Another one? she thought with frustration and a flash of fear. *Or maybe it's the same one. I might be in its territory. At least it seems distracted by something else.* Darting close to a steep rise that veered away from where the bird had flown, Hasefi remained alert, scanning the air for any signs of danger.

This is a pretty barren area, Hasefi thought nervously as her eyes flickered over the relatively flat ground ahead. She clambered down a shallow slope before she stood at the edge of the small clearing. Two cliff-faces rose on her sides with another jutting out ahead, breaking the clearing into two different paths. One led down, the slope steep enough for the snow to fall away and reveal rocks jutting away from the mountainside. The other continued ahead with a curved wall of rock leaning over it. It twisted off so she couldn't see where it led.

Hasefi followed the twisting path to her right since it gave her some cover from the bird in case it flew by. Unfortunately, she soon found that it fell off at a dead end. She only looked for a heartbeat or two before turning, the view she caught presenting a horizon revealing nothing she hadn't already seen before. *Are you sure there's more out there?* she asked Sefonis as she moved back to the clearing so she could follow the other way out. *I don't understand how the world can be so big and yet have nothing of what you described to me.* She found herself once again doubting his words, wondering if he had been describing a fantasy world to keep her distracted from the cold. *Everything else he ever told me was always real. He wouldn't make something up, would he?*

Hasefi made it to the slope and began jumping down from rock to rock until she reached the mound of snow at the bottom. She jumped over it to a shallower patch of snow and continued on.

Eventually, when her legs ached from moving for so long, she allowed herself to slump against a tall rock that twisted out of the ground and connected to the bulging mountainside a few pawsteps away.

I guess I can't expect to have two *good days,* Hasefi thought as she closed her eyes. *I just wish those wolves hadn't shown up. I let them catch me off-guard. I should have known better.* She forced her eyes open again, knowing her hunters could appear just as suddenly as they had that morning. *And there's still a monster-bird nearby. Does it ever end?*

I just need to gather my strength again, she thought sternly before she could fall into despair. *I ate yesterday, so it won't take so long.* She let her eyes close again. *I'll just wait a few heartbeats.*

When Hasefi opened her eyes again, she was horrified to find that the sky was darkening. She shot to her paws and looked around in alarm.

What happened? She looked up and saw the light of the sun glaring around a mountain peak. *Why is it so low? I didn't fall asleep! Did I?*

Hasefi ran ahead, looking around in bewilderment and terror. *I am the luckiest lynx in the world,* she thought. Every shadow and sound made her jump and she grew more panicked as the night crept closer. *I can't stay out here much longer. I need to find somewhere to stay.*

When Hasefi couldn't stand being out in the dark any longer, she slunk towards a huge rock formation that made her think of a giant lynx's ear. She entered the small curved clearing within it and pressed herself against the wall. Cold claws ran through her fur, threatening to curl deeper into her bones. *What if it's too cold tonight?* she thought. *It seems to be getting warmer and the sun stays out longer, but it's still so cold. I can't believe I fell asleep. With wolves around? What's wrong with me?* She was a little surprised she hadn't heard any faint warnings whispered to her, but she was also still trying to figure out if the voices were even real or not.

I need to try and get some sleep tonight so I can move again tomorrow. I haven't been able to follow the sun, so I'll have to try and make up for it. She let out a small sigh and buried her nose in her fur. It took a while, but she eventually managed to fall into an uncomfortable sleep.

When she woke the next day, she felt as if she had hardly slept a heartbeat. Wariness had woken her multiple times and her body was frozen. She had to rub warmth back into her legs before she could use them and even then she was still stiff.

How long can I keep going like this? she thought as her despair broke through. She squeezed her eyes shut and let out a growl. *I have to keep going,* she told herself. *This mission is all I have.*

Hasefi continued along her path as the sun moved along its own. She was relieved to find there were no signs of the wolves. Or any other predators, for that matter.

When the sun reached its peak, Hasefi tucked herself into a narrow crack along the ground so she could conserve some of her strength. Then she was on the move again, following a curving path towards a summit that led directly towards the horizon where the sun rose. She paused on the top to peer around, willing any sign to appear to show that she was close to the end of her journey. But there was nothing.

Keep going, Hasefi, a voice whispered to her, causing her ears to twitch in surprise.

I will, she responded. *Am I close?* Her words were unanswered, but she had assumed they would be. With a determined nod, she scurried down from the summit until she was walking along a narrow snowy path that wound between two rock-faces. It slanted down and opened up into a short ravine. At the bottom, a scent caught her attention.

Hare? she thought with excitement. Even though she was still fairly satisfied from her meal the day before yesterday, Hasefi couldn't help but try and find which direction the hare was in. *If I can have a meal of hare today, I will be the happiest lynx ever.* She had to stifle a purr as she remembered the first time she had tried some. It had been the tastiest thing she'd ever eaten and she would always ask the hunters to bring her one when they went out.

"Tenarli," she whispered quietly as the name came to mind. *She would always bring me hare if the hunters managed to catch one.* A faint scuffing sound like claws against snow pushed the memory aside and Hasefi focused on finding her prey. *Where is it?* A tiny cry sounded and Hasefi watched as a blur of white flashed a few paces away, fleeing out of the short ravine. Hasefi's ears flicked back in irritation.

So much for that, she thought. *But I should get out of here, in case it wasn't me that scared it.* Hasefi followed the hare's path out onto a somewhat flat stretch of snow. Instead of continuing along the hare's prints, Hasefi found a thin rock ledge she could leap onto and follow to keep from leaving prints. It brought her higher up the side of a cliff until it was too steep to follow and she had to leap onto a new ledge jutting out below her. The path was rough, but didn't rise so steeply. Feeling fairly secure, she allowed herself to sit down and acknowledge the disappointment that was growing within her after missing the hare.

I haven't had fresh hare for moons, she thought irritably. *And it's one of the few animals that aren't bigger than me. Not anymore, at least.*

Don't let one mistake ruin your day. The voice that entered her mind was Kilarsa's, echoing a memory from moons ago. *If you do, then you'll never give yourself the chance to grow better.* Hasefi relaxed as her tribemate's comforting words soothed her. She smiled with an ache in her chest, wishing the gifted lynx was there to add just a little bit of magical warmth to help ease her disappointment.

She never let me give up, no matter how difficult our journey got. I don't think I would have learned how to hunt if it weren't for her encouragement. And now look at me! I caught a mountain goat on my own.

Even if it was a little young, an amused voice said.

Hasefi snorted. *It was still twice my size,* she argued, her whiskers quivering. The voice didn't return, but she was nevertheless satisfied with knowing that something—whatever they may be—was still watching over her.

Movement caught Hasefi's eye and she watched in bewilderment as the hare shot past below her. Instinct caused her to look down from where it had come and she felt her heart flutter with terror as three black shapes moved swiftly across the snow.

Panicked, Hasefi crouched on the ledge, hoping the wolves wouldn't see her. *How are they here? Sunblind hare! Why did it have to lead the wolves here of all places?* Hasefi knew that if the hare had nowhere to run but back the way it had already been frightened, it was unlikely she would have better fortune trying to escape the wolves.

They're distracted. I need to hurry. Hasefi forced her paws into action and hurried along the ledge. She saw a place ahead where she could jump across the ground below and possibly escape on the other side, but she couldn't tell if it was a dead end.

If it is and they see me when I jump, then I'm trapped. Hasefi crouched at the edge, trying to determine if dropping down and running the way the wolves came would be wiser.

"Lynx!" a bark sounded and Hasefi's fur spiked with fear. "Above!" Howls rang through the air as the wolves kicked up snow, abandoning their pursuit of the hare and charging towards Hasefi. Her decision made, she bunched her legs under her and leaped.

A terrified cry left her jaws as she realized she had misjudged the distance. Her forepaws landed on the edge while her hind legs dangled in open air.

"You're dead meat, lynx!" one of the wolves snarled. Hasefi managed to hook her rear claws to the rock, but they kept slipping every time she tried to pull herself up.

"Sal is going to tear you apart like he did to the rest of your group!"

"There's nowhere to go, little pup!"

Hasefi's struggling grew more frantic as she felt her foreclaws slipping. *Don't let go, don't let go!* she thought desperately. *Please don't let go!*

The sound of snapping jaws and the faint disturbance of air near her hind legs gave her a burst of strength that let her scrabble up onto the ledge. She let out a relieved breath and peered down at the wolves.

"Go!" one barked at the others and they disappeared the way they had come. The wolf glared up at Hasefi and bared its teeth. "You can't run forever!"

"Neither can you, mutt!" she spat. *At least, I hope not.* Without waiting for a response, Hasefi whirled around and followed the trail, praying it didn't end abruptly.

To her relief, the walls sloped down and the path opened up into a steep ridge that led towards a broad summit. Hasefi was panting when she finally reached the top, but she felt secure when she collapsed in the snow to catch her breath.

That feeling evaporated as the savage howls and barks of wolves sounded. Hasefi shot to her paws and peered down the steep slope she had come from. To her utter dismay, two of the wolves were slowly scrambling up the mountainside to where she stood, quickly joined by the third.

I thought wolves were terrible climbers! she thought. As if her thoughts were as powerful as a gifted's, one of the wolves slipped and tumbled down the slope.

"Tef!" one of the wolves cried after it. Then it looked back to Hasefi. "You'll pay for that, you slippery lynx!"

The remaining two wolves clambered higher and higher. Hasefi looked around, trying to find a way to escape. But one side of the summit ended in a sheer fall and if she tried to climb down the way she had come, the wolves would meet her.

What do I do? What do I do?! She paced the edge, trying to find an angle she could use to avoid the wolves. *Maybe the others will fall before they reach the top,* she thought. She watched the wolves hopefully for a moment, but their loathing snarls and determined gazes were uninterrupted by loose rock or snow.

Wait. Hasefi looked around until her gaze landed on a small boulder just within reach of her paws below her. *What if I made an avalanche?* Hasefi crouched and carefully reached a paw towards the boulder. She tried to push on it, but it wouldn't move. *There's nothing blocking it,* she thought, briefly getting up to see why it wouldn't move. *It must be too heavy. Maybe if I try jumping on it....* Hasefi crouched before the boulder again, preparing to leap. The wolves weren't far, so she knew if her plan didn't work, she was indeed dead meat.

"What are you doing, lynx?" one of the wolves snapped. Hasefi realized there was fear in its amber gaze. "You can't stop us!"

"I hope you're wrong," she murmured. Then, with a deep breath, she leapt at the boulder, smacking it as hard as she could with her paws. She felt a surge of strength ripple through her when her paws made contact and the boulder shifted immediately. It slid, shaking the mountain as it moved, and Hasefi turned to jump back onto solid ground. Frightened yelps sounded as her paws sank into the snow and she smirked with satisfaction.

That's right, you mangy—

"Oof!" Hasefi's paws slid out from under her and she landed on her flank as the snow beneath her fell away. She tried to scramble to her paws before she went with it, but her claws found no hold. With a terrified yowl, Hasefi went over the side of the mountain after the boulder she had knocked down.

Pain lashed through her every time she hit rock. Snow blinded and choked her. Hasefi thrashed wildly, trying to stop her fall. Every heartbeat that passed seemed to be her last as she waited to hit something big enough to knock the life out of her.

Sefonis, help! she screamed silently. *I don't want to die!*

Hasefi gasped as she hit something that stopped her abruptly and she went limp, dazed by the violent fall. Her body shuddered with pain and she was helpless for a moment as her hind legs were battered with snow and rock. When she was able to recover enough to move, she pulled her lower half in before it could drag her back with the avalanche. She watched it rush past, burying any signs of the wolves ever being there.

By the stars, what did I do? She got shakily to her paws and gave the pillar of rock she was leaning against a grateful look.

The ground shook harder and Hasefi jerked her head up the side of the mountain where more snow had been shaken loose. *I need to move.* She limped away from the avalanche, narrowly avoiding being swept up as more snow and rock fell towards the pillar that had saved her life.

She moved farther from the avalanche until she could hardly feel it beneath her pads. Then she collapsed against a ridge, trying to catch her breath.

My whole body hurts, Hasefi thought, trying and failing to check herself over. *I can hardly breathe.* She slumped to the ground despite her instincts telling her to keep moving.

"Sefonis," she whispered. "I don't know if I can keep going. The wolves keep getting closer and I don't know if I can keep staring death in the face like this." She didn't get a response and she let out a whimper. *Maybe it would just be better if I joined them.* Despite the thought, she forced herself to her paws and continued walking.

If I had a piece of prey for every time I almost died, I would never go hungry again. She snorted softly. *I must have shaken that whole mountain. There's no way those wolves made it out. But how in all the stars did I?*

Hasefi's legs gave out suddenly and she collapsed into the snow. She tried to drag herself through it, but cold quickly drained the strength from her body and she went limp. Red spread through the snow around her and she wondered if the avalanche did more damage than she thought.

Maybe I'll just rest here for a moment, she thought. *Nothing will be around after an avalanche, right? Maybe I'll wake up and everything will be fine. Like yesterday. Or maybe I'll see my tribe....* Hasefi started letting her eyes close. The ground seemed to sink away from her and darkness slowly filled her vision. Blood and snow entered her mouth and she choked, her eyes opening fully.

What? she thought frantically as she realized the ground *was* sinking beneath her. *I'm not even near a slope! How is this happening?* Hasefi clawed desperately at the snow to keep from falling into it, but her claws couldn't find a grip. The snow swallowed her, dragging her into empty air where claws of darkness wrapped around her. Then they closed and slammed her into unconsciousness.

Chapter Three

Pain throbbed through every hair on Hasefi's pelt as she woke. The most prominent, however, was the agony in her leg which was stuck beneath her flank.

Where am I? she thought, too dazed to open her eyes. *What happened?* The feeling of her claws slipping through snow as it swallowed her entered her pounding head and she let out a low moan. *Oh.*

She forced open her eyes and was met with mostly darkness. Fear flickered through her as she couldn't make out whether or not the pit she had fallen into was wide open, or if the walls were a mere pace or two away.

Death can lurk in any shadow, the warning words echoed in her mind and her heart started to pound.

Don't let fear take you, Sefonis's words joined the others and she closed her eyes, drawing in slow breaths to try and calm herself down.

I use tunnels and caves all the time, she thought. *This is no different.* When she felt calmer, Hasefi tried to lift her head, but pain shuddered through her and she gave up quickly. *Okay, I don't need to get up.* She opened her mouth slightly and tasted the air. It was mostly stale, thick with the scent of blood, but she could detect a faint breeze that she figured was from above. Her eyes slid over so she could just make out the faint outline of a long hole above her where the dark, cloud-filled sky rendered the moonlight almost invisible. *I'm such a sunblind kit,* she scolded herself. *I knew snow could hide pits like this. I should have been more careful!* A weak sigh left her jaws. *I have to try and get out.*

Hasefi tried moving again, but her body responded with the same torment. Her left foreleg was the worst, but she couldn't move her head to look at it. *What do I do?* she thought helplessly. *If I don't get out of here soon, I'll either freeze to death or some predator will find me.* Hasefi shuddered as a worse thought entered her mind. *Or the wolves.* She couldn't bear to think of what would happen if the wolves came across her helpless like this.

If I hadn't been cheating death for the last four moons, I would be astonished by how I'm still alive. She looked up again. *If it's nighttime, then I've been out all day...or much longer.*

After another failed attempt to get up, Hasefi had nothing else to do but sink into her own thoughts. *I just need to let myself recover,* she told herself. *I did just survive an avalanche, after all. Some rest will help.*

Overwhelmed with pain and exhaustion, it was easy to slip into unconsciousness. However, cold and hunger prodded cruelly at her, waking her up what felt like every few heartbeats. She fought for sleep until the dull light of the hindered moon retreated so the stronger light of the sun could break through the clouds and reveal more of the pit she lay in. The light helped her feel more alert and she tried looking around again.

I still can't see the sides, she thought as she squinted at the darkness looming around her. *But I can see me.*

Hasefi managed to lift her head and get a better look at the state she was in. She was sprawled within a small mound of snow, her hide hardly even warm enough to melt the snow that partially buried her. She tried to shake it off, but lifting her head alone was already difficult.

Her gaze moved to the foreleg that was trapped underneath her. She couldn't roll off of it because just the thought of doing so made the pain immensely worse, but she could tell it was bent at an unnatural angle. *It's broken,* she thought, recalling a time when one of her tribemates had fallen off a ledge and down the side of a cliff. Fortunately, they were able to reach him, but Hasefi had glimpsed one of his hind legs twisted beneath his robes with the bone sticking out before Sefonis averted her eyes. *At least he had other gifted to help him,* she thought, wincing at the dried blood caking her fur and staining the snow around her. *I don't think mine broke like that, but I'm still utterly helpless.* She lowered her head back to the snow, barely noticing the cold as it numbed her cheek. *If there's another entrance, I'm as good as prey.* She let out a breath, stirring the snow in front of her nose.

Is this it? she thought suddenly. *Am I going to die? I can hardly feel my body and what I can feel hurts. Is this what dying is like?* She felt fear as she explored the idea, her tribe's death as vivid in her mind as the day it had happened, but she found a dark hope swelling eagerly within her. *Is it over?*

It can't be, she thought quickly. *I have to finish my mission. I need to follow the rising sun. I can't let my tribe down.* Yet, despite her desperate thoughts, she couldn't find the strength to even think of how to escape. A dangerous claw of despair curled into her chest.

I've already failed, haven't I? she thought, imagining Sefonis before her. *That's why I'm here, isn't it? I've already failed.* Her thoughts were met with cold silence and she closed her eyes in defeat. *I don't want to die,* she admitted. *But I'm not sure I want to live, either. I need your help, Sefonis. What do I do?*

Silence.

Maybe dying doesn't have to be so bad. Maybe it'll be like falling asleep. Hasefi flinched as she watched her tribe die again, her mind playing out the events carved into her mind. *I can't imagine what it felt like for them. I just hope the pain went away when they did. Will it go away for me? Where would I go? Will I go to my tribe? Will we be with our ancestors? What if they don't want me because I failed? What if I don't go anywhere?* Fear rippled through her again and she whimpered. All she wanted was the comfort of her uncle's warm fur and his soothing tongue.

I can't do this anymore, she thought. *I've been following the rising sun longer than my tribe did. I don't even know if my tribe or the ancestors are watching over me or if I've been imagining them this whole time. What if I've been alone? What if there's no point to continuing?*

A weak bout of whimpering shook her flanks, only making the pain she felt worse. "I'm scared," she whimpered. "I don't want to die here. I don't want to be alone. Please, Sefonis, I need you. Why did you have to go?" Forgetting about the cold and pain she felt, Hasefi sank into her grief. It opened wide like the jaws of a giant creature and swallowed her whole, forcing her into a darkness she couldn't escape from. A darkness she wasn't sure she wanted to escape from.

"Look ahead! We have reached the Broken Peak!" Kilarsa's voice roused Hasefi and she tried to peer around to see what the gifted was talking about. The tribe was in a wide valley filled with snow too deep for Hasefi to walk in. Despite that, her uncle lowered her into it. She started to protest, but when she lifted her head and looked up the sloping path ahead, she quickly forgot about her cold paws.

She'd seen it in the distance—Kilarsa kept reminding her it would show the tribe which way home was, but she never thought anything could be so big.

It was a mountain bigger than any of the others they'd seen, but it had somehow split almost in half. The giant crack ran through the mountain in a jagged line until it reached the end of the valley, providing a path right through the Broken Peak.

The two points at the top leaned away from each other, one shorter than the other. They were so high up that Hasefi had to tilt her head all the way back to see them.

"This is it?" A lynx with white robes and a white band beneath his ears leaned towards one wearing similar apparel with a hood.

"Almost," the hooded lynx responded. "The Broken Peak is only half the journey."

"Regardless, perhaps we should stay for a while," Sefonis spoke. Hasefi watched her uncle as he swapped a glance with the white-hooded lynx, then approached Kilarsa and the fully-armored Hykalof. She felt a prick of envy for their armor, wishing she had something like that to protect her from the cold, but she was told she wasn't strong enough to wear her own yet.

"You look cold, Highchief," the hooded lynx murmured, approaching her. Did he read my mind? Hasefi wondered. She gave him a shrug, still distracted by what was happening.

"We're home?" she asked him.

"No, dear kitten. But we are close. Do you remember your prophecy?" Hasefi paused, trying to remember what the other lynxes had said countless times before. But her mind was filled with snow. She shook her head slowly.

"I'm sorry," she told him.

"You don't need to apologize," he comforted. "Here, I will remind you while you warm up." He crouched in front of her, pushed back his hood, and looked to the snow rising up to her shoulders. Hasefi watched with awe as his orange eyes began to glow. Then he parted his jaws and an orange mist trickled from his mouth.

The mist danced around Hasefi, passing through the snow around her and melting it until she was standing freely in an oval. Then the light moved to her, spreading through her fur and warming her up.

"Thank you," she purred.

"My pleasure, dear lass." His eyes still glowing, the hooded lynx sat up. "Half a moon ago, your mother was visited by our ancestors and was told a prophecy. Do you remember that?"

Hasefi narrowed her eyes in thought. "I remember you telling me. And Sefonis. And...the others." Her whiskers twitched with embarrassment, knowing the lynx she couldn't even remember the name of probably thought she was dumb for always forgetting. But he offered her a sympathetic purr.

"There's no need to be ashamed, Hasefi. You are still young and you have travelled far for one of your age." Hasefi felt a little bit of pride at his words. "They told her 'the first Heir to the Highchief will lead a destiny beyond the river.'"

Hasefi's ears twitched with curiosity. "That's me?" she asked and the hooded lynx nodded. "But Kilarsa said the Broken Peak would show the way. How does she know? Did the ancestors visit her, too?"

He shook his head. "No, but they visited one like her. He is an Elder like her, gifted by the ancestors. He told her the Broken Peak would lead the way."

Hasefi peered past him to see the mountain, but she couldn't find anything that stood out. "How does a mountain show the way?" She noticed the lynx's eyes flicker and the light warming her cooled for a heartbeat. Then it returned and the lynx looked towards where Hasefi's uncle and the others were talking.

"That is for her to find out," he told Hasefi. She wasn't satisfied with his answer, but before she could speak, the ground started to shake.

"Dahsefer, what is that?" the other white-clad lynx came over to them, looking around nervously.

"Avalanche." It was Sefonis who spoke, returning to them with Kilarsa and Hykalof close behind. "We'd better brace ourselves—this valley is the perfect place for one to come down."

"I'd better lend my strength to the other gifted," the hooded lynx, Dahsefer, told Hasefi. She nodded, understanding. The light from his eyes faded and the warmth around her with it. But she was too distracted by the sudden wariness the other lynxes were displaying to notice.

"What's happening?" she squeaked to her uncle.

"Nothing we can't handle," he told her. "The snow is just feeling a bit restless—it'll pass soon."

Hasefi opened her mouth to respond, but the shaking in the ground suddenly turned into a deafening cracking and she instinctively flattened herself against the snow.

"The mountain! It's falling!"

Hasefi's eyes darted up to where she could see the divided top of the Broken Peak. To her terror, the shorter side was slowly sliding away from the other, bringing with it rock and snow.

Sefonis stepped into the little area Dahsefer had melted for Hasefi and crouched protectively over her. She pressed her paws against her ears, the sound of the mountain falling ear-splitting.

Why is the mountain falling? *she wondered frantically.* Is it going to hurt us? *The ground shook harder and she dug her hind claws deep into the snow.*

After what felt like days, the ground began to settle and the thunderous crashing had faded to a low rumble. Hasefi dared look up when she felt Sefonis move and was relieved to find the other lynxes looking fine.

"The mountain fell away from us," Hykalof stated, jerking his chin toward Hasefi's right. She saw that only part of the mountain had collapsed and the Broken Peak still bore two halves. "But it could have loosened nearby snow and rocks. We may yet be in danger."

"Hykalof is right," Sefonis agreed. "Kilarsa and Dahsefer, you and your gifted remain alert in case anything else happens."

"We will," Dahsefer responded. His gaze moved to Kilarsa who was staring in the direction Hykalof had indicated.

"Kilarsa?" Sefonis murmured. "Is everything alright?"

The gifted lynx turned her head, her eyes glowing in a way different from how a gifted's normally did. "The Broken Peak has shown us the way," she breathed. She looked away again, her eyes narrowing against the sunlight, before continuing. "The rising sun will lead us home."

Hasefi's eyes slid open, Kilarsa's voice echoing through her head. *Home,* she thought. *Am I home?* She looked around, but her surroundings confused her. The echoing in her head seemed to be reverberating through the darkness around her, getting louder and louder. She felt the ground shaking again until a deafening crack resounded through the air, but as a voice that reminded her where she was.

"Lynx!"

Wolf, she though with immediate dread. *They've found me.*

"Lynx! Wake up!"

Hasefi's eyes slid up to where the light was partly blocked above her. A black face with a long muzzle and yellow eyes pointed down towards her. Its teeth flashed in the bright light as it opened its jaws to call out again. "Lynx! Your eyes are open—you're alive! Thank the moon!"

He can't be one of the wolves from the avalanche. More must have come when the others didn't return. But that means...how long have I been here?

"Lynx, can you hear me?"

"Of course I can hear you—that's the whole point of barking obnoxiously, isn't it?" she snapped, wondering if he could smell her fear-scent. *Is he going to kill me? He seems glad I'm alive. The other wolves mentioned Sal wanted me for himself. But why? I'm just some lynx!*

"Can you move?"

Hasefi glared up at the wolf.

"I'm not going to come out just so you can take me away," she hissed. "You'll have to get me yourself." There was confusion in the wolf's expression and he paced the length of the hole a few times before settling again. "What, too afraid to come down and fetch me?" she sneered.

"It wouldn't do either of us any good if we both got stuck."

"Mostly you, because you'd lose your eyes pretty quickly, I figure." The wolf flinched and Hasefi felt some of the fear that was making her heart pound fade. *He's smaller than some of the other wolves. Is he alone? Usually they travel in twos or threes. Where are the others? Could they be getting Sal?* The idea of being found so helpless by their leader sent a shiver of icy terror through her. *Why does Sal want me dead so badly? Is he upset that I managed to escape? What will he do if he does get me?* The thought was too horrifying for her to dwell on. *Maybe if I'm lucky, I'll die before he does.*

When Hasefi looked up towards the wolf, she found that he had disappeared. *There's no way I can try and escape. Even if I found a way out, he or some other wolf is probably keeping watch.*

Hasefi tried to move, but her limbs barely responded to her. Dismay rippled through her and she let out a defeated breath. *I'm going to end up just like my tribe.* She went limp and closed her eyes.

"Lynx?"

Hasefi flinched at the wolf's voice, then glared angrily up at him. "Think I'll die before Sal gets here? Did he threaten to tear you apart, too?" she taunted. The wolf seemed affected by her words and she felt a tiny sliver of satisfaction.

"I really hope that doesn't happen," he responded. "Just…try to stay awake, okay? I won't be long." Before Hasefi could snap another retort, he vanished. Her defiance quickly faded into defeat again and she went limp with exhaustion.

Before, I was trying so hard to live and escape the wolves. Now, I'm still trying to escape them, but I'm trying to die instead. The memory of what the wolves had done to her tribe played in front of her yet again, every image she had seen just as vivid. She also saw the giant wolf that had killed her uncle, still certain it was Sal.

Suffering the same fate as her tribemates was the worst thing she could think of. The wolves' giant fangs and burning eyes never left her alone, even when she thought she had managed to lose her hunters for a time.

Is there a way to fall into death like falling asleep? she wondered. *That wouldn't be so bad then, right? But my tribe fought so hard to keep me alive. Would they understand I had no choice if I was able to explain it to them? Surely they don't want me to face the same fate if I don't have to.* Receiving no direction and not knowing what else to do, Hasefi tried to relax as if she were sleeping for the night, but her pounding heart and the throbbing pain she felt kept bringing her back. Eventually she let out a frustrated whimper and her eyes flickered open. *Sefonis, please.*

Trapped and hopeless, Hasefi watched the light change within the pit until it dimmed into faint moonlight. Her will darkened with it until dangerous thoughts touched her mind like a careful lick over a wound, giving her glimpses of how she could escape into death. Sometimes she thought she had found the courage to follow them, only to realize she hadn't twitched a muscle. Despair only clawed deeper until Hasefi was sure her chest had been torn open to spill out onto the snow.

"Look, wee lass." Sefonis's voice suddenly filled her head, speaking words she had heard him say before. *"Do you see the stars? Those are our ancestors watching over us. Even when you can't see them, they can always see you."* Instead of comforting her, Hasefi felt guilty and she couldn't look through the crack above to see if there were any stars visible through it.

"I don't see the point in fighting anymore," she told the air around her. "Even if I somehow made it out of here and past the wolves, what's stopping something like this from happening again?" A tiny flicker of anger let her eyes slide up and she saw a single star peering back at her. "If you're really watching over me, then why won't you help me? You keep telling me all these things…but now you're silent." Her anger strengthened and her claws twitched. "If you're watching over me, then why did you let my tribe die in the first place?" The only response she got was a slight whisper from the breeze that swept by above and she deflated. "I'm sorry."

"It's okay."

Hasefi twitched with surprise as the wolf's voice floated down, then she twisted her face with hatred. "I wasn't talking to you, mutt," she growled.

"Then who?"

"Can you just let me die in peace, please?"

The wolf disappeared and Hasefi frowned, wondering if he was actually obeying. *Huh. That was easy.* She closed her eyes, wondering if she could convince the wolf she was actually dead if he came back.

Something landed on her and she cried out, expecting to see the wolf on top of her about to sink his giant fangs into her throat. Instead, she watched as the limp body of a hare slid off of her and down the mound until it stopped just within reach of her claws.

"Sorry," the wolf called. "I didn't mean to hit you."

"Am I just a part of your prey pile now?" she hissed with fury and humiliation.

"What? Wolves don't eat lynxes."

"No, you just tear them apart until there's nothing left but fur and blood!" Hasefi watched as the wolf visibly recoiled, looking sick. She narrowed her eyes. *What's his problem?*

"Why do you keep saying things like that?" he asked her.

Hasefi narrowed her eyes further. "Like what?" she snapped.

"Like...scary, bloody, violent things!"

Hasefi snorted. "Because that's how you live, isn't it?" she sneered.

"There is no moon I would ever do something like that under!" he protested, looking genuinely shocked. Confusion started to weave its way through Hasefi's fear and anger and she began wondering if perhaps there was something she was missing.

"What do you want, then?" she asked, forcing herself to sound somewhat calmer.

"To help," he told her.

"Why?"

"Why wouldn't I?" he responded, looking confused.

"Because I'm a lynx and you're a wolf."

"I don't see why that has to mean anything," he murmured, glancing away.

Hasefi stared at him, utterly bewildered. *Who in the stars is this wolf? Maybe he's...got a softer mind?*

"You should eat," he told her. "You need to keep your strength up."

"Why?"

"So you can get out," he explained.

Hasefi narrowed her eyes as a thought entered her mind. *What if he's trying to fool me? What if he's trying to get me out on my own so he doesn't have to risk himself?* Hasefi bared her teeth. "Forget it, wolf. I'm not going anywhere."

"Please—"

"Leave me alone, you irritating long-snout!"

The wolf's jaws slowly closed and he backed away until Hasefi couldn't see him anymore. Instead of feeling relieved that he was gone, she found herself a little disappointed. It seemed ridiculous and she tried to dismiss the feeling, but for some reason she couldn't. *He's a wolf,* she told herself sternly. *Wolves don't care about anything. He's just pretending. It's not real.*

Her stomach tightened, bringing her attention back to the hare lying near her claws. *I won't eat,* she thought determinedly. *Especially not some wolf's lousy prey.* Yet she couldn't help but lick her lips as the sweet scent of prey-blood drifted to her nose. Hasefi squeezed her eyes shut. *Ignore it,* she hissed silently. One eye opened slightly and she let out an annoyed snort. *Why did it have to be hare? Maybe if I take a couple bites it'll be easier,* she decided. With a grunt, she reached out with her good forepaw and hooked the hare with a claw. She slowly dragged it towards her muzzle until she could stretch her neck to take a bite. The rich taste coated her tongue and she let out a pleased hum. *How long have I been down here?* she wondered. *It's been a while since I've eaten.*

When she finally managed to pull away from the hare, she was surprised and dismayed to find there was little more than bones left. She gave them an annoyed look and kicked them away before bringing her paw to her face and washing it.

Hasefi woke up to sunlight streaming down over her fur. She'd managed to uncover herself from the snow and scrape it away so it wasn't leeching what little warmth she had left. But the stone beneath her felt just as cold as the snow and she was beginning to think she'd never feel some parts of her body again.

The sunlight and the tiny amount of warmth it shed on her was suddenly blocked as a black-furred face poked through the hole.

"Lynx!" the wolf called excitedly. "You ate! How are you feeling?"

"I'd be better if I could feel the sun on my fur," she growled, managing to push herself up so she wasn't lying on her flank.

"I'm sorry," the wolf said, ducking. The light blinded Hasefi and she let out an annoyed hiss. "Do you think you can walk?" he asked.

"Does it look like I can?" she snapped. The wolf gave her an apologetic look. "Look, wolf, I'm not falling for it. Just do us both a favor and back off."

"Falling for what?" he asked.

"This act. I know you're just keeping me well enough to make it for when Sal comes. Just...back off."

"Who's Sal?" The wolf's questioning tone was so genuine Hasefi couldn't help but believe that the wolf was truly oblivious. She squinted up at him.

"Really?" He shrugged. "You don't know who Sal is?" *Maybe I'm wrong and Sal isn't anyone important. But all the other wolves sure seem to think so.*

"Are they a lynx, too?" he asked. "Were they with you before you got trapped?"

"No…" She tried to find any evidence that the wolf was trying to trick her, but she could only see puzzlement and curiosity in his expression. *Could a wolf be good at hiding their emotions? Do they even have emotions?* "You really don't want to take me away?" she asked him.

The wolf shook his head.

"Then why are you here?"

"I told you—I want to help," he insisted.

"How did you know I was down here?"

The wolf hesitated long enough to make her suspicious. "There's blood up here," he explained. "I recognized it as lynx blood. I didn't think lynxes traveled this far into the mountains."

"Well, they do," she sighed, resting her head on the ground.

"Were you abandoned?"

Hasefi's head snapped back up to glare at the wolf. "Why would you say that?"

"Why else would you be alone?"

Hasefi shot him a wordless snarl.

"I'm sorry," he told her.

"You must be alone, too, if you're not here to hurt me," Hasefi hissed. "Were *you* abandoned?"

There was hurt in the wolf's eyes and he retreated until Hasefi couldn't see him anymore. She laid her head back on the stone, his words circling in her mind. *Who does he think he is, asking if I've been abandoned? My tribe would never do such a thing! He has no idea who I am.* Hasefi's expression softened and she lifted her gaze up towards the hole above. *He has no idea who I am. All of the other wolves know exactly who I am. What if he really is trying to help? But why would he help a creature he doesn't know?* She watched the hole, waiting for him to appear again, but the wolf was nowhere to be seen. "I'm sorry," she murmured, but he wasn't there to respond this time. *Maybe I've finally pushed him away.*

What if he's seen other lynxes before? she wondered. *Maybe he knows the place I'm looking for. Would he tell me? Maybe the ancestors sent him to me. But why a wolf? Why not another lynx—or any other creature, for that matter? Sefonis, what do I do?* Her words were lost to the air and she felt painfully alone. *Maybe I could try talking to the wolf...if he comes back.*

As the light began to fade from the hole, Hasefi was faintly relieved when the wolf poked his head into the pit once again. He didn't say anything like she was expecting him to, though. She pretended not to notice, but soon grew uncomfortable under his watchful gaze.

"What are you doing?" she asked.

"Trying not to bother you," he responded.

"Well, you're not doing very well." He looked away and Hasefi felt a brief flash of fear that he would leave again. "I mean, you don't have to sit in silence."

"Every time I say something you get upset," he pointed out.

"Yeah, well...I think I'm beginning to see things...a little differently."

He cocked his head. "What do you mean?"

"Maybe...there is a way out." She could see delight in his amber eyes which seemed so foreign in the kind of gaze she was so used to seeing hate and rage in.

"I haven't found anything around here," the wolf admitted. "But I'm sure there's something!" he added quickly. "I won't give up on you."

Hasefi snorted. *I was so ready to give up on myself, yet here is this wolf who's practically as determined as my tribe to keep me alive.* Narrowing her eyes, Hasefi pushed herself up. After a few grunts and slips, she managed to sit up.

Her vision blurred and she tried to shake her head and clear it, but it only made her dizzier. "Maybe I should lie down a wee bit longer," she decided.

"I'll go hunting again," the wolf offered. "You need strength. There's a full moon tomorrow," he added as if it were something she should be looking forward to. *What does that have to do with anything?* Hasefi thought faintly. Instead of responding to his words, she sank heavily onto her side and let her vision darken until she ceased to feel anything.

Chapter Four

"Sefonis, what is an 'uncle'?" Hasefi asked as Sefonis cleaned the fur on her flank.

"Well," he began, pausing for a moment. "An uncle is the brother of one of your parents."

Hasefi rolled onto her back and rested her forepaws under his chin. She frowned thoughtfully before continuing. "I thought you were my parent."

Sefonis moved his head and Hasefi caught him watching her with surprise and dismay. She sat up and gave him an apologetic look.

"I'm sorry," she told him. "I didn't mean to make you upset."

"No, wee lass. It's not...." Her uncle's expression twisted with pain, causing Hasefi's chest to tighten with guilt.

"You don't have to say anything," she told him, wanting him to be happy again. "I was just curious, is all. It's not important." However, her words only seemed to hurt him more.

"It is important," Sefonis told her quietly. "I just didn't think about it and...well, you're still so young—"

"I'm two and a half moons!" she couldn't help blurting. "I'm not that young."

Sefonis let out a small purr and nosed her cheek. "Well, you certainly are the bravest kitten I've known," he chuckled.

Hasefi puffed her chest with pride, then frowned at her uncle. "What other kittens have you known?"

Sefonis let out a sigh and sat up, his gaze not quite meeting hers.

"Is something wrong?" she asked him worriedly. "Did I do something?"

"No, of course not," he quickly assured her. "You're not to blame." He was silent for a few heartbeats. "Do you remember your mother?"

"I remember you and the others telling me about her," Hasefi admitted.

"Right. And you know that she's your parent?"

"Yeah, but...." Hasefi frowned at the ground, trying to find the words she wanted to say. "I always thought a parent was someone who cares for their kittens."

"They are," he admitted. "But sometimes things happen. Sometimes parents have to do something difficult, when it is asked of them." Hasefi waited for him to elaborate, but she could see a mixture of grief and anger changing his face. She decided it was time to bring an end to the conversation her uncle was struggling to get through.

"So...you're my mother's brother, then?"

"No," he told her. "I'm your father's brother."

"Fath...er...." Hasefi's eyes flickered open, but she was no longer at her uncle's side. She couldn't make out where she was and felt utterly disoriented and groggy. A voice filled her ears, but it was strange and she couldn't understand what it was saying. She tried to look around, wondering if Sefonis was calling to her, but she had little strength.

"Lynx?" The voice came into sharp clarity and Hasefi recalled where she was, the realization dropping on her like a mound of snow. "Lynx! Oh, I thought you—are you okay? You weren't moving."

Hasefi squinted as she looked up to where the wolf was peering down at her, his expression twisted with fear. She could see his claws as he leaned precariously over the edge to stare down at her.

"What are you barking for?" she croaked, surprised at how weak her voice was. She coughed faintly and let her head rest on the ground again.

"Please, lynx, you need to get up."

Exhaustion weighed down on Hasefi, making it more difficult to keep her eyes open.

"Lynx, don't sleep again." The wolf's whimpers and frantic scratching faded away above her. Snow fell onto her, but she didn't have the strength to flinch as it melted into her fur.

Hasefi's eyes closed, her mind echoing with fragments of her tribe's voices. *A prophecy,* Hasefi thought. *I'm part of a prophecy. But I have no idea what it means. I don't even know what 'river' means. And my parents? I've thought about meeting them, but I never thought about who they could be. But...one of them was a Highchief like me. Could they still be out there?* Her eyes flickered open and she was bewildered to see that the light had faded from the pit. *I've been here for so long.* Her thought seemed to float away, as if her mind couldn't hold itself together anymore.

Is this *what dying feels like?* she thought. *It's not so bad.* As her eyes flickered closed again, something stirred the fur in her ears. They twitched as she tried to understand what it was. The sound grew louder, swirling through the air in the pit and caressing her fur like her uncle's soothing tongue when he licked the snow from her fur after a snowfall. Her eyes flickered open, widening with realization.

It was a voice. A wolf's voice.

It's him. He's...howling, she thought. *But not like the howls the other wolves make when they find prey. This is...different. It's actually kind of...beautiful.* She thought it would be hard to admit that to herself, but she found that she was drawn to the wolf's ghostly melody.

Hasefi managed to push herself up slightly and pricked her ears so she could hear more clearly. *I didn't know wolves could sing like this,* she thought with wonder. Her surprise only strengthened when she realized the wolf was howling actual words. She sat straighter, determined to hear them. They floated just out of earshot, like snowflakes in a breeze that were about to land in her fur only to be swept away. Hasefi dragged herself from the mound of snow that had been her sleeping place for longer than she knew and stretched herself towards the hole above.

She picked up his words and went completely still, her breaths slow and soft so she could hear him.

> I howl, I howl, to the full moon this night,
> To the bright white light of the ancestors.
> Full moon, full moon, will you hear my words tonight?
> I know my past is dark,
> I know I bear his mark.
> Yet, you led me to this place,
> And I know not what I face.
> So these words this night are going to be
> For her, she needs help, she needs the will to fight,
> To rise up, tall, brave, and free.
> I ask this of you, because I want to do what's right.

The wolf repeated the words and Hasefi felt as if she was hearing them for the first time each time. Amazement rippled through her with each change in the wolf's voice and she could only sit in silent shock.

As she listened, she realized there was a sadness in his tone, a desperation that stirred something deep within her. *How can a wolf feel like this?* She thought in shocked disbelief. *They talk and think, but do they actually feel?* The answer was obvious as his voice floated to her ears, growing louder as if he was letting out more of himself with each word.

He *does, at least. And, I can feel it.* Hasefi's chest continued to tighten at the fraught hope she heard in his voice, appalled by how this creature—a wolf of all things—could express such deep emotion.

He was hurt, she realized. *Something must have happened to him. Like me. Did he lose someone? Could wolves have tribes? Are there more than just the wolves hunting me?* Hasefi felt a prick in her heart as a thought entered her head. *He asked if I was abandoned. Was he?* His words offered her no answers, only more questions.

He's asking for help. Help for me. He's speaking to ancestors. Do wolves have ancestors? And why would he ask them to help me? She froze when the wolf's howl faltered, only to return again, sounding more desperate now.

Why does it sound like he's running out of time? she thought worriedly. Her thoughts took a full turn and her eyes widened. *What if he's trying to save me from the other wolves? From...Sal?* she wondered. *He didn't seem to know who Sal was, though. But what if the other wolves are close? And he's trying to get me out before it's too late? I've never heard the other wolves sound like this before. This wolf is...different.*

Hasefi's head jerked to the side as she examined herself, realizing with surprise that she had managed to get herself where she was without really noticing. *I have some strength,* she thought. *I need to use it.*

Gritting her teeth, she slowly got her paws underneath her, holding her left foreleg up so it didn't brush the ground as it hung crookedly. The three supporting her shook, but they held her up.

There has to be a way out of here, Hasefi thought. She limped further away from the snow mound until her whiskers brushed rock. She followed the wall around the line of light that lit up the blood and snow in the middle of the pit. Each step felt like it would be her last before her legs gave out, but she forced herself to push aside her weakness and press on. Finally, the wall fell away and she felt the air change around her as she entered a narrow tunnel.

The wolf's voice changed and she stopped, pricking her ears to listen. He was holding the last few words longer than he had before. Then, instead of repeating his words, they changed.

> The night is fading, I cease my howling
> Thank you, full moon, for listening.

He told me about the full moon. Is this why? Did he want me to hear him? Hasefi's foreleg gave out and she fell against the rock beside her. *I don't have much time. I need to get out of here.* She pushed herself up and continued on, keeping her ears pricked for the wolf who had gone eerily quiet. Worry built within her and she urged her legs to move faster.

The air is stale here. But this is the only way out of the pit. There has to be something. Hasefi pressed onwards, step by limping step, following the tunnel as it sloped gently up and curved to the left. It started to open up and thoughts of bigger creatures being able to fit in there with her fluttered in her head.

If anything else were here, I'd know by now. She refused to acknowledge that the fact nothing had come in implied there was no way for anything to come in. Or out.

After a few more paces, Hasefi's legs went limp and she slumped to the ground. She tried to get up, but quickly gave in to the weakness she felt. *Where is the wolf?* she wondered. *I thought he'd be checking on me by now.* She was surprised when fear flickered through her. *What if he can't? His howls would be heard from far away. What if something else heard him? Sunblind wolf.* She managed to push herself up so she was sitting. *I have to try and get out. He was trying to help me—I have to do the same.* Yet, as she tried to step forwards, her paw slipped in snow and she fell back to the ground.

I can rest here, she decided, shivering as icy claws dug into her. *Just for a heartbeat or two. Besides, I've been sleeping in snow for stars know how long and I've been okay.* She started to close her eyes, then quickly opened them. She stretched her paw forwards and curled her claws through the snow.

Snow, she thought. *In the cave.* She looked around even though all she saw was darkness. *There has to be a way for it to get in.* She tasted the air, but it was mostly stale. *Maybe it's blocked,* she thought, feeling stronger with hope. She dragged herself forward until she started to climb deeper into snow. *Yes! This is a way out! It's just caved in!*

"Lynx?" The wolf's voice echoed behind her. "Lynx, where are you?" Overwhelmed with hope, Hasefi said nothing as she clawed at the snow. She could do little to dig herself out with one paw and she soon doubled over with exhaustion. *I need help.*

"Wolf!" she called before she could give herself a chance to think twice. "Wolf, I'm here!"

"Lynx? I hear you! Where—?" He cut off and Hasefi waited. Heartbeats passed and she wondered if something had happened. *What if he saw something? We're making an awful lot of noise and he said my blood was up there.* "Lynx, keep talking!"

"I'm here!" she called, putting all of her strength into her voice. "I found a tunnel, a way out, but it's caved in! I can't dig through it, I need your help!" She paused, waiting for a response, but none came. "Wolf, I'm here! Come—"

"I found you!" The wolf's voice no longer echoed behind her, instead sounding faintly in front of her, muffled by the thick wall of snow. "Just hold on!"

Hasefi shuffled backwards as she heard claws digging frantically through snow. Blurred moonlight began to show through, flickering as the large bulk of the wolf moved while he worked deeper and deeper into the cave.

Hasefi was beginning to feel light-headed and she leaned against the cave wall for support. The wolf's voice grew stronger as the light continued to filter in through the snow, but Hasefi was already limp with relief.

It's okay, she thought. *I'm going to be okay.* Large black paws broke through the snow and the light was blocked almost entirely for a brief moment. As the figure moved towards her and darkness filled her vision, a tiny flicker of doubt entered her mind and she wondered if perhaps she had made a mistake in calling to a wolf for help.

Chapter Five

"I can't get warm," Hasefi whimpered.

"I know, wee lass," Sefonis rumbled sympathetically. "You have a fever. Dahsefer is searching for some herbs to help heal you."

"Can't he heal me without them?" Hasefi pointed out.

"Aye, but it requires strength and we need to save all the strength we can."

Hasefi closed her eyes and snuggled further into her uncle's sandy brown fur. As she kneaded it with her paws, she realized he was trembling slightly, as if he was struggling to get warm, too. She hesitated, feeling guilty for trying to draw away his warmth.

"Are you cold?" she asked.

"Only a wee bit. Don't worry about anything but resting, okay wee lass?" Sefonis's words confused Hasefi since he was always telling her that, as the Highchief, part of her duty was to make sure the rest of her tribe was well before herself. Sometimes she would go around and ask how the other lynxes were, but sometimes she was too cold or too tired and left them alone for a day.

Or, in this case, three days.

We haven't been able to go anywhere because of me, *she thought. Our journey home is taking longer because I'm sick. Determination trick-led through her and she pushed herself to her paws.*

"Hasefi?" her uncle murmured.

She met his surprised gaze and was dismayed to see her own ex-haustion reflected in his. A terrible thought went through her mind. I'm not the only one who's sick. As if the thought uncovered the truth that was being hidden from her, Hasefi heard the rasping coughs and sneezes echoing through the tunnel her tribe had taken shelter in. I need to take care of them, she thought. Hasefi stepped forward and touched her nose to her uncle's fur. She could smell the sour scent of sickness and feel the heat coming off his pelt despite his shivering. There was also another scent there, one that made her fur prickle. She breathed in deeply, trying to determine what it was.

Wolf.

Hasefi was on her paws immediately, her claws flying at the surprised and fearful yellow eyes that flashed by her. She let out a wordless snarl and leaped back only to find one of her legs wouldn't respond. As she looked down to see why, realization flooded through her and she stared at the creature before her.

"Wolf," she gasped as he raised a paw towards the blood welling on his muzzle. He made no other movements and she relaxed slightly, letting herself sit with her broken leg stretched awkwardly out. "Why were you so close to me?" she demanded.

"You kept mumbling that you were cold. I…was just trying to help," he explained, licking the blood from his paw and returning it to the ground.

"Well, it might be best if you stay a few pawsteps away," she told him. *Or maybe ten.*

"I think I've figured that out," he said with a nervous chuckle. Silence floated between them and she watched as he awkwardly nosed a small clump of snow away from his paws. Hasefi kept her eyes on him, still wary that he would try something.

What do I do? she wondered. *He's a wolf.* Her fur rippled with unease as she glimpsed the white of his teeth poking from his lips and the piercing yellow eyes that studied the ground. *But he helped me.*

"You're pretty fast for a three-legged pup," the wolf murmured suddenly, his eyes darting to her then away again.

Hasefi narrowed her gaze. "What did you just call me?"

"Er, sorry," he blurted, straightening. "Kit, right? That's what lynxes call their...pups?" He cocked his head. "Or are you just a really small lynx?"

"I'm a kit," she said quickly, wondering what he was trying to do. When there were no answers in his expression, she tried talking. "A pup is a wolf-kit, then?"

The wolf nodded.

"Makes sense," she muttered, recalling the word being used by some of the wolves that were after her. Her thoughts grew more concerned at the thought of them. *More wolves are bound to come soon. But maybe they'll be short-pawed after that avalanche. Maybe it'll give me some time to recover. More than I've already had.*

"You don't like wolves much, do you?" the wolf asked, drawing her from her thoughts.

Hasefi's mouth opened, but she hesitated, not entirely sure how to answer. "Uh, no..." she admitted slowly. "I mean, I haven't had much reason to. Until now, I guess. Um, thanks," she added awkwardly. The wolf shrugged and silence fell between them again. "Um...I guess you like lynxes?" she tried.

"I've never really met one," he admitted. "I've seen a couple from a distance, but I never actually talked to one." Amusement lit his amber eyes. "You have funny accents."

"So do you," she retorted, trying to sound defiant. However, she couldn't stop her whiskers from quivering slightly. The wolf stuck his tongue out partly before his expression grew serious. He glanced down the tunnel, then returned his gaze to her.

"How did this happen?" he asked, his eyes darting over her. "You look like you did more than just fall into a hole."

"Yeah," Hasefi admitted. "It sort of started with an avalanche."

The wolf nodded with understanding. "Explains why there's no other creatures around here. The only thing scarier than a mountain lion is an angry mountain."

Hasefi immediately felt pride and jumped on the opportunity to boast about her feats to a wolf. "More like an angry lynx," she purred, sitting back on her haunches and giving her good paw a nonchalant lick. The wolf frowned with confusion. "I knocked a rock down the mountain and made the avalanche." His eyes widened and her pride only strengthened.

"Why would you ever want to do that?" he gasped. "Avalanches and landslides and anything to do with the mountains themselves falling apart is something no creature can expect to survive! You're lucky to be alive," he added sternly.

Hasefi snorted, returning to three paws. "I think *cursed* is the word you're looking for."

The wolf narrowed his eyes in disbelief. "A lynx-kit, injured and bleeding, tucked safely away in a cave to be found by a random wolf willing to give her a paw? Sounds pretty lucky to me. Unless it's more than just luck?" His expression changed suddenly and the questioning gaze he gave her seemed to ask for an answer she wasn't sure she should give. *Is he thinking of magic? Does he think I'm gifted?*

But I don't have a star on my chest...would a wolf even know of magic? He mentioned ancestors while he was howling last night.... Didn't he say something about being led here?

"How did you find me?" she decided to ask. "If I was so safely tucked away?"

The wolf's nose twitched and he looked to the ground, poking a piece of ice with his claw. "The falling moon guided me," he explained.

Hasefi studied him, his response bringing forth a set of new questions. *Why would a creature just follow the moon? Why would he sing to it? Could he really have ancestors?* She stared at him in disbelief.

He met her gaze, looking embarrassed. "I'm not making this up," he told her, mistaking her expression.

If the falling moon led him here and the rising sun led me *here...were we supposed to meet? But that doesn't make sense. My whole tribe was following the sun.*

"What does that face mean?" the wolf asked uncertainly.

"Why are you alone?" she demanded, trying to find even a single answer amidst the confusion whirling in her mind.

The wolf tilted his head. "Why are *you* alone?" he returned somewhat defensively.

Hasefi gritted her teeth, reluctant to answer. "Why did you help me?" she tried instead.

"I couldn't just leave you there," he pointed out.

"Why not? If it were you down there, I wouldn't have done anything."

The wolf flinched and looked away. "I guess it's a good thing it wasn't me, then."

Hasefi watched him closely, seeing the way he flattened his ears and how his lips curved into a frown as if she had actually hurt him. *Maybe wolves are more like lynxes than I thought.*

"Why are you staring at me?" the wolf asked.

"I didn't know wolves could be so…soft," she replied.

He lifted his head. "I didn't know lynxes could be so tough." He nodded towards her, his eyes on her leg again. "That can be dangerous. You might want to clean it."

Hasefi only nodded.

"Will you be alright if I go and hunt?"

"I don't need you to watch over me," she snapped, though she quickly regretted her words. *Why does he suddenly want to hunt?* The wolf twitched his ears before he turned and left the tunnel. Hasefi wanted to call after him, worried that he would be dangerous out of her sight, but decided it would probably be good for her to think while she was alone.

I'm still weak, she thought. *But I'm not as cold. Thanks to him, I guess.* She got up and limped towards the opening that led outside. She tasted the air, the wolf's scent still making her paws itch with the urge to flee. Other than that, though, the air was clean of any other scents.

What do I do now? she wondered. *I won't be going anywhere anytime soon. And…this wolf really does seem intent on helping me. I mean, if he really meant what he howled last night…. Maybe I should ask him about that.* Hasefi glanced towards where his prints led out of the narrow clearing. Something dark in the snow caught her eye and she looked to where blood trailed through the snow until it fell away through a long crack in the ground.

I can't stay long. If predators don't come first, wolves will. She looked back to where the wolf had disappeared. *Assuming they won't be returning with him.*

What if he doesn't come back at all? The thought popped into her head and she was surprised at the fear it made her feel. Hasefi laid her broken leg carefully in the snow and began to gently rub snow on it, the cold soothing the pain as she wiped off the blood. *Why would he stay?* she pointed out to herself. *Except to help? But I still don't understand why he would want to and he seems just as unwilling to offer answers as I do. What secrets could a wolf have?* Hasefi rolled the question around in her mind until her leg was mostly cleaned of blood. It was difficult to touch the part where her leg was unnaturally bent, even with her tongue, so she just pushed some snow over it and let it melt, numbing the pain a little and soaking the blood with it.

Maybe there's no reason behind us meeting, she thought. *But I probably would have died if we didn't. Maybe my ancestors sent him? But why a wolf? If I'm on the path home, why not just another lynx?* Hasefi let out a long sigh, her head pounding with the cyclic nature of her questions. She swallowed a couple mouthfuls of clean snow in case part of it was dehydration, but she figured she was just overwhelmed by the thoughts swirling in her mind.

I'm tired and hungry and cold, which is normal, but now I can't do anything about it. I have to wait for the wolf to return—if he does—if I want to eat. But...can I trust him? Hasefi trudged back to the cave where she curled up away from the snow, rubbing warmth back into her fur.

What else can I do, though? If I'm going to finish my tribe's mission, I have to get better. And he's my best chance of letting that happen. So I have to trust him. She let out another sigh and let her eyes close halfway, watching the opening before her. *I can't trust him, but for some reason he wants to help me. I have to take advantage of that, at least. And maybe I can find out more about wolves in general to avoid them better.* Hasefi's mind darkened. *I can't let him know about the other wolves—he might side with them if he knew they were after me.*

Determined to shorten the time she would have to depend on the wolf, Hasefi decided to get some sleep to help herself heal.

The wolf returned to the cave before dusk—alone, to Hasefi's relief—dragging a mountain sheep that had tiny brown stubs where its horns were beginning to grow. Her stomach growled eagerly as he dropped it before her and took a step back.

"Nice catch," she told him instinctively, echoing the words Sefonis always used when the hunters brought in food. The wolf looked pleased by her praise. Hasefi leaned forward to take a bite, but she hesitated before her teeth grazed its flesh. "Have you eaten?" she asked.

"I'll eat later," he told her.

Hasefi narrowed her eyes. She was about to shrug and dismiss it, but she hesitated again. *A Highchief's duty is to ensure her tribe is well before herself.*

He's not my tribe, she thought. *But he did help me. And there's plenty here for both of us.* Hasefi straightened.

"You eat first," she told him.

The wolf shook his head. "I'm not hungry."

"I may be a kit, but I've been on my own long enough to know that every creature is always hungry." They held each other's gazes until the wolf cocked his head.

"Lynxes are stubborn," he commented before settling down beside the sheep.

"And you better remember it," she responded, feeling proud of herself for overcoming him. The wolf shrugged and dug into the prey.

"So," he said after swallowing a mouthful. "How does a lynx-kit end up in the mountains alone?"

"How does a wolf-pup end up in the mountains alone?" she returned.

"I'm not a pup," he argued.

"I've seen wolves before," she said before she could stop herself. *Just go with it.* "You're big, but not that big."

"I bet I look pretty strange, too," he said with a chuckle before taking another bite.

Hasefi frowned, not understanding. "Well, not really."

The wolf looked up at her in surprise. "Really? Black fur?"

"Can wolves have different fur?" Her response seemed to disturb him and he stopped eating, his gaze fixed on the sheep's bloodied fur. "What is it?"

"You've seen wolves in the high mountains?"

Hasefi stiffened, searching for an answer. "Well, around, I guess," she stammered, trying her best to seem nonchalant. "Just like you've seen lynxes. From...a distance." The look he gave her made her uncomfortable and she wondered if she was capable of making it to the entrance before he caught her. *Changing the subject is more likely.*

"I heard you," she said quickly. "During the full moon, I mean," she added when his intense gaze flickered with confusion. "I heard you howling."

"I'm sorry," he told her, glancing away. "I tried to move away so I wouldn't bother you."

Hasefi stifled a breath of relief as he seemed to let go of the topic of other wolves. "No, it's okay," she told him. "I didn't mind. It was nice. I mean, I liked it. Or...." Hasefi trailed off, embarrassed.

"You understood?" he offered.

"Some of it," she admitted. The wolf's expression reminded her of the one Sefonis would have every time she had to rub feeling back into her numb pads.

"I'm sorry," the wolf sighed.

"For what?"

"What you've been through. And I don't just mean this," he added, nodding at her broken leg. "I can't imagine what the high mountains are like for a kit."

Hasefi was silent, unsure how to respond.

The wolf touched a paw to his muzzle. "That looks a few moons old."

Hasefi touched her own paw to her face, feeling the three lines that ran from her right brow to her left cheek. Pride rippled through her and she sat a little straighter.

"I got this from a monster-bird," she said importantly. To her dismay, the wolf's gaze lit up with amusement.

"A monster-bird?" he chuckled.

"Yes! The things that circle in the sky and have strange brown fur, giant yellow eyes and even bigger claws! And they're, uh, three lynxes big!" The wolf laughed and Hasefi deflated, feeling humiliated.

"That's an eagle," he told her.

"An eagle?" she repeated sulkily. The wolf's mirth faded and he looked at her seriously.

"Wolves don't have to worry about eagles or hawks or anything like that except when they're really young. How did you survive?"

Some of Hasefi's pride returned. "I had this stuff called armor when I was younger," she explained. "It protected me like a hard pelt on top of my actual one. The mon—uh, eagle tried to grab me, but it couldn't find a grip on my armor. I clawed at its wings until it let go and found shelter before it could recover. But it gave me this before I was safe." Hasefi touched the scar again, pleased by the admiration in the wolf's eyes.

"Wow, a lynx-kit who already has her first battle scar."

"Come on, you can't be that much older," she pointed out. "If you're still a pup."

"I'm not a pup. And I'm seventeen moons," he told her, chuckling when her eyes widened with surprise.

"I thought you were younger," she admitted.

The wolf cocked his head. "How old are you?"

"Seven moons," she admitted after a moment of hesitation. Now his eyes stretched wide with surprise.

"Seven?" he cried. "By the moon, how have you survived? No creature is safe in the high mountains! Let alone a tiny pup smaller than any of the prey around!"

"Not all prey," Hasefi pointed out. "I guess I'm just lucky, like you said."

The wolf narrowed his eyes. "It has to be more than luck," he told her. "Something is watching over you."

Hasefi frowned. "Like what?"

"Have you ever heard of the idea of spirits?" he asked.

Her frown deepened. "Like...ancestors?" she murmured warily and the wolf nodded enthusiastically.

"Exactly! There must be ancestors watching over you. My ancestors are what told me to follow the falling moon," he explained.

Surprise rippled through Hasefi and she took a moment before she spoke. "How can a lone wolf have ancestors?" she pointed out.

"How does a lone lynx-kit know about ancestors?" he returned.

Hasefi gave a short snort. "We seem to keep finding questions like this," she sighed.

He nodded, clearly not intending to reply.

Maybe I should take a step back and try this again. What would I say to another creature I just met that didn't want to kill me right away? She thought for a moment before the answer hit her like snow falling off a ledge above.

"Hasefi."

"What?" the wolf asked, tilting his head.

"My name is Hasefi. Not, uh, 'lynx'."

His eyes lit up and he looked pleased. "My name is Kolahn."

"Kolahn?" Hasefi echoed. "That's a weird name."

"So is Hasefi," he told her and she snorted. Kolahn pushed the remaining sheep towards her. "I'm full."

Hasefi narrowed her eyes at him. She decided he was telling the truth and began to dig into the warm prey. "Can I ask how long you've been alone?" she asked carefully.

"Only if you're willing to answer the same question," Kolahn replied.

Hasefi thought for a moment before nodding.

"About seven moons," he stated.

"About seven—? That's my whole life," Hasefi gasped. "I couldn't imagine surviving that long on my own. It's been...four moons for me."

Kolahn looked upset by her answer. *Does he not believe me?*

"Do you...do you have somewhere to go?" he asked hesitantly.

Hasefi frowned with puzzlement. "Like a home? Don't you think I'd be there if I did?" *I can't tell him about the rising sun because I'll have to tell him about my tribe...and then what happened to them.* "What about you?"

"I have a home," he admitted.

"So why aren't you there?" Hasefi glanced around the cave they were in. "Unless...this is it?"

"Because of the falling moon," he explained.

"Right. Which led you to me. So...are you returning home, then?" Hasefi found herself afraid of the answer he might give. *If he does go, what will I do? I can't take care of myself, not like this. But...can I really stay with a wolf?* Her instinct to survive was telling her to stay and run at the same time and she didn't know which to do.

"I'm...not sure. I can't leave you like this." She felt a flicker of relief, but she hid it by frowning at her meal. "Unless...you'd prefer I was gone?"

"No. I mean...I can't hunt," she added slowly, avoiding his gaze. "I'll need help until I'm better." When she found the courage to look at him, she saw a sorrowful look she didn't understand. "But you don't have to."

"I don't mind. It's...nice to talk to another creature."

Hasefi took a bite and nodded. "Yeah," she agreed. "It is." Silence fell again, but Hasefi found it wasn't as uncomfortable as before. She was able to eat relatively relaxed, though she kept an eye on Kolahn the entire time. The wolf seemed to grow interested in the snowflakes that were beginning to fall outside. Eventually, he returned his attention to her. When he didn't speak, Hasefi decided trying to prod about last night.

"Why were you howling?" she asked.

Kolahn glanced away and Hasefi assumed he wouldn't answer, but then she heard him take in a small breath. "It's...a wolf thing," he began slowly. "When the full moon is out, we howl to it. Every wolf has a different song and their song always changes. Sometimes it's an apology, sometimes it's a cry for help. Sometimes it's just a respectful prayer."

"What was yours?"

Kolahn didn't meet her gaze.

"It sounded like all of those."

"It...was," he admitted.

"You wanted them to help me. Your ancestors. But you sounded as if you didn't get a lot of their help."

Kolahn didn't respond, his gaze clouding.

"Well, I think it worked," she tried. "I mean, here we are."

His ears perked up slightly and he focused on her again. "You're right. Here we are."

Hasefi lowered her head to take another bite and she chewed it thoughtfully. *There's a lot to this wolf,* she thought. *Hopefully it's nothing that'll put me in danger. If I'm not already in it.*

When nothing remained of the mountain sheep but bones, Kolahn helped her remove the remains outside and showed her how to bury them so no other predators were attracted by the scent. Then she returned to the cave, curling up as best she could with her broken leg, and watched the wolf as he sat near the entrance.

"You can rest if you'd like," he told her. "I can keep watch."

Hasefi nodded, but she didn't close her eyes.

The wolf cocked his head. "Did you want me to go somewhere else? Are you cold?"

"No," she said quickly, a little irritated by his questions. "I'm just not used to having another creature around while I sleep. Or at all, for that matter."

"Neither am I," he murmured.

Hasefi opened her mouth, feeling like she should say something, but no sound left her jaws and she closed them. Then, with a sigh, she lowered her head onto her good paw and, after a few more heartbeats, was able to close her eyes and sink into sleep.

Chapter Six

The sweet scent of prey blood woke Hasefi from her slumber. She kept her eyes closed for a moment, imagining Sefonis was coming to wake her for the day's meal. But when a voice spoke her name, it wasn't her uncle's.

"Sefi? Are you hungry?"

"You know the answer to that," she groaned, forcing her eyes open. "And it's *Ha*sefi." Her gaze landed on the hare he dropped near her. "You must be some sort of expert hare hunter. I've had more hare this last quarter-moon than I have my whole life."

Kolahn let out a breath of laughter as he sat down. Hasefi peered past his bulk and saw the fading light outside. "You've been out all day."

"Hunting in the high mountains isn't easy," he pointed out. "But you know that."

Hasefi shrugged and pulled herself closer to the hare. She tested her broken leg, but it felt the same as it had when she was in the pit.

"Broken bones take forever to heal," she grunted with annoyance. Kolahn gave no response other than a sorrowful look. Stifling her impatience, Hasefi settled before the hare. Instead of taking a bite, however, she looked to Kolahn. "You know I won't eat until you have," she told him. Kolahn rolled his eyes and bowed his head towards the hare.

"You need it more than I do," he mumbled around a mouthful.

"If you lose your strength, neither of us will be eating." She couldn't keep some of the bitterness out of her tone and the wolf gave her another sorrowful look. "Stop looking at me like that."

His eyes quickly darted away, focusing on the cave wall as he chewed. After a few moments of silence, Kolahn stood up and moved away from the hare. "I'm not eating anymore," he told her. "You have to have some."

Hasefi shrugged and dug into the prey. She stole a glance at him as he moved towards the entrance to keep watch.

She was beginning to feel more comfortable with the wolf around, though she still kept a close eye on him. It was clear there was something more to him, but Hasefi knew she had her own secrets. They hadn't talked much while she recovered and anything they did say was practically meaningless. A part of her was relieved since the wolf seemed content enough to ignore her shadows as long as she ignored his, but Hasefi knew it was only a matter of time before some of hers revealed themselves.

I'm surprised there hasn't been any sign of the other wolves. They seem to disappear as suddenly as they appear. Again, she wondered if Kolahn had anything to do with it.

He would have done something by now, if he intended to. And he certainly has no reason to be so kind to me, I would think. Unless there's something about how his ancestors happened to lead him here. But ancestors wouldn't let harm come to other creatures, right? We couldn't have the same ancestors. So how does that possibly work? Could his have talked to mine? Is that possible? What if he's lying about having ancestors? Then how would he know of them? Hasefi's head was beginning to hurt and she let the confusion sink to the back of her mind. *Regardless, Kolahn seems harmless enough. I mean, I don't even think he likes killing prey.*

Hasefi looked towards the wolf again, trying to battle the conflicted feelings she had. *I want to learn more, but he won't talk unless I do. What could I ask that I wouldn't have to answer in return?*

Hasefi's ears perked up when something came to mind.

"What is your home like?" she asked.

Kolahn's head turned until he was looking at her. He seemed to assess the question before answering. "Well…it's a cave," he began. "Bigger than this one. There's a waterfall that fills a pool beside it, which turns into a stream that leads through the valley. The valley is filled with trees and grass and there's so much prey. I like to call it the Great Valley," he added shyly.

Hasefi gave him a dubious look.

"What?" he asked, his fur twitching.

"Waterfall? Pool? Trees? I think you're just making up words."

Kolahn stared at her with bewilderment. "You don't…?" he trailed off, his expression utterly baffled.

Hasefi shook her head, wondering yet again if the wolf's head was full of nonsense. *It would make sense to why he's helping me.* She frowned, suddenly feeling as if she'd dealt with this before. *Sefonis,* she realized. *He mentioned…trees, was it? He used those words before. It's the place he told me about. What if Kolahn lives there? He keeps saying 'the high mountains' as if there could be other places. What if Sefonis was right? What if the place Kolahn lives is the place I'm supposed to go? That would make sense as to why my ancestors led me to him. Kolahn said he saw other lynxes before. This has to be it!*

Hasefi masked her excitement by sitting back on her haunches to lick the fur on her chest. Then she peered at Kolahn.

"What is a…tree?" she asked warily, not knowing what his reaction would be. The wolf cocked his head before responding.

"They're kind of like some of the shrubs that you've probably seen up here. Except they're really tall—taller than...ten wolves! And they're straighter, with a trunk in the middle and branches spreading out around it until they end in a tip at the top. But some trees are different."

Hasefi frowned, trying to imagine what he was describing, but it looked really silly in her head and she guessed trees weren't that silly since he was describing them like they were amazing. "Okay...a waterfall?"

"You know when snow melts it turns into water?"

Hasefi nodded.

"Well, a lot of snow melts and it runs down in streams and rivers. These sometimes pour over a cliffside."

"A waterfall," Hasefi murmured. "At least the name describes it." Despite her words, she had a hard time imagining the little drops shaken from her pelt after a long day of walking being plentiful enough to join together and pour over a cliffside. "How far is your home?" she asked.

"It's a couple moon's journey," he responded.

Hasefi stopped chewing for a moment, shocked by his answer. *That's a long way away. Did he really follow the moon for that long?* Her ears twitched. *I've been following the rising sun for a good while, too, I suppose. And that's not including the time with my tribe.*

"I could take you there."

"What?" Hasefi blurted, her mouth still half-full.

"I mean, if you wanted. I just thought...maybe it'd be nicer than staying up here in the cold." The wolf looked away in embarrassment while Hasefi studied him through suspicious eyes. *Why would he ask that? Maybe he's trying to be friendly, but I can't leave my path, nor can I risk telling him about it. Unless going with him is my path....*

"There's no way I'm going anywhere while I'm like this," she decided to say, indicating her broken leg. The wolf nodded and said nothing else, letting silence settle within the cave.

Hasefi wasn't sure what else to do but finish her meal. Kolahn brought his attention to the entrance again, leaving her alone.

Maybe I should go with him, she thought. *At least until we leave the 'high mountains'. It's my best chance. But will he suspect something if I agree to go? Maybe he'll just assume I'm tired of being in the cold.* Hasefi's thoughts shifted. *Could it be real? Somewhere that's warm? Without snow?* Excitement began to bubble up within her again. *There's so much I haven't discovered yet and I feel like I've travelled the world.* Hasefi sat up after she finished the hare and started washing her fur. *I'll have to be careful, but maybe staying with this wolf for a wee bit longer wouldn't be a bad idea. Once I reach this new place, the rising sun will show me where to go.*

Feeling more content than she could remember, Hasefi gave a long stretch and started to wash her chest. She opened one eye to peek at Kolahn, wondering how to tell him her decision, only to find the wolf was already watching her.

"Yes?" she asked suspiciously, straightening.

"Lynxes are so weird," Kolahn murmured.

"Explanation?" Hasefi asked, her wariness turning to amusement.

"You could roll in the snow and it would clean your pelt faster," he told her.

Hasefi let out a laugh before raising her good paw so she could lick it. However, the wolf showed no signs of humor and she hesitated. "Wait, really? Is that how wolves clean?"

In response, Kolahn ran out of the cave.

Hasefi limped after him, curious. Laughter bubbled out of her mouth as the wolf dove into the snow, thrashing his legs as he rolled around. By the time he stood up, he looked like a wolf with white fur.

"Starlight, aren't you freezing?" she chuckled. He bounded up to her side and shook his fur out. "Hey!" she squeaked, half stumbling, half ducking away. "What is up with you?"

"Just thought I'd give you a paw," he explained, sticking out his tongue in a goofy expression. Hasefi found herself laughing yet again, her stomach beginning to hurt from it.

"I did not know wolves could be so silly," she giggled.

Kolahn positioned himself so his front legs were stretched across the ground and his tail was in the air, swinging back and forth. His tongue hung out again and Hasefi shook her head and turned back into the cave, unable to bear laughing any longer.

"You're so strange," she chuckled as she retreated. "And I think I'll stick to my methods, thank you," she added, giving her snow-dusted chest a lick.

Kolahn straightened with a nonchalant shrug. "Whatever you prefer," he told her as he padded back into the cave after her.

Hasefi settled back down and resumed her wash. She kept one eye open to watch the wolf, witnessing his silly mood slowly fade into a somber expression. She was quiet, pretending not to notice, until Kolahn began to speak.

"Sometimes we will groom each other," he admitted. Hasefi sat up straight and listened intently. "To socialize. Or sometimes to comfort." He laid down a few pawsteps away, not quite close enough that she wanted to move away, but enough that her muscles remained tense. Kolahn seemed to hop out of whatever his mind had put him into and he gave her an amused look. "But snow or water works pretty well."

Hasefi studied Kolahn for a moment, wondering if there was something she could say to get him to talk more. *Obviously he had others before. Where did they go?* But she knew there was nothing she could do. "I'm not plunging myself into any snow or...water any time soon," she told him through narrowed eyes.

Kolahn chuckled and laid his head on his paws.

Hasefi resumed her wash, pondering his words. She tried imagining wolves having a system like her tribe did. *If I'm right and Sal is a leader for the other wolves, then they must have some sort of structure, but what about champions like Sefonis and Kilarsa?*

A sound caught her attention and she jerked upright, her ears perked as she tried to figure out what was echoing faintly against the cave walls. It was familiar, but instilled both wonder and terror in her at the same time.

Howling.

Hasefi's fur spiked with fear and she stood, staring at the entrance with wide eyes.

"Wolves," Kolahn observed, lifting his head and following her gaze. "I didn't really think there were others so high in the mountains." His gaze moved to her and concern changed his expression. "You don't have to worry," he told her. "Howls can travel far through the mountains. Besides, they probably wouldn't come near us."

Hasefi crouched and stared at the entrance, half expecting a wolf to stalk in at any moment. *We can't stay here any longer,* she thought. *We have to move. But where can we go? I can't tell him about the rising sun. Can I?*

"Sefi, are you okay?" Kolahn asked, getting up.

"I'm...I can't stay here," she told him. "I have to go."

He cocked his head. "Why? Where do you have to go?"

Hasefi's claws curled against the stone. "There's a lot we don't know about each other, Kolahn," she said through gritted teeth. "I'm leaving. Whether or not I leave alone is up to you."

"Are you sure you can walk?" he asked, his eyes on her leg.

"I'll have to try. I've had a quarter moon to recover my strength. All that's left is this." She lifted her injured leg. "We just need to move for a bit, then I'll rest again." The wolf still looked doubtful. "We've been here too long. Surely you know staying in one place can be dangerous?"

"It's dark," he pointed out. "Which is also dangerous."

Hasefi gave outside a reluctant look. Her fear tempted her to try and use the safety of darkness to cover her as she fled, but instinct reminded her that there were others that knew the shadows better than her.

"Then I'll move at first light," she stated.

Kolahn studied her with his yellow gaze and Hasefi prayed that he wouldn't ask anything else. To her relief, the wolf nodded and settled down again with a thoughtful expression.

"I'm sure it's hard to imagine a kit having secrets," she said with a nervous chuckle, hoping he wouldn't come to some conclusion that would put her in danger.

"No," he said to her surprise. "It's not hard to imagine."

Curiosity tugged Hasefi's whiskers as Kolahn's gaze grew distant and he looked outside, but she knew it would be wiser to accept silence.

Completely alert now, Hasefi watched the entrance, scrutinizing every shadow and flinching at every sound.

"You should at least try and sleep," the wolf eventually spoke, giving her a worried look.

She didn't say anything.

"Are you afraid of the wolves? I can keep watch."

"You are a wolf," she breathed, shifting her weight as her body grew stiff from staying still so long. She could feel Kolahn's gaze on her and she met it, her nose twitching nervously. Understanding softened his troubled expression and Hasefi felt a flicker of uneasiness. "What?"

"Nothing," he told her. "Just let me know if you get tired. I will make sure nothing comes close. You can trust me, okay?"

"Kolahn, I can't," she murmured. "You saved me...but I don't know you."

The wolf flinched and she could see the hurt in his eyes. She waited for him to argue, to insist that he would watch over her, but the wolf merely lowered his head to his paws. Hasefi watched him even after he closed his eyes, unable to determine if his reaction bode well or not. *He thought of something just a few heartbeats ago,* she thought. *What did he think of?*

Hasefi's eyes flickered to the darkness outside and she felt the urge to poke her head out and peer up at the stars. *That would be foolish,* she thought. *Besides, the stars don't need to see me to hear me.* She waited for a voice to tickle her ear fur, giving her a sign that they felt her reaching out, but the air was still.

Sefonis? she asked. *Are you here? With me?* Silence sat heavily around her. *I need you,* she told him. *I don't know what to do and I'm at the mercy of a wolf.* She looked to Kolahn, then her claws. *Well, kind of at his mercy. But he might be able to take me to the place you spoke of. His ancestors led him here. Why would they do that? Were they even trying to lead him to me? Or did he just happen upon me?* Hasefi shook her head. *I can't figure this out on my own, but I can't get any answers from him. Maybe I have no other choice but to trust him. At least as much as I already have been.* Hasefi paused, waiting for a sign from her uncle—or any of her ancestors—but the only presence she could feel was the wolf's.

With a quiet sigh, she focused on the darkness outside. Exhaustion tugged at the edges of her mind, but she was too afraid of being caught by wolves especially after her dread when Kolahn first showed up.

Eventually, the shadows began to lighten up and the first rays of sunlight sparkled against the snow. There were no other signs of wolves, but Hasefi knew better than to be hopeful. She stood, prepared to wake up Kolahn, but the wolf lifted his head.

"Time to go?" he asked. Hasefi was silent as the wolf stood and stretched. When he met her gaze again, he looked upset. "Do…you want me to go?"

"I don't think I have a choice," she admitted. He looked to his paws and she felt a little guilty. "I mean, it's nice to have some-one watching my back." Kolahn gave her a delighted look and she couldn't help but feel a little happy. She jerked her head to the front of the cave. "Come on."

Hasefi ensured it was safe to exit the cave, then led the wolf out and into the cold. "Are we going a certain direction?" he asked warily.

"I'll lead," was all Hasefi said. Kolahn remained silent as she tasted the air again, ensuring there were no threatening scents. She frowned at the thick clouds hanging low in the sky, masking some of the taller peaks.

With a deep breath, Hasefi glanced towards the rising sun. She kept an eye on Kolahn, but he didn't seem particularly interested in what direction she chose. Nevertheless, she decided to move adjacent to the rising sun, just to be careful.

After a while, Hasefi found a path that split and she stifled a relieved breath when one way curved towards the sun. She did her best to appear nonchalant about choosing the path, peering at Kolahn out the corner of her eye. The wolf seemed focused on the foggy ground above them and she relaxed slightly.

It's almost been half a moon since he found me, she thought. *If he was going to do something, he would have done it by now.* She looked to

Kolahn again. *I want to trust him. There's something about him...something like me. But...he's still a wolf.*

What if I told him about my tribe? The thought made her hesitate and she hit her broken leg on a rock jutting out of the snow. Hasefi let out an irritated hiss and crouched as pain throbbed through her leg.

"Are you okay?" Kolahn asked, quickly coming to her side.

"I'm fine," she snapped, flinching away from him. "I just wish this cursed leg would heal!" Kolahn gave her a sad look and she let out an annoyed snort.

"We could try herbs," he murmured.

"Herbs," she echoed, forcing herself to calm down. The word was familiar to her and it only took a few heartbeats before she remembered what it meant. "Plants, right? Plants that heal? But we're not gifted. I mean...." she gave the wolf a wary glance.

"We don't need magic for herbs to work," he told her. Surprise rippled through her, but she pushed it aside, not wanting him to see it. *Do wolves have gifted?* she wondered. *Maybe that's why it was so easy for the other wolves to break through the barrier around my tribe. But wouldn't they have found me easier, too?*

"I don't know how to find herbs," she told him.

"I know where we can." He hesitated.

"Where?" she urged, knowing each moment they continued to remain in place gave her hunters a chance to catch up.

"In the Great Valley."

Hasefi frowned. *His home? Why there? Couldn't there be somewhere else?* Hasefi hesitated. *If I agree, then he might think it's just to heal my leg. He won't suspect what my real mission is.* She met his wary gaze.

"Where is it?" she demanded.

"That way," he told her, pointing his nose the opposite way Hasefi had been travelling ever since she recalled her tribe's mission.

Disappointment filled her, but it was quickly replaced by confusion. *That can't be right. He said he followed the falling moon here.* Hasefi resisted the urge to give him a wary look and decided to try something else.

"Is there somewhere else these herbs could be?" she asked. "Do the, uh, high mountains end somewhere else?"

"Sure," the wolf admitted. "Just a quarter moon that way. But unfamiliar territory can be dangerous," he added as he jerked his head adjacent to the rising sun, in the direction they had come.

Hasefi looked down at her leg. The wound itself looked fine, but it was clear something inside was still broken and it didn't seem to be getting better at all. *I might have no choice,* she thought. *Especially if I want to finish my mission.* She looked to Kolahn. *He seems willing to let me choose where to go, so he can't be trying to bring me into a trap. But it still doesn't make sense. I just have to be ready.*

"Okay," she said. The wolf looked surprised. "But I get to lead."

"I could get us there faster," he pointed out, but Hasefi shook her head. Then she limped past him and began their journey in a new direction.

However, it wasn't long before exhaustion began to overwhelm her and Kolahn padded ahead to lead the way. She wanted to stop him, but she knew if she tried, he'd insist that she rested. So she followed, dragging her paws through the snow, ignoring Kolahn's suggestions to stop, until she finally collapsed into the snow.

"Sefi?" The wolf bounded to her side. "Sefi, are you okay?" Before she could react, he gently nosed her flank. She wanted to bat at his muzzle and get him away, but her paw was slow to respond. "Can you stand?"

"Obviously not," she hissed, though it sounded more like a gasp. Kolahn nosed her again and she was surprised at how gentle his touch was.

"Let me help," he said, tucking his nose under her shoulder and carefully pushing her to her paws. When she was up, he gave her his side to lean on. "There's an overhang back the way we came. We can shelter there."

Hasefi wanted to protest, but she couldn't. Instead, she let the wolf lead her back along their tracks until they veered off towards the overhang. There was a small area underneath where snow was absent and a scraggly bush with branches like twisted claws was growing from the side. Hasefi pushed away from Kolahn and sank beside the bush. The wolf laid down a couple pawsteps away, his gaze focused outside.

Hasefi wanted nothing more than to fall deep into sleep, but she forced herself to keep her head up. *If he wasn't here, I would have been left out there for a predator to find me,* she thought, appalled. *Kolahn is the only reason I'm alive—why I might stay alive, right now.* When she peered at the wolf again, she found him sitting dutifully, his eyes sweeping over their surroundings. *Like Hykalof, whenever he kept guard,* Hasefi thought. She let herself imagine that the wolf's black fur was actually the armor of her tribemate. But when a breeze whispered past, her image was broken as Kolahn's fur rippled in the wind.

I should thank him. Without giving herself a chance to think twice, Hasefi pushed herself up onto shaky legs and sat beside the wolf. He gave her a shocked look and opened his mouth, but she spoke before he could.

"Thank you."

Kolahn stared at her for a couple heartbeats before giving her a slow nod. "Maybe we should take it slower tomorrow," he told her.

Hasefi didn't respond as she imagined the other wolves finding their tracks and catching up to them. *I'd be helpless. What would Kolahn do? Would he help me? Or them?* Another thought entered her mind. *What if we came across lynxes that wanted to hurt him? Who would I help?* She looked to Kolahn, whose gaze had returned to watch outside their shelter. *Wouldn't I owe it to him to try and help? But I couldn't reject my own kind. Could I? What would be a reason they'd want to hurt him? Would I help them if they were hunting him since he was a kit? A pup? But lynxes wouldn't do that, right?*

As she watched him, the same question that had made her hesitate earlier came to mind again. *What if I told him what happened? Then I could see how he reacts. And maybe I wouldn't be so nervous around him, assuming he's not like the others. But there's something he's hiding, too. Maybe he'll tell me if I tell him.* She stifled a sigh and her mind hardened again. *I don't know this wolf. I can't trust him. I can't let my guard down. That's exactly what got me here in the first place.* Hasefi got up and moved back to where she had curled up by the small bush. She looked to the wolf one last time before lowering her head to the ground and closing her eyes.

Chapter Seven

"Does it hurt?"

"Of course it hurts, you giant furball!" Hasefi flinched away from Kolahn's careful prodding and gave her twisted leg a nursing lick. "And it won't stop. My leg is healing on the outside, but the inside still feels the same." Her ears flattened with frustration. "I just want to be able to walk again." Kolahn started to give her a sorrowful look, but he masked it as Hasefi opened her mouth to snap at him again.

"We just have to keep going," he told her quickly. "Once we get to the green mountains, we can find some herbs that will help." He gave her leg a worried glance. "Especially if it becomes infected or something."

"Infected?" Hasefi asked, trying not to sound frightened.

"It'll stop healing and get worse. Infection has a terrible scent, so we'd notice. You just have to keep it clean."

Hasefi nodded, trying to ignore the urge to sniff her leg for any signs of infection. Kolahn continued forwards again and Hasefi limped to his side.

"So, which...herbs will help?" she asked. Kolahn hesitated, causing Hasefi to feel even more afraid.

"Comfrey?" he said more as a question than a statement. "Or is it chervil?"

"You can't be asking me," Hasefi murmured quietly.

Kolahn shook his head. "I know what it smells like, I just get the names mixed up."

Hasefi relaxed slightly, but she still gave her leg a nervous glance. *It'll get better,* she told herself. *I just need to be patient.* She looked to the sun which was beginning its descent.

"How much longer?" she asked. Again Kolahn hesitated and Hasefi grew irritated. *It was better when I didn't have to depend on someone else! Then I wouldn't be so panicked all the time.*

"A couple days?"

Hasefi stumbled in front of the wolf and glared at him. "I know how the moon works," she growled. "We've been moving for a quarter moon already and you said it would only take that long." His gaze flickered briefly to her leg and bitter understanding rippled through her. "Right, it's my fault. Nevermind."

"I didn't say—"

"You didn't have to. Everything you think is on your face."

Kolahn's eyes darkened and his ears flattened. Hasefi flinched as his lips curled slightly and he spoke in a half growl. "Not everything."

"Sorry," she quickly apologized, dark memories flickering in her mind. "I wasn't trying to be mean." To her relief, Kolahn's expression softened and he gave her a sympathetic look.

"I know," he told her. "It's not your fault." His words were empty to her, even though she knew he meant them. With a defeated sigh, she sat heavily in the snow and hung her head. "You're getting stronger every day," he pointed out.

Hasefi gave him a miserable look. "What's the point of getting stronger if my leg stays the same?" Kolahn's mouth opened, but Hasefi stood and turned away from him. "Come on, I don't want to slow us down more than I already am." She waited until Kolahn slowly moved past her, taking the lead. She still didn't feel entirely relaxed with him choosing their path, but she knew if she had continued to lead, she would be slowing them down even more.

I'm useless, she thought. *If the other wolves caught up, I couldn't run. I'd be helpless. Maybe it would have been better if I died in that pit.* She quickly shoved the thoughts aside, knowing they were just as dangerous now as they had been when she was on her own. Instead, falling into old habits, she kept alert for any signs of food or danger.

It's so much easier having him, she thought grudgingly with a glance at the wolf. *Monster-birds—eagles haven't bothered me ever since he found me. And he can scent danger before I can. It's almost like I'm with my tribe again.* Her mind darkened and she glared at the wolf. *But I'm not.*

Hasefi unsheathed her claws as she thought back to the three wolves that had been chasing her before she met Kolahn. *I've killed wolves,* she thought suddenly, surprise rippling through her fur. *But they weren't up close. I'm not even sure if they really did die. But I remember the fear on their faces. They* can *die, I know that. But could I...?* She watched Kolahn closely, studying his movements. She noticed his ears prick every time there was a sound, his nose twitch when she guessed he picked up a new scent. *Maybe I could learn to fight a wolf,* she thought. *Maybe I won't have to run away forever.*

Her thoughts quickly faded when her attention moved to her left leg and she stifled a defeated sigh. *I won't be fighting anything until this stupid leg gets better.* She pushed the thought aside and focused on the shallow slope Kolahn led her down. Her mind started to wander to what these 'green mountains' might look like, but with his description of trees and waterfalls, she still had a hard time imagining it.

"Kolahn?" she asked, catching up to him.

"Yes, Sefi?"

"What else is there? Outside the, uh, high mountains, I mean. Are there other...plants?" He gave her a wary look as if trying to figure out if her question was real. Hasefi's ears flattened. "Oh, shush. I know I'm hopeless!"

"Sorry," he told her. "I'm still baffled you haven't seen the forests."

"And I'm still baffled that there's more to the world than rock and snow. What are 'forests'?"

"They're beautiful," he said. "But I don't think I can explain it to you—not if you really want to understand. You'll just have to see for yourself. But it won't be long before the mountains begin to change. We might even see some trees by tomorrow."

"Really?"

"Yes. That's what forests are mostly made of. Lots and lots of trees...."

Hasefi nodded slowly, even though she couldn't picture what he said.

"After that, the mountains will get shorter and rounder and eventually there will be parts between them where no snow reaches during the warm season."

"Warm season?"

Kolahn's expression became distraught and he stopped.

Hasefi's ears twitched uncomfortably. "What?"

"I'm sorry," he murmured.

"For what?"

"For what you've been through," he explained. "Whatever it may have been."

"You've said that already," Hasefi responded, rolling her eyes.

"I know," he admitted. "I...I hope I can show you a better life than what you've been given."

Hasefi tilted her head. "Why?"

Kolahn shrugged. "No creature should have to suffer the high mountains alone—no creature like us, I mean. Lynxes and wolves don't belong here. I...there's just so much missing that you don't know."

Hasefi's ears flattened. "I'm not stupid."

"That's not what I meant."

"I know," Hasefi sighed. "I just...never realized there was so much more beyond...*this*." She gestured at the peak they were beside. "There's so much more I should know."

"Not should," Kolahn said. "Could. There's so much more you *could* know. But that goes for any creature. No creature could possibly know everything there is to know about the world. It's just impossible." He gave her a wary look. "If you let me, I could teach you what I know."

Hasefi frowned at the snow and flexed her claws deeper into it. Then she raised her head and nodded.

"I'd like that."

The wolf gave her an excited look and he hopped once in the snow.

Hasefi purred with amusement and started to move again. "I don't think I've ever seen a creature this happy."

Kolahn gave her a shrug. "I like being able to help," he told her.

Hasefi nodded, studying him as he kept pace with her. *Kolahn is the opposite of any wolf I've ever seen,* she thought. *I really am the luckiest lynx in the world.*

"So, what are some of the things you know, then?" she asked him.

"Well, I don't think there's much about the high mountains that's left to teach you. It's fairly simple up here—survive. But in the forests, it's different. Prey is more plentiful—and there's more kinds of it. There's predators, of course, like eagles and mountain lions. There's not much of those around the valley. I haven't even seen a mountain lion in my lifetime."

"Mountain lions," Hasefi echoed. "You mentioned that before. What are those?"

"They're terribly dangerous," he told her. "You might have picked up their scent before—I think they're the only creature that actually likes the high mountains. They're cats, like you, but they're bigger than any wolf and have reddish brown fur and piercing eyes. Their fangs can crack stone and their claws can leave gouges in the rock."

Hasefi perked her ears. "I've seen one of those before."

Kolahn gave her a dubious look.

"No, really. They have black-tipped ears, right? And white muzzles...long tails."

Shock changed the wolf's expression.

"I have!" Hasefi insisted. "I...I was hiding from...from some dangerous creatures and then a monst—a mountain lion came and scared them away." Amusement was creeping into the wolf's expression now and Hasefi rolled her eyes. "Oh, please."

"What was that?" he asked.

Hasefi shook her head, refusing to answer.

"Monster lion?"

"Monster-*cat,* actually," she growled with mock annoyance.

Kolahn chuckled until the humor in his eyes returned to doubt. "It's a miracle that you're alive, then," he said seriously.

"You've also said that before, too," Hasefi said with an exasperated sigh, too aware of how many times she had eluded death.

"It's true. You are being watched over."

Hasefi shrugged and they continued on in silence for a little while.

"Are there new predators in the forests?" she asked, still wanting to know more about the forests so she knew what to expect.

"Not really. There's other dangers." The wolf suddenly stopped and Hasefi stumbled with the effort of trying to stay beside him. "There's bears."

"Bears?" Hasefi echoed.

"They're rare, like mountain lions, though you won't see them in the cold season when there's snow around. And they're just as deadly as mountain lions. Imagine a giant boulder with paws."

Hasefi had to hold back a chuckle as she imagined a boulder charging at them.

"Bears are serious," Kolahn told her sternly.

"I can't say I'd be too afraid of something I'd call a monster-boulder," she giggled and the wolf gave her a disapproving look. "Okay, maybe some of the fur on my neck would tingle at the sight of a boulder with paws." Kolahn let out a defeated sigh and Hasefi gave his shoulder a playful nudge. "Hey," she said as a thought came to her. "You said you've never seen a mountain lion. How do you know what it looks like?"

"My father told me." The moment the words came out of his mouth, the wolf seemed to regret them. He immediately fell into silence.

"I don't remember anything of my parents," Hasefi admitted slowly, wanting to make the wolf comfortable enough to talk, but wary of revealing too much. "But I had an uncle," she added carefully. "He told me a wee bit about my parents, but not much." She went quiet and Kolahn gave her an unreadable look, still silent. "Did your father see a mountain lion?"

"I don't know," the wolf admitted finally. "He would just tell us stories to scare us into staying in our den at night."

"Why would he do that?" she gasped, giving the wolf a horrified look.

"Tell us stories?"

"Scare you? That sounds horrible!"

Kolahn snorted softly. "Well, it's better than being snatched away in the night by some predator," he pointed out.

Hasefi's ears twitched indecisively. "Maybe." She thought back to the nights she had with her tribe where she would settle down with her uncle and they would just talk until she fell asleep. She never really listened to what he said since she was more focused on warming herself, but she loved falling asleep to the sound of his voice.

"Sefi?"

"*Hasefi*," she groaned.

"Too long."

She glared at him and he gave her a mischievous look. "What is it, you silly wolf?" she sighed, her whiskers twitching with amusement. The wolf hesitated for a moment before continuing.

"Why don't we take a break and I'll see if I can find some prey?"

Hasefi could tell that the wolf hadn't asked what he really meant to, but she didn't press and just gave him a simple nod.

"Okay. But let's find somewhere secure, first." Her whiskers twitched. "If a bear comes, I want to be somewhere a boulder can't squeeze into."

Kolahn gave her an unimpressed look and her whiskers quivered playfully.

When they found a place where the face of a peak had collapsed and two rocks leaned against each other to form a sheltered space, Hasefi settled down and Kolahn went off in search of food. Hasefi took the time to wash her fur, giving her leg extra care as she sniffed for any warning scents that might indicate the infection Kolahn had mentioned. But her leg seemed completely fine except for the fact it was still broken.

How much longer will it take? she thought. *All my other wounds are practically gone. Even my leg is on the way to looking okay on the outside, but the inside won't fix itself.* She stretched out her leg, trying to lay it as flat as she could along the ground. Her teeth gritted as pain throbbed through her limb. When she couldn't bear stretching it farther, she used her other paw to gently feel it.

That's...the bone, she thought. She let out a small hiss as she got to where her leg was twisted. *I can feel a lump here. Is that bone? Why hasn't it fixed itself?* She put a little bit of pressure on it, but quickly retreated and let her broken leg relax. *Prodding it isn't going to help anything. I just need to wait until we can use some of the herbs in the green mountains.* Hasefi rolled onto her flank and rested her head on the cold ground. *I just have to wait.*

When Kolahn finally returned, Hasefi found that she had dozed off. The sound of the wolf's claws on stone roused her and she lifted her head.

"Did the hares outrun you this time?" she tried to joke when she saw his empty jaws. However, she could hear the disappointment in her own voice.

"Don't worry," he told her. "Prey will be growing more plentiful soon. We've been moving down, so it'll be getting warmer. Actually I think we're closer than I thought. We might see one of the forests before sunpeak tomorrow."

"Really?" Hasefi asked, unable to completely hide her excitement. He nodded with an amused look. *I'll finally know what Sefonis was talking about. I'm getting closer to the end of my mission—I can feel it! Once we're in the forests, maybe I'll find signs of other lynxes.* Hasefi lowered her head slightly. *Would it be far enough away from the other wolves? Would they track me down all this way?*

"Kolahn?" she murmured, getting up so she was sitting.

"What is it?"

Hasefi hesitated, knowing if she used the wrong words, she could be putting herself into danger. *But I have to know.*

"Are there other creatures in the forests?" she asked. "Creatures like us, I mean? Lynxes? Wolves?"

The wolf sat down and lowered his head so his gaze was level with hers.

"I can't say for sure," he began. "But I've travelled a lot these last seven moons and I haven't come across any other wolves. I haven't seen any lynxes, either. Except you."

Hasefi nodded, feeling both relieved and disappointed at the same time.

"What are you worried about?"

"I'm not worried," Hasefi argued, narrowing her eyes angrily at him.

"Yes you are." A glint of humor lit his eye. "I can see it in your face."

"You think you're so clever," Hasefi groaned.

"I am!" Kolahn's tongue hung out and Hasefi's whiskers quivered with amusement. He settled down again and looked at her seriously. "Is there anything I can do to help?"

"I just wish I didn't feel so helpless," she said quickly, not exactly lying. "I've just been fending for myself for so long, being injured like this makes me think I'm a dead cat walking—or limping, I guess."

"Have hope," he told her. "You won't have to be so wary with me to watch your back." His friendly expression became uncertain when Hasefi shook her head.

"I don't understand," she told him. "Why? Why watch my back? Why help me?"

"I like helping other—"

"I know, I know, you said that. But why?"

Kolahn didn't respond.

Hasefi snorted with annoyance that wasn't entirely directed at him. "Another one of those questions neither of us will answer."

Kolahn didn't meet her gaze.

Feeling a little guilty, Hasefi sought a way to relieve the tension she'd caused. "Can you fight?" she asked him.

He gave her a confused look and tilted his head. "I've never fought anything before," he admitted slowly. "Why?"

"Just curious. I've tried to teach myself," she added when he started to move his attention elsewhere. "After that eagle attacked me, I thought it would be good to know how to defend myself. But it's hard when everything is so big."

"Being small can have its advantages," Kolahn pointed out. "It makes you faster. You can get into places other creatures can't."

Hasefi's ears twitched impatiently. "I've figured that much out." She stifled a defeated sigh and was about to lay back down when Kolahn spoke again.

"I could help teach you, if you wanted," he offered slowly. "I don't know much, but...we could try. If it would make you happy."

Hasefi straightened and nodded eagerly. "That would be great!" She hesitated, trying to mask some of her excitement. "I would appreciate that, I mean."

Kolahn snorted softly with amusement. "How about we start tomorrow?"

Hasefi frowned and looked down at her leg. "I won't be much good until my leg is healed," she pointed out. She lifted her head just as the wolf looked away. "We'll have to wait until then."

"It might be wiser to try with your injury," he told her. "If you ever did get into a real fight, you'd probably get injured one way or another, right? Learning to fight with one might not be so bad."

Hasefi gave a lopsided shrug. "I guess." She settled onto her side and rested her head on the ground. With her leg, she hadn't been able to curl up like she usually would to keep warm when she slept and she found she was getting tired of sleeping uncomfortably on her side. She watched enviously as the wolf curled up. *Please let my leg get better.*

The next day, Hasefi forgot her interest in fighting for a time when she noticed that the peaks were growing significantly rounder. *Can the mountains get flatter?* she wondered. *It'd be a lot easier to travel.* It wasn't long after she saw the strangest thing ever.

"What in the stars is this?" she gasped, walking up to what she could only describe as a giant, pointed bush. The branches were straight and reached out from the giant brown stalk in the middle. She tilted her head to see the top as it waved slowly in the faint breeze. There was snow weighing down some of the branches and the ground underneath was littered with the strange little green lines that covered the branches.

"That, Sefi, is a tree," Kolahn told her as he came to sit beside her.

Hasefi lowered her nose to sniff the little lines, then poked them with a paw. "So this is what you and Sefonis were talking about. This is pretty amazing," she admitted, looking up again. "And there's more?"

"Look."

Hasefi followed the wolf's gaze down the mountainside and saw that more trees dotted the snow. Her attention returned to the snow at her paws and she sniffed at the lines again.

"These look like they could be painful if you step on them wrong," she murmured, lightly putting a paw over one.

"Pine needles are actually pretty soft when they cover the ground," Kolahn told her. "Besides, your pads will get used to it when you get older. At least, I think so. I'm not sure if lynx paws are different from wolf paws." He lifted his paw and looked at the pads on the bottom. Hasefi turned towards him and sat back on her haunches to lift her good forepaw beside his.

She was surprised to find that her paws were wider than his, but not quite as long. She also saw that his pads were more exposed than hers, but Hasefi's paw was fluffier and the black of her pads was mostly hidden in white fur. She moved her paw to Kolahn's and carefully ran it over his.

"Your paw is so tough," she gasped. "How do you feel anything with it?" The wolf chuckled. "And your claws—why do you keep them out?" Hasefi flipped her paw over again and unsheathed her claws, seeing that they looked much sharper than his and curled more, too.

"I can't do that," Kolahn explained.

Hasefi looked at him, startled. "Are your paws broken?" she asked worriedly.

He laughed again, shaking his head. "Wolves can't move their claws like that," he explained.

Hasefi frowned. "That seems inconvenient. Don't they get in the way?"

He shrugged and lowered his paw. "Not when you're used to it."

Hasefi lowered her own paw, but stayed on her haunches. When she looked up at the wolf again, she realized how close she was to him and twisted to move away. Unfortunately, she fell ungracefully into the snow.

"Are you alright?" the wolf asked, clearly trying to hide amusement.

Hasefi let out a frustrated huff and pushed herself up. "I'm fine," she snapped. "I just...wish I never broke my stupid leg." Her anger quickly dissipated and she hung her head with defeat. A gentle touch on her ear made her look up and she saw Kolahn flinching away.

"Sorry, I just...wanted to comfort you," he said with an apologetic look.

"It's okay," Hasefi told him. "Thank you," she added quickly.

The wolf tilted his head with a warm look.

I didn't know a wolf could have that look, she thought. "Let's keep moving," she said, feeling awkward. He nodded and trotted past her. Hasefi followed, quickly becoming lost in awe as she studied each tree they walked past.

As they continued down the slope, the trees grew more plentiful and the snow was covered in little pine needles. There were patches where the snow was completely gone and Hasefi made a game of hopping over each one. She quickly grew tired of it, however, when she slipped and jarred her broken leg, causing her to follow the wolf in sulky silence.

The call of an eagle caused her to look up sharply, but she quickly relaxed. *It won't bother me with Kolahn here. I've hardly had to keep an eye on the sky since he found me,* she thought, looking to Kolahn who was just a couple paces ahead. *It's nice to have someone else to watch my back. I don't think I've ever been this relaxed.* Hasefi hesitated, reminding herself that Kolahn was still a wolf. But she couldn't help but realize how comfortable she was becoming with him around.

There was always the little voice that reminded her of what he was, but as the snow became shallow and the trees thickened, the voice grew fainter and fainter. It was like having him around filled a part of her she didn't realize she'd been missing.

She even started worrying less about predators. She continued the habits she had picked up from experience and the advice of her mysterious helpers, but she did so with more confidence than when she'd been alone. And there were no signs of Sal and the other wolves which let Hasefi wonder if she had finally left them behind for good. *How far would they really go to get me? Would they leave the high mountains? Do they know that this flatter ground and these trees are here?* Her thoughts shifted. *These 'green mountains' are closer than*

I thought, but they're not toward the rising sun. I never would have went this way if it weren't for Kolahn.

As the sun lowered itself out of sight, they reached a place that confused Hasefi at first. Her initial thought was that the ground fell away up ahead to some giant fall and Kolahn was about to tumble over the edge. But then her mind righted itself and she realized there were still trees and other plants growing ahead. There was just no more snow. She bounded ahead and looked warily at the green and brown ground that revealed itself. She rested the shoulder of her broken leg in the snow so she could reach out with her good paw and touch the little green plants that stood up straight.

"What is this?" she asked as Kolahn came to a stop beside her. "It's kind of soft."

"It's grass," Kolahn told her.

"Grass," she echoed, putting her paw flat on it. She pushed herself up and limped forward so she was standing completely on it. She unsheathed her claws and let them sink into the soft brown ground underneath.

"It's...weird."

"That's earth," Kolahn murmured, giving her a look mixed with warmth and amusement. Hasefi sat back on her haunches to lift her paw and saw that some of the brown still clung to her claws. She shook it, giggling when a piece landed on Kolahn's muzzle and he sneezed. With a playful squeak, Hasefi lunged ahead. Kolahn's pawsteps sounded behind her as he followed. She quickly slowed as exhaustion weighed her down, but Hasefi was too caught up in her surroundings to grow frustrated.

With the sun at the horizon, the angled light made the shadows of the trees stretch strangely across the ground. She was fascinated by them and every new thing she discovered. Hasefi absorbed every detail of everything her eyes caught. The things that interested her most were the different plants that came into view. Bright green leaves of different sizes made her wonder if the tiny, gray bushes in the high mountains even qualified as plants. There were some with colors that made her think of the sky when the sun was below the horizon and strong smells floated from those parts. Her head was getting dizzy with the new scents and all the new information.

I didn't know there were so many colors or smells or things, she thought. A rustle sounded ahead and she froze, her ears pricked as she scanned the ground ahead for any sign of movement.

"It was just a falling twig," Kolahn assured her when he caught up to her.

Hasefi's ears twitched uneasily. "There's so much cover for predators," she realized unhappily.

"And just as much for us," the wolf pointed out.

Hasefi gave a lopsided shrug and continued forwards, though more warily now.

"And more cover means more prey," Kolahn added.

That point made Hasefi pause again as she opened her mouth to taste the air.

"I think I smell prey," Hasefi said excitedly. Then she frowned. "But I don't know what it is."

Kolahn lowered his nose to the ground and started to sniff. He moved a few pawsteps forward, his muzzle sweeping the ground until he started to follow a path.

"That's deer," he told her, lifting his head. Hasefi came beside him and lowered her nose to the ground the same way he had. The scent was stronger there and she followed it until she could make out hoofprints in the earth.

"Is it like goat?" she asked. "Or sheep?"

"Sort of. Deer have short brown fur. The males have antlers, which are like horns that look like bushes without leaves. The females don't have them."

"Think we could get a meal before dark?" she asked, eagerly sinking her claws into the earth.

"Worth a try," he agreed. Kolahn lowered his head and continued to follow the trail. "It's still fairly fresh," he murmured quietly. "We should be alert."

Hasefi nodded and waited for him to move a few steps before following. She tried her best to remain silent, but each time she stepped forwards, she couldn't help but think she'd start another avalanche with how heavily her good paw hit the ground. Not wanting to scare off the deer, she fell back another pace so she could watch for Kolahn's signal.

The trail started to lead back into the snow, but soon curved down the slope. The trees continued to grow thicker and various other plants provided even more cover that made Hasefi think anything could be watching them from just a few steps away. She noticed even stranger colors on some of the plants, some she couldn't even name. It was difficult not to get distracted by them, but she managed to keep herself focused on Kolahn and the strengthening scent of the deer.

The wolf suddenly stopped, his tail lifting. Hasefi halted and peered past him, straining to see what might have alerted him. A brown flash caught her eye and she saw the flank of a creature that reminded her of the sheep and goats she had tracked in the snow, but with much shorter fur and thinner legs.

Hasefi waited for Kolahn to make a move. The wolf watched the deer for a moment, his body as still as a rock. Then he took a couple slow steps forward. Hasefi shifted, trying to catch a glimpse of the deer's face. She tilted her head, straining her neck to see past Kolahn.

Her leg gave out and she slipped onto her side, causing Kolahn to jump and the deer to straighten and flee through the trees.

"Broken stars!" Hasefi hissed, giving her injured leg a painful shake. Kolahn looked at her with flat ears and she growled wordlessly at herself.

"Are you alright?" he asked her.

"No!" she snapped. "I'm more useless than the first moon I was on my own." She tried to get to her paws, but her good leg wouldn't hold her weight and she slumped back down.

"Just take a heartbeat to rest. We've been moving a lot more these last few days than we did before. You just need to build up strength."

Hasefi could only hiss with frustration, knowing and hating that what he said was true.

He came over and carefully nosed her good foreleg. "You've been relying on it to carry half of your weight."

"Yeah, I realize that," she spat. He withdrew, but his sorrowful expression only frustrated her more. "What's the point of being saved if I can't even stand?" The wolf flinched as if she had made a retort towards him. "I'm starting to think this is never going to heal."

"Don't lose hope," he pleaded. "We've already reached the beginnings of one of the forests. I call this Edgewood. By sunpeak tomorrow, we'll start to see more of the plants that grow within. The herb we need usually grows by water, which we'll see, too."

Hasefi glared at her leg, her ears flat.

"Please, Sefi. I know you're stronger than this."

She drew in a deep breath. *He's right. We just have to make it a little farther. Soon I won't have to deal with this anymore.* Hasefi let out the breath in a long sigh.

"Edgewood?" she murmured. Kolahn turned his head, looking embarrassed. "That's kind of a neat name. Why that?"

"Well, these are the woods closest to the edge of the world."

Hasefi's eyes widened. *The edge of the world? I knew I was close! That means home must be close, too, right?* Excited, Hasefi pushed herself up so she was sitting. "Will we see the edge?"

"No," the wolf told her. "The edge is that way and the high mountains take over again before you can see it." Kolahn pointed his nose towards the rising sun and Hasefi's curiosity grew. *The rising sun was leading us to the edge? Home must be there. But it wouldn't be in the high mountains, would it? Maybe it's at the edge of...Edgewood.*

After she was able to stand again, Hasefi gave the wolf a nod and Kolahn continued leading the way. As Hasefi followed, she tried to make use of her broken leg a little more to keep some of the weight off her right foreleg, but the pain soon became unbearable and she reverted to relying completely on her good one.

Once darkness flooded the sky, Kolahn stopped at a spot where a tree had fallen and the end normally in the ground was torn up, reaching out like twisted claws. Hasefi squeezed through them into the small sheltered space they made. Kolahn came in after her, curling up as far away as he could which was only a couple pawsteps away. Hasefi saw that some of the tree's claws were poking into his pelt.

"That can't be comfortable," she said. The wolf gave a seemingly nonchalant shrug, but Hasefi could see the discomfort in his face. "I'm not going to make you sleep with those pricking your pelt. Come here," she added hesitantly.

Kolahn looked at her with uncertainty before shifting closer until their pelts brushed.

"Better?" she asked.

He nodded slowly.

"Good." Hasefi lowered her head, her nose close to the fur on his flank. After a moment, she felt him lower his head near her hind paws. The warmth from his body being near reminded her of Sefonis and she fell asleep with a faint purr in her throat.

Chapter Eight

"It's sunpeak," Hasefi pointed out with a glance at Kolahn. "I don't see this herb."

"We haven't come across any water yet," the wolf explained. "But we will soon. I'm pretty sure there's a lake not far from here."

After tasting the air and getting overwhelmed by myriad scents, Hasefi pricked her ears, wondering if a 'lake' made some sort of sound. But she heard nothing outside the rustling of branches and the strange chirping that Kolahn had explained was made by tiny little birds.

"So all of this is Edgewood? What other forests are there?"

"There's two others that I know of. The one I live in is the Great Forest."

"In the Great Valley?"

"Sort of. The forest covers a lot more land than the valley does."

Hasefi nodded, understanding. "How about the other one?"

"I haven't been to it, but from what I've seen of it, it looks dark and dangerous. I call it Darkwood."

"Darkwood," Hasefi echoed. A smirk came onto her face. "It's a good thing I didn't name it."

Kolahn gave her a confused look.

"I'd probably end up calling it Monsterwood."

The wolf let out a bark of laughter. "That actually makes it sound scarier," he pointed out.

Hasefi snorted. "How big is your home?" she asked him.

"Big enough I thought to call it the 'Great Valley'."

Hasefi snorted again and tried to peer through the trees to find any signs of water, but she only saw forest.

"It won't be much longer," Kolahn assured her again.

"You said your home was a couple moons away, right?" Hasefi asked, wondering if she could satisfy a curiosity that had been itching at her mind.

Kolahn nodded.

"But if you followed the falling moon to me, that means you would have been far from home already." She watched Kolahn closely as she spoke, but his expression didn't turn guarded.

"I like to explore," he told her. "I...decided I wanted to leave home for a bit, so I did."

"Why did you want to leave home?" she asked with surprise.

Kolahn shrugged and this time his expression did become unreadable. Knowing the conversation was over, Hasefi moved her attention to where they had left the snow behind. Then a thought came to her and she froze.

"Kolahn?"

"What is it?"

"What do we do when we're thirsty?" she asked. "There's no snow to eat."

Kolahn lifted his head and his nose twitched as if he were sniffing for something. Then his eyes lit up and he gave a little bounce. "Come on! I'll show you!"

Before Hasefi could reply, the wolf darted away. She let out a surprised squeak and limped after him. It was difficult to keep up, but he didn't leave her sight. Hasefi pushed herself, ignoring the pain in her leg and focusing on following the wolf.

Something glinted between the trees, sort of like the sun sparkling off snow, but with a different intensity. The space ahead seemed open and she grew nervous, wondering if Kolahn was running straight towards a dangerous area. *He said there weren't as many predators in these green mountains. But there has to be some watching a clear area like that, right?*

"Kolahn!" she called, but her voice was lost with the wind. Hasefi put on a burst of speed, but Kolahn only ran faster. "Sunblind wolf, come back!"

Suddenly, she burst out from the trees and almost stumbled into Kolahn as the wolf came to a halt. Hasefi lurched to the side to avoid hitting him, but still hit the ground as she lost her balance.

"What is up with you, you crazy wolf?" she gasped, getting to her paws and shaking her pelt. "Is your head full of stars?" Hasefi realized the wolf was watching her and she fluffed her pelt out, wondering if there was still some grass or dirt stuck to it. "What?" His eyes flicked to something behind her and she turned. The grassy ground gave way to a line of strangely smooth rocks that dipped towards what looked like liquid ice shimmered in the sunlight. Hasefi's eyes widened and she crept closer. *Is this all water?*

"You said this was a… a lake?" Hasefi asked.

Kolahn stepped beside her and nodded.

"But what does this have to do with eating snow?" To her amazement, the wolf bent his head and lapped at the water.

"It's way better than eating snow," he told her when he lifted his head.

Hasefi gave him a doubtful look, but started to lower her own head.

Before she was close enough, she was terrified to see a face peering back at her. With a surprised yowl, she stumbled back.

"I think there's a lynx trapped under there!" she cried. "What do we do?" She looked to Kolahn for an answer, but the wolf was laughing. "Kolahn, this isn't funny!"

"It's your reflection," he told her between chuckles. Hasefi's ears flattened with humiliation even though she didn't know what he was talking about. "It's just the water showing you."

"Showing me what?" she demanded, wishing he would quit giggling.

"*You*. It's showing you *you*. Look." Kolahn leaned over the stream. "See? It's me."

Hasefi crept beside him, watching the water warily. She saw another wolf peering back at them. It cocked its head the same time Kolahn cocked his.

"It *is* you," she murmured, realizing that she recognized his face in the water. "So that's…me?" She leaned over the water and peered down. Two green eyes looked back from a gray face. The muzzle was white and there were two large ears with black tuffs on them. They twitched the same time she twitched her own ears. Three lines stretched across the muzzle, making the face look vicious. "I'm kind of scary looking," she murmured.

"You're telling me," the wolf said. "When I first saw you, I was afraid you'd claw my eyes out."

"I'm pretty sure that thought went through my head. More than once," Hasefi admitted. She head-butted Kolahn's shoulder when he looked at her nervously. "Don't worry, I wouldn't do that now. As long as you don't give me a reason to, anyways," she added wryly. Hasefi straightened and pricked her ears. There was a faint sound that seemed to be coming from the left, but the lake curved inwards and trees blocked her view. "What is that?"

Kolahn followed her gaze, his own ears pricked. "It's the stream that feeds this lake," he explained. "I can show you."

Hasefi followed the wolf alongside the lake until they rounded the trees and came upon a large, shallow rise.

Water was trickling down it, creating pools in flat areas and pouring over the sides, zigzagging until it finally fell into the lake by their paws. "Is this a waterfall?" Hasefi asked curiously.

"Yes. But there's some that get so big and pour from so high up the water turns to mist before it even hits the ground."

Hasefi tilted her head, not entirely understanding what he meant. "Will we see one?"

"Probably not," he admitted. "There's a waterfall in the Great Valley, but it's not quite *that* big," he added hesitantly.

Hasefi wasn't sure how to respond, so she decided to change the topic to why they had come to warmer territory in the first place. "So where is this herb?"

The wolf's gaze scanned the side of the lake, then he brought his nose to the ground. "We need to look for a plant with hairy green leaves and hanging purple flowers." Kolahn's expression turned apologetic when Hasefi twitched her ears, hesitating. "Erm, what part of that did you not understand?"

"I understand," Hasefi replied defensively. "I'm just...not sure what you mean by 'purple'." She gave her chest an embarrassed lick.

"Really?" he said with a surprised look. "You've probably seen it before. In the sky, when the moon is returning to sleep or waking up."

Hasefi frowned thoughtfully. "Are you talking about a color?"

The wolf nodded. "Come on, I might be able to show you if we can find some."

Hasefi nodded and followed him back the way they had come.

Along the way, Hasefi tried to take in all the new scents that were around her. Most of them were foreign and she had no idea what they were, but every now and then she'd find one that was familiar in a way she didn't understand.

It's like I've been here before, she thought. *But I don't remember any of it. Maybe it was before the memories I do have, when I was still really young.*

"Sefi!"

Hasefi returned to the present and limped over to Kolahn. The wolf was standing beside a plant with dark green leaves that pointed out like ears and pieces that dangled which, like Kolahn said, reminded Hasefi of the darkening sky.

"This is…comfrey?" she asked.

"I think that's what it's called," Kolahn replied. "The roots will help your leg heal." He began digging at the base of the plant, carefully pulling out roots with his teeth.

"How does it work?" she asked. "Do I touch it?"

Kolahn dropped a mouthful of roots beside her and gave her a wary look. "You have to chew it up and lick it into your fur."

Hasefi screwed up her face in disgust. "That can't be right," she told him. "Why would I ever put a plant in my mouth? Also, why would I ever spit it back out onto myself?"

"It's the way herbs work for us," the wolf tried to explain. "I don't know *how* it works, I just know it does."

Hasefi gave him a repulsed look, but lowered her head to sniff the roots. She coughed as thick earth scent choked her. "Can I at least get the dirt off?"

"You could wash them in the water," Kolahn suggested.

Hasefi straightened and pawed the roots toward the lake. Then she took one in her claws and lowered it into the water. She flinched as the cold seeped deep into her paws, but made no other reaction as she rubbed the root until it was clean. She tossed it back onto the grass.

"Do I have to use all of this?" she asked, looking reluctantly at the pile.

"I don't think so. Just enough around the break."

Hasefi nodded and lowered her nose towards the root. She hesitated, narrowing her eyes. Then she straightened.

"Do I really have to do this?" she asked, searching the wolf's gaze for any signs of trickery. *What if this is a joke?* she thought.

"I can chew it up for you," he offered and Hasefi quickly shook her head.

"There's no way I'm letting you lick my fur." She let out a sigh. "Alright, here I go." She picked up the root with her teeth and bit down. Her nose wrinkled as her teeth sank into it and a bitter taste entered her mouth. Hasefi chewed until she decided it was enough.

Screwing up her face, she spat the contents of her mouth onto the wound on her leg. Then she carefully licked the pulp into her fur, wincing as the visible wound began to sting.

"This doesn't feel okay," she told Kolahn. "Are you sure this is right?"

"It's supposed to hurt a little," he told her. "It won't last long."

Hasefi continued to lick the pulp until it coated the wound. She did the same with another root, then sat back. "How long does it take?"

"I'm not sure," the wolf admitted. "You'll probably have to keep doing this for the next few days."

Hasefi felt her heart sink, but she did her best to hide it.

"We can find somewhere to stay and bring the rest with us so you can use it."

Hasefi nodded after giving the sun a reluctant glance.

"I think there's a cave not far." Kolahn picked up the roots and led Hasefi towards where the sun was beginning to descend. The lake widened and Hasefi looked across the water to the other side. There was a line of trees before the ground sloped sharply upward, then rounded out at the top of the mountain. There were no trees on the top, just boulders and gravel.

Kolahn turned away from the lake and brought her into the trees again. They came across a spot where three giant boulders came together amongst a group of fallen trees to create a sheltered space between. Hasefi saw that a path had been left behind the boulders where small trees were now growing. *They must have fallen down the mountain,* she thought. *That would have been terrifying to be around.*

The wolf entered the makeshift cave and laid the roots on a little ledge that jutted out from one of the boulders. Then he turned to Hasefi as if waiting for some sort of reaction.

"This will work for now," she said slowly, not sure what he was expecting from her. "At least until my leg is healed."

Kolahn's gaze flickered away and he nosed the roots so they were lined up more neatly. Hasefi gave her shoulder a lick, unsure what to do now.

"I'll go find some food," Kolahn decided finally. Hasefi nodded silently as he slipped past her. She turned and watched him disappear, then settled down on the dappled ground outside the cave.

I hope this comfrey works fast, she thought, looking to her crooked leg. *Then I can get back to my mission.* She glanced towards where Kolahn had went. *He wants me to stay with him,* she thought. *But he knows I'll leave the moment I can take care of myself again.* Hasefi felt a claw prick of guilt, but she quickly pushed it aside with a snort. *What does it matter? I didn't ask for his help. If he expects something from me, then he shouldn't have helped me in the first place.*

While she waited for the wolf to return, Hasefi decided to take a nap inside the cave. However, rustling soon woke her and she was surprised to see Kolahn dragging a young deer over.

"That didn't take long," Hasefi told him. "I barely closed my eyes."

"There will be a lot more prey around here with the lake," he explained after letting go of the deer. "All sorts of creatures come here to drink."

Hasefi's ears flattened slightly. "Like predators?"

"Yes," he admitted. "But they're not as common around here. We're probably the scariest things around."

Hasefi's ears twitched uncertainly, but she said nothing more on the matter. She waited until Kolahn had taken a bite of the deer, then took her own.

"I didn't know the world could look like this," she told him, peering past his bulk to the trees and grass outside. "There's just so much."

"We could explore tomorrow," he offered. "And I could teach you what some things are called and where certain prey likes to hide. I could also teach you some hunting techniques, since hunting in the forests is different than in the high mountains." A pit began to grow in Hasefi's stomach as the wolf spoke and she couldn't meet the wolf's excited gaze. "Unless…you don't want to?" the wolf asked.

"I do," she told him. "It's just…" she trailed off, not knowing what to say. Her instincts warned her not to get used to this new place, but it wasn't for the same reasons it had been before. They weren't warning her of threats that might happen upon them or of getting caught by her hunters. They were warning her of getting attached.

"It's okay," the wolf said, bringing her out of her thoughts. "There's no rush for anything. We can take our time."

Hasefi's gaze flickered away as she thought about her tribe. *When my leg is better, I have to continue my mission. But…that'll take time and it would probably be wise to at least learn about this new territory.*

"Thanks, Kolahn," she told the wolf.

When they finished eating, they moved outside to watch the sky darken and the stars come out. Hasefi felt uneasy with the different shadows and sounds that came from the forest, but Kolahn seemed relaxed, so she tried to let herself do the same.

The moon showed over the mountain tops, shining scattered white light through the trees. It was a claw in the sky that was growing gradually bigger with each night. *I've been traveling with this wolf for over half a moon,* she thought. *And I've seen more than I have in the last four.* She looked to Kolahn and was fascinated by the comfort of his presence. *I want to trust him,* she thought without meaning to. *He brought me here. He's cared for me. He's...almost like a tribemate. But he's a wolf...so what would that actually make him?* Hasefi tilted her head at the moon again as a new thought entered her mind.

"Kolahn?"

"Yes, Sefi?"

"Do you sing every full moon?" she asked.

Kolahn followed her gaze to the moon in the sky before responding. "I try to." He turned his gaze to her. "You have ancestors, right?"

Hasefi nodded once.

"What do you do to communicate with them?"

"Well," she began, thinking of the mysterious help she'd had before he showed up. "I don't...howl or anything. I just talk to them like they're here, I guess."

Kolahn nodded. "I'll do that sometimes," he agreed, surprising her. "Some nights I'll pray, too."

"What do they say to you?" she asked.

Kolahn cocked his head slightly before responding. "They don't really *say* anything. They...don't actually..." His eyes clouded for a moment. Then he blinked, reverting to normal. "They sort of just show signs. Like the falling moon."

"How did you know to follow the falling moon if they didn't tell you to?"

"I just…felt it. Its light fell upon my face in the night and woke me. The first thing I saw was the path it lit ahead and I knew I had to follow it."

Hasefi shrugged.

"Do…your ancestors say anything to you?"

"No," she said quickly, looking to her paws. "But I like to talk to them a lot." *Assuming it's them I'm talking to, anyways.*

Kolahn nodded and the two fell into silence. Hasefi focused back on the sky as more of the stars began to reveal themselves. She imagined that each one was one of her tribemates looking down at her. They felt distant and she wondered if it had to do with not thinking about them as much as she usually did. *I haven't even had much for nightmares in a while,* she realized. *I've been too focused on worrying about Kolahn turning on me and this star-cursed leg. What if they think I've abandoned them? Certainly they can't be pleased that I'm with a* wolf *of all things?*

I'm not turning my back on you, she thought firmly, staring up at the brightest star she saw. *I just need to heal and I can't do that on my own.* She closed her eyes and took in a long breath. Then she let it out and laid in the grass, relishing its warmth and soft touch against her fur. *I just need to be patient.*

Chapter Nine

Hasefi rubbed her cheek against the bark of a tree to scratch an itch that was bothering her. When she was satisfied, she sat back and looked into the forest, aware of every shadow and every needle and leaf that shifted in the wind's gentle breath.

It was Hasefi's fourth day living by the lake, but there was still so much for her to get used to. Every day she found something with colors she had never imagined or a scent that was entirely new to her.

She never strayed far from the cave when she was on her own, though. Hasefi was still afraid that if she let herself completely relax in this new territory, it would rise against her in the form of a bear or some other threatening creature.

Like a wolf.

"Sefi?" Kolahn slunk into view, the scent of prey on his breath. "There's a couple of hares in the cave when we're done."

"I still don't think it's a good idea leaving prey lying around like that," she growled.

"It's not lying around," he pointed out. "It's inside the cave."

Hasefi gave an unsatisfied shrug, but decided there was no use arguing. "Alright," she said, unable to completely hide the excitement building up within her. "Let's give this a try." They left the trees and moved to a grassy clearing beside the lake. There was plenty of room to run around and the grass was long and soft beneath her pads.

"Like I said," Kolahn began warily. "I don't really fight and I've always tried to avoid any violent situations, so I'm not sure how much I can actually teach you."

Hasefi smirked. "You've already taught me plenty," she pointed out, unable to hide her pride. "Your claws aren't as useful as mine, so you rely on your teeth more when it comes to hunting or, if it should occur, fighting. You also have really thick fur, so a simple swipe isn't going to do anything. If I want to land a meaningful blow, I have to aim it well and get close."

Kolahn looked at her with surprise. "That's really clever," he told her.

Hasefi shrugged. "Fighting isn't just about *fighting*. You have to be smart about it."

Kolahn eyed her. "But it still is about the *fighting*. It's easy to lose your senses when you're in battle."

"How would you know?" Hasefi pointed out.

"Well, it just seems like that would happen, I guess," he said with a shrug.

Hasefi snorted with amusement and gave his shoulder a teasing swipe. "You're right. But I have had my fair share of battles." Hasefi brought her paw to her face.

"More than just an eagle?" the wolf asked.

"Hunting is a battle, Kolahn. You know that, but it might not be as hard for you since you're bigger. Even hares were dangerous to me, once."

"Hares are dangerous to any hunter. I knew a wolf who was blinded in one eye when her catch fought back."

Hasefi shuddered, thankful she had never suffered such a fate.

"But you're right," Kolahn continued. "Maybe we both have more experience than I thought."

"I learnt to use my size. I'm faster than most of the things that are bigger than me, stronger than the things that aren't." Hasefi's ears twitched and she looked down to her leg. "Or I used to be." There was no longer any sign of trauma on the outside, but her leg was still bent and walking remained a struggle. It was, however, less painful to use and she was growing hopeful that she wouldn't have to stay by the lake much longer. "But, like you said, injuries will happen. I'll learn how to deal with a lame leg for now, in case something like this happens again."

The wolf nodded silently. Hasefi stood and limped a few steps away before facing him again. Kolahn watched her and they ended up staring at each other until Kolahn looked away awkwardly.

"How do we start this?" he asked her.

Hasefi's ears twitched and she put on a thoughtful face, trying to pretend she had a clue.

"Well, I suppose whoever knocks over the other wins."

Kolahn crouched slightly and Hasefi was blinded for a moment by the memory of a wolf pushing its way through the snowy barrier and flashing giant fangs.

"Sefi?"

As soon as she returned to the present, Hasefi lunged towards the wolf. He flinched backwards and Hasefi batted his cheek before limping out of reach. Kolahn shook himself and resumed his crouch, his lips raised slightly and his eyes flashing uncertainly. *He's not anything like the other wolves,* she thought briefly. Hasefi darted towards him again, but Kolahn stepped sideways and used his head to knock her on her side. Hasefi got to her paws and shook out her fur.

"Not bad," she told Kolahn and he stuck his tail in the air as he reached out with his paws. "Again?"

He straightened and gave her a nod.

They tried a few more times before Hasefi let out a frustrated growl and clawed the ground. "I'm too slow," she hissed.

"Maybe if you try a different strategy?" Kolahn suggested.

"I *have* been. But this star-cursed leg keeps stopping me! I just wish it would heal faster." She let out a defeated sigh and sank to the ground.

"We could take a break from this," he offered. "Maybe we could take a walk?"

"Because walking is easy," she growled. The wolf flinched and she forced some of her anger down. "Sorry. Yeah, maybe a walk will help." She got up and limped towards the lake and followed its shore. Kolahn followed in silence, staying a couple steps behind her. Hasefi could feel his gaze burning into her fur and she had to resist the urge to snap at him. In an effort to avoid that, she tried to make conversation to distract herself.

"You've been here before, right?"

Kolahn trotted up to her side before replying. "Yeah. Not long ago, actually. I had just passed through here towards the high mountains when I started following the moon."

Hasefi looked at him with surprise. "Really?"

He nodded.

"So you didn't even follow it for a full moon?"

"I guess not. Did you think I had?"

"I had thought before you'd left your home to follow the moon...but you were already close by." She hesitated. "What made you decide to travel so far from home in the first place?" She knew she'd asked him before, but thought she might have different luck with the answer this time.

"I told you, I like to explore," he murmured, looking away.

Hasefi narrowed her eyes. *Maybe, but that's not the whole truth.* Hasefi knew there was no point in trying to find answers from him, so she let the topic go in search of another one.

However, her frustration with her leg returned and it built up until she felt like she was going to explode. Wanting to let out the energy, Hasefi pushed on ahead, veering off into the trees and leaving the lake behind. As she ran, she tucked her twisted leg against her chest so it wasn't jarred after each step. Her right foreleg got tired quickly, though, and she had to stop when she reached a little clearing where the sun shone on the grass that rose from the pine-needle covered ground.

Various flowers and shrubs surrounded the clearing, coloring it with bright greens and pretty yellows and blues. The gentle breeze and the peaceful surroundings gave her a chance to calm down and she sat in the middle. Her ears twisted back as she listened for Ko-lahn, but there was no sign of him. *He's probably giving me a chance to be alone,* she thought.

Hasefi's eyes were attracted to a small plant that grew a few pawsteps into the clearing. She had never seen it before and got up to look at it. The leaves were long and dark and many, curling into the base of the plant and putting the ground beneath into darkness. Rising above the leaves were bunches of flowers that reminded her of the night sky when the moon was rising, sort of like comfrey, but lighter. The flowers drooped differently, too, opening up to reveal yellow insides.

Wanting to remember this plant in case it turned out to be another herb they could use, Hasefi leaned towards it and sniffed. A terrible bitter scent caused her to recoil and she twisted her face with disgust. *No helpful plant would smell like that, right?* she thought.

"Hasefi, stop!"

She froze, her eyes darting around as she tried to find what had caused Kolahn to call out to her. Something poked her side and she let out a startled squeak as Kolahn herded her back into the middle of the clearing. She quickly recovered and ducked away from his nose, her fur fluffing up as she gave him a baffled look.

"What is with you?" she demanded. "Is this a game?" Despite her words, she could tell by the wolf's face that whatever was happening was serious.

"I'm sorry," he told her, sounding breathless. "I forgot to tell you. There are other threats." He paused for a moment and Hasefi shook her head, not understanding.

"What threats?"

"Wolfsbane."

Hasefi continued to look at him blankly. Kolahn jerked his head towards the edge of the clearing, in the direction of the plant she'd been inspecting.

"I don't see anything," she said flatly.

"Plants can be just as harmful as teeth and claws," he explained. "In this case, even more harmful."

Hasefi snorted with amusement and looked to the plant. "What, is it going to trip me? I already do that on my own." Kolahn's ears flattened slightly and she saw there was still no humor in his expression. "Are you being serious?"

"Just touching wolfsbane can kill a creature, Sefi," he said quietly. "Did you touch it?"

"No," she replied slowly, getting a little nervous. "That can't be possible, though."

"Some plants heal, some kill. I don't know how, but they just do. Are you sure you didn't touch it?" he asked.

"Yes!" she gasped. "Why? What would happen if I did?" She gave the plant a scared look, but still couldn't see how *flowers* and *leaves* could harm her.

"You would get sick," he explained. "It would get worse and worse until you die. Even smelling it can make you sick."

Hasefi's ears went flat. "I may have…sniffed it," she admitted quietly.

Kolahn gave her a frightened look.

"I'm not going to die, am I?"

"No," he said quickly, sounding panicked. Hasefi winced. "You won't," he assured her. "You just might get sick. I'm sorry, I should have warned you."

"Let's go back," she decided, trying to control her voice.

Kolahn nodded and moved past her towards the cave. Hasefi gave the plant, wolfsbane, one last look before quickly following him.

They moved in silence, but Hasefi could see Kolahn's attention focused on her, even though he was clearly making an effort to hide it. She didn't care, though, since her attention was also focused on herself as she waited for some sign she was getting sick. The one time she ever had been ill was in the mountains when the rest of her tribe had been similarly afflicted. But it had just been a sore throat, coughing, and exhaustion, then. Now, she couldn't imagine what it might be that could lead to death.

I can't die now, right? I just found the kind of place my uncle kept telling me about and I still have to follow the rising sun. I can't die.

When they reached the cave, Hasefi didn't feel any different than before she had sniffed the wolfsbane other than scared.

"How are you feeling?" Kolahn asked her and her ears twitched with annoyance.

"I'm fine," she said shortly. He hesitated before giving a slow nod and moving towards the entrance again. "Where are you going?"

"I'm going to remove it," he explained. "The less wolfsbane in the forests, the better."

Hasefi shook her head. "Isn't that dangerous?"

"Maybe, but it'll be just as dangerous to keep there. If one of us is careless, or if prey happens upon it and becomes our next meal—"

"Okay, I get it. But you're not doing it alone."

Kolahn's eyes flickered to her leg. "It's too dangerous for you—"

"I know I can't help," she snapped. "But I'm not going to sit here and wait to see if you come back or not." Hasefi stood and jerked her chin in the direction of the lethal plant. Kolahn stood still for a moment before giving in with a sigh.

"We should find a branch," he told her. "Something I can use to get it out of the ground."

Hasefi nodded and they searched the forest for something that would help. It wasn't long before Hasefi found a fallen branch with a small fork at the end and a thick base for Kolahn to hold. He picked it up with his jaws and they headed towards the clearing.

When they entered, Hasefi watched a fuzzy little winged creature Kolahn had called a 'bee' hanging on the bottom of one of the wolfsbane's flowers. As they approached it, the bee flew into the air, buzzing lazily away.

"You're sure wolfsbane is lethal?" she asked him. Kolahn merely nodded and Hasefi decided to settle with the fact that it probably was.

The wolf angled himself near the plant and began using the branch to uproot it. Hasefi stood back to avoid any parts that were flung about as he dug. It was a long process, but eventually Kolahn had removed the wolfsbane from the ground so it was lying limply on its side.

"Now what?" Hasefi asked.

"Now we bury it deep in the earth."

Hasefi watched the wolf as he moved a couple paces away and began digging. He didn't stop until the hole was almost as big as him and he was panting with the effort it cost. Then, he used the stick to push the plant into the hole and started filling it in again. Hasefi came forth and helped scoop some of the earth over the wolfsbane, eyeing it until it was no longer visible.

"How do you know about wolfsbane?" she asked as they continued to paw more dirt into the hole.

"I was told," he admitted.

"Did your father tell you a story about it?" she dared press. Kolahn shook his head. Hasefi waited for him to explain, but he remained silent. She said nothing more until the hole was filled and Kolahn stomped on the earth a few times.

"At least I never had to worry about killer plants in the high mountains," she murmured. Kolahn gave her an apologetic look, but she spoke before he could try and apologize. "I think I'm going to sit by the lake for a bit."

"Would you like company?" he asked.

Hasefi shook her head, pretending not to notice the hurt in his eyes. "I won't be long. Meet you at the cave?"

Kolahn nodded and she left him alone in the clearing. When she reached the lake, she lapped up a few mouthfuls of water, then stared at her reflection.

I almost died. Again, she thought. *But not because something was hunting me or a mountain was angry. I was almost killed by a plant. Leaves. Flowers. All because I didn't* know. Hasefi's ears flicked. *Everything else was easy to figure out because it already seemed dangerous. But a plant? What other dangers are out there? What more do I need to know to survive in this place?* Hasefi sighed, knowing that, despite dodging death, it wasn't truly the wolfsbane that was making her feel anxious.

The rising sun. Every day that passes that I don't follow it is making me feel more and more impatient.

"Sefonis," she barely dared whisper his name partly because she was afraid Kolahn would be listening and partly because she was afraid her tribe was angry with her. "I can't go yet," she told him. "I have to wait until I'm better. But Kolahn..." She looked in the direction the wolf had disappeared. "Leaving him will be hard. He helped me and he seems so keen on continuing to help. I know he's a wolf, but he's not like the others. I know him." Her heart sank and she lowered her head. *I don't know him. I don't know where he came from. He still hasn't told me. But I haven't told him, either.*

Hasefi raised her head and peered into the darkening sky. *When I'm better, I'll go. I haven't lost sight of our mission. Home isn't going anywhere, right? There's no point in hurrying and risking myself to get there if I don't have to.* She looked to her leg and carefully sniffed it. The coat of comfrey she had put on earlier had mostly rubbed off, so she got up and went to where she and Kolahn had stored the roots in the cave. The wolf was nowhere around and Hasefi felt a prick of guilt. Then she pushed it aside and applied the comfrey. After a fresh coat was on, she went and grabbed one of the hares Kolahn had left and returned outside.

When she finished, she found herself feeling restless. She thought about running into the trees, but she knew she wouldn't make it far with her leg. Instead, she noticed a low hanging branch from one of the trees a few paces away. She hopped over to it until she stood directly underneath it.

She leaned back on her haunches and tried to swipe at the branch, but it was too high. She lowered herself to her paws again and tried to hop up to reach it, but it was still too high. She flicked her ears and gave her chest an embarrassed lick before turning back towards the cave. Then she stopped.

If I ever had to face the other wolves, I'd need to be able to jump on their backs where it's harder for them to reach. Hasefi looked back towards the broken branch. She turned herself and crouched. She tried to put weight on her injured leg, but quickly resorted to tucking it into her chest. She stared at the branch, breathing slowly as she gathered her haunches beneath her.

She leaped forwards, bounding once before leaping into the air with her good paw stretched towards the branch. She felt her claw brush the bark and let out a victorious yowl. However, she hit the ground awkwardly and rolled a couple times before landing on her flank.

Hasefi pushed herself up, growling at the branch. *If I can't land a jump, I'll be torn up, too.* She crouched again, taking less time before she charged and leapt for the branch. Her paw missed it by a whisker-width, but she managed to stay on all three paws when she landed.

I need a balance between strength and control, she thought, echoing the words that had been whispered to her when she'd learnt to hunt while she was on her own. She lowered herself a third time, her eyes focused on the branch. She thought of the wolf that had killed Sefonis, the one she guessed was Sal. Hasefi imagined the branch was Sal's muzzle as he stared down at her. Gleaming teeth and loathing yellow eyes appeared in her head. Instead of being scared, however, she felt angry. Hateful.

Hasefi launched herself into the air, letting out a hiss as her claws extended to their full length. To her surprise, her pad smacked the branch and her claws dug into the bark, causing it to rip away from the tree and hit the ground as she did. Hasefi stumbled slightly with the branch underneath her, but she managed to remain upright. She ducked as needles fell from above, hitting her pelt and the ground around her. With an amused breath, she shook herself out and released the branch. Pride welled within her as she looked at her catch.

Maybe one day I could actually face Sal and the other wolves, she thought. *Maybe I won't have to train just to defend myself.* Rustling caught her attention and she trotted back towards the cave. Kolahn appeared a moment later, his expression holding his usual delight when he approached her. Hasefi gave him a friendly rumble as he took out the other hare and laid it near her.

"I don't think the wolfsbane affected me," Hasefi told him as he started to eat.

The wolf nodded agreement. "We'd probably start to notice signs by now."

"Good. I'm tired of being crippled. Getting sick would just make things worse."

Kolahn nodded again, but his expression was glazed.

"Is there anything else I should be afraid of in the forests?" she asked.

"Not in Edgewood," he told her. "There might be some other poisonous plants, but they're only harmful if you eat them. The denser forests might have some more harmful stuff, like bugs."

"Like bees? You said they could...sting, right?"

"Yes," he agreed. "But we're still high up in the cold, so there isn't too much to worry about. But the Great Forest is lower in the mountains where it's warmer. Things like spiders can be dangerous if they bite you."

"What's a spider?"

"There's all kinds and they can be any color, but they always have eight legs. You'll know when you see one."

Hasefi shuddered. "Eight legs? That doesn't sound pleasant. How big are they?"

"Like I said, there's all kinds. But the biggest I've ever seen is hardly the size of my paw."

Hasefi's ears flicked with surprise. "Something that tiny could kill us?" she wondered. "You wouldn't even see it coming."

"They don't go out of their way to attack," the wolf assured her. "Just don't step on one or walk through its web."

Hasefi's whiskers twitched with uncertainty and she couldn't help but scan the ground around her. "I think I'm starting to miss the high mountains."

Kolahn chuckled softly and Hasefi let out a tiny snort. They were silent for a bit while Kolahn finished his meal, buried the remains, and licked his jaws clean. Then the wolf looked over to her with an amused expression.

"Sefi?"

"What?" she asked with narrowed eyes.

"Why are there pine needles in your pelt?"

Hasefi's ears went flat and she twisted her head to look at her flank. Sure enough, needles were still stuck in her pelt and embarrassment warmed her fur.

"Um, well, there's a perfectly logical explanation for that," she said hesitantly, earning a chuckle from Kolahn. "There is!"

"What is it, then?"

"I was…fighting a dangerous creature?"

"A dangerous creature?" Kolahn echoed, his eyes sparkling.

"That looked like a branch…."

Kolahn snorted and shook his head while Hasefi rolled her eyes. "Did you win?" he asked.

Hasefi raised her head proudly. "I did. He didn't stand a chance."

Kolahn laughed again and Hasefi felt warmth spread through her again, this time from affection.

"I remember this time when I was a pup and a leaf blew into my den," Kolahn began with a hint of a smile. "It was huge and I had never seen anything like it—I thought it was going to attack my brothers. So I pounced on it and woke them up."

Hasefi laughed, imagining the annoyed looks Kolahn probably received for his heroic actions. But she also soaked in every word, wanting to know every detail about his past.

"Sounds like you were the hero they needed, even if they didn't want it," she purred. To her dismay, the wolf's expression waned and he gave a half-hearted laugh.

"Yeah," he murmured, his gaze on his paws. Hasefi opened her mouth, but she didn't know what to say. To her relief, Kolahn spoke. "Did you want to try practice-fighting again tomorrow?" he asked.

"Yes please," she said eagerly.

And so they did.

It was a slow process, but Hasefi was getting used to her lame leg and was able to work around it. She was also pleased to see that the wolf was learning just as much as she was and was growing more comfortable with fighting. He even seemed to enjoy it sometimes. Hasefi enjoyed it quite a bit herself, but every time she tripped or stumbled, she was reminded that she was as helpless as a newborn kit. It didn't help that her leg seemed to be making no progress in healing, even after another quarter moon.

"Broken stars!" she spat, raking her claws through the ground only to jar them against a rock. She had tried to feint to one side to surprise Kolahn with a blow to the cheek, but she had lost her balance and teetered towards the lake until her paws splashed into the freezing water.

"Maybe we should rest for a moment" the wolf decided.

"I have been resting!" Hasefi snapped, shaking her paws angrily. "But nothing is happening! This leg won't heal! I'm going to be lame forever!" Hasefi let out an angry huff and sat heavily on the ground.

"Did you want to try hunting?"

"So I can scare off all the prey again?" She let out an annoyed growl when Kolahn looked at her helplessly. "Why do you always give me that look?"

"What look?"

"The look that makes me think I really will be lame forever."

The wolf's ears flattened and he looked away.

Hasefi felt her heart drop and her anger was jarred into fear. "I won't be, will I?" she asked quietly.

"Sefi...I...I'm not sure if...." He trailed off and Hasefi felt despair wash over her.

"I'm crippled." she breathed. "I'm going to be crippled forever."

"I'm sorry," he whimpered. "I didn't want to say anything because I thought maybe it would heal. But, without a gifted, I don't know what to do."

Hasefi sank to the ground, her eyes staring ahead into nothing. "I should have died in that pit."

"No, don't say that," the wolf pleaded. "We can learn to work around this."

"I don't want to work around anything, Kolahn. I've been running my whole life and now I can't even walk! You can't expect me to keep going like this." *How can I finish my journey to the rising sun if I can barely walk?*

"You have to. You've made it this far!" He paused and Hasefi gave him a dull look. "You don't have to run anymore."

Hasefi's ears flattened and she looked away. "You don't understand," she sighed.

"Maybe not," he agreed. "But I'm not going to let you give up." He sat himself barely a pawstep away from her muzzle.

"Why not?"

"Because you're my friend." The wolf's words brought a memory to the front of Hasefi's mind and she let herself sink into it, relishing the presence of her tribe, no matter how faint.

The memory took her to one of the many nights when there was hardly enough food for a single lynx, let alone a tribe. Sefonis had pawed over his portion to her despite not having eaten the last time there was food. Hasefi had always eaten without question, but that night she had hesitated and looked up at her uncle.

"Why won't you eat?" she had asked.

"I'm not hungry, wee lass."

"That's a lie. I can hear your belly rumbling." She flattened her ears. "Why are you giving it to me?"

"You need your strength," he explained.

"For what? I'm small. You need more because you're big."

Her uncle didn't respond then and she wondered if she had made him upset.

"I just think we should all eat, at least," she said.

"You will make a brilliant Highchief," he murmured, his eyes glowing.

"So you'll eat?"

Sefonis shook his head.

"Why not?"

"Because you're family, Hasefi, and it is my duty to protect and care for you, no matter what. Your life comes before mine."

Hasefi stared at her uncle for a moment before shaking her head.

"I still think you should eat."

Sefonis's laughter echoed through Hasefi's mind as she returned to the present. There was an ache in her chest that was almost pleasant and she let it linger for a little longer. *If there's a tribe out there, I need to show them I can be worthy of the title I was given. I can't let this get in my way.* Hasefi lifted her head again, widening her eyes so she was giving the wolf a bewildered look.

"Kolahn?"

"What?"

"What's a 'friend'?" she asked.

The wolf's mouth opened, but no sound came out right away. He got to his paws and gave her a baffled look.

"You don't know what a friend is?"

Hasefi let out a soft chuckle and the wolf narrowed his eyes suspiciously.

"Of course I know what a friend is," she murmured. Then, she slowly pushed herself up and met the wolf's gaze again. "And, well, I guess you're mine, not that I've really had a friend before."

Delight glowed in the wolf's yellow eyes and he stuck his tongue out in that goofy smile. He quickly relaxed, however, when Hasefi lowered her head, and sat down again.

"You know," he began. "I was hunting this one time and I came across a deer that had a twisted hoof. In my head, I was thinking it would be an easy catch since something like that could never outrun me. So, when I went after it, I didn't worry much about running. Which was why I lost the deer."

"Really?" Hasefi asked disbelievingly.

"I had underestimated it and it cost me a meal."

Hasefi looked down at her leg, this time without the usual hatred she felt. "I've been underestimated," she murmured. "Because I'm small. And young. It's probably why I'm still alive."

"It doesn't have to be all bad," Kolahn told her.

Hasefi sighed, making a decision. "There's something I need to tell you."

Kolahn's eyes darkened.

"I wasn't some kit lost in the mountains. I had a path."

The wolf tilted his head in confusion.

I can't tell him everything, yet, but I can tell him about my mission, at least. "I was following the rising sun. Because my ancestors told me it would bring me home."

"The rising sun?" Kolahn echoed. His eyes widened. "The falling moon...our ancestors led us to each other."

Hasefi shrugged. "My mission isn't over," she pointed out. Kolahn deflated slightly, but Hasefi was determined to continue, now that she had begun. "I still need to find this home. I have a mother and a father, Kolahn. I don't remember them, but I think they're where the rising sun is leading me."

"But your leg will make it difficult," he pointed out.

"Yeah, I realize that. But if it's not going to get better, there's no point for me to wait anymore."

"A moment ago you said you would rather be dead."

"A moment ago you were trying to convince me I shouldn't give up." She gave him a challenging look, wondering why he had shifted suddenly. But the wolf offered no answers as he looked away. *He wants me to stay with him, but he can't expect that to actually happen, right?* she wondered. *I know he saved me and I know this has been nice, but I have a home. I have a family. And he's a wolf.* "If you had family you could go back to, wouldn't you?"

"Without hesitation," his voice was barely a whisper.

"So you have to understand when I say I have to do this. Whether or not it's alone is up to you."

The wolf gave her a surprised look. "You'd do it?" he asked. "You would go, even if I don't agree to help?"

Hasefi felt a lump in her stomach at the wolf's words, but she forced herself to remain firm. "What other choice do I have?"

"Stay. With me. We could go to my home in the Great Valley and I could show you my territory. It's much better than this.

Wouldn't you like that?" There was desperation in the wolf's voice which made Hasefi start to feel her own desperation.

"Lynxes died for me to get where I am," she said through gritted teeth. "I can only promise to do the same. I owe it to them. Their deaths can't be in vain."

"But they weren't. You're alive. And happy. Aren't you happy?" The panic in the wolf's tone made Hasefi's heart twist, but she resisted the urge to give his shoulder a comforting rub with her cheek.

"Kolahn, you saved my life and offered me a home. You have a kindness I didn't know could exist in the world beyond my own kind. But you have to understand that I have a mission. I can't abandon it for a simple life. There's more to me than you know. Just like there's more to you than I know."

Kolahn hung his head.

"Please, Kolahn."

"Sefi, there's nothing towards the rising sun," he whispered. "It's just ocean."

Hasefi shook her head. "I don't know what 'ocean' is, but I can't let that stop me. Besides, you can't believe that there's absolutely nothing. I know now that the world is bigger than I could ever imagine, even if we are on the edge. You couldn't have explored all of it in the last eight moons."

Kolahn didn't respond and Hasefi stifled a disappointed sigh. Not knowing what else to say, Hasefi rose and slowly turned towards their cave.

"When do we leave?"

Hope flared through Hasefi like the first rays of sunlight at dawn. She quickly took control of her excitement and faced Kolahn again.

"Tomorrow," she told him. "At dawn."

The wolf nodded once, lifting his head. She could see there was pain in his eyes even though he was trying to hide it behind a determined expression.

"We will see your mission done," he told her. With that, he moved past her into the cave. Hasefi watched him, wishing she could help him feel less reluctant.

He has to understand, she thought. *If it was the other way around, I would help him.* Hasefi hesitated. *Wouldn't I?* She peered behind her into the trees with a frown. *If I had no one to go to, no mission to follow, would I help him with his?* She looked back to where Kolahn was settling down on his side of the cave. *What mission would a wolf have? Except to follow the moon to an injured lynx?* Hasefi gave her pelt a shake and pushed the thoughts aside. *I can't worry about that. I have a mission to finish.* She glanced into the sky, noticing a full moon was rising. Hasefi felt a pang, knowing Kolahn probably had no intention of howling tonight.

I'm sorry, she told him silently. *But I have to find home. For my tribe.*

Chapter Ten

The moment Hasefi's paws touched snow, she began to regret deciding to leave Edgewood. *I was hoping I had left the snow behind,* she thought. *But Kolahn did say the high mountains wrap back around.* She stifled a disappointed sigh. *This is for my tribe,* she told herself. *They all suffered much more than cold paws.* She looked ahead to where Kolahn was scouting a few paces in front. He had been uncharacteristically quiet since they left yesterday morning and it only made Hasefi feel guilty. *He didn't have to come,* she thought with annoyance, but it quickly dissipated. *Maybe he just needs space to think.*

She focused her mind on keeping her legs moving. Traveling through snow and across slippery rock was difficult, but Hasefi moved carefully. *It's better to show up late than not at all. Besides, home isn't going anywhere.* Hasefi tilted her head curiously. *Home. I haven't had a place I could call home.* She thought briefly of the cave she and Kolahn had stayed in, but quickly pushed it aside. *That was just a shelter. My home is wherever the rising sun leads.*

A rock blocked Hasefi's path and she jumped onto it. She stopped for a moment to try and peer at the path ahead, but it revealed nothing. *I wonder what ocean is,* she thought as she returned to the ground, placing her paw in Kolahn's prints. *Kolahn said it was the only thing there. Is it big? Is it a mountain? Maybe 'ocean' is a wolven word.*

She thought about asking the wolf, but suppressed her curiosity, knowing the last thing she wanted was to annoy him right now.

The day pressed on, still in silence. It made Hasefi think of her time alone, when the only time she used her voice was to talk to the voices in her head or to snarl at wolves. But it was still different having a physical presence nearby, knowing there was someone to talk to who was watching her back as much as she was watching his. *I don't want to travel like this,* she thought. *I have to try and talk to him.* She bounded towards the wolf, only to skid to a halt as he froze. Hasefi limped to his side, following his gaze to where large prints crossed their path.

"Mountain lion," Hasefi whispered. Kolahn's nose hovered over the prints.

"The scent is stale," he murmured. "But we need to be careful."

Hasefi nodded, trying to push aside her fear. The glimpse she'd had of a mountain lion didn't haunt her like her tribe's murder, but it made her fur prick and her legs shake when she thought about seeing something like that again.

"Kolahn, what if we come across one?"

"I doubt we will," he told her. "Mountain lions are practically never seen."

"Or, the chances of living after seeing one are small."

Kolahn's ears flicked.

"But there has to be some chance, right?" she pressed. "Otherwise scary stories for pups wouldn't exist."

"We'll be fine," he told her. "Like I said before, I've never seen one and I've explored plenty of land in the high mountains." His words calmed her somewhat, but she kept her ears pricked for any sounds while her eyes studied every shadow and crevice. However, her desire to continue talking to Kolahn divided her attention.

"So you've explored all the way to this...ocean?" she asked. "How far away is it?" She winced when the wolf's expression fell somewhat.

"It's a few sunrises away."

Hasefi's whiskers twitched with surprise. *Maybe my home is before it. But does that mean it's in the snow? Maybe the green mountains will come back before we reach this ocean.*

"Are there other warm places in the world?" Hasefi asked. "Like Edgewood and your valley?"

"The mountains on the other side of the valley flatten out and there's open space where you can see a long way."

"Flatten out? Like they're squished?" Hasefi asked, giving him a dubious look.

"Sort of."

Hasefi tilted her head, but the wolf said nothing more. Finally, she gave up and fell back a few steps.

Before the sun was hidden by the peaks behind them, they found a large cave hidden behind a boulder to sleep for the night. Kolahn murmured about going hunting and left Hasefi sitting in darkness.

He doesn't want to talk to me. Is he mad at me for wanting to go back to my tribe? Wouldn't he want to return to wherever he came from? He said he wasn't always alone. What if I told him about my tribe? Would he tell me what happened to him?

Hasefi was deep into her mind when Kolahn returned and she didn't notice until he dropped a scrawny hare at her paws. She frowned at it, once again regretting her decision to return to the unforgiving cold.

"It's all I could find," he told her. Hasefi pushed it towards him, but Kolahn turned away. "I'm not hungry."

"Well, neither am I." Silence floated between them and Hasefi drew in a deep breath. "Kolahn, what's going on?"

The wolf continued to study the ground.

"Does it have something to do with why you're alone?" she dared ask him.

"No," he said quickly.

"Then what? Why are you upset?"

He lifted a paw and pushed a tiny rock with his claw.

"Kolahn, I don't want us to part like this."

"So you *would* leave me?" The hurt in his expression when he looked at her was sharp enough to pierce her heart. Hasefi opened her mouth, but nothing came out. "Did I do something wrong?"

"Kolahn, no. It's not like that. Don't you understand?"

He hung his head, one eye towards her, but not meeting her gaze.

"I've told you," she tried. "This is my purpose. The…lynxes I was with before… they're gone now, but their mission still lies with me. I have to complete it. It'll weigh on me until I do."

"But what happens if you do find other lynxes?" he whimpered. "What happens then?"

Hasefi hesitated. She'd always known she would stay wherever the rising sun led her, but it didn't seem quite as simple now that she had Kolahn. Even though her mind told her she'd join whoever waited at the end of her journey, another part of her made her think otherwise.

"I'd join them," she said quickly, startled that she was thinking twice about her tribe's mission.

"And that's it? I would just go home?" he asked.

"Maybe you could be with us?" Hasefi tried.

"Wolves and lynxes don't mix well, Sefi. You know that better than anyone." His words sent icy claws through her and she shot to her paws.

"What in the world makes you say that?" she snapped.

Kolahn met her gaze, his head low so their eyes were level. "The lynxes you were with were killed by bl—by wolves, weren't they?"

A mixture of fear and anger whirled through Hasefi and her lips pulled back in the beginnings of a snarl. Kolahn only reacted by closing his eyes and nodding as if having proved something.

"So you knew, huh? Why didn't you say anything?"

Kolahn didn't respond which only made Hasefi angrier.

"Is it because you're hiding something about what happened?" she hissed. "Are you responsible—?"

"No!" All of a sudden Kolahn was looming over her, his eyes as fiery as the ones that haunted her dreams. "I'm not like those wolves. And I never will be!"

Hasefi shrunk back against the cave wall behind her, preparing to defend herself if she had to. But Kolahn quickly retreated and hunched a few steps away from her.

"I didn't say anything because I was afraid you'd ask about me," he whispered.

"I didn't say anything because I was afraid you'd turn on me," she replied just as quietly.

Kolahn flinched at her words.

"But I'm beginning to think I was wrong about that," she added slowly.

Kolahn was silent.

Hasefi settled on the ground. Her fur was still spiked from his outburst, but her fear was changing directions. "What happened?" she asked gently.

"I can't tell you," he said quietly but firmly. "You just have to know I'm nothing like them, okay?"

Hasefi opened her mouth to ask how he knew about the wolves that had murdered her tribe, but when she saw the desperate look in his eyes, she stopped.

"Okay," she told him. "But this doesn't stop my mission. I need to follow the rising sun home, Kolahn. I don't know what I'll do when I find it," she added when misery entered his expression. "But I don't think I'll know until I do." The wolf kept his attention focused on his paws. "Kolahn, you're my friend. Maybe a moon ago I wouldn't have thought twice about leaving you behind, but that's not how it is now."

Kolahn pricked his ears and turned his head towards her.

"We'll figure something out, okay?" she assured him. "For now, let's just figure out why my ancestors were so intent on what lies at the end of the rising sun." She waited for Kolahn to respond. He was still and she was prepared to give up and sleep for the night, but he finally spoke.

"You know I want you to be happy, right?" he whispered. "I really do."

"I know. But you want you to be happy, too."

"I'm selfish," he growled.

Hasefi shook her head. "No, you're *alive*. No creature wants to spend the rest of their life alone, you know I understand that. I wouldn't just forget you—you're too important."

Kolahn finally lifted his head and met her gaze, his muzzle tilted down as he looked at her.

"You've done so much for me, Kolahn. I owe it to you."

"You don't owe me anything," he murmured. "You've already given me more than I deserve."

Hasefi held his gaze for a moment. Then, she stepped forward and buried her nose in the fur on his cheek and she felt him rest his muzzle on her shoulder. "You deserve to be happy, Kolahn," she told him.

The wolf drew away and their gazes met. "Let's finish this journey," he told her. Warmth spread through Hasefi and she gave the wolf a grateful look.

"Thank you."

Kolahn leaned toward her and gave her cheek a lick. She let out a surprised squeak and jumped away

"I'm sorry," he said, withdrawing.

"It's okay," she told him. "Why isn't your tongue rough?" she asked.

Faint amusement entered his expression. "Because I'm not a cat."

"Really?" she asked, giving her shoulder a lick to compare.

"Um...?" Kolahn asked with his head cocked.

"No, I mean obviously I know you're not a cat! Wolves are just so weird."

Kolahn chuckled and stuck out his tongue.

Hasefi stuck out her own. "Thith ith what a tongue thould be like."

Kolahn barked with laughter and Hasefi felt a sense of relief that things were okay again. She turned to grab the hare and placed it between them. Kolahn settled down and lowered his head towards the hare. Hasefi took a bite when he drew away and they fell into comfortable silence. She could still see there was reluctance in the wolf's expression, but affection and determination were stronger.

The following day, they travelled much more comfortably. There was still silence, but it was relaxed and would often be broken by a small comment that didn't always relate to their journey at all. But as each step took them closer to the end, Hasefi felt excitement ripple through her fur.

There could be lynxes anywhere! she thought. Hasefi looked at every print, waiting to find ones like her own. Every shadow that moved she peered at, hoping to see a friendly feline face peering back. But, so far, there were no signs of other lynxes.

They would have to keep themselves hidden, she thought. *They wouldn't want to meet a mountain lion or wolves or something.* Hasefi realized with surprise that she hadn't worried about the threat of wolves despite returning to the high mountains. *Maybe I really have escaped them,* she thought hopefully. *Even if I did see them again, once I find other lynxes, I won't have to be afraid anymore.*

Her mind shifted to the thought of her parents. She didn't remember anything from them—the only blood she knew was Sefonis. An idea came to her mind and she looked to her companion.

"Kolahn?"

"What is it?" The wolf stopped and let her catch up.

"Did you have an uncle?" To her surprise and dismay, his gaze darkened and his lips lifted in the beginnings of a snarl.

"Not one worth mentioning."

"Right…sorry," she murmured.

The wolf relaxed and gave her an apologetic look. "You had one, right? Sefonis?"

Hasefi looked at him with shock. "How do you know that name?" she demanded.

"You've said it before," he explained. "And…you've murmured it in your sleep, too."

Hasefi's fur twitched with embarrassment.

"Did he take care of you before?"

"I don't want to talk about this, Kolahn," she said, caught off-guard. The wolf shut his mouth immediately and returned his attention ahead. Hasefi watched him for a few moments before following.

He's figured out quite a bit about me even though I've hardly said anything. Or maybe I haven't been as careful as I thought. She frowned. *I still don't know anything about him!* Her ears twitched. *Well, that may not be true. He's told me he had a family. A mother, a father. Brothers. He knows there's wolves out there and he has an obvious fear of being left alone. Could he have been a part of the other wolves and they let him go or something? But he's nothing like them. Maybe that's why he's alone now.* Hasefi glanced at the wolf before making a decision and catching up to him.

"I never knew my parents," she admitted to him. "My uncle, Sefonis, was the closest blood I had." She paused. "Did…you know what your parents were like?" Hasefi watched as Kolahn's gaze grew distant, a wistful flicker in his yellow eyes.

"My mother was beautiful," he whispered. "And she was so kind to everyone, regardless of who they were. My father…I didn't see much of him. But he would talk to my brothers a lot and I would listen. He told stories. Sometimes they were scary, but sometimes they were inspiring. And they always taught a lesson." Kolahn's eyes darkened and he went silent, coming to a stop.

"Sefonis was like that for me," Hasefi murmured. "He gave me a lot of advice—sometimes I still hear his words. He never really told stories. But he would always say things like 'a Hi—a lynx needs to care for others before herself,' or 'a lynx must be able to make difficult decisions to help those around her.'"

"It sounds like Sefonis taught you well," Kolahn murmured. "If you've been alone as long as you said, then you would have been pretty young when…." He trailed off into silence.

"His words were all I had," she pointed out. "I guess you pretty much know my story now," she added. To her disappointment, the wolf added nothing and she had nothing else to do but fall into her own thoughts.

Hasefi thought about Kolahn's description of his parents. *He loves them,* she thought. *He misses them. And he told me he would do anything to be with them again. But he said his mother* was *beautiful and his father* would *talk to his brothers. Are they dead?* She tried to imagine herself not only without her tribe, but without any other lynx to go to. Now, at least, she had the rising sun to follow. *But Kolahn doesn't appear to have anything. I was the only thing his ancestors offered. What if I'm supposed to help him, too? He's obviously not the last wolf. Maybe there are others out there for him.*

"Something interesting is happening in your head."

Hasefi was startled out of her thoughts, realizing they were still sitting silently in the snow.

"I was just admiring the shape of the rocks," she replied.

"I don't think so. You make faces when you're thinking."

Hasefi's fur fluffed with embarrassment. "No I don't," she protested and Kolahn grinned at her.

"Yes you do," he insisted.

Hasefi rolled her eyes and got up. "Come on, you silly wolf. Let's not waste sunlight."

They continued along, following the rising sun, then leaving it behind them as it fell slowly towards the horizon. Eventually, their path led them to a set of hoofprints that were particularly fresh.

"Time for a hunt?" Hasefi asked with excitement.

"A lone mountain goat can be fast. We'll have to corner it."

Hasefi nodded and opened her mouth, tasting the prey's scent. Then she let Kolahn lead her a pace away from the tracks so they wouldn't stumble upon the goat and startle it.

It wasn't long before Kolahn halted, his tail lifting to stop Hasefi. She crouched lower, waiting for his signal. His ears twitched, indicating she join him at his side. When she was there, she could see the goat nosing the snow where a resilient bush grew.

It's trapped on one side, she thought. *But if we ran after it now, it could escape that way.* She looked to the left where the ledge their prey stood on lowered into a narrow path. The ledge itself was surrounded by a half circle of rock, almost as if an unfathomably large lynx made of stone was extending a claw along the ground and she and Kolahn were standing on the toe. *If I block the open area, then it has nowhere to go but to Kolahn.* Hasefi twitched her ears toward the narrow path and Kolahn gave her a tiny nod. She backed away, putting some distance between her and the goat so she could sneak into position.

It was difficult to be completely silent when she relied on her right foreleg so much, so she didn't move up far enough to see the goat. She could, however, just see Kolahn's muzzle when she looked up and waited. He jerked his head in the direction of the goat and Hasefi lunged forwards.

"Come here, goat!" she cried. A startled bleat sounded and she watched as a flash of white went past her. She swiped at it, but her claws met only air. Another cry left the goat's mouth as Kolahn stood up to meet it. His jaws flashed forward before the goat could try and turn away and he brought the prey to the ground, moving on top of it so it couldn't twist away from his grasp.

"Nice work!" Hasefi commented as she joined Kolahn. The wolf let go of the prey and looked away, seeming faintly disgusted. "Oh, come on, you have to stop feeling bad. It's just prey!"

Kolahn whipped his head around to glare at her. "Prey are still creatures! They feel fear and pain just like we do!"

Hasefi recoiled, surprised by the wolf's intensity. "Okay, you're right. But it's food."

Kolahn's expression quickly changed and he retreated a couple steps. "I know, sorry. Don't mind me."

Hasefi gave him a worried look, but he was clearly intent on moving on.

"There's a spot over there we can eat," he suggested. "Nothing can sneak up on us there." He picked up the goat and Hasefi helped him drag it to a short, wide pillar of rock that was just a leap away from an edge connected to where they stood. Hasefi made the jump first so she could stabilize Kolahn when he followed. Then he laid the goat down and they began to eat.

"Kolahn," Hasefi began slowly. He looked up at her questioningly. "Why do you think we're like this?"

"Like what?"

"You know…why are we different than prey and mountain lions and eagles? Why don't they talk like us or…or think like us?"

"I don't know," the wolf admitted. Hasefi was unsatisfied with his answer, but she didn't press, afraid he might snap at her again.

By the time they were finished eating, the sky was already darkening, so they found a nearby crevice to take shelter in. It was narrow enough that they couldn't keep their fur from touching when they went inside, but Hasefi barely noticed. Kolahn's strange mood showed no signs of having ever existed and they talked half the night away discussing hunting techniques and how it was much more comfortable to stalk with soft pine-needles and grass beneath their paws.

On the fourth day, Hasefi woke up feeling different. Somehow, she knew this would be the final day of their journey. *Whatever the rising sun was leading my tribe to is here. Our home is here.* Most of her thoughts were on meeting her parents. *Since I'm a Highchief, does that mean one of them is, too? Isn't that what the prophecy said?* Hasefi narrowed her eyes, trying to remember it. *'The first Heir to the Highchief will lead a destiny beyond the river.' I'm an Heir? So that means one of my parents is a Highchief.* A flicker of delight went through her. *I know what a river is now. Kolahn said it's like a stream, only much bigger and deeper.* Her excitement shifted. *Maybe these lynxes will be able to explain why my tribe left in the first place.*

She could hardly contain herself as she imagined what it would be like to see another lynx and how they would greet her. *I'll have to make sure they aren't frightened by Kolahn. But I haven't seen another wolf in over a moon. What if there aren't any here?* Her whiskers twitched with delight. *That would be one less thing to worry about.*

What if they could fix my leg? she thought, but her hope quickly diminished. *But it's been broken for so long. What if they can't?* Hasefi pushed the thought aside, not wanting to go through the despair of knowing she would be crippled forever again.

What would I say to them? she wondered. *Would they remember me? Maybe I'll have to introduce myself. Would they know my name? Surely my parents would, right?* Hasefi stopped, suddenly feeling afraid.

"Sefi?" Kolahn asked, retracing his steps to stand in front of her.

"What if they don't remember me? My parents?" she asked. "What if they forgot? Like I forgot them?"

The wolf's face softened and he sat down. "A parent would never forget their pup," he told her. "Something tells me letting go of you was the hardest thing they did." She could hear a tightness in his voice as if he was straining to talk. "I'm sure they would know exactly who you are if they saw you."

If?

"They *will* see me," she growled. "Even if they don't remember, they'll see me." She turned away from the wolf and led the way. He took her position at the rear even though she was slower than him.

Hasefi remained alert for any signs that she had finally arrived in the place her tribe was headed to, but the only thing that changed was a strange, faint tangy scent in the air. *Maybe it's a new place in the world, like Edgewood. It smelled strange, too. Maybe the home we were looking for isn't in the cold and snow after all.* She climbed a narrow winding path and pulled herself up onto a ledge. Hasefi looked ahead and saw a strange blue texture between the peaks. *What is that?* She looked to the sun which wasn't even halfway to its peak and saw the blue was right below it. *This is it!* she thought.

Hasefi leapt off the ledge and ran forwards, ignoring Kolahn's surprised yelp from behind. She pushed herself to run as fast as she could, ignoring the pain in her broken leg. She leaped over rocks and snow and crevices, bounding from one ledge to another until she finally skidded to a halt on a flat piece of rock that ended in a sheer fall.

Her heart sank into her paws as she gazed out at the massive stretch of blue before her. Sunlight bounced off of it, scattering in all directions in a sickly beautiful manner. Closer to the mountains, ice and snow reached out like desperate paws, breaking off as they stretched further into the mass of blue.

This is ocean, she thought. *Endless blue, like the sky. This is the edge of the world.* Her legs swayed and she backed away from the ledge. The world seemed to spin around her as questions ravaged her mind.

Why did the rising sun lead me here? Did I go too far? Did I miss my home? Did I do something wrong? Am I too late? Did something happen? Where are they?

"Sefi?"

"Kolahn, we have to go back," she told the wolf, already beginning to return the way they had come. "I think we passed them. We must have. The sun couldn't have led me here. There's something we missed. I'm not surprised, really, the mountains are so huge and you can't really see far. Maybe we could take a different way, in case the place my tribe was looking for is just a few steps in a different direction. It has to be, Kolahn. I—" she halted as Kolahn stepped in front of her, his expression distraught. "We just have to keep looking," she insisted, trying to move around him. "They're here, I know they are. I can *feel* it. They have to be here, Kolahn."

"Sefi, wait."

"No, I've waited long enough," she argued, getting past him and continuing. "What if they moved like my tribe did? What if I was supposed to be here sooner? What if I failed because I didn't leave earlier? I should have come here, I shouldn't have waited. Why did I think I had time? Maybe there's tracks we can follow…or a scent or something, right? There has to be a sign. There has to be…right?" She stopped as her entire body began to tremble, claws of despair curling into her. Hasefi turned towards the wolf. "Why aren't they here?" Her voice was barely a squeak as her throat tightened painfully.

She didn't avoid Kolahn this time as he moved towards her and pulled her in with a paw. Hasefi buried her face into his chest, overwhelmed with disbelief.

"Why aren't they here? What if something happened? What if I was supposed to come sooner? What if they were killed, too? What if I was supposed to warn them?"

Kolahn said nothing and despair washed through her as she refused to accept that she might be the last lynx. *I can't be. I can't be!* Confusion rippled through her and her thoughts were aimed at her ancestors.

"Why did they lead me here?" she whimpered. "Why did the ancestors bring me to nothing?"

"Ancestors work in mysterious ways," Kolahn murmured.

"Why? Why did my tribe have to die? Why did I have to live? If this is the destiny I'm supposed to lead, then I don't want it!" The words circled in her head, turning her despair into the deep pain of betrayal and she pushed away from Kolahn to glare at the sky.

"Why did you lead me here if there was nothing? Why did you let my tribe die? Why did you let me live? You told my mother I would have a destiny beyond some stupid river—is this what you meant? Are you so cruel? My tribe *died* for me! Why would you let this happen? Why didn't you help us against the other wolves? Against Sal?" Hasefi's anger suddenly froze into a cold fury and she lowered her gaze to the snow.

"Sal did this," she whispered. "Sal made this happen."

"Let's find somewhere to rest," Kolahn suggested, but Hasefi ignored him.

"He deserves to suffer for what he did." Hasefi's claws curled into the snow and she welcomed the cold that stabbed into her pads. "Maybe it's time he and the others finally found me."

"I don't know what you're saying," Kolahn said nervously. "But I think we need to find somewhere to think this out."

"I'm going to rip him apart just like he did to my tribe," she snarled. "Just like he did to Sefonis!"

"Hasefi, please," Kolahn insisted warily. "This isn't right. I know you feel betrayed. I know you want revenge, but, trust me, that's not the path you want to follow."

"Don't pretend you understand!" she snapped, letting her fury run unchecked. "I watched my tribe get torn apart limb by limb while their blood melted the snow around them! I watched their throats get ripped out and saw the light die from their eyes! When that mountain lion gave me a chance to escape, I went back because I didn't know what else to do! I had to walk over my own uncle's legs in order to get to him because he had been scattered like leaves! I slept beside what was left, his blood soaking my fur because I didn't know what else to do! So *don't* pretend you understand!" Hasefi shoved past Kolahn, limping slowly away from the ocean.

I have nothing now, she thought. *My tribe won't talk to me anymore. There's no more lynxes. All because of wolves. I'll make them pay for this. I've killed wolves before. Killing all of them couldn't be that hard. I've spent so long running away afraid, but now I'm going to march right back and tear my claws through the throats of every single one of those wolves. Especially Sal's.*

Chapter Eleven

"Why?" Hasefi glared at the stars above her. "Why did you let this happen?"

Silence met her and she curled her claws deep into the snow.

"Why won't you answer me? Who else was talking to me during all those moons I was alone? Was it you playing some cruel joke? Or was it my tribe? Did you stop them? Or maybe they realized what you did and abandoned you? *Answer me!*" With an angry snarl, Hasefi clawed at the rock in front of her, hardly noticing the pain as she wrenched her claws. She let out a long sigh and sat, her head hanging. The fact that anything could pounce on her at any moment and take her away didn't even make her ears twitch.

But if I were killed, I'd never get the chance to make the wolves pay, she pointed out to herself. With another sigh, she lifted her head and glared at the snow around her, daring something to try and attack her. *I have enough anger inside of me to fight a mountain lion.* She stood and turned to look into the large cave behind her. She could just barely see Kolahn's outline and saw that his paws were over his ears.

He hasn't said a word to me since this morning. Is he afraid I'll do something? She felt a tiny sliver of guilt. *I'm not sure I wouldn't. And yet he's still with me. Poor wolf. He doesn't know where else to go.* Her ears flattened. *And neither do I.* She sat down and hung her head again, finally feeling the mix of ice-cold fury and sun-hot rage settle into dark, hard misery.

I have absolutely nothing, she thought. *My tribe is gone. The ancestors have abandoned me. And I may very well be the last living lynx in the world.*

"Sefi?"

Hasefi gave no reaction to the wolf's quiet voice. She remained hunched with her ears flat as he slowly crept out of the cave to sit in front of her.

"Sefi, I'm sorry."

"For what?" she hissed. "You didn't kill my tribe or lead me on some meaningless journey."

The wolf flinched and Hasefi gritted her teeth. *It's not his fault. He doesn't deserve this.* She let out a sigh, forcing out some of her anger with it. She still couldn't look at him, but she was able to keep her voice low and monotone when she spoke.

"Do you think ancestors could be evil?"

"Evil?" the wolf echoed as if the word itself embodied its namesake. "I don't know. I don't...think so."

"Well, mine are."

"What? What about Sefonis?"

"No, not my tribe. They would never let something like this happen if they could help it. But my ancestors never gave me anything. They just let my tribe die. They abandoned us. So I'll do the same to them."

"Maybe there's something else," the wolf tried, but Hasefi shook her head, refusing to listen to anything he would use to argue.

"The wolf that killed my uncle, he was the biggest of them all and I'm pretty sure he was the leader. I heard the others talk about a wolf named Sal. I think that's him." Hasefi's gaze moved in the opposite direction of the edge of the world. "I wonder where Sal is now," she growled. "I've only ever encountered the wolves in the mountains that way." She jerked her head in the direction she was looking. "Maybe I'll find them if I keep going that way."

"You're not coming back to the valley?" he whispered.

"The valley?" she asked, confused.

Kolahn fidgeted. "I thought…maybe you'd come home with me, since…."

A flash of anger raked through Hasefi. "Why should I?" she snapped. "My mission failed. All I have left is to avenge my dead tribe. Even if I die trying, at least I'll be with them again."

Devastation twisted Kolahn's face and Hasefi tried to calm down a little. *He hasn't asked anything about Sal or my tribe. Does he know something? Or is he just scared of how I'll react?* She stifled a sigh and got to her paws.

"I'm tired." She limped past him and curled up on the opposite side of the cave from where he had been. He followed soon after and, to her relief, resumed his position there.

The next morning, they continued their trek in silence. Hasefi spent most of her time in her head, trying to think up new moves to use in a fight against a wolf. *Maybe it would be wise to join Kolahn in the valley so we can train,* she thought. *But Kolahn doesn't seem intent on helping me.* She frowned. *If he really is going to let me go alone…well, I might not be able to. I can't hunt for myself. Stars, I won't be able to fight a wolf! What am I thinking?* She stopped, letting Kolahn catch up to her.

"Is everything okay?" the wolf asked quietly.

"If I come with you to the valley, can we keep fighting?" To her surprise, relief relaxed the uncertainty in his expression.

"Of course," he told her. He started to move away, but she stopped him by touching his flank.

"Thank you for helping me this far, Kolahn," she told him. "I know this hasn't been easy for you, either."

"You mean a lot to me, Sefi. All I want is for you to be happy," he said. Her ears twitched.

"Even if that's avenging my tribe?" she dared ask.

Kolahn hesitated, then turned and stood directly in front of her. "Sefi, I know more about what you're feeling than you think," he began slowly. "It's dangerous. It can consume you if you're not careful. It can turn you into something you don't want to be."

"Like what?"

"The kind of creature that tears a tribe apart."

Hasefi gave the wolf a warning glare.

"I don't want to watch you become that," he explained.

"You know, it's hard to understand how you really feel when you still won't share your past with me," she growled. "And why haven't you asked me anything about what I've said? Do you know something?"

Kolahn was silent.

"Still nothing. Whatever." She brushed past him, her ears flat with frustration. *If he won't talk to me, then I won't talk to him.*

As the sky began to darken, Hasefi found an icy tunnel that led to a small, sheltered hole in the rock behind. As she moved towards it, Kolahn wordlessly slipped away. Hasefi curled up in the shelter, feeling a numbness spread through her as she settled.

Maybe Kolahn is right, she thought. *Maybe I just need some time to figure out what I'm going to do next. But what else can I do but stay with him? I'm not even fully grown. Sal would bat me around like I was nothing. Like he did with them....* She lowered her head to the ground and let out a soft sigh. *I just need to figure this out. But I'm too tired to think now.*

She closed her eyes, prepared to doze off, but her fur kept itching and her paws twitched restlessly. Hasefi gave an annoyed huff and rolled onto her other side, squeezing her eyes tighter as she willed sleep to come.

It continued to elude her.

What is wrong with me? she thought irritably as she sat up. Hasefi glared at the stone below her paws until she let out a defeated sigh. *I'll just wait until Kolahn comes back.* She moved to the entrance and watched the snow outside the tunnel, looking for any sign that Kolahn was returning. *He won't try hunting for long,* she thought. *It's getting dark.*

She waited, watching the sky darken until the ground was thick with shadows. But there was still no sign of Kolahn. *Where is he?* she wondered, growing faintly worried. *Maybe he's struggling with a big catch.* Hasefi's stomach rumbled at the thought. *Maybe he needs help?* She stepped out of the tunnel and looked to where his tracks led away. *But what if he's stalking something? What if I startle him?* A smirk crept onto her face and she lowered herself into a crouch. *Maybe I can use this as practice for when I really am hunting wolf.*

Hasefi followed his steps for a while, then put some distance between her and them when she could so she wouldn't bump into the wolf. Her mouth was open, tasting for scents. His was still fresh and she could taste the faint scent of snow hare. *He would have noticed it, too. Maybe he ran after it.* She continued to follow, but there was no sign of any fear-scent along the way. The hare's scent grew stronger until Hasefi slowed her pace even further. *I must be practically on top of it now,* she thought. *Maybe Kolahn is hunting it.* She looked around, but his steps continued to lead ahead to where the ground sloped down into a narrow ravine. *The hare must be down there. So where is he?*

A slight scratching sound made her freeze. Her ears perked as she tried to identify what exactly it was. *Kolahn?* she wondered. Holding her breath, she made her way to the edge of the ravine, step by limping step.

To her surprise and dismay, she saw the fluffy brown and white fur of a hare as it dug into the snow. It stuck its face into the hole it made, then hopped ahead to repeat the process. Hasefi watched it with confusion until it noticed her and fled.

"Kolahn?" she asked, growing more nervous. "Kolahn, where did you go?" She looked back to his prints where they led to the edge of the ravine farther down the opposite way the hare had run. Hasefi went over, seeing that his paws had skidded like he had gone in sudden pursuit of something. *Maybe there was another hare?* she wondered. Hasefi opened her mouth to see if she could scent another hare, but all she got was fear-scent.

Kolahn's fear-scent.

He didn't go after something, she thought, feeling her heart stop. *Something went after him!* Her head jerked up and she searched for any signs of other creatures, but there seemed to be none. *Wolves would be obvious,* she thought. *It must be a mountain lion. Or maybe a bear. Either way, he needs help now!* Hasefi slid in the snow as she jolted herself into a run, following Kolahn's tracks along the edge of the ravine. *He didn't come back,* she thought. *He didn't lead it to me.* Her thoughts were pushed aside as a half-terrified, half-agonized yelp sounded.

Hasefi had to clamp her jaw shut to keep from calling out the wolf's name. She came to a halt when she glimpsed the reddish brown fur of a mountain lion in the ravine. Kolahn's tracks showed he had clearly slipped into the ravine, but Hasefi couldn't see him over the mountain lion's bulk.

What do I do? her mind screamed. *What if Kolahn is already dead? I heard him, he can't be, right?* Hasefi tried to get a better angle, but there was a large pillar of rock that blocked her view of the front half of the mountain lion and whatever was in front of it. *Fallen stars!* She crouched at the edge of the ravine and risked stretching her neck out until she could see. There was a flash of black fur followed by a whimper. It was all she needed.

Hasefi launched herself off the edge and landed directly on the mountain lion's shoulders. It let out a grunt of surprise which quickly turned into pain as she dug in her claws to stay on. The mountain lion shook itself, but Hasefi kept her grip by burying her teeth into its neck.

"Sefi, what are you doing here?" she heard Kolahn gasp.

"Saving your furry tail!" she growled through a mouthful of fur and blood. "Now move!" She watched as Kolahn darted to one side, but the mountain lion quickly blocked his path. *Don't touch him!* Hasefi raked her hind claws down the mountain lion's back and it shook her again. Her lame leg gave out, but she managed to stay on with her teeth and other foreleg, getting her balance before the mountain lion shook again.

"Sefi, you need to get off! We need to run!"

"No kidding, furball! Move!"

The mountain lion jerked underneath her and she felt something crush her broken leg. Hasefi could do no more than gasp as the mountain lion used its jaws to rip her off and toss her away. Pain smashed through her as something hard stopped her momentum and she crumpled to the ground, unable to move.

"Sefi!" she heard Kolahn's voice. "Sefi, get up!" His voice grew fainter each time he called her name. *He's running away,* she thought with relief. Her vision darkened around her and she watched the sky swirl with the peaks above until everything melted into nothing.

Agony greeted Hasefi the moment she started to wake up. She let out a weak moan, imagining that she was still somehow in that pit and Kolahn had never showed up to save her.

"Sefi?"

"Not the pit," she gasped, forcing her eyes open. Kolahn's face was close to hers. "You're stealing my air," she coughed and the wolf backed away, looking faintly relieved.

"I thought you wouldn't wake up," he murmured and she snorted.

"Are you kidding? I always wake up. Even when I don't want to," she added quietly, despair curling into her like hunter's claws.

The wolf's expression grew grave. "You didn't want to wake up?"

"Why would I? I have nothing now."

Kolahn recoiled slightly.

"My tribe is dead," she continued flatly. "Our mission was a failure. The ancestors have abandoned me. I'm in *pain*. What else do I have?"

The wolf hung his head, his ears drooping.

"Kolahn?"

"What about me?" he whispered.

"Hm?"

"You still have me," he whispered.

Hasefi winced, realizing how stupid she had been. "I'm sorry, Kolahn. I never meant it like that."

"Then what did you mean?" he asked, surprising her as his eyes flickered with something she didn't understand.

"I...I don't know," she admitted. Kolahn sighed and went limp again. "Kolahn, I'm sorry." She tried to move, but her body protested sharply and she let out a whimper.

"Don't move," he told her. "You took a hard hit."

Hasefi closed her eyes and drew in a shallow breath. "Yeah, I noticed." She opened her eyes and examined Kolahn. "You look fine, though." To her surprise, Kolahn shifted further into the darkness of the cave they were in. Hasefi looked around, bewildered. "How did we get here?"

"I brought you here," Kolahn explained.

"Okay…but how did you fight off a giant monster-cat?"

"It left."

"You expect me to believe that?" Hasefi scoffed.

Kolahn merely shrugged. "Maybe it lost interest."

"Right, a predator loses interest in prey where prey is scarce. Kolahn, what happened?"

"I told you. I don't know what else to say. It's the only explanation that makes sense, isn't it?"

"Maybe. Unless it isn't the only one." Hasefi narrowed her eyes, but the wolf wouldn't meet her gaze. "Are you gifted?"

"What? Of course not! Bl—I would have a crescent moon on my forehead if I were. Didn't you say the first mountain lion you saw didn't take any interest in you?"

"Yeah, but there was also a huge pack of wolves that would fill a belly much better than a tiny, hungry kit. Not to mention the easy meal that was *my tribe.*" Hasefi let her head fall to the ground again. "I don't know what to do anymore, Kolahn." The roof of the cave seemed to spin and she let her eyes move with it as she watched.

"Maybe settling down in the valley wouldn't be such a bad thing," the wolf suggested. Hasefi moved her gaze to Kolahn. "At least for the first step," he added.

Hasefi's mouth was partly open as she tried to find something to say. But she could only agree with him. "Okay," she sighed. "Maybe you're right."

"But you need to heal before we worry about that," he told her.

Hasefi narrowed her eyes at him again. "Seriously, how do you have no wounds?"

"I do," he replied quickly. "They're just hidden in my fur."

Hasefi's eyes narrowed further.

"Maybe I should go hunt," he decided.

"Yeah, because that worked out so well last time." Hasefi tried to push herself up again, but even lifting her head was difficult.

"We need to eat," Kolahn pointed out. "Especially you. You need your strength."

"Yeah, but if you get killed, I have no one to keep me fed."

"Well, I won't be keeping you fed if you don't let me," he insisted.

Hasefi rolled her eyes. "Just stay for now. Please," she added when he started to argue.

"For now," he agreed hesitantly.

Hasefi relaxed when he laid down a couple steps away. She was prepared to slip back into sleep, but the desire to remain awake a little while longer forced her eyes open.

"Kolahn?" she asked.

"Yeah?"

"Do you know Sal?"

The wolf didn't respond.

"Please, just yes or no. I need to know. I won't ask anything else."

"I don't know who Sal is," he finally admitted.

Hasefi felt a sense of relief even though his answer didn't help her figure out where he had come from.

"Like I said," she began. "I think Sal might be the one who led the attack on my tribe. For a while I didn't say anything about him or the other wolves because I was scared you would turn to him the moment you knew what he did. But I know now you're the exact opposite of what he is. You wouldn't have done that to my tribe." Hasefi felt a little pang in her chest and her eyes glazed over as memory seeped into her mind. "The Tribe of the Second Divide. That was what we called ourselves, I think. I heard some of the lynxes say it."

"You have a pretty good memory," the wolf said quietly.

"Well, not really," she admitted. "I was reminded of a lot of stuff after they were gone." Confusion glittered in the wolf's eyes. "I heard voices," Hasefi explained hesitantly. "They gave me advice and warnings, too." Still, the wolf looked doubtful. "But they don't anymore. Haven't for over a moon, actually. I thought it might have been my ancestors, but I know now they don't care. So all I can think of was that it was my tribe talking to me."

"Are you sure?" Kolahn asked.

"Sure of what? That it was my tribe?" Hasefi asked, feeling her own confusion. The wolf hesitated before replying.

"Suffering something traumatic can really affect a creature, especially one so young. If you heard your tribe talking to you after…."

Hasefi narrowed her eyes. "You think I'm crazy?"

"Not crazy, no. But if you think you're hearing their voices, it's probably just your own mind. And being alone for a long time is difficult for creatures like us."

"Sure, but I'm not imagining voices," she told him. "They've said things I didn't know before."

"We learn things every day that we didn't know before. Sefi, it's not so strange. I used to hear my brothers' voices when I…when I was alone. You said they stopped about a moon ago, right? When I found you in the pit?"

"Well, yeah, but I'm sure there's a reason."

"There is." Kolahn looked at her meaningfully and Hasefi turned her head away. "I think they've gone now that you have someone else with you."

Is he right? she wondered. *Was it all in my mind? But I've felt my tribe, too. I've felt them watching over me. Was I alone that whole time? Sefonis?* She waited for some sort of response, but she felt nothing from her tribe. No presence, no whispers. They were nowhere to be found.

I can't believe that, she protested. *There has to be something.* But she couldn't find any reason better than what Kolahn had given her for the voices to remain absent.

Hasefi turned away from Kolahn and hid her face in her fur. She pretended to fall asleep, but she was wide awake with the idea that she'd been alone ever since the wolves took away her tribe.

The following day, Hasefi woke to find the wolf gone. She let out a frustrated growl, but couldn't help but feel a little relief that he might come back with something to fill her belly.

I'm starving, she thought. *When was the last time I ate?*

While she waited, Hasefi focused on pushing herself up and examining the damage done to her. The first step took forever since her broken leg was rendered useless by the gaping bite mark in it and the rest of her body complained with every movement. However, she refused to give up and finally managed to sit herself up against the wall of the cave.

Her head spun and she waited to see if she would pass out. Her vision cleared and she took in a few deep breaths, ignoring the pain it caused.

My fur is clean, she thought as she examined her pelt. She ran a paw over her head and saw just a little trickle of blood staining the white fur on her paw. *There's no way.* Her gaze moved to her injured leg, which she realized was only covered in fresh blood. *Kolahn must have kept my fur decent,* she thought, remembering when he had mentioned the possibility of infection. She wasn't sure how she felt about the wolf grooming her, but she decided there was no point in getting worried or being angry about it so she forgot about it and went to work cleaning her leg. It took her until the wolf returned, carrying nothing but disappointment.

"You're up," he observed.

"You didn't listen to me," Hasefi growled, lowering her leg as Kolahn sat near the back of the cave.

"I couldn't wait any longer," he admitted.

Hasefi frowned. "Any longer?" she echoed. "How long has it been?"

"We've been here for six nights."

Hasefi's heart skipped a beat and the ground swayed beneath her paws. "We can't stay here any longer!" she gasped. "We have to move!"

"You still need to rest," he pointed out.

"That won't do us any good if we get killed!"

The wolf suddenly hung his head, looking utterly defeated.

Hasefi felt a claw prick of concern and forced her urgency aside. "What?"

"Can we stop arguing?" he asked quietly.

The claw prick deepened into guilt. "I'm sorry," she told him. "I just...wish things could be easy for once." She cocked her head when Kolahn snorted. "What?"

"You and easy? I could never see it."

Hasefi flinched, offended, but the wolf continued.

"You would get bored so fast. How long did we stay by the lake?"

"Half a moon, I think?" she responded, relaxing.

Kolahn chuckled. "When we get to the valley, I'll be surprised if we stay longer than that before something new comes up."

"Well, maybe I'll surprise you, then," she murmured, her gaze moving past him.

The wolf looked up hopefully.

"Maybe I need to take a break from missions and adventures."

"What about Sal?" he asked carefully.

"As far as I know, the only creatures he and the other wolves can terrorize are us and prey, so he can wait until I figure out how to take you down."

Kolahn smiled faintly and Hasefi felt the tension that gripped deeper than her muscles begin to loosen.

"I'll rest," she told him. "But only for a few more nights. We have to move."

"Okay. How about the morning before the dark moon we leave?"

Hasefi nodded agreement and settled down again.

It wasn't long before Hasefi slipped into sleep. The next couple sunrises went by quickly as she spent most of it asleep. Kolahn managed to hunt down a little bit of food for her to eat while she healed. When the fourth sunrise came, the morning before the dark moon, both of them were eager to leave the cave and Kolahn helped her out.

"Wait, the ravine is right there," she murmured as she noticed the drop to her left. "Is that blood?" she gasped, moving away from Kolahn. "By the stars! There's so much! And nothing was drawn by the scent of it?"

"Let's move before something *does* come," the wolf urged. Hasefi stumbled back to him and let Kolahn lead her away from the ravine.

"Last time I saw something like that was from my tribe," she murmured quietly.

"A lot of it is yours," he said quickly.

"There is no way that's true. I don't even think that much blood exists inside me. Right?" She looked to her injured leg. She couldn't put any weight on it and it was still bleeding. Drops of it fell into the snow and she winced. "I'm going to lead another mountain lion right to us," she said. "Or maybe the same one."

"Let's not think about that. We just need to get away from here and find somewhere else to stay."

Hasefi heard the urgency in his voice and began to wonder if it was more than instinct that drove him. *What if he's had a past with mountain lions?* she wondered. *What if he lied to me about never seeing one before?*

"You know what I just realized?" Hasefi said as they hurried along a winding path. "Now we can share scary stories with our kits and pups."

"Let's get out of the high mountains, first," Kolahn responded. Hasefi watched his expression to see if there was any reaction to prove her thoughts might be right, but his face was unreadable.

"I understand why a parent would scare their young," she continued. "But, mountain lions aren't as scary as you made them sound."

"What do you mean? That mountain lion threw you like you were no more than a scrap of fur!" he exclaimed.

"But it bleeds like us, Kolahn. It's just a creature, not a monster. Creatures can be killed."

"Please don't tell me you want to kill a mountain lion," he said.

"No," she assured him, her voice quiet. "I'll save that for Sal."

Before the sun could reach its peak, Hasefi began to grow too tired to move. When she collapsed, Kolahn carried her by the scruff until they came upon a large crevice in the ground that ran further underneath the rock.

"You can't fit under here," Hasefi mumbled as the wolf tucked her underneath the rock.

"It's okay. If I keep my head low, nothing will see me." His gaze moved to her leg which was leaking blood onto the ground. "We need to stop that. Maybe we could put snow on it." Before Hasefi could question him, he jumped out. Kolahn quickly returned with a mouthful of snow which he gently spread over her leg.

"Oh, that feels nice," Hasefi sighed. Kolahn jumped out a second time to get more, then settled in the space open to the sky, watching her leg closely.

"Let me know if it gets too cold," he told her.

"Mhmm," Hasefi hummed, her eyes drooping. A random thought entered her mind, waking her up slightly. "Do you only howl to the full moon?"

"What do you mean?"

"Would you howl at a half moon? Or a dark moon?"

"Maybe," he murmured. "If I really needed to tell the ancestors something, I guess. Why?"

"You didn't howl last full moon," she reminded him. "What if they are waiting to hear you?"

Kolahn moved his face away into the shadows. "I don't think they would wait for me," he told her.

"Why not?" she asked, but he didn't answer. "Yours seem more intent to help than mine do."

Kolahn flinched.

"I think you should howl tonight."

"I could draw unwanted attention," he pointed out.

"You had no problem when I was in the pit."

The wolf shuffled uncomfortably.

"Will you sing?"

"I don't think I can, Sefi. I'm sorry."

Hasefi let it go, knowing that it was merely her anger with her own ancestors driving her curiosity. "You're lucky," she sighed. "Your ancestors seem to actually listen to you. Maybe I should try praying to them, instead."

"I wonder if a lynx could learn to howl," Kolahn chuckled.

Hasefi snorted. "I doubt it. I know we're known for our battle-cries, but I don't think it'd be as pleasant if I started screeching at the full moon." She let out a hoarse purr when Kolahn laughed.

"I wonder if my ancestors would hear you," the wolf continued more seriously.

"You think they might?" Hasefi asked. "What would that mean, then, if they did?"

"I have no idea," he told her. "I guess…that they would accept you as one of us?"

"A wolf?" Hasefi said with amused disbelief. "It wasn't so long ago that being a wolf was the last thing I'd ever think of."

"I think you'd make a great wolf," Kolahn said and Hasefi rolled her eyes. "You be like a…a wolfcat!"

Hasefi let out a burst of laughter that made her body ache. "A wolfcat?" she echoed, trying to settle herself down to keep from aggravating her wounds more.

Kolahn nodded eagerly.

"Right. Whatever you say, you silly wolf."

He stuck his tongue out and Hasefi let out a content sigh, lowering her head again and letting her eyes slide closed.

"A wolfcat," she murmured again. "Something tells me I'm going to hear that again."

The response she received was in the form of an affectionate lick on her shoulder and she started to purr again. The wolf shifted until their fur brushed and Hasefi welcomed the warmth as it seeped into her. Despite the pain throbbing throughout her body, she was able to fall easily into slumber.

Chapter Twelve

Hasefi woke with a heavy heart and didn't even have the will to open her eyes. She'd dreamt that she was lost in the high mountains again, but as her current age. She called for her uncle, but when he didn't respond, she tried her other tribemates. But none of them would respond and she found she was rapidly forgetting their names when she tried to call out to them. The first thing she did when she escaped the horrible dream was ravage her mind for her uncle's name.

"Sefonis," she whispered immediately. "I didn't forget you."

"Sefi?" Kolahn's voice caused her eyes to flicker open and she looked blankly at him from underneath the rock she laid beneath. "Are you okay?"

"Bad dream," she admitted. She wasn't going to elaborate, but when it was clear he was waiting for her to continue, she did. "I thought I'd forgotten the names of my tribemates. I...I can't forget them. But now that my mission is over...I just feel so lost. And empty."

"I felt that way when I was on my own for the first time," Kolahn admitted, but Hasefi gave her head a tiny shake.

"This is different. I had something to hold onto before, something to keep me going. But now, I have nothing. I'm alone."

"You're not alone," the wolf said firmly. "I'm here and I'm not going anywhere."

Hasefi sighed and closed her eyes. "I know. I know, I'm sorry. I just…can't help it. I think…I think a part of me thought that by finishing my mission, it would bring back my tribe. It's stupid, but—"

"Having hope isn't stupid," the wolf told her.

"Isn't it? If you're just disappointed in the end?"

"Hope is faith. You asked me before why we're different than other creatures and I think it's because we have faith. Creatures like us have been given the gift of believing and loving and knowing. Otherwise your tribe would never have been able to exist in the first place. And without that pain you feel now, they wouldn't be able to live on with you."

"They died because they had faith in me…and I failed."

"They died because they loved you. You were everything to them," he told her.

A wave of despair rolled over Hasefi. "They were everything to *me!*" she protested.

Kolahn reached a paw towards her and she laid her own over it, ignoring her stiff limbs. When she was able to control herself a bit better, she spoke again.

"Maybe it'd be better to be like a mountain lion or a goat and just focus on surviving."

"I know you don't believe that," Kolahn murmured. "And I'm not saying they don't feel loss—of course they do. But for us, I think it just runs deeper."

"Too deep," she sighed.

"You'll be able to move on. I know you're strong enough—you're the strongest, bravest creature I have ever met. I have never seen another creature face a mountain lion, let alone a tiny kit!"

"I'm not tiny," Hasefi snorted.

"You're pretty small."

Hasefi swiped weakly at his muzzle and he let out a chuckle. Her mood quickly faded as a new thought entered her mind. "What about Sal?" she asked.

Kolahn cocked his head and gave her a puzzled look.

"Why is he like us, too?" she elaborated. "Creatures like that can't have ancestors, right?" A claw of fear entered her heart. "Could he have gifted wolves?"

"No," Kolahn answered quickly and seriously. "Wolves like him have abandoned their ancestors. And gifted come from ancestors."

Hasefi relaxed slightly and tried not to worry about what things would have been like if there had been gifted wolves trying to track her down.

"But you haven't abandoned yours," she said as a statement rather than a question.

"I would do anything for them," he answered anyways.

Hasefi nodded. "Well...I know I can't say the same. The only spirits I care about are the ones that suffered cold and hunger with me. I'm just not sure if they're watching over me...."

Kolahn looked upset by her words, but he didn't say anything.

Hasefi pulled herself into the open crevice where Kolahn laid and she looked out at the blue sky. "I think I believe they were with me, before. I can't think otherwise."

Kolahn looked like he was going to say something, but his mouth remained closed.

"And maybe they led me to you, somehow," Hasefi continued. "If there isn't anything out there for me—no new home, no parents— then they must have done what they could to give me happiness." Hasefi looked to the wolf. "I think it was the last thing they could do for me." She touched her nose to the wolf's cheek and rested against his flank. "Thanks for putting up with me," she murmured.

"It's not 'putting up with you'," he told her. "It's being here when things are rough for you."

Hasefi gave his cheek a lick and pulled away. "I think you are the most patient creature ever," she told him.

Kolahn shrugged with a smirk.

"Let's get out of here, shall we?" she suggested.

Hasefi was able to make it through the rest of the day before exhaustion overwhelmed her. Kolahn had also come across an injured eagle while he was hunting and Hasefi examined the bird with surprise.

"It's smaller than I remember," she observed. Kolahn only wrinkled his nose and she chuckled. "Come on, bird isn't that bad."

"At least this one actually has some meat on it," he grumbled.

Hasefi chuckled again and began plucking some of the feathers from its body.

"I just don't like sneezing every time I try to take a bite," the wolf said, eyeing the feathers.

"That's why you pluck the feathers before you take a bite." Hasefi shook a feather off her claw and it floated towards Kolahn. The feather suddenly attached itself to his nose and the wolf sneezed, giving Hasefi an irritated look. "Well, when you try to sniff the feather like that, you can't blame anyone but yourself."

"I wasn't sniffing it," he muttered.

Hasefi laughed and tucked into the bird.

The following day, Hasefi began to recognize some of the landmarks they passed. *We'll probably pass the lake by tomorrow if we keep this pace up,* she thought hopefully. *Then we'll be on our way to the Great Valley.* Feeling energized, she pushed herself away from Kolahn and walked on her own.

It wasn't long before she had to return to his side and use his shoulder to stay upright. A wave of exhaustion flowed through her and she snorted. *That was a mistake.* Kolahn stopped suddenly and Hasefi barely managed to keep herself from falling over.

"Kolahn?" she looked up at him, but his attention was focused on something ahead. Hasefi looked, but she couldn't see anything. She opened her mouth and tasted the air.

Mountain lion.

A deep growl sounded and Kolahn jerked to the side. Hasefi stumbled into the snow, but managed to lift her head and watch as a mountain lion revealed itself from behind a jagged rock.

"Kolahn!" Hasefi gasped. "It's the same one!" she was shocked to see half healed wounds covering its body, not including the ones she'd given it on the back of its neck and shoulders. "By the stars, what happened to it?"

"Run, Sefi!"

Hasefi was jarred to the moment six moons ago when Sefonis had said the same thing.

"Not again," she growled, pushing herself up and standing beside the wolf.

"Sefi, please!" he begged. "I'll be right behind you."

Hasefi ignored him and let out her own growl towards the mountain lion. It hesitated, as if surprised or amused by her reaction.

A loud snarl sounded, but the mountain lion's jaws were hardly open. Then, to Hasefi's utter amazement, another mountain lion landed beside the other and reared up to bring its giant forepaws down. The first mountain lion met it with an angry snarl and the two were locked in combat as they dug teeth and claws into each other's flesh.

Something shoved Hasefi aside and she glimpsed Kolahn's black fur as he nosed her away. "Move! We need to get out of here!" he gasped.

Hasefi started to run forwards, but her gaze was brought back to the mountain lions. The injured one was shoved into the snow while the newcomer pushed itself up. Its gaze met Hasefi's for a moment and she saw something that was eerily familiar. Then the pinned mountain lion raked its cheek with giant claws.

"Hasefi, you moon-eyed pup, move your tail!"

Teeth clamped down on Hasefi's scruff and she was dragged until she finally had the sense to put her paws under her and run.

"Stay where I can see you," she gasped to Kolahn as he moved behind her. To her relief, he came to run beside her and they fled through the snow until Hasefi collapsed, her body aching and her chest heaving for air.

Kolahn located a place nearby where a rock was held up against another with a mound of snow obscuring the space beneath and they moved under there for cover.

"Kolahn," Hasefi gasped when her breathing started to regulate. "That mountain lion—it looked at me!"

"It probably would have eaten you if it wasn't after the other one," he said seriously. "Why didn't you run?"

Hasefi shook her head and spoke between gasps. "No, I recognized it!"

"Yeah, it was the one that attacked us before."

Again, Hasefi shook her head. "The other one," she panted. "It was the same one I saw before. When my tribe was…. The one that scared off the wolves so I could get away. It was the same one from all those moons ago!"

Kolahn gave her a look of utter disbelief.

"You have to believe me!" Another thought came to mind. "What if it's like us?"

"Sefi, we have other things to worry about right now. I don't know what you're trying to make happen here, but we need to keep our minds straight if we want to survive this."

Hasefi opened her mouth to argue, but Kolahn gave her a stern look and she ceased. "Okay, you're right. I'm sorry." She went limp, still trying to catch her breath.

"You are the luckiest creature in the world," Kolahn murmured. "Whether you think so or not, your ancestors are doing more than watching over you."

"If anyone is helping me, it's my tribe," Hasefi corrected. "And your ancestors, perhaps, since they actually seem decent."

"You really shouldn't talk about your ancestors like that," Kolahn told her with a frown.

"If they don't like it, then why don't they come tell me themselves?" she challenged. "If they're so powerful?"

"They don't work that way. They can't just come at the whim of every creature."

"Right. The slaughter of a tribe just isn't important enough for them," she scoffed.

"Sefi—"

"Are we staying here for the rest of the day?"

"Only if you need to," the wolf murmured.

"Stars, no. I felt like I was running for eternity, but I'd be surprised if those mountain lions weren't just around a corner. Let's get out of here." She pushed herself up and they resumed their trek through the high mountains.

On the next day, they reached the place where trees began to grow and, soon after, where the snow gave way to more plant-life. Hasefi felt a wave of relief wash over her strong enough that she actually stumbled and Kolahn used his muzzle to keep her from falling.

"Are you alright?" he asked.

"Yeah, just a little dizzy," she admitted. "Let's take a moment to rest."

The sky was already darkening when they huddled under a tree. Hasefi looked down the slope to where the forest started, her paws itching with the desire to be down there.

"Should we wait until morning?" Kolahn asked.

"I don't want to," Hasefi admitted. "But I think that would be wiser." She gave a sigh and lowered her head to the ground. "Maybe we can get some herbs on this wound," she murmured. "It hurts."

"At least it's not bleeding anymore," the wolf pointed out.

Hasefi hummed agreement, feeling herself slip further into unconsciousness.

"You know what I don't miss?" Kolahn asked.

"Hm?" she hummed absently.

"The snow."

"Well, don't look behind you," Hasefi warned. "Otherwise you might be disappointed."

Kolahn snorted and Hasefi gave a faint chuckle. Something touched her cheek and she opened her eyes despite not remembering closing them.

"How are you feeling?" the wolf asked.

"Well, this might surprise you, but I'm kind of tired. Sleep might be good for me." She shifted her head away from his muzzle and closed her eyes again. Then she opened one eye and peered at Kolahn. "Everything alright?"

"I just want to make sure you're okay," he told her.

"Well, I don't think I'm quite there yet, but I will be." A tiny purr of amusement rumbled in her throat as Kolahn continued to look at her worriedly. "Goodnight, you giant furball." Kolahn gave her shoulder a lick and she closed her eyes.

"Sleep well, Sefi."

When Hasefi woke again, Kolahn was prodding her shoulder with his nose, his expression very worried. "Can't I rest?" she moaned, trying to push him away with a paw.

"Sefi, it's almost sunpeak." Her ears perked up and she lifted her head.

"Really?"

"Are you sure you're okay?" the wolf pressed.

Hasefi pushed herself to her paws, wobbling slightly, but managing to stay upright. "Yeah. I just haven't had the chance to really recover, I guess. Maybe we can stop at our cave by the lake," she suggested when he looked at her seriously.

"Your leg doesn't seem to be healing very well," he pointed out.

"Good thing it was already lame," she pointed out. "Maybe that's why."

Kolahn's expression didn't change.

"We can put some gross plants on it when we get farther down," she assured him. "Stop worrying."

"Sorry, can't do that," he told her.

Hasefi rolled her eyes, but was relieved when Kolahn left the shade of the tree and began descending down the slope. Hasefi followed more slowly, willing her legs to hold her up until they reached the area where the giant boulders lay.

"Are you sure you're okay?" Kolahn asked. "You're moving slower than yesterday."

"Kolahn, if you ask me that one more time, I will swipe at you with my claws unsheathed. We were going down a steep slope, you silly furball—of course I'm moving slow!"

Kolahn shrugged and continued, throwing concerned glances in her direction. Hasefi focused on following him down, but couldn't help but worry that maybe something was off. When the wolf was carefully lowering himself from a rock to the roots of a tree growing sideways, Hasefi paused to examine her leg.

She sniffed it first, finding that there was nothing that seemed strange to her. *But I don't know what to look for,* she thought. *Well, I'd probably notice if something was wrong.* She carefully licked the skin around the wound. It was swollen and tender, but seemed fine, otherwise. *I'm just being paranoid because Kolahn is. I have had so much happen in this last half moon that it would be crazy not to think I'd be having a hard time moving around.* As if to prove her point to herself, she hurried along the path Kolahn had taken until she caught up to the wolf. Then she gave him a confused look. "Why have you stopped?"

"Bear," was all he said. Then his muzzle pointed to the right and he crept towards a tree with some of its lower branches broken.

"Woah, something big passed through here," she murmured. "Bigger than a mountain lion, even." She opened her mouth and tasted the air. Her nose wrinkled and she immediately clamped her jaws shut. "Well, if that's bear, I won't be forgetting their scent anytime soon. I might suffocate if we don't move away soon."

"It's fresh," Kolahn panted, his eyes wide with fear. "It looks like it was heading towards the valley. But why? Bears don't usually come *from* Edgewood. Why would it come from the snow?"

Hasefi limped up in the direction the bear's path led and sniffed. "Don't be so sure," she choked dramatically. "It's stronger up here. I think it was coming *into* Edgewood."

"Seriously, Sefi, you need to learn that a little bit of fear can be good."

Hasefi returned to his side. "Sure. Wow, what is that acrid scent? Is that more bear?" Hasefi gagged, moving away from Kolahn in case she did vomit. When she looked back, she saw the wolf's nose close to the ground. "How can you breathe?"

"Sefi, I think I know why a bear is here."

"Okay. Continue."

"It was running," he said.

"Running?" she scoffed. "Something like that was running? What would make a huge creature like that afraid?" To her surprise, Kolahn bounded away. Hasefi jolted into a run, not wanting to lose him, especially if either of them did come across this bear. The wolf came to a sudden halt on a rock that jutted out of the slope, allowing a view of the mountains ahead.

At first, she couldn't tell what the wolf was looking at, but then she noticed something in the sky that didn't quite seem right. She narrowed her eyes until she could make out the strange, low-hanging dark cloud that hung over Edgewood.

"That's strange fog," she observed.

"Not fog," the wolf panted, clearly having issues catching his breath. "Smoke."

"What's smoke?" she asked.

Kolahn's gaze darted around before he responded. "It comes from fire," he explained, continuing as she opened her mouth to ask what 'fire' was. "Fire is worse than any creature or plant that could kill you."

Hasefi gave him a disbelieving look, but she could see the horrible mixture of terror, dismay, and hopelessness in his expression.

"It is merciless," the wolf gasped. "It feeds on anything alive, turning it into ash while releasing that dark, suffocating smoke. Anything in its path is doomed and fire can never be sated. It'll destroy homes and clans in its wake."

"Including a valley?" Hasefi asked slowly. The wolf gave a tiny nod. "How do we stop it?"

"Didn't you hear me?" he asked, his voice high with panic. "Nothing stops it! It only has one weakness which we have no control over."

"What is it?"

"Water."

"So if we stick to streams and lakes, we'll be fine, right?" Hasefi tried, but Kolahn shook his head.

"Fire can jump over them or move around if it has to. It always finds a way forward. Our best protection will be the snow."

"There has to be something we can do," Hasefi protested. "I mean, we did just survive a mountain lion attack. Two, practically."

"Sefi, this enemy doesn't bleed. It doesn't think or feel. It's not a creature. It just feeds. This is one thing you can't sink your claws into."

"Okay, okay, I hear you. So what do we do?" she asked him.

Kolahn's gaze moved in the direction of the valley. "We have to run until it dies."

"It can die?"

"Sometimes rain from a storm can kill it, but if not that, then it might die of starvation. Without more life to feed it, it will eventually wane. But it moves so fast and covers so much territory...." The wolf trailed off and Hasefi shuddered, trying to imagine what this 'fire' might look like.

"Have you seen it?" she asked Kolahn. The wolf shook his head. "Another story, then? From your father?" To her surprise, Kolahn shook his head again.

"A story, yes," he admitted. "But not from my father. Let's go—we don't have time to waste."

Hasefi followed the wolf wordlessly as he led her through Edgewood. His gaze was glued to where the smoke hovered in the sky, which made Hasefi more alert to their immediate surroundings so nothing caught them by surprise. However, she couldn't help but glance nervously ahead, knowing the direction they travelled brought them not only closer to this fire, but to Sal and the other wolves. *They were in the high mountains,* she assured herself. *Not here.*

As they continued through the day, the acrid scent that had been mingled with the bear's grew more prominent in the air. The smoke from before travelled fast and, by the time they found shelter for the night, was almost upon them.

Even though she knew Kolahn was easy to spook, there was something about his utter silence that unnerved Hasefi. *It really scares him,* she thought. *More than anything else we've faced. But he said he'd only heard of fire in a story. Could he be lying? Is there something he's not telling me?* Her whiskers twitched. *Something else, that is?*

Hasefi moved her attention to the dark cloud looming above the trees nearby. She could feel her chest tightening as if she had been running for a long period of time. *Kolahn said it was suffocating,* she thought. *Could it kill us? Is it wise to move in the same direction as it? He said we could retreat into the snow if we had to...but that would bring new dangers.* She looked to Kolahn, wanting to voice her fears, but the wolf was curled up on his side of the hollow staring bleakly into nothing.

"The world is really scary," Hasefi murmured instead.

"You have no idea," Kolahn sighed, laying his head across his paws. Hasefi gave him a questioning look, but he closed his eyes. She studied the wolf, dismayed at how defeated he looked. *None of this has been easy for him, either,* she thought. *And now he's scared he might lose his home.* She peered through the bushes surrounding them in the direction they travelled, seeing there was still no sign the fire had come upon their path. *Poor wolf. And I've been too involved in my own matters to even notice.*

Hasefi got up from where she had settled on the other side of the hollow and moved over to him, settling in the crook of his belly. Kolahn raised his head, giving her a surprised look which quickly changed to affection. The moment Hasefi relaxed her muscles, she was surprised to find how relieved she felt to lay down as if the day's trek had taken more out of her than she expected. She soon fell into a deep slumber that wrapped around her like the possessive claws of a hungry predator.

Chapter Thirteen

"Hasefi, you need to get up. It's time to go." Sefonis's voice broke through Hasefi's sleep and she flattened her ears.

"Can't we stay longer?" she pleaded. "I'm tired. And cold."

"We all are, Hasefi. But your tribe needs you to get up. Home won't come to us." There was a tone in her uncle's voice she didn't recognize so she opened her eyes and lifted her head to search for an answer in his expression. She frowned.

"Why are you scared?" Something passed through his expression and he crouched, giving her an intense look that she couldn't interpret.

"We'll stay another day, okay?" he told her. "But we need to move tomorrow."

"Okay," she agreed, quickly curling up again. She heard him walk a few steps away to where some of the other lynxes were in the tunnel they had taken shelter in. Hasefi had no idea how long they had been there, but it seemed to get colder with each day.

"How is she?" a deep voice asked, catching Hasefi's attention.

"I can't tell," she heard her uncle respond. "She insists on staying, but I can still see light in her eyes. Broken stars, Hykalof, a kit doesn't belong out here! What lynx would send any tiny kitten into the cold like this? Let alone their own?"

"She was only obeying the word of our ancestors," Hykalof said calmly.

Hasefi's uncle let out a sigh. *"Well, I can't say I'm too fond of their words right now. We haven't even reached this Broken Peak. It didn't look so far. We've been out here for almost half a moon!"*

"It isn't easy," Hykalof agreed. *"But the Highchief chose us because we are strong. And so is her kit. Hasefi will make it. It is her destiny."*

Am I sick? *Hasefi wondered.* I just feel cold. What's so bad about that? *Guilt touched her heart and she squeezed her eyes tighter.* I'm going to get lots of rest today so I'll be strong tomorrow. Then Sefonis won't be so worried. *She focused on getting stronger, imagining that she was somewhere warm. But her body began to ache and her stomach churned as if she'd eaten bad prey. Her fur grew hot and her throat was dry, causing a weak cough to leave her jaws.*

"Sefonis?" Hasefi croaked.

"Sefi, thank the moon!"

Hasefi forced her eyes open and was confused to see a fluffy black face with golden eyes looking down at her. "Can you hear me?"

"Sefon...is?" she asked, wondering where he and Hykalof had gone.

"It's Kolahn. Your leg is infected. I'm going to see if I can find some herbs farther in the forest." An image of ominous darkness reaching through the sky entered her mind and she reached out a paw towards the wolf.

"Not...safe. Stay..."

"I can't, Sefi. You could die."

"You...die."

Kolahn gave her cheek a quick lick. "I'll be back, okay? Just don't fall asleep. Stay awake."

Hasefi's eyes closed the moment the wolf left her sight. She started to slip away into nothing, but something drew her back.

When she opened her eyes, she found that another figure stood before her.

"Sefonis," she whispered, her voice slurred.

"Wee lass," her uncle murmured, watching her with distraught eyes. "I'm so sorry."

"It's okay," she told him even though she didn't know what he was apologizing for. "You don't ever have to be sorry for anything," she continued, wavering between the world of the living and the not.

"I'm here now," her uncle insisted. "You see?"

"I remember," she purred faintly.

"No, Hasefi. I'm here with you. Really here."

Hasefi was roused slightly by his words and she frowned. "I'm dreaming, right?" she asked, beginning to realize she didn't remember having this particular conversation.

"Aye," Sefonis told her, "but I've come to you."

"Why?" Hasefi asked, trying to get her paws underneath her.

"Don't move," he told her. "Just talk to me, okay?"

Hasefi blinked with confusion, studying her uncle more clearly. "Sefonis?"

"Aye." There was desperation in her uncle's expression, but Hasefi was confused by the lack of pupils in his yellow eyes and what she could only describe as starshine along his silver plated armor. She let her eyes follow the intricate black lines along his chest and shoulders, then moved up to the line of fur along the top of his helmet.

"It's you, isn't it?" she murmured.

"Aye, wee lass, it is."

Hasefi stared for another moment before letting out a wordless whimper. She tried to move towards him, but her uncle came to her so she could press her head against the armor over his.

"How?" Her voice was hardly more than a whisper as she was overcome with emotion.

"I tried so hard," Sefonis told her, his voice cracking.

"I know," she told him. "But—" she pulled away from him. "I failed you. The rising sun didn't lead me anywhere."

"I know," he murmured, his gaze moving to the ground.

"Then why were we following it? Why did you let me continue?"

"I...I tried to help. But...the rules are different here and..."

"Our ancestors," Hasefi whispered and her uncle nodded. "They didn't want you to warn me?" He shook his head and she felt a flicker of anger. "I'm not surprised. They really don't do much, do they?" Sefonis chuckled slightly and Hasefi let out a purr. "I miss that sound." Sefonis's amusement faded and he simply gazed at her. "I miss you," she told him.

"I miss you, too," he whispered. His gaze suddenly flicked away and Hasefi watched his affection turn into a mix of irritation and fright.

"Is everything alright?" she asked.

His gaze returned to her and he resumed his warm expression. "Of course," he told her gently.

Now Hasefi flashed him an amused look. "You know...I'm not a blind little kit anymore," she told him, her eyes fluttering as they began to feel heavier.

"You were never blind," Sefonis laughed softly. "You could always see right through me or any other lynx." Sefonis's warm gaze held hers and she could see a sadness there. But there was pride, too.

"Something tells me you can see much more than just 'through' me, now."

"You are a brave lynx, wee lass. Brave and strong. You have faced more in your kithood than many will face in their lifetime. The world is a dangerous place, but I know you will stand firm."

"Always," Hasefi agreed. "Because I have you at my side."

Sefonis's gaze glowed with affection and he pressed his armored head against hers again. Hasefi closed her eyes, relishing the touch. She breathed in, tasting his comforting scent and letting herself believe for the moment that she was back with her tribe and that she had just had a really horrible, intricate nightmare.

"Sefi." Kolahn's whisper broke her out of her mind and into a world of dizziness. She could smell the thick scent of smoke, but there was also a sweet scent that reminded her of some of the plants Kolahn had taught her about. She tried to move her head, but the dizziness only grew worse. She closed her eyes, feeling exhausted. "Sefi, stay with me." She tried to open her eyes, but she could only manage to get them to tiny slits. "You know, there's a lot that I haven't told you," the wolf said quickly. "But I just don't know what to say." Kolahn paused, but when he spoke again, it barely felt like a heartbeat later to Hasefi.

"I had something akin to what you did," he explained. "Except they call themselves a clan." Interest caused Hasefi to perk up a little and her eyes flickered open. "I was about ten moons when I had to leave them, so I remember quite a bit." He went silent and Hasefi felt a faint pressure along her broken leg. She winced and closed her eyes, willing the hurt away. Kolahn's voice returned and she focused on it to try and ignore the pain.

"There are usually two leaders," he continued. "The Lord and the Lady. One would be of the royal family while the other was their mate. Their pups would later be judged to determine the next Lord or Lady. Until then, they were known as the princes and princesses of the Clan.

"After them, there are Alphas, which were in charge of certain aspects of the Clan. The Rogue Alpha handled stealth and hunting. The Warrior Alpha handled combat and defense. And then there was the Seer Alpha. They were one of the gifted given by the ancestors. Each Alpha is the oldest of their order."

Hasefi twitched, wanting to speak, but her voice failed.

"Each Alpha took charge of their respective sections. The wolves in those sections would also teach the tenderpaws which were the pups that reached ten moons. Pups got to choose what they would be."

Hasefi closed her eyes as the wolf's words painted an image in her mind. But instead of seeing wolves, she saw her own tribe. She imagined what life would have been like if they had all made it to a home like the one Kolahn described to be the valley. The thought carried her away until she felt as if she were merely a feather floating on a light, warm breeze.

Chapter Fourteen

"What do you see?"

Hasefi squinted at the mountain ahead as she studied the deep orange glow that outlined it where more and more smoke continued to pour into the sky. She stifled a disappointed sigh.

"More smoke," she answered Kolahn. "And the glow is getting brighter. It's kind of like the sun." She still had a hard time imagining the destruction Kolahn described that fire could do. Especially when it just looked like light.

"We might have to move, soon. How's your leg?"

"Kolahn, it's been over a moon—there isn't even much of a wound anymore." Hasefi gave the wolf an amused look when his serious expression didn't change. "Trust me, I'll let you know the moment there's the tiniest change in my recovery." She returned her gaze to the fire, her mind wandering to where it had been ever since she'd escaped death once again.

He had a clan. A group, like I did. There was a time where I never would have thought wolves could be as organized as we were. But where did they go? She focused on the fire again. *Could it have been fire? But Kolahn is afraid of so many things, it could be anything! Mountain lions, bears, fire—what happened?* She itched to ask him about it, but she didn't want to cross a line, especially since things were beginning to feel normal between them again since they had reached the ocean.

He told me so much about it—I know he was just trying to keep me from slipping away then, but did he think I wouldn't remember it? He hasn't talked about it. Is he waiting for me to? Or hoping I won't? Her gaze moved to the wolf. Kolahn was arranging their temporary shelter so it was more comfortable to sleep in. *Will we even be sleeping in them tonight? The smoke is getting thicker here. We might even have to move into the high mountains if it keeps up.* She stifled a groan.

When the wolf finished, he came to sit beside Hasefi, but his gaze was on her instead of the fire. "Why do you like watching it?" he asked.

"You said it could move faster than I think," she reminded him. "Someone should keep an eye on it. And...I just can't wrap my head around it."

"I hope you never have to," he sighed.

Hasefi gave him a suspicious look. "You said you just heard a story about fire, but you sound like you've experienced it."

Kolahn was silent.

"Is it just another one of the many things I don't know?" Her tone wasn't meant to be unkind, but the wolf still looked away as if she had hurt him.

"You haven't said anything about what I did tell you," he murmured.

Hasefi's whiskers twitched with surprise. "I assumed you wouldn't want me to."

Kolahn shrugged.

"Can I ask you about it?"

He didn't respond.

"I won't ask what happened," she assured him. He was still silent, so Hasefi just continued. "You mentioned different roles in the Clan. What was yours?"

"Pups became tenderpaws at ten moons," was all he said.

Hasefi tilted her head. "Okay. What would you have liked to be?"

The wolf raised his head and his eyes had a wistful glimmer in them. "I wanted to be a rogue, like my brother."

"What was your brother's name?"

"I had two," he told her. "Norahn, who wanted to be a rogue. And Mokahn."

"What did Mokahn want to be?"

"I don't know. He never really talked to me." There was a sadness in the wolf's eyes and Hasefi felt her heart clench.

"I'm sorry," Hasefi whispered. "I…you had so much more time to know your clan. It must have…it must have been unbearable to lose them."

Kolahn's gaze darkened and Hasefi stiffened. But his next words had nothing to do with what they were talking about.

"We should move into the snow in the morning," he murmured quietly. "I'm going to hunt." The wolf left Hasefi alone to think about what he said. She was beginning to think whatever Kolahn went through was worse than anything she'd been through thus far.

I can't blame him for keeping it a secret. Not only is it painful, but he might be trying to protect me. If I could keep him from learning even scarier horrors than what we've faced, I would. What other 'stories' does he know?

Kolahn came back later with a hare and they ate before retiring to the partial den to preserve their strength for the following morning. Hasefi was up first and was disappointed to notice breathing was more difficult than yesterday and her eyes watered as the smoke stung them.

"Kolahn," she murmured, running her paw gently along his shoulder. "Kolahn, we should get going." The wolf woke with a cough and Hasefi took a step back as he gave his head a shake.

"It's getting worse," the wolf gasped.

Hasefi led the way out of their shelter and looked down the way they had been travelling for the last moon.

"We can't go back," Kolahn rasped before she could ask anything. "We can't risk running into the mountain lions again."

"Okay, but if we go into the high mountains here, we could run into the other wolves. I don't think mountain lions would track us down this far," she added, but Kolahn merely shook his head.

"Then we'll keep moving towards the valley."

Hasefi opened her mouth to argue, but she knew that it would prove as successful as it had for the last moon.

I don't understand what it's like to care about a place so much, she thought. *Could a home really be worth dying for? I guess I've risked half my life trying to find mine...but I also had no choice. Kolahn does. He has me.* She felt a flicker of sadness as she watched him move away from their shelter, his eyes glazed over and staring into nothing.

As they continued their trek through the next few days, Hasefi began to notice the forest growing denser. Some of the trees looked like giant bushes and the brush beneath them grew more plentiful.

"Are we in the Great Forest now?" she asked Kolahn.

All he responded with was a nod.

Later that day, Hasefi found that they were both having a hard time breathing, so, against her instinct, she suggested they move higher into the mountains. They reached snow just as the sun began to descend, casting an array of colors than glittered along the ground.

She got up early the next morning to watch the smoke again. It was strange how it changed the sky and the sun. She'd found to her surprise that the sun was a lot smaller than she'd thought. It was merely a tiny ball of light in the sky, which was made clear as its brightness was muffled by the smoke, causing an eerie orange glow to descend upon the ground. However, Kolahn had told her it was still dangerous to stare at the sun, so she did her best not to.

She could still taste smoke in her mouth and she let out the odd cough every now and then, but the cooler air in the high mountains helped ease the tightness in her chest.

"It's so huge," she couldn't help but murmur as she followed the long golden line that stretched through the mountains. It seemed to extend forever, like an unfathomably huge sunset that stretched from one side of the world to the other. "But it's rained several times since it started," she pointed out.

Kolahn shrugged. "This fire is too strong for just rain," he said, his voice monotone. "We'll just have to wait and see what happens."

Hasefi's ears twitched uncertainly and she gave the fire a nervous look. "It's been here for so long. What if it never goes away?"

Kolahn didn't respond.

Hasefi searched for something to say to try and comfort him when an idea came to mind. "Could you ask your ancestors?"

"What?" he asked, giving her a puzzled look.

"Could you ask them for help?"

"I don't think so."

"Why not?" she pressed.

"I just can't, okay?" he snapped.

Hasefi flinched and returned her attention to the fire. *Could Sefonis help?* she wondered. She hadn't heard from him since he'd spoken to her that night when her leg was infected, so she wasn't able to satisfy all the new questions his presence had given her. But that didn't stop her from trying to reach out.

Sefonis? she thought. There was no answer and she glanced towards the wolf before walking a little ways off. "Sefonis?" she tried again. There was still no response, but she decided to continue anyways. "I'm in a bit of a predicament here," she began somewhat awkwardly. "I don't know what kind of things you can do now...but you helped me when I was dying. So now I'm wondering if you could help me with something else. With the fire." She paused. "Kolahn's home is ahead—that's where we're heading—and he's afraid it will be eaten by the fire. I...I don't want that to happen because I don't know what that'll do to him. So...if you're able...could you lend a paw?" She gazed into the sky, searching for an answer to her plea, but there was none. *He can hear me,* she assured herself. *I just have to be patient.*

She returned to Kolahn who was still staring ahead. She watched him, studying the frown his lips were curved into and the way his brow hung heavily over his eyes.

He hates fire, she realized. *Not like he's scared of bears and mountain lions. He actually hates fire. Kolahn, the wolf who feels bad killing prey, actually hates something. Fire must have taken his clan.* Sorrow swept through her. *It would have taken his home, too, which is why he's afraid of losing the valley. I can't understand how he feels. My home was wherever my tribe settled for the night. Or the places where I slept alone. Or wherever Kolahn and I have stayed.*

A sudden thought came to her mind and she moved towards the hollow that had been dug out for her to sleep in. Kolahn's eyes had closed and she thought he had fallen back asleep, but they flickered open when she stepped near him.

"Kolahn," she began. "I was thinking and, well, I realized I would rather travel everywhere with my tribe than live in one spot alone. Or, now, I'd rather travel with you."

The wolf lifted his head and looked at her with dull yellow eyes.

"What if that means...home isn't a place," she continued. "But a feeling? The kind of feeling you have when...you're with your tribe —or clan. Or when you're with another creature you care about. Is that silly?"

Faint amusement flickered in the depths of his gaze and Hasefi felt a little bit of joy ripple through her.

"That's not silly at all," he murmured. "It's...wise. You're a wise little puppy."

Hasefi gave his nose a gentle bat and Kolahn nosed her shoulder until she fell over. When she got to her paws, she quickly grew serious, holding Kolahn's gaze.

"I don't know what it's like to lose a home," she told him. "But I do know what it's like to lose everything I care about. If the valley is lost, remember we still have each other."

Kolahn's gaze glimmered with affection, but Hasefi could see that he was still upset.

He'll get better. Just like I did, she thought. *I'll make sure of it.*

Chapter Fifteen

"Kolahn, look!" Hasefi leaped away from his side and jumped onto the rock above where they had spent the night. Kolahn's head poked out from under her and she could barely suppress a delighted yowl. The mountains where darkness was rising was no longer glowing. "It's weakening!"

"Don't get too excited yet," the wolf warned. "It probably just changed directions. Fire lasting this long doesn't just suddenly die, unless it has eaten everything. A storm might help, or it'll just make it worse."

"A storm," Hasefi echoed. "I never understood snow falling from the sky, but water? And I hate how it soaks into my fur. But you said a storm is different than just rain, right? The clouds make sound?"

"It's thunder," he told her. "It usually follows lightning."

"Which is lines of light that stab out of the clouds," she said disbelievingly. "If everything you've mentioned hadn't come true before, I wouldn't believe you for a second."

Despite Kolahn's previous warning, Hasefi noticed the smoke beginning to fade, revealing a frontline of heavy clouds that looked as if they had swallowed the smoke. She watched eagerly as they marched closer to where they were staying just inside the high mountains where Edgewood wrapped around the Great Forest. The air beneath the clouds was obscured by heavy rain.

"There's your storm," she said triumphantly when she noticed a brief flash in the clouds followed by a faraway rumble.

Kolahn looked out from under the rock, but he still didn't look convinced.

"We could probably return to the trees," Hasefi pointed out. To her dismay, Kolahn just lowered his head back onto his paws. Hasefi got up, preparing to leap down to his side, but decided against it and just sat back down.

What do I do? she asked herself. Then her gaze went to the darkening sky above her. *He didn't try hunting today. He hasn't even decided to leave so we can continue towards the valley. What if he loses his will? Like I did in the pit? How do I help him?* When the sky offered no answer, she returned her gaze to the weakening fire. *Whatever that fire has done to the other side of the mountain is beyond what I can imagine. But if I'm right and fire is what haunts his past, then he knows exactly what's over there. Maybe if I can see, I can understand.* Hasefi jumped down from the rock and stood in front of Kolahn. The wolf didn't react to her, so she went straight to the point.

"I want to see."

The wolf's nose twitched and his eyes slid over to give her a puzzled look.

"I want to see what the fire did."

He raised his head with a frown. "That's not a good idea," he told her. "Even if it seems to be out, there could be areas still on fire. Why would you want to see? I can't imagine it's pleasant."

"Can't imagine?" Hasefi echoed. "Or can't experience again?"

Confusion entered the wolf's expression again and his jaws were open slightly as if he were going to say something. Then understanding changed his face and he let out a soft sigh. "Fire has nothing to do with why I'm not with my clan," he told her.

"Then what? You talked about your clan, but ever since this fire came, you've been too upset to do anything—you haven't even gotten up today! What is bothering you if not the fire?"

The wolf shook his head and lowered it again. "It's more complicated," he told her. "I didn't 'lose' them. Not like you lost your tribe."

"So, what? Are you saying they're still out there?"

Kolahn didn't answer her.

"I want to understand, Kolahn. Please let me!"

"This is my fault," he whimpered.

Hasefi settled in front of him, her face close to his. "What is?"

"All of this. It's because of me."

"The fire?" she asked disbelievingly.

"And the mountain lions. Ever since you've been around me, you've just been getting hurt."

"You can't blame yourself for that," Hasefi told him, surprised and a little put off that her wellbeing had made him this depressed. "I wouldn't be here if it weren't for you."

"I was selfish," he continued. "I just...didn't want to be alone. And now...all you've done is suffered these last few moons and...it's because I'm too much of a coward to tell you the truth."

Uncertainty pricked Hasefi's pelt and she had to resist the urge to get up.

"What truth?" she asked quietly. *Could he somehow be involved with Sal?* she thought immediately, old fears beginning to rise. *Maybe he really was formerly with Sal's group. Was that his clan?* "What are you talking about?" she urged him.

"You're going to hate me," he told her.

"I highly doubt that."

"You *should* hate me!" Kolahn shot up onto his paws, making Hasefi jump back. His yellow eyes were suddenly ablaze, replacing the abject misery that had been there before. "You have no idea what I am!"

"Yes I do," she argued, her voice soft but firm. "You're a kind, friendly wolf that helped a kit stuck in a pit when she wanted nothing else but death. You're the wolf that used his strength and time to take care of her, who saved me from being eaten by mountain lions and who comforted me when I thought I lost everything."

Kolahn's uncharacteristic fury quickly diminished and he lowered himself back down. "You don't understand," he told her firmly.

"So let me. Kolahn, whatever you say now won't change the fact that, when this fire dies, we're both going to go to your valley, hunt some food, and have a nice, relaxing evening." She waited, but the wolf continued to remain silent. Hasefi stifled a disappointed sigh and closed her eyes. *Why won't he just let it out?*

"Your tribe's name was Tribe of the Second Divide, right?" Kolahn said finally.

Hasefi nodded. "I have no idea what that meant, though," she admitted.

"My clan had a name," he admitted. "It was Clan of the Gray Wolf."

Gray Wolf? Hasefi thought with puzzlement. *That doesn't make sense.* She kept her mouth closed, however, letting Kolahn continue.

"Despite what you've seen, wolves aren't supposed to be black. They're supposed to have gray fur with white underbellies and paws. You actually look more like a wolf than I do," he added with a sad chuckle. "Wolves with fur like mine, fur the color of darkness, are touched by evil."

Hasefi glanced at herself, unable to imagine Kolahn with her fur.

"There is a story that my mother told me when I began to ask why I couldn't leave the den with my brothers," he continued. "It's about the first black wolf. There was a point when the Clan was suffering difficult times. Food was scarce and their territory was constantly threatened by…by other predators. Numbers were diminishing as wolves died from hunger and sickness. The Clan was hopeless and they looked to the only place they could."

"Your ancestors," Hasefi murmured before she could stop herself.

"Well, *their* ancestors. The moon has no room for black wolves." He was silent for a moment before continuing. "The Clan prayed and howled, begging for an answer to their suffering. And then they were given one.

"A Watcher—that's what we call the spirits—came to the Lord of the Clan, saying that 'two pups will be born under the light of the half moon, reflecting its form in the sky, and one will rise to defeat the darkness that threatens the Clan.' Sure enough, when the half moon came, the Lady bore two pups. They resembled the moon they were born under—one had fur akin to the half that shone upon her, while the other had fur of the hidden half. The Clan saw this as one of the greatest gifts from the Watchers. Their names were Eilwyn and Resahn, respectively.

"The princess and prince grew up as any other pup did, but the anticipation of which wolf would be chosen to take charge of the Clan was more intense than any royal pups before them. However, when they began their training, the choice seemed obvious.

"Resahn was strong and smart. He quickly beat the Alphas in training and even managed to outwit some of the gifted. Eilwyn was a formidable wolf, but she never had the same talents her brother did.

"When the Lady fell ill and joined the Watchers, the Lord decided it was time to step down and choose which wolf would be declared the next ruler. Resahn had many feats beneath his paws, including saving the Clan from extinction. He was admired by all the wolves—they worshipped him as the prophesized wolf sent by the Watchers. Also, princes and princesses were required to have a mate by the time they were twenty moons and Eilwyn had failed to adhere to that rule. Thus Resahn was made Lord.

"Leadership was shared equally between mates, but Resahn's mate was not one any wolf expected to become leader. She was a very average wolf with little will to do much beyond daily duties. But this was overlooked by the rest of the Clan as their admiration for Resahn shadowed their concern over his choice of a mate. It wasn't long, however, before the purpose of his choice was made clear.

"The moment Resahn became Lord, he made known his true desires for the Clan. He had come to hate the—the things that had hindered them before. He declared war on them, turning the Clan into an army to fight off any little thing that threatened their borders.

"At first, it didn't seem particularly terrible. But his desire to drive away any other predators soon caused him to ignore certain rules of the Clan and enforce new ones. Pups were a requirement of all wolves—Resahn had many mates and forced other males to do the same. Pups were made into tenderpaws at five moons instead of ten and they were all forced to be warriors. No gifted were given to the Clan during this time and the Seer Alpha seemed to be in line with Resahn.

"While Eilwyn remained the sole white wolf, more black wolves were born into the Clan and not all of them were of his blood. Soon the Clan could hardly be called Clan of the Gray Wolf. Over half of them bore fur like his. And it was soon discovered these black wolves had the same strength as Resahn.

"The Clan was confused by this turn of events. The Watchers had said a new wolf would be born to face the darkness brought upon it. But the confusion came from the fact they thought the darkness was something outside the Clan. Not the wolf they thought would save them from it.

"Soon, wolves began looking to Eilwyn for answers. But Eilwyn seemed prepared to stand by her brother in all of his plans. The Clan was thriving, but no wolf was truly happy unless their fur was black.

"Resahn had led his wolves into a final battle to secure the new borders of his already huge territory. But his sister suddenly turned to face him with the intent to kill. Resahn was able to stop her, but then the Seer Alpha struck the blow she had intended, using magic to destroy the Lord. The battle ended and the wolves returned home.

"From there, the Seer Alpha and Eilwyn took lead of the Clan, repairing the damage her brother had done. During this time, Eilwyn had found a mate and became the true Lady of the Clan.

"The black wolves, scattered by the loss of their leader, had been kept as prisoners by the Seer Alpha until he and Eilwyn decided what would be done. Eilwyn decided that the Clan would not stoop to murder their enemies like Resahn had and instead cast them out to live their own lives. Should they return, however, they would merely be inviting death.

"Despite the victory over Resahn, black wolves continued to be born in the Clan. This forced the Lady to create a rule that black wolves would be kept until hunting age to give them a chance in the wild by themselves. But they couldn't remain within the Clan since they were touched by the evil of Resahn and whatever dark force had created him."

Kolahn ended with a shaky breath, suddenly looking like a frail old wolf with an inherent hopelessness in his gaze. As Hasefi stared in utter bewilderment, she saw how broken Kolahn really was.

"By the stars," she whispered, unable to find other words to respond with. "I..."

"That's why you can't stay with me," he told her, his voice strained. "I'm evil. Bad things happen because of me."

Hasefi shook her head, words stuck in her mouth. They made her throat ache until she finally found the ability to speak again.

"No. Kolahn, the last thing you are is evil."

"You don't understand—I *am* evil. I *feel* it. Whenever I fight, whenever I hunt, I *feel* it. It's trying to get out. I'm scared I won't be able to keep it in. I...I could be like the wolves that took your tribe."

"No," Hasefi said firmly. "No, you're not evil. Kolahn, you've just been told about evil. I've seen it. And you're not evil." Kolahn opened his mouth, but Hasefi didn't give him a chance to talk. "Killing for food is one thing, but killing to kill is what evil is. Inflicting pain for joy is evil. Sal and the other wolves, that's what they do. They've given in to whatever dark feeling it is you have. But you're not like them because you choose to fight it. You fight the urge for bloodshed—you don't even like hunting because of it. And that makes you *good*."

"But I don't know how much longer I can keep it in."

"You don't have to worry about that, because I can help."

Kolahn looked at her with wide, scared eyes. "Why?" he asked. "Why would you help me?"

"You know why."

"But...I lied to you. How can you trust me?"

"You did it because you wanted to protect me," she told him.

Kolahn shook his head. "I did it because I wanted you to stay with me. I didn't...want to be alone again."

"And no creature can blame you for that. I'm sure I would have done the same thing in your place," Hasefi pointed out.

Kolahn shook his head, but he said nothing more. Hasefi felt her heart break at the sight of the defeated wolf and she pressed her nose to his cheek.

"Your clan is blind for throwing you out," she insisted. "They should have been able to see that you weren't like the others. This

Eilwyn seems to be getting rid of black wolves because of how she feels about her brother."

"Resahn was evil," Kolahn growled. "And he's inside me."

Hasefi moved to meet the wolf's eyes. "Your names are alike. Was he…your father?"

"I was born after he was dead," was all he offered.

"You know what I think?" she said.

Kolahn's ears twitched.

"I think your clan should have tried to help you and your kind. Instead of deciding to throw you out—even the ones involved during Resahn's time—they should have tried to help you fight it. To help you control what you feel. Not just toss you aside to succumb to it."

"You don't understand what Resahn did," he told her quietly.

"I think I understand better than you do. My tribe was massacred, remember?"

Kolahn lowered his head.

"I'm not going to leave you, Kolahn."

"You can't trust me."

"Well, I do. You saved my life more than once. And you gave me a reason to keep going—again, more than once—when I thought I'd lost everything. I'm not leaving your side, no matter how hard you try to push me. Now, you and I are going to leave this snow behind and go to the valley and bathe in a nice patch of sunshine and stop letting our pasts haunt us."

The wolf said nothing.

"Okay?"

He drew in a long breath, then let it out slowly. "Okay."

"Great. And maybe we can find something to eat along the way, I'm starving."

The wolf got up, but his expression was still distraught.

"Kolahn?"

"Let's go," he said and walked out from under the shade of the rock. Hasefi watched him for a moment before following him, keeping a close eye on the wolf.

They didn't end up hunting along the way, but hunger was the least of Hasefi's worries. Her focus was on Kolahn as he moved silently down the slope into Edgewood, his expression fixed on something only he could see.

I could never have imagined this was what he was dealing with, she thought. *He still has his clan, but returning to them means death because they think he's evil. Why would his ancestors even let something like that happen? Why would they give them this supposedly great white wolf, then this terribly evil black wolf to doom all other black wolves?*

Maybe we were both abandoned by those we were supposed to believe in. But he still believes. How could he still believe in them?

The wolf suddenly stopped and Hasefi gave him a questioning look. Kolahn was staring at his paws and he crouched with a whimper.

"I can't do this," he told her.

"Can't do what?"

Kolahn just shook his head and Hasefi felt a flare of anger directed at the wolves who had tossed him out, particularly the one he called Eilwyn.

"Kolahn, your fur doesn't define who you are," she told him sternly. "Your actions do. There were lynxes in my tribe that had black in their fur. They also had white and orange and brown and gray. I don't know how it is for wolves, but having white or black fur doesn't define you as good or evil.

"It's even in your story. Nobody saw Eilwyn as the savior because Resahn was the one performing all these heroic acts to help the Clan. In that, *he* was seen as good. Eilwyn wasn't good until she actively tried to kill her own brother to stop his evil. Even this Seer was originally seen as bad because he helped Resahn until he landed the killing blow. It doesn't make sense. Your clan judges you by your fur with a story judged by action."

Kolahn's gaze slowly moved to meet hers and she could see the conflict there. It slowly changed until there was a faint light there.

"Sometimes I forget you're barely ten moons old," he whispered. Then a tiny flicker of amusement entered his gaze. "You are kind of like a wolf," he added suddenly.

"How?" she asked him with a disbelieving look.

"You're starting to sound like one."

"Well, yeah, what do you expect? All I've been able to listen to is your obnoxious accent for the last three moons."

Kolahn chuckled slightly and Hasefi rolled her eyes.

"Wolfcat," he teased.

"Right, I'm a wolfcat, sure. Unless maybe you're a lynxdog."

Kolahn shook his head. "Wolfcat sounds better."

Hasefi let out a mock sigh of annoyance which quickly turned into an affectionate purr. "You're going to listen to me, right?" she asked, growing serious again. "You're not with your clan anymore and I'm not with my tribe. So we can make our own rules. Our own stories."

Kolahn nodded slowly. "I'd like that."

Hasefi rubbed her cheek along his shoulder and he nosed her flank.

"Now, I'd like to see what all the fuss is about for this valley of yours."

Chapter Sixteen

Hasefi flinched as cold droplets fell on her fur, seeping into it and sending cold shivers through her body.

"One thing the high mountains didn't have was this," she muttered, ducking under a tree for cover. Kolahn stopped to look at her, not even seeming to notice the rain as it soaked his pelt.

"It's better than fire," he pointed out. Hasefi shrugged, forcing herself to leave her cover and continue walking with him.

"I just wish it didn't make me so cold" Hasefi sighed. "It's different than snow-cold." To her surprise, Kolahn gave her shoulder a playful nudge and she teetered off balance. "Hey, no fair!" she cried, trying to look annoyed.

Kolahn let his tongue hang out, then he bounded ahead.

"That's how you want to play? Well, you asked for it." She veered off through the trees, following the slope they were descending into what Kolahn told her was the beginning of the valley.

She could hear him nearby and altered her path so that there was always brush between them so he couldn't easily pounce on her.

He knows this place well, she thought. *He'll know shortcuts, so I'll have to do something unexpected.* Hasefi continued to evade him for a little longer until she bounced off a tree and shot past the wolf, causing him to let out a startled yelp. Hasefi let out a short yowl in victory as he stumbled to a clumsy halt and she was able to gain some ground.

It wasn't long, however, before her legs tired and her lungs ached from breathing in the still smoke-tainted air.

It's been almost a half moon since these storms started coming, Hasefi thought. *How much longer until they clear the air?* She pushed the thought aside as she came across a stream that cut through the forest. She looked down both ways, then noticed a faint rumbling amidst the downpour.

Kolahn said there was a waterfall by his home. Hasefi started heading in the direction of the roar, hoping she'd find a nice dry place to lick the water from her fur.

As she moved, the rain began to ease and the sun peeked through the clouds. By the time she came across a small, steep rise where the stream trickled over, the rain had slowed into a faint drizzle. She climbed awkwardly up the ridge and soon came to a point where the trees broke away, revealing a beautiful clearing.

A waterfall bounced down the side of a cliff until it splashed into a large pool in the center of the clearing. The end of the pool fed the stream that had led Hasefi there. The grass was long and soft and various flowers and sweet smelling plants grew within the clearing.

The thing that amazed her the most was the network of tunnels along the cliffside around the waterfall. It looked like most of it had collapsed and a lot of the pathways had crumbled into nothing, but it was clear a large, intricate cave system had existed there.

This would have been perfect for my tribe, she thought wistfully. Her gaze moved to the large gaping mouth on the right of the waterfall. She saw a flash of black which surprised her.

Did he just decide to run home after I tricked him? she thought with amusement. *You shouldn't give up so easily, silly wolf.* Hasefi stepped into the clearing, her mouth open to call out to the wolf.

Her jaws snapped shut and she threw herself back into cover, her heart pounding.

No, she thought. *No, this can't be.* She peered through the leaves of the bush she hid in until she caught sight of the black fur outside the cave. Another figure had joined it, their voices carrying through the air to her ears.

They're here, she thought with panic. *How are they here?* She angled her ears as far forward as they would go, trying to catch their words.

"Vek was right," the first murmured, her gaze flicking towards Hasefi, making her duck. Fortunately, the wolf made no sign that she'd noticed anything. "The smoke did lead us to something."

"How in the shadows did he figure that out?" the other asked, glancing in the direction where faint smoke still floated down the other side of the valley. "After all these moons, too?"

"He hasn't been here in a while," a third voice said as the speaker revealed himself by leaving the cave. "His scent is stale and his bedding unused. He might have moved on to new territory."

"Are you sure it was another like us?" the first wolf asked doubtfully. "It's not like the Pack to miss a new outcast."

"Especially for this long," the second added. "He obviously made this place home for a while."

"Could he know about us?" the first continued. "Would he be trying to avoid us?"

The second wolf snorted. "Under what moon would a wolf avoid his own kind?" he scoffed.

"Under what *sky,*" the third wolf growled. "The moon abandoned us, remember?"

The second wolf just rolled his eyes.

I have to find Kolahn. Hasefi turned back into the forest and hurried to where they had separated. There was no sign of her companion, so she decided to try tracking him down. *There's still a bit of rain—maybe it'll mask any sound I make. Hopefully it'll wash away my scent, too.* Hasefi opened her mouth to taste the air, both relieved and dismayed to find that Kolahn's scent was already difficult to pick up. Regardless, she pressed her search, hoping she didn't come across a different wolf again.

What if he doesn't realize they're here? Or they find him before I do? Will he be in the same danger I am? There was a sound nearby that made her duck. Hasefi carefully limped to a bush with branches that stretched far from its stem. After hiding underneath, she peered out, trying to determine what the sound had been.

It could be a squirrel, she thought. *Kolahn said they could be alarmingly loud sometimes.* Despite her thoughts, she glimpsed the thick black fur of a wolf. Several sets of paws padded through the brush, indicating there were more than just a few wolves scouting Kolahn's valley. *They're scouring the woods. What if Sal is here? Would he be? Why are they here in the first place? Are they still looking for me? They don't know I'm here, yet. But they know Kolahn was.* Hasefi shrank closer to the middle of the bush. *Where is he? I can't stay here, but I can't leave him!* Indecision racked her mind and she felt as if claws were trying to tear her two ways.

Something heavy fell on top of her and fur smothered her mouth and nose. She tried to let out a yowl to warn Kolahn what was happening. Then she realized nothing was.

"Sefi, it's me." Kolahn moved off of her and she got back to her paws. "Sorry, I didn't want you to call out and alert them."

"Kolahn," she gasped. "Oh, thank the stars." She pressed her head against his chest. "What do we do? We can't stay here. They know you've been here and I think they want to find you. I don't know how many wolves are here. What do we do?"

"We need to get somewhere safer, first," Kolahn told her.

Hasefi nodded agreement and moved away from him.

"We'll move towards what's left of the fire," the wolf continued.

"Towards?" Hasefi echoed, feeling a ripple of surprise and fear.

"No creature would willingly follow it. It's the safest way we can go."

"Except that fire will eat us if it gets the chance," Hasefi argued, wondering if Kolahn had forgotten his own fear of the fire.

The wolf paused. "The fire is weakened," he said finally. "If it hasn't already died. It'll be easier to avoid than these wolves. We don't have much choice."

Not wanting to stay there any longer, Hasefi just nodded and Kolahn led her away. They crossed the stream and moved up the shallow slope towards where the smoke had been coming from.

The acrid tang grew thicker, tightening Hasefi's throat. She did her best not to cough on it so she wouldn't lead the other wolves straight to where they were. The ground grew steeper as they went further, but it didn't reach as high as the ground they had travelled on the other side of the valley.

When they were near the top of the mountain and Hasefi thought she would collapse with the strain of breathing, Kolahn stopped and moved along a ridge that jutted out from the slanted ground with a hole carved just above it as if a giant creature had scooped a pawful of ground from the mountain. Hasefi hopped in after Kolahn, looking back down into the valley to where she could see the waterfall disappearing into it.

"I'm so sorry," she whispered. "They're probably still looking for me. This is my fault."

"No," Kolahn told her sternly. "It's not your fault."

When Hasefi turned to face the wolf, she saw that he looked afraid, but she was surprised to see the amount of anger that twisted his face.

"What are we going to do?" she asked. "We can't stay here. It won't be long before they pick up our scents and we both know how eager they'd be to track me down once they realize I'm nearby." She peered into the valley, but the forest was too thick to make out anything below. "We can't fight all of them." Hasefi clawed the ground beneath her in a spurt of frustrated rage. "I don't want to run anymore!"

"So don't."

Hasefi's ears twitched with surprise at Kolahn's words.

"This is my home," he continued. "I'm not giving it up—not because of them. They've already taken too much from others."

"But what can we do about it?" Hasefi pointed out. "There are way too many of them to take on. And you're not exactly a fighter, not to mention I only have three working legs."

"Maybe we don't have to fight."

"Kolahn, these wolves murdered my tribe without reason—I don't think they know anything but violence."

The wolf held her gaze and Hasefi found something in his eyes she couldn't understand.

"Are you sure they attacked without reason?" he asked.

Hasefi was silent, confused.

"Do you know why they've been hunting you?" he pressed.

"I don't know—because they're evil?" Hasefi offered.

Kolahn shook his head. "You told me evil comes from action. But action comes from reason. What reason does Sal have to hunt you?"

"I don't know," she said again. "Maybe he's angry I got away."

"Tracking you down for moons just to satisfy an irritation? There has to be more."

Hasefi frowned at the ground, knowing Kolahn had a point. *Why* would *they keep hunting me? Why did they kill my tribe in the first place?*

"I'm not sure knowing would really help us out," she pointed out. "Besides, it's not like we have any way of finding out."

"That might not be true."

Hasefi gave Kolahn a confused look. "What, do you want to just walk up to them and ask?" When Kolahn's expression didn't change, Hasefi felt her heart drop. "Kolahn, they'd kill us."

"You, maybe," he admitted. "But I'm like them."

"No, you're not. You're the opposite of what they are."

"They don't know that."

"Okay, well, even if you did ask and then for some strange reason Sal told you why he was after me, what would that do for us?"

"Maybe we could stop them."

Hasefi just stared at Kolahn in utter bewilderment. His gaze didn't waver, glowing with determination. She realized he was standing tall, despite his wet fur, looking more confident than she had ever seen him.

"What did you do with my timid wolf friend?" she whispered.

"I think this is what I'm supposed to do, Sefi," he explained. "When my ancestors, the Watchers, led me to you, I didn't really understand why. But now I think I do. They want me to stop Sal. He may not be able to harm my clan like Resahn did, but that doesn't mean the life outside should suffer. Black wolves never should have come to be."

"Okay, but what could you possibly do to stop them?"

"I don't know," he admitted. "But if I find out what their purpose is, maybe we can find a way. Don't you want to stop them, too?"

Hasefi stared at him in disbelief, but she couldn't deny the rage that still boiled deep within her belly every time she thought about what the wolves had put her through.

"Maybe this is our chance," Kolahn said.

"I don't know if it's worth it, though," Hasefi argued. "It is a huge risk and, yeah, we make a pretty great team, but neither of us have what it takes to take on even one of them." Hasefi narrowed her eyes when Kolahn's gaze flickered away for a brief moment. "Do we?"

"There's more to wolves like me than our fur and size," he murmured. "The darkness that's inside, it makes us stronger. And helps us heal faster."

Hasefi blinked with surprise. "Really?"

"In the high mountains, when the mountain lion attacked…."

Hasefi's eyes widened. "So you *did* fight it off, didn't you?"

"Sort of. It could've turned me into fresh meat, but it didn't seem keen on risking a fight, so I just gave it enough injuries until it backed away."

"So…what's taken me a moon to heal, took you a quarter moon?"

Kolahn shrugged.

"By the stars that would be useful," she sighed enviously. "But these wolves have that same advantage," Hasefi pointed out.

"Except they succumb to it," he pointed out. "And it controls them. If I manage to control it, maybe—"

"Maybe what? You take down as many as you can before they kill you? No. You said there might not have to be violence. What else is there?"

Kolahn hesitated before replying.

"I don't think they want to harm me," he started slowly. "If they're looking for me, they might be trying to recruit me."

"How can you be sure?"

"What reason would they have to kill one of their own?"

"The fact that you're not one of their own," she pointed out sternly. "Kolahn, I really don't think this is worth it. We've stayed in so many different places, I don't see—"

"I can't leave my home, Hasefi," he growled, causing her to recoil. "I will not leave her."

Hasefi shook her head, not understanding. "Her?"

"If I manage to get in and figure out what they're doing…we might be able to get some help," he continued as if his outburst had never happened.

"From who?"

"My clan."

"Right, because they'd be so willing to help one of the wolves they outcast," Hasefi snorted.

"I think if they knew what kind of threat the other outcasts have become, they would do something about it. I know they would. It would be their responsibility."

"You really think so?" Hasefi asked doubtfully and he nodded. "But what risk does that put you in?"

"Returning…means death."

Hasefi let out an exasperated groan. "Is there any way we can go that *doesn't* put your life at risk? Like leaving this alone?"

"I told you, I can't," he insisted. "This is what I'm supposed to do."

Hasefi shook her head, but she was beginning to realize that arguing might be futile. "So you'll leave me alone while you go on this crazy mission of yours? What happens if you don't come back?"

The wolf was silent for a long while.

"Follow the stream that way," he told her, jerking his nose in the opposite direction of the waterfall. "The valley drops off into a wide forest. Just below is where the Clan is."

"Really?" she gasped.

"If I don't come back to you, then you need to go to them and tell them what's going on. Ask for Lady Eilwyn."

"Kolahn—"

"They're not fond of lynxes, but they wouldn't do anything until they understand why you've come to them. They'll listen to you."

"Kolahn, just shut up for a heartbeat, please."

The wolf was silent, but Hasefi found she had no words to use. She stood with her jaws parted, lost in the rush of what was going on.

"Sefi, please. I have to do this. For my clan. For the Watchers." Kolahn tilted his head and warmth entered his eyes. "For you."

"Fallen stars," she whispered, moving forward until her face was pressed into his chest fur. His foreleg draped over her shoulders and she shut her eyes, trying to hold back the emotion she was feeling. "You know this doesn't make sense, right, you sunblind wolf?" she mumbled into his fur. "You're too good, you know that? It's going to get you killed."

"I'll be back," he murmured into her ear. "Give me until tomorrow's moonrise. If I'm not back before dark, go to the Clan of the Gray Wolf." Kolahn pulled away, his gaze serious as he held hers. "We're going to stop Sal."

Hasefi nodded, beginning to get a hold of herself. "What if they get too close and I need to move?" she asked.

"I'll find you," he said firmly.

Hasefi nodded. "Okay. Kolahn?"

"What?"

"Don't die, okay? I can't lose you. You're everything I have, you know?"

He nosed her cheek. "I'll be back," he promised. Then he stood. Hasefi's heart skipped a beat and she felt the urge to block his way or curl her claws into his fur so he wouldn't leave. But she forced herself to remain where she was.

"What are you going to do?"

"I'll go to them," he told her. "And I'll tell them the truth. I've returned after a long journey in the high mountains."

"What if they ask about me?"

Kolahn paused for a moment. "I won't know what they're talking about."

Hasefi's fur twitched nervously. "Would they believe you?"

"Lying is something I can do," he said, not quite meeting her gaze. "Now, I should get going so they'll be too preoccupied to notice you've been here."

Hasefi nodded. She wanted to say more, but her voice wouldn't work. Kolahn seemed to understand and he rested his chin on her head.

"I'll be back before you know it." He turned away, then hesitated. A flash of hope went through her as she thought perhaps he had changed his mind, but the expression her gave her was serious. "Don't come after me." Before she could respond, he was gone. Claws of despair sunk into Hasefi's chest and she felt the suffocating pressure of loneliness surround her.

Just until moonrise, she told herself. *Maybe sooner. I just have to wait.* The last thought didn't sit well with Hasefi, but she knew getting herself caught would ruin Kolahn's plan. *It's not even much of a plan,* she thought. *But he believes this is what he has to do.*

Hasefi poked her head out of the hollow, getting wet in the weak rain no longer the worst of her concerns. There was no sign of Kolahn or any other wolf. She sat on the edge and looked out into the valley, trying to glimpse a flash of black fur. But the shadows of the forest and the rain made it too difficult. Her gaze went left to follow the stream away from their home.

All I see are trees, she thought. *But he said it leads to his clan. How far away are they?* Hasefi's curiosity quickly faded as she returned her attention to where she could glimpse the waterfall that fed the stream. *Is Sal down there? His wolves said the smoke led them here. How would they think of that? Could they have some sort of ancestors?*

Hasefi eventually retired back into the hollow to sleep for the night.

When she woke, the rain had stopped and the smoke was significantly thinner. She stepped out onto the ridge outside the hollow and breathed in the wet scent of the forest, enjoying the taste of fresher air. It was still dark, but the first rays of sunlight were beginning to enter the sky and shine orange light over the valley.

She was able to hunt a meager meal of squirrel when the critter practically ran across her paws, but hunger wasn't at the front of her mind.

There were no signs of wolves—friendly or not—which made her think Kolahn was right and they were focused more on him than scouring the area further. *That'll change once they find my scent,* she thought. *I have to remain alert.* She fell into old habits, but a small voice nagged at her, reminding her she wasn't alone. It was almost worse than when she had been alone, because it made her belly twist with worry and her heart flutter with fear.

As the sun followed its path, Hasefi felt the weight of her loneliness begin to weigh down on her. She had the urge to say something to break the silence and found herself looking instinctively to the clouded sky above.

"Sefonis," she whispered. "Watchers. Whoever's out there." She paused, but there was no response to indicate she was being heard. She shifted uncomfortably, aware of her displays of anger she had shown to the sky before. "I don't know if anyone's listening, but if you are, I have to ask you something." Hasefi glanced into the valley. "My friend believes he's been given a mission by you and he believes it's the right thing to do—which it is. But I don't think the risk is worth it." She went silent for a few heartbeats, gathering her thoughts. "I want to stop Sal. I want to make him suffer for what he did—more than anything. But…I don't believe that's worth Kolahn's life. Or mine." She studied her paws before lifting her head up again. "Which is why I need to ask you one thing. And that's to protect him. Okay? I need you to protect Kolahn. He's a good wolf, no matter what color his fur is or whatever darkness might be inside him. He's *good*." She waited, but there was no response. After a few more heartbeats, she let out a defeated sigh and hung her head.

She thought of her vision of Sefonis, but with his lack of presence since that night, she couldn't help but wonder if he had merely been the result of her feverish mind reflecting her wistful thoughts.

Kolahn is really all I have, she thought. *My tribe is gone. I know that. All I have is him. I can't lose him—especially not to Sal.* There was hopelessness in her heart and she thought maybe she should try and track where he had went, but she managed to convince herself otherwise and she retired to the hollow to try and sleep the time away.

She settled so she could still see the sky and laid her head on the ground with her eyes on it. A final thought went through her head before she closed her eyes.

Bring Kolahn back to me.

Chapter Seventeen

Hasefi's gaze flicked to where the stream led, only to move quickly back to where the waterfall was. She had been watching it intently since the sun had begun to change the color of the sky as it settled for the night, waiting for any sign of her companion.

She'd moved farther along the mountain since Sal's wolves had begun showing up near the hollow. They weren't search parties, however, and moved directly towards where the fire was still giving off small puffs of smoke every now and then. *Maybe they're setting up a camp,* she thought. *But why would they go toward the fire?* Hasefi wasn't sure if they even really lived in the mountains or had always just been on the move like her. They also seemed to be leaving the valley as if Kolahn's presence was all they had needed from it. *Which means they probably never found any trace of me.*

Hasefi shifted restlessly, urging Kolahn to appear below in the direction of the hollow. But nothing moved except the trees as they swayed softly in the breeze.

Where are you?

She stood, tempted to scout out the edge of the forest, but she forced herself to sit down again. *I can't. If I got caught, it could put him in danger, too. But what if he's already in danger?* Her claws churned up the grass beneath her paws and she let out an impatient breath. *What if he needs my help? What if waiting makes me too late?* Hasefi got to her paws again, then gritted her teeth. *What do I do? Going might risk him, but not going could also risk him!* She looked up at the sky. *What do I do?*

A yelp sounded a few paces away and Hasefi sprang into action. She moved higher up the mountain, her ears angled towards where the sound had come from. The trees were spread thinner here than in the valley since the ground was so steep, but still provided decent cover. She found one to slink behind as she peered ahead, her eyes wide as they looked for any sign of movement.

But it was sound that came to her.

"You idiot, watch where you're walking," a wolf growled, her tone cold.

"I hate this cursed land!" another voice snapped, tinged with pain. "Why did *we* have to come here?"

"You know why. Now pull that thorn out of your puppy-soft pads and get moving."

There was a wordless whimper.

"What?!"

"I can't. It's too deep." Another yelp sounded and Hasefi ducked farther behind the tree as a wolf came into view, limping on three legs. The paw he held in the air oozed blood onto the ground below. "Why did you do that?"

Another wolf came into view, this one bigger than the first with a cold yellow gaze. She spat on the ground and gave the younger wolf an irritated glare.

"Now it's out. Let's keep moving. Sal wants this area checked out for any predators so we're not caught off-guard in our new home."

New home? Are they planning to stay here permanently?

"What about the lynx-pup?" the young wolf muttered, limping in the general direction Hasefi was hiding.

"Her trail was lost moons ago," the bigger wolf growled. "I'm just looking forward to when Sal finally gives it up and we can actually move forward with the plan."

The plan? Was Kolahn right? Is Sal up to something? Hasefi backed away from the tree, knowing she would be discovered if she stayed any longer. She turned and hopped away as silently as she could.

"Wait."

Hasefi froze as the younger wolf spoke excitedly.

"I smell lynx."

"You foolish pup, you just think you can. There's no way—" The older wolf cut off and Hasefi winced.

Broken stars.

She lunged forwards, running along the mountain. An excited howl sounded behind her and she urged herself to go faster. *They'll catch up soon,* she thought. *I have to do something!* Hasefi came to a halt when she saw a wall of rock in front of her, blocking her path. She turned just as the two wolves appeared, their gazes burning with excitement.

"Well, what do you know?" the older wolf growled with a pleased grin. "The little lynx appears to us and we're not even looking for her. Sal will be pleased."

"Look at her," the other snickered. "She's crippled. How is she still alive?"

"I guess that new wolf wasn't lying after all," the bigger wolf pointed out. "And he was right—she was foolish enough to stick around and wait for him."

Doubt crept through Hasefi's mind. *Kolahn told them I'd be waiting for him? They must have hurt him.*

"If any of you touched a hair on his pelt I'll—"

"What, exactly?" the older wolf asked. "There's nothing you can do, little lynx. You can't even stand properly."

Hasefi heard Kolahn's voice brush her mind and she leaned even more on her good leg.

"Well, you can't even track properly," she sneered. "How does a 'little lynx' evade a pack of big bad wolves for, what, seven moons now?"

"I think I understand why Sal wants to be the one to kill her," the younger wolf growled.

"You can't run, little kit," the older wolf snarled, advancing on her.

Hasefi felt her muscles tighten of their own volition as if another creature was taking control of her. For a moment, she thought the bigger wolf might be gifted and was somehow controlling her, but something tickled the fur inside her ears and she quickly realized it wasn't the wolf she felt.

"You're right," Hasefi admitted. "I haven't been able to walk the same ever since I threw an avalanche at the last wolves who tried to take me."

The bigger wolf snorted, but Hasefi saw a glimmer of uncertainty in the younger wolf's eyes. Energy rippled into her, filling her with something both familiar and strange. She lowered her head, holding the gazes of both wolves as she growled softly. "But that won't stop me."

"Stop you from what?" the wolf sneered. Her words had barely left her mouth when Hasefi dashed forward, slid under the bigger wolf, and leaped towards the younger wolf. He ducked, but Hasefi's paws kicked off the tree beside him and she landed on the younger wolf's back, digging her claws and teeth into his flesh.

"Get her off of me!" he yelped, shaking himself. The older wolf leapt to his aid, but Hasefi slipped off the smaller wolf and limped out of reach.

To Hasefi's surprise, the bigger wolf was by her side in a single bound and buried her teeth into Hasefi's shoulder. Hasefi let out an agonized cry and dug her claws into the fur around the wolf's cheeks, but the wolf didn't let go.

Claw out her eyes!

Hasefi moved her good foreleg and raked her claws through the wolf's left eye. The wolf released her and Hasefi scrambled to her paws, turning to face the younger one as it advanced on her.

"You think you're stronger than us?" he growled.

"Not at all." Hasefi dodged him as he lunged towards her throat and raked her claws along his flank. "But a mountain is." She turned her back on him as he charged at her. Hasefi kicked out her hind legs, sending him sprawling down the mountainside with a terrified howl.

"Mav!" the remaining wolf screamed. She turned her furious gaze on Hasefi, revealing the bloody mess that was her damaged eye. "I'll kill you!"

"What, and risk Sal ripping you apart, too?" Hasefi hissed.

The wolf responded with a wordless snarl. Her face twisted into a murderous expression, her remaining pupil stretching wide so her eye was almost black. She almost seemed to grow bigger and Hasefi wavered as the wolf transformed into one of the creatures that had taken her tribe away. The wolf lunged and Hasefi tried to move out of the way, but the wolf shouldered her and threw her off balance. Before Hasefi could recover, teeth dug into her good foreleg and she was jerked violently as the wolf shook its head.

I will not break another leg! she screamed inwardly, trying to twist herself to get a grip on the wolf. But the wolf continued to shake her until it felt like all of her bones were jumbled randomly within her pelt. *She won't stop until I'm dead!*

So die.

Hasefi went limp, her teeth gritted as the wolf shook her for a few more heartbeats before tossing her against the mountain. She twitched as she slid onto level ground near the wolf's paws.

"You don't play dead very well," the wolf growled. "I can see your flank moving."

"Death and I have a hard time getting along," Hasefi growled as she shot up, nailing the wolf in the jaw with her shoulder. To her dismay, the wolf barely even staggered at the blow and quickly sank her teeth around the back of Hasefi's neck. Hasefi gasped as she was lifted off her paws. She tried to jerk the wolf off balance, but the wolf's teeth only sank deeper and Hasefi could feel blood flowing down her shoulders. She reached back with one paw and curled her claws into the soft flesh of the wolf's nose. The wolf let out a muffled growl and dropped Hasefi, allowing her to get to her paws. Panting with pain and exhaustion, Hasefi turned to face her opponent.

"Get ready to see those other lynxes we killed," the wolf sneered. Her words were slurred and hardly comprehensible as if she was losing the ability to speak. She reared up on her hind legs and Hasefi charged into them, sending the wolf sprawling over her. Hasefi quickly clawed her way onto the wolf's flank and sank her teeth into the wolf's throat. The wolf let out a strangled cry and thrashed against the ground, but Hasefi didn't let go until the wolf's movements faded into weak shuddering. She stepped off and glared at the dying wolf, each heartbeat bringing strength into Hasefi despite her wounds.

"You can't kill me," the wolf choked. "You're a crippled lynx-pup."

"Don't underestimate your prey," Hasefi gasped, stumbling back from the dying wolf. She slumped to the ground, but her wounds didn't seem to be affecting her like they should. *Something is happening to me,* she thought, her gaze moving upwards to where stars were beginning to appear. *That wasn't me fighting—I didn't know some of those moves. Sefonis, you're here, aren't you?* Hasefi pushed herself up, marveling at how both her forelegs, one broken and the other bleeding, held her up as if they were as strong as ever. She started to turn away, lost in bewilderment, but recalled what the wolf had said about Kolahn. She was watching Hasefi and bared her teeth when she approached. "What did you do to him?" Hasefi demanded.

"To who?" the wolf spat, blood pooling on the ground around her jaws.

"To the new wolf?" Hasefi said.

The wolf's lips twisted in a malicious grin made more sinister with the blood that coated them. "We didn't do anything." The wolf coughed once and a flood of blood left her jaws before she grew suddenly still. Hasefi saw that the blood had soaked into her white paws, turning them red, but her mind was elsewhere.

Didn't do anything? Then why would Kolahn say I was waiting for him? Hasefi glared at the wolf. *She's lying. I have to find him. What if he's already dead? I still have to try.*

Hasefi looked up the side of the mountain. *They were scouting the area for predators. I think the other wolf said more of them had come here. Could Sal's whole group be nearby? I'm going to find him.* However, her legs gave out as whatever energy had entered her before the attack was fading and she slumped to the ground. *No, not now! I have to get to Kolahn!* She closed her eyes, willing strength into her body, but all she could feel was the pain of her wounds returning.

"Sefonis, help me!" she gasped. When nothing happened, she wondered if she had been wrong about her tribe's help. *No,* she told herself. *I know it was you. I heard you!* She forced her bleeding leg under her, hissing against the pain. Her hind legs moved underneath her, then her broken foreleg. Agony throbbed through her, but she proceeded to stretch her twisted leg as if the more pain she felt, the better her tribe might be able to help her.

As she rose, the agony in her legs and the other bites she endured faded to a tolerable amount. Her ears were tickled by soft, indiscernible whispers and she felt a presence settle within her. She closed her eyes, letting the strange energy beneath her pelt flow through her. Then she opened her eyes and glared at the path ahead.

Let's go find Kolahn. She climbed up the slope as if she'd hardly suffered a scratch, her new strength supporting her.

When she got to the top of the mountain, she was horrified to see what lay before her. The forest fell way to an open field of black and gray ground with naked trees stabbing into the air. Some had fallen and were blackened and half eaten, hardly recognizable as trees at all. Hasefi glimpsed the white of a skull poking out of the strange ground, its eye socket facing her.

This is what fire does? she thought. *What is this?* She touched the strange ground with her paw, finding it was quite soft. When she lifted her paw and examined it, the strange soil was plastered to it, mixing with the blood still leaking through her fur. *It eats everything and just leaves behind...this?* She gazed out, taking in the destruction before her. *Sal is here,* she thought, her mind darkening. *This place is perfect for him.* Hasefi's eyes moved to where some smoke was rising ahead and she moved towards it. *Would he stay near fire?* she wondered. She remained alert as she moved towards the unknown creature Kolahn had described, waiting for it to reveal itself to her.

She climbed a shallow rise and jumped down the other side to land near what was a fallen tree with strange light underneath it. Hasefi crept towards it, noticing the heat that came from it.

"It really is like the sun," she breathed. She reached a paw towards the strange glowing rocks under the tree, but had to retreat when the heat bit her paw. In her heightened state, it was barely noticeable, but she could feel the sensation of something unpleasant against her pad.

Enough playing. I have to find Kolahn. Hasefi straightened and tried tasting the air, but smoke and death clogged her throat, making her cough. She looked around, trying to find prints or fur, but there was no sign of wolves. *Maybe they're not here. They could still be in the valley. I could try following where those two wolves came from.* She backtracked until she was on the edge of the slope leading down the mountainside. As she walked, doubt entered her mind.

Even if I do find them, what can I do? I can't fight them. The whispers increased and Hasefi's entire body shivered as if a cold wind had passed over her. Her determination hardened and she glared ahead defiantly.

I just took out two wolves. What's a few more? She continued onwards, feeling both clear-headed and crowded at the same time.

Eventually, she came to a part of the mountain that seemed to still be on fire. The smoke was thin, but Hasefi noticed some light dancing along the ground where some half-burnt wood lay. Ahead of it was a line of fire that was consuming some other plants that still clung futilely to life. She watched it for a moment, fascinated by the strange thing that writhed before her. Then it reached out towards her and she leapt back, barely avoiding her whiskers getting singed.

That's fire, she thought. *But a lot smaller than what ate this forest.*

She turned away from it, intending to walk at a safer distance, but a flash of shadow caused her to duck behind the burning wood. She peaked out and saw a wolf scanning the area in front of it, its ears perked as if it had heard something.

They blend in so well with this weird soil, she thought. *And all the burnt trees. I have to be more careful.* Hasefi crept slowly along the ground on the other side of the fire from the wolf to where the orange tongues were bigger. The wolf moved away from the fire and she was able to sneak by.

Not long after she left that wolf behind, several more appeared. These ones seemed to be doing combat training—but without stifling their blows. One wolf stumbled back, bleeding from its shoulder and cheek as it moved away from another wolf whose teeth were stained red. *Hurting each other just makes each other vulnerable for the real fight, doesn't it?* she thought. Some of the whispers she heard shifted as if responding to her before moving to their normal patterns. Hasefi continued to move along, keeping an eye out for wolves on her side of the fire. Fortunately, they all seemed to be on the other side.

"Sal."

The voice sent a chill through her, both because of what it said and the way it was said. It commanded attention like how Hasefi would expect an adult lynx to say a kit's name when it was misbehaving.

Hasefi peered through the fire and froze when her gaze landed on a particular bulk.

Sal. It's him. He's right there. Hasefi saw again her uncle facing the giant wolf and a part of her wanted to leap through the fire and fight him herself. But another part of her wanted to flee.

I can't run. Kolahn is here somewhere. They must be keeping him prisoner. That's why he hasn't come back.

"Walk with me."

Hasefi returned her attention to Sal and the other wolf that was too close to the fire for her to see properly. She watched as Sal obediently joined the wolf's side and they began walking. *Who is this other wolf?* Hasefi wondered, confused as to why he would speak to Sal in such a way.

"What do you think of this place?" the other wolf asked.

"Well," Sal began slowly, uncertainly. "It's barren. There's little if any prey and we have to walk a while before we find water."

"Is that all?" the other asked, not unkindly.

"I think…it would be better if we stayed somewhere else," Sal continued.

"And where would you think?"

"In…in the valley?"

The other wolf stopped and Sal gave him a nervous look, not at all acting like the savage creature Hasefi remembered him as. *Who is this wolf?* she wondered again, trying to get a better look at him.

"Right," the other wolf replied after several long seconds. "The valley would make a great home. The only thing is it's taken. Taken by the very thing you've been hunting for too long now." *Are they talking about me? I never had the chance to live in the valley yet.*

"I don't see how that stops us from using it."

"Yes, and that's why I do the thinking. What do you think will happen if this kit finds her home overrun?"

Sal was silent.

"She would leave it behind without thought. But if we abandon it, she might yet see hope."

"But she won't return," Sal pointed out. "Not if she knows we're here."

"No, of course not. But she also won't leave it." The other wolf began walking again and Sal quickly moved to join him. "It's like dangling prey in front of a hungry pup that knows it can't have it, but won't leave as long as the prey remains." He paused for a moment. "But perhaps I *am* wrong, since none of your wolves have managed to find her." *They* are *looking for me?*

"Her scent is present," Sal said quickly. "We're close. She just manages to stay a step out of reach. And the rain has made it difficult...." Sal trailed off and Hasefi could hear the other wolf sigh softly.

"And what of this new wolf?" the other wolf continued. "He claimed he could track her down."

"Yes," Sal admitted. "But I'm not sure—"

"You can trust him? Interesting. I've felt that way about another wolf in the Pack for the last seven moons." They stopped again and the other wolf moved closer to Sal, allowing Hasefi to get a better look. She was surprised to find this other wolf was a little smaller and didn't even seem to bear any scars. *Sal could take him down easily, couldn't he? Why is he letting this wolf treat him like this?*

"We're closer than ever to finding her," Sal blurted.

"You better be. We don't have time to deal with loose ends like this. This never would have been a problem if you hadn't turned your hunting party into a raid."

Hunting party?

The other wolf's head jerked up suddenly. "What are you doing?"

Hasefi followed his gaze and was surprised and relieved to recognize Kolahn slinking by a trio of wolves with their heads close together in conversation. Kolahn quickly straightened when he heard the wolf's voice.

"I was just going to find some water," he explained, surprisingly relaxed. Hasefi started to feel unnerved when she watched him trot easily over to the two. *He's clearly okay,* she thought. *So why did he tell them about me?*

"Sal mentioned living in the valley, where we'd have more things like food and water," the wolf told Kolahn who cocked his head and gave Sal a confused look.

"If we're in the valley, Hasefi will stay out of sight. She's expecting me tonight, so it won't be long before she comes out of hiding."

Hasefi went rigid and her breath caught in her throat. *Kolahn?*

"What do you know?" the other wolf chuckled. "That's what I said! I'm glad there's at least one other wolf with more than just a bunch of muscle beneath their fur. You know, Kol, when we catch this kit, Hasefi as you call her, you will have accomplished something that even the strongest of us failed to do."

"Being strong isn't a skill," Kolahn responded. "How you use it, is."

"Exactly," the other wolf said, obviously pleased. "Wolves like you, Sal, succumb to the darkness that lives within us. You let it use you. But wolves who know and understand what lies beneath our fur are the ones that will bring us victory. We don't need a wolf who can stagger a mountain lion to find this kit—we need a wolf who can think like her."

"Well, apparently this kit had no trouble facing a mountain lion," Sal mumbled, twisting his face with disgust at Kolahn.

"I believe it," the other wolf said. Sal looked at him with surprise. "You've given this kit the most dangerous weapon a creature could ever wield. You left her with nothing but one thing, one thought—the very thing we've thrived on for countless times longer. This kit wants revenge." The wolf let out cackle. "And she's coming for you." The wolf moved farther away from the fire, revealing the rest of himself. Hasefi had to grit her teeth to swallow a gasp as she saw that the wolf's eyes weren't amber like the others.

They were red.

"And you know what the most interesting part about all of this is?" The wolf stood beside Kolahn, close enough that Hasefi wondered if they hadn't known each other before last night. "She's managed to get our own kind in on it."

Hasefi's blood froze, immune to the fire burning just a pace away. She could see Kolahn's gaze drop just like her heart as her dread shifted completely.

"This is your doing, Sal," the wolf continued. "Because of your lust for violence, our own kind has been compromised and we have a new enemy."

"But she's just a kit!" Sal blurted.

"Something tells me she's hardly a kit anymore," the red-eyed wolf said. "It's been seven moons and you're trying to hunt down a three-moon old kit when you should be looking for an adolescent lynx. This is why you're the teeth and I'm the mind of the pack. We thrive when we work as one. But you stopped that when you decided to taste lynx."

"I thought it would be good for our wolves to take out a big target," Sal protested.

"Except they didn't. They missed one little part and we're still trying to take her down." The red-eyed wolf looked to Kolahn, looming over him with a dangerous glint in his unnatural gaze. "I believe you know where she is. You've just been stalling."

Kolahn just flattened his ears, saying nothing.

Do something! Hasefi urged her friend. *You chased off a mountain lion, chase them off!* Hasefi tried not to imagine what kind of power this older wolf might have, especially when she knew a wolf like Sal was afraid of him.

"We will find her," the red-eyed wolf growled. "And we will tear into her while you watch. But not because I want you to suffer," the wolf added in a soothing tone as leaned closer to Kolahn. "You see, we are born out of pain. Out of darkness. We were abandoned by our own ancestors the moment the energy of life was given to us. And yet they let us live on, thinking the threats of those who cast us out would be enough. But they are wrong.

"The Clan already knows we are strong, but we are also resilient. We breathe pain, our blood burns with the fire of rage. Some wolves aren't strong enough to control it. But some wolves aren't strong enough to use it, either. You hide from it. You've locked away who you really are. But I know how to unleash it. You think you're capable of caring about another creature. I'll show you you're not. You were born after Resahn's reign, so you never tasted the glory of battle. I will change that."

Kolahn was still silent and Hasefi had to grit her teeth to keep from screaming at him. Even when the wolf crashed down on Kolahn and buried his teeth in his throat, Kolahn did nothing more than yelp.

You horrible, mangy dog! I'm going to claw your eyes out and tear out your throat! Hasefi's claws curled into the ground, keeping her rooted instead of diving through the fire to unleash her fury on him. The strength that was surging through her, keeping her upright despite her injuries, pulsed and she shuddered with the effort of staying in place. The voices she heard stabbed painfully loud through her mind, but the pain only fueled her rage. She watched with utter loathing as the wolf straightened over Kolahn's twitching form, wondering if she had nothing to lose if she did let go of the ground.

"When we find this kit," the wolf growled to Sal. "I will be the one who kills her, not you, understand?"

"Yes, Vek," Sal gasped.

Vek, Hasefi thought with loathing, too filled with fear and rage to care about the defeated expression on Sal's face. But, despite the anger that burned through her like whatever this wolf had described ran through their blood, Hasefi was able to keep her mind in check and the energy in her faded until it was just enough to keep her up.

I can't take on this whole group by myself. Neither of us can—even if Kolahn did chase off that mountain lion, he won't defend himself. He's too afraid of himself. Nothing can scare off these wolves except—oh.

Chapter Eighteen

Hasefi let out an agonized yowl, gritting her teeth as she listened to it echo off the peaks that rose ahead of her. She looked around, half expecting a group of wolves to appear.

I'm surprised they haven't, she thought. *I feel like I've been yowling loud enough to wake my tribe from death.* Hasefi stretched her jaws wide, this time adding some words to her yowl.

"Help! Someone help me! I'm lost and afraid and hurt! I'm helpless! Come find me!" She crouched, trying to recover her fading strength as her words echoed around her. *I don't know how much longer I can keep this up.* She ignored the urge to check her wounds, feeling that she would collapse if she knew the extent of them. The strength her tribe was giving her, if it was indeed them, seemed to be fading and every step was harder than the last. *At least my blood might help me.*

Hasefi straightened and tasted the air, looking for any sign of a mountain lion nearby. *The fire scared off the bear we had scented. There's still smoke—I'll have to go farther if I want to find anything.* She glanced backwards to where the crest far behind her hid the damage the fire had done. *But I'm already so far away—even if I found a mountain lion, I can't expect to outrun it before I got back to the wolf camp.*

A sound ahead of her caused her head to snap forward, but a mixture of disappointment and relief quickly filled her as she watched a squirrel climb a nearby tree, chattering angrily at her.

I'm going to get myself killed. But what other choice do I have? Face the wolves alone? Let them take Kolahn? Anything I do will just lead to death, whether it be quick...or not. She took in a deep breath, forcing herself to keep going. *This is my only option.*

Hasefi continued moving, each step taking her farther from Kolahn.

She reached a small stream of water that flowed between a deep, narrow ravine. She followed it downstream until it brought her to an edge where she could look down into the valley.

I'll get his home back, she thought. Her gaze moved to the moon that was creeping behind the distant mountains ahead. *I would hardly have a chance of making this work in daylight, let alone while it's dark. But I can't wait until then.*

Hasefi hopped over the ravine, letting out another yowl until her throat felt as if she had scooped up a mouthful of pine needles and swallowed them. *Fallen stars, what am I thinking? Maybe I am going mad.* Her thoughts went to the mountain lion she had recognized and she found herself wondering again if perhaps it was different than the others. *It technically saved me twice,* she thought. *Surely that can't be coincidence? What if mountain lions are like us?*

Hasefi snorted, amused with herself and again wondering if she had gone mad. *But if it were true, it would make this a lot easier,* she pointed out to herself. *It could be the only way this succeeds.* She tried to ignore Kolahn's words when he had argued that mountain lions weren't like them and she was being immature.

I need something *that'll work,* she thought. *Anything. I just need Kolahn back.*

Hasefi continued until she decided she was too far from the wolf camp. She started to follow the direction the stream came from, putting the valley behind her. She tasted the air again, praying that she'd find a trail to follow.

Deer? Prey might lead me to something if I injure it. Hasefi knew that if her own blood and yowls weren't working, another injured creature wasn't any more likely to help. *But I have to try* something.

She followed the scent to where two rock-faces cut into the side of a low peak. The path twisted until it came to a dead end where Hasefi found the deer nibbling on a bush among a pretty patch of colored flowers.

If I get any closer, I'll scare it. It won't be able to get away, but it might hurt me trying and I'm not sure how much more I can take. Maybe if I wait, I can pounce as it walks by and then follow wherever it goes.

She settled behind the curve leading to where the deer ate. After a few moments, she peeked at it and found it was still eating. *Please don't take long. Hopefully it'll catch my scent and try to run.*

Her gaze fixed on where the deer would pass in front of her while her mind began to wander. *What are they doing to Kolahn? Vek sounded like he wanted to keep him alive...but what if he changes his mind? Kolahn said he heals fast, so that blow wouldn't kill him, would it?* She bowed her head for a moment. *Kolahn told them I was waiting. But Vek knew he was a spy. If Kolahn really wanted to betray me, wouldn't Vek have known?* She flattened her ears. *Do I really think Kolahn would betray me? He said he'd tell them the truth. Maybe that's what he was doing. But he said he wouldn't tell them about me. And...he sounded like he wasn't coming back. Well, he won't be now. Not unless I do something.*

Hasefi peeked again at the deer, debating whether or not to risk going after it now. Then she watched a shadow hover over it until the biggest creature she had ever seen landed on the deer, crushing it without it having the chance to call out.

The mountain lion slowly rose, the muscles beneath its heavily scarred pelt tensing with pure strength as it straightened. Hasefi was rooted to the ground in terror as it slowly turned to face her, its black eyes devoid of anything but murder.

You'll do.

Finding her paws, Hasefi fled through the winding pathway until she burst onto open ground. She was so filled with terror her pain was forgotten and she almost lost sight of her plan. The mountain lion's paws shook the ground every time they hit and it let out a petrifying snarl. She urged her legs to move faster, her lame leg jamming the ground to offer what little speed it could add.

After jumping the stream, her eyes caught a large jagged pillar of rock rising from the ground. It stretched wide along the ground and she could see a crevice leading into it. She had noticed it earlier and knew there was another opening on the other side. *If that runs all the way through, it'll bring me back towards the wolf camp and give me more ground.* She veered towards it, hearing the mountain lion's claws rake earth and rock as it skidded past her when she turned.

She was able to put some distance between her and the mountain lion while it recovered its speed, allowing her to dive into the crevice safely and follow the tunnel within towards the faint light that shone ahead.

It could trap me in here if I'm not quick enough, she thought. *I need to move!* Hasefi pushed herself faster, fearful her legs would give out at any moment. She left the safety of darkness behind her and returned to the open ground leading towards the crest where the fire was still trying to burn.

Something felt off as she ran and she looked around, wondering if there were wolves nearby. She needed every breath she had, so she couldn't taste the air, but she couldn't see any sign of black fur around her. Hasefi's ears swiveled back and she came to a halt, panting as she stared at the open ground behind her.

There was no sign of her pursuer.

Where in all the stars did it go? she wondered, growing nervous. She looked towards the tunnel she had used. *Did I lose it?* Without warning, her body gave out and she fell to the ground, breathing heavily. She was fully aware that she was an easy meal if the mountain lion appeared, but for some reason the massive creature was nowhere in sight. She had no idea how long she laid there, but when she was finally able to get her shaking legs beneath her, night was fading from the sky and the sun was beginning to reveal itself.

Still unable to catch her breath, Hasefi staggered back towards the tunnel, expecting the mountain lion to jump out at any moment and crush her like it had the deer. But she reached the tunnel unhindered.

"Where did you go?" she asked, leaning against the rock for support, then peering into the tunnel. *It didn't get stuck trying to follow me, did it?* Not wanting to come face to face with an angry mountain lion that had managed to get itself stuck, Hasefi slowly rounded the rock until she came to the end where the crevice led into it.

It was empty.

Mountain lions don't just disappear, do they? Hasefi bowed her head, fighting the urge to collapse. *Kolahn,* she told herself. *For Kolahn.* With a short breath, she retraced her steps until she could see the earth her pursuer had churned up as it ran. Disbelief caused her to snort as she saw the mountain lion's tracks end as if it had stopped abruptly. She lowered her nose to the ground and found the scent grew fresher along the path back.

Did it give up? She followed the scent, keeping alert as she returned to the place the deer had been. *It could pounce on me at any moment. Could a mountain lion set up a trap like this?*

When she passed the corner she had used to hide from the deer, she was surprised to find the mountain lion tearing away at the prey's flesh. Hasefi instinctively ducked to her original hiding spot, overcome with bewilderment.

It just gave up? she thought. *I suppose there's no reason to hunt more prey when you already have some. But a deer won't fill up a mountain lion, will it? At least not one that big.* Hasefi paused. *I have to try again.*

She took a few more moments to gather what scraps of strength and courage she could, then crept out of hiding. Everything inside of her screamed at her as she stalked towards the mountain lion. Its gaze snapped up and she froze, but it did nothing more than growl at her.

"Hey," Hasefi began, her voice strained with exhaustion and fear. She swallowed hard before continuing. "Can you understand me?" The mountain lion continued to watch her, but it made no reaction to her words. Its murderous stare showed no signs that it was even remotely akin to her. Disappointed, she changed her strategy.

"Hey, you giant furball. Don't you want more to eat? That deer doesn't look like it'll fill even half of your belly. You might want to add some more while you can."

The mountain lion watched her for a few more heartbeats. Then it lowered its head and continued eating.

"Really? Are you just going to ignore me?"

The mountain lion's ears twitched.

Hasefi stepped closer and it snarled viciously, making her jump. "What if I try stealing your prey? It looks mighty tasty."

The mountain lion kept an eye on her as it tore a piece off of the deer.

Hasefi shuddered. *That wouldn't be so terrifying if I couldn't imagine myself in that deer's place.* Swallowing her fear, Hasefi dared another step forward. This time, the mountain lion rose slightly, its eyes gleaming with violence.

"Come on, chase me," Hasefi squeaked. She lifted her paw, but it didn't even touch the ground as she staggered backwards to avoid the mountain lion's claws as it swiped in her direction. Hasefi stumbled a few paces away until she realized the mountain lion wasn't following.

"Seriously," she gasped, crouching to gather herself. "I thought running from you would be the hard part." She hesitated, feeling as what little strength remained in her faded. The whispers that were brushing the fur in her ears had left, too. *There's no way I can hope to succeed without help. But I have no other choice.* After a few moments, she returned to the mountain lion. Its eye watched her as it ate. *I could wait it out,* she thought. *But I'm not sure I have that kind of time.* She stared at the mountain lion, silently urging it to get up. When it didn't, she let out a long sigh.

I'm going to get myself killed.

With a grunt of effort, Hasefi jumped towards the rock beside the mountain lion, then used her hind legs to launch herself onto its hunched back. The mountain lion rose abruptly, throwing Hasefi to the ground. She got to her paws and swiped hastily in its direction, catching its nose with her claws. A deafening screech filled the small area and Hasefi turned to run.

Pain exploded through her flank as a heavy paw slammed into it, sending her crashing into the wall. Hasefi slumped to the ground dazed, waiting for the blow that would kill her. Instead, a shower of gravel fell from above, causing the mountain lion to duck to avoid getting hit. Hasefi struggled to get her paws underneath her and let out a desperate yowl. A flicker of strength rippled through her and she was able to get up, wasting no time in hauling herself away along the narrow path and into the open.

Another angry screech sounded behind her and she knew the mountain lion wouldn't be giving up on her now. However, terror overwhelmed her as its shadow fell over her and she was knocked to the side. Hasefi rolled across the ground, her paws thrashing as she tried to get a hold of herself. When she was upright, she came face to face with the mountain lion, its hot breath choking her.

Help me! her mind screamed. *Don't let me die now! I have to save Kolahn!* As the mountain lion lunged, she ducked under its chest without volition and slipped away. Without her command, Hasefi's legs sprinted for the stream and she was able to jump over it before the mountain lion began to catch up again.

I can't die here! she yowled silently as the voices surged through her head. *I have not come this far to die! Sefonis, you've done everything to keep me alive up to this point—I need you to make sure I stay that way, just for a little longer!* Hasefi gasped as she felt a flood of strength move through her. Her legs pumped harder, her broken leg and wounds unable to hinder her. She was brought to the crevice she had used before, each step giving her new confidence.

She darted into the tunnel, barely spending a heartbeat in it as she flew through the exit. The mountain lion landed beside her and her determination wavered.

"Run, wee lass." Sefonis's voice filled the air beside her and she saw a figure running with her. Not having the breath to speak, Hasefi could only meet his eyes with hers.

He's here, she thought. *He answered.* Another figure appeared beside her uncle's, transparent like him but her eyes as sharp as starlight. *Kilarsa.* All around her, the echoes of her tribe appeared, running with her.

My tribe, Hasefi thought, her heart filling. *They're here to help me.* Hasefi realized she was slowly putting distance between her and her pursuer. *They're here to end this.*

Several figures appeared ahead and Hasefi felt a flicker of anticipation as she swiftly flew towards them. When the wolves noticed Hasefi running towards them, her tribe shimmered out of view, but her strength only grew. All of the anger she had felt since the rising sun had proved meaningless rose up and flowed from her jaws in a yowl.

"This is for my tribe, murderous dogs!"

One of the wolves started toward Hasefi, but let out a terrified yelp and fled. Hasefi quickly passed it, not looking back when an agonized howl tore the air.

The other wolf had started running the moment it saw her and now Hasefi was beginning to gain on it. When she neared, she swiped at the wolf's foreleg, causing it to stumble. Now Hasefi hesitated to watch as the mountain lion pounced onto it, ripping into its flank without bothering with a killing blow.

"Hey scar-pelt! There's more where that came from!"

The mountain lion made no reaction to her words, but when another group of wolves appeared, it abandoned the twitching wolf and charged. Hasefi watched as the trio darted in different directions. The unlucky wolf the mountain lion chose to follow suffered a fate of a dismembered leg followed by a ripped out throat.

Hasefi ran past the mountain lion, catching its attention again and leading it towards the wolf camp. *I have to find Kolahn,* she thought. *I can't let the mountain lion get him.*

"It's the lynx!" a voice cried when she could see the line of fire that bordered their camp. A terrified yelp followed and Hasefi watched a wolf run by her, its eyes wide with fear. She relished the look on the creature that had once haunted her nightmares.

Hasefi came upon the area she had followed Vek and Sal to, except now she was on the same side they had been. Fire rose in front of her, weaker than before but still licking the air with dangerous orange tongues. Wolves were scattered around her, their faces twisted with surprise.

"Mountain lion!" a howl pierced the air and wolves were scrambling around, forgetting Hasefi as she scanned the fire line, searching for any sign of her friend.

Yelps and screams assailed Hasefi's ears and the stench of blood filled her nose. For a moment, she was back in the mountains with her tribe, watching them get murdered before her eyes. But when she saw a wolf get taken to the ground in front of her, she was jolted back to reality.

"Kolahn!" she called. "Kolahn, I'm here! Where are you?" She whipped around, looking for him or something that would lead to him. There wasn't any sign of Sal or Vek, either, and Hasefi wondered if perhaps they had chosen now to leave the camp.

"Come on, you stupid pups!" A jolt went through Hasefi as a voice rose into the air, filled with hate and anger. "We don't call ourselves greater wolves for nothing! Lift your tails from between your legs and face this threat!"

Hasefi turned and saw Sal's bulky form on top of a rock near the fire, his shadow dancing erratically at his paws. Some of the wolves near him began to gather, the fear in their eyes flickering into rage. *I can't let them recover.*

A battle cry left her jaws and she charged towards Sal and the other wolves. The one closest looked at her in utter bewilderment and was helpless as she charged into its flank, her given strength knocking it easily onto its side. She leaped away to the next wolf, climbing onto its back and jumping to a third where she buried her teeth into its shoulder.

Something slammed into her back and she was wrenched from the wolf. She fell heavily onto the ground, but was able to roll away from the jaws that snapped where her throat had been.

"You!" The word was filled with utter hatred and Hasefi felt a similar feeling hardening in her gut.

"That's right," she growled, getting to her paws to face Sal.

"Make sure that mountain lion doesn't get near us!" Sal commanded to the nearby wolves and they hesitantly moved to where the mountain lion was swinging a wolf through the air.

"Sending off the other wolves to die so you don't have to?" Hasefi sneered. "For some reason I pictured you a lot less pathetic."

"I'm going to rip you apart just like I did to your little group."

"And risk Vek doing the same to you? I don't think so," she hissed.

For a brief moment, uncertainty flickered through Sal's gaze, but it was quickly smothered by rage. "Who cares? You've been a thorn in my pad all these moons. I will suffer no longer!"

"Suffer?" Hasefi screeched. "You think *you've* suffered? I watched every creature I knew die before me! I've spent over half of my life running in fear! I never even thought of revenge because I was too afraid to die!" Her voice lowered and her anger grew more focused. "Until I met someone who made me realize dying was not the worst thing that could happen."

"So you want to kill me?" Sal scoffed. "You can't."

"I'm not the little kit you think I am."

"You're not the invincible creature you think you are," the wolf returned.

Hasefi shook her head with a dark chuckle. "Oh no, I just brought that with me." She felt a flicker of satisfaction as Sal's gaze moved towards where the mountain lion was facing three wolves that were trying not very successfully to circle it. When he returned his gaze to Hasefi, there was new rage burning there.

"You have delayed our plans too long!" he growled. "If it weren't for you, we would have dominated all of the other wolves and lynxes by now! I'm going to tear you into scraps!"

"Yeah, you said that. And yet you're still standing there."

Sal let out a wordless snarl and lunged at Hasefi. She was caught off-guard by his speed and barely managed to duck away. His teeth snapped a whisker-width from her cheek and she raked claws across his muzzle. Sal was unfazed and shouldered her back, causing her to stumble.

He was upon her instantly, but Hasefi sank her teeth into his leg until they grazed bone. Sal let out a furious howl as she slipped away, taking a few steps back to recover. She was hardly given a heartbeat as Sal leaped towards her. Hasefi rolled away and swiped his flank as he soared past.

"Stay still!" he snapped, whirling around and aiming his jaws at her shoulder. Hasefi moved towards him and latched onto his throat, but he quickly shook her off. Hasefi tried to roll further out of reach, but the wolf stood over her. Hasefi used her forelegs to keep his jaws away from her throat while her hind legs raked his belly.

Her efforts didn't seem to hinder the wolf even though Hasefi could feel warm blood flowing down her legs and along her belly. His jaws clamped down on her broken foreleg and she let out an agonized yowl. Sal jerked her onto her side and Hasefi felt his teeth brush her throat. Before they pierced her flesh, however, she heard him yelp and he was no longer over her.

Hasefi forced herself up on three legs and watched as the mountain lion dragged Sal by his tail. The wolf's gaze flashed with fear before returning to rage and he jerked free of the mountain lion's jaws. As he turned to face it, Hasefi saw he wasn't much smaller than the mountain lion and wondered if there was a chance he could win.

She watched as the mountain lion reared up and Sal darted underneath it. However, as it came down, he dodged out of the way and bit down on one of its forelegs. The mountain lion snarled and buried its teeth into his shoulder. Sal tore himself free and reared up so he could clamp down on the back of the mountain lion's neck. It shook him off and he fell onto his side. The mountain lion's fangs were aimed at Sal's throat, but the wolf's jaws closed around the bottom half of the mountain lion's mouth. Hasefi watched in utter shock as Sal jerked his head and a crack sounded. The mountain lion quickly moved off of him, its mouth hanging open at a strange angle. Sal got to his paws and moved towards the mountain lion again, but it landed a hard blow across his cheek, sending him sprawling to the ground.

The mountain lion crouched over the dazed wolf and sank its claws into his flanks, making a strange gurgling sound like it was trying to growl. A wolf ran over, however, followed by another. The mountain lion moved off of Sal and slowly began to retreat, letting out warning snarls from its crooked jaw. The wolves followed after it and Hasefi watched until they disappeared. Then she limped to where Sal was laying, his breaths uneven gasps and his black fur coated with blood.

"How...are you...still standing?" he forced out as his eyes followed her.

Hasefi stood over him, glaring down at his defeated form. "Because of you," she murmured and her tribe began to appear around Sal. The wolf didn't seem to see them, but when Hasefi spoke again, a different terror entered his expression.

"You will not kill another innocent creature," she said, the words not her own but those of Sefonis.

"Nor torment another kit," Kilarsa hissed.

"You have no ancestors," Dahsefer said almost as if scolding a misbehaving kit. "Who knows where you will go? Perhaps your soul will fade into nothing. It would be more than you deserve, if that is so."

"You should have killed me that day," Hasefi told the wolf, taking back her voice.

Sal's gaze softened as the fear left, fading into utter defeat. Then his eyes dulled into death and his flanks ceased moving.

Kolahn. Her tribe disappeared with the thought and Hasefi looked around, searching for a sign of Kolahn. As she did, she saw the remains of her attack.

Wolves were scattered among the clearing, some unmoving, some trying to drag themselves to their paws. One wolf was screaming as he pawed desperately at the ground, his lower half being eaten by flames. Hasefi's eyes skimmed over all of them without stopping until she noticed a place in the fire where it bulged out.

Hasefi limped over and saw that broken logs and branches had been arranged in a tight circle, allowing the fire to feed around something that had been put in the middle. With a jolting mixture of relief and dismay, Hasefi realized the unmoving thing was Kolahn.

"Kolahn," she said, raising her voice over the crackling of the fire. The wolf didn't respond and she tried again. "Kolahn, it's me, Hasefi. Kolahn?" *He's not dead. He's not.*

Hasefi took a few steps back, then charged forwards. She leaped through the fire, grunting as her legs were engulfed briefly by the flames. When she landed next to the wolf, the pain was forgotten and she licked his cheek.

"Kolahn, it's me. Wake up." Hasefi blinked, a memory coming to the front of her mind made vivid by the presences just out of sight.

"Sefonis?" Hasefi recognized the silver armor with intricate black design on the plating, but what resided within had been mauled into nothing but flesh, fur, and blood. Hasefi looked around until she found the helmet with black fur on top, her uncle's dull gaze staring out.

"Sefonis?" she crept up to his helmet and peered into his face. "Are you awake?" She knew he wasn't, but she couldn't acknowledge—couldn't comprehend—the idea that her uncle wasn't with her anymore. "Sefonis, I'm cold."

Hasefi curled up beside her uncle's cheek, comforted as his warmth melted the snow around her and soaked her fur.

"Sefonis, wake up. Please wake up. I don't know what to do. Sefonis?" She gave the tuft of fur sticking out the bottom of his helmet a lick, but he didn't respond. With a whimper, Hasefi laid her head against his. The moment she closed her eyes, she saw the image of all the lynxes strewn about the snow like her uncle was, so she closed her eyes tighter, trying to banish the image.

I'm just having a nightmare, *she thought.* When I wake up, Sefonis will be here to rub warmth into my fur. And Kilarsa will make some light with her magic. And Tenarli will have fresh prey. It'll all be okay when I open my eyes....

"Kolahn, don't make me go through this again. I swear by the light of the stars—" Hasefi's words ended with a gasp as the wolf's ears twitched. "Kolahn?"

"Sef…i?" Kolahn started to raise his head, but it fell back down. He turned it so his gaze was on her and it widened. "Sefi…what happened…to you?"

Hasefi looked down at herself and saw that her fur was soaked with red. If she hadn't known the color of her fur, it would have been impossible to tell what she might have looked like. "Not all of this is mine," she told him. "At least, I don't think it is."

"Sef...." Kolahn's eyes started closing, but Hasefi crouched closer to him, shoving her face close to his.

"No, don't sleep yet, Kolahn. We need to get out of here. Can you get up?"

Kolahn's legs twitched and went still.

"Come on, you have to try."

Kolahn's legs tensed again, this time moving until they were under him. Hasefi helped him stand up, staying with him until he stopped swaying precariously.

"We need to clear the fire," she told him.

"I can barely breathe," the wolf rasped.

Hasefi gritted her teeth, looking to the fire around them. *It only feeds on what's alive.* Hasefi turned slightly and kicked the soft soil onto the burning wood. After a few pawfuls, it began to weaken and she was able to nudge one of the still hot branches aside, making a hole for them to get through.

"There. Come on."

Kolahn limped after her, moving agonizingly slow. Hasefi forced herself to wait, watching anything that moved. Then the wolf stopped, his eyes growing wide with horror as he looked around the camp.

"What happened here?" he coughed.

"I'll tell you later."

Kolahn didn't move, his head slowly turning as he scanned the carnage around them. "Please tell me this wasn't you," the wolf whispered.

"Vek hurt you. I was afraid I was going—" She was silenced by the horrified look Kolahn aimed at her.

"What have you done?"

"I found a mountain lion and...and brought it here. Kolahn, I thought they were going to kill you. I—"

The wolf limped past her as if she'd suddenly ceased existing.

"Kolahn?" Hasefi caught up to him, but he made no reaction to her presence. "Kolahn, say something, please."

The wolf stopped, his dull gaze staring emptily at the ground ahead. When he lifted his head, his eyes were filled with abject dismay.

"What you did…what you've done here…this is evil."

Chapter Nineteen

Evil.

The word played over and over again in Hasefi's mind with Kolahn's strained, horrified voice. She hadn't been able to do much but sleep the last half moon since her tribe's strength had faded from her body and she had sunk into unconsciousness for a whole quarter moon.

Kolahn had avoided her since they made the decision to move into the valley, knowing the wolves wouldn't be bothering them anytime soon. The wound in his neck must have healed before she had woken from her long sleep because he kept hunting for her. Yet she never saw him.

I don't know if he's angry with me, afraid of me, or even just tired of me. He always comes when I'm asleep. Hasefi tried to get up, but her legs were too weak. She couldn't even move her broken leg because it had deep bite wounds that she was afraid would get infected. But Kolahn supplied her with plenty of herbs to treat herself with and she kept it as clean as she could, since there was nothing else for her to do.

He thinks I'm evil, she thought. *I'm not, am I? If I were, then why did my tribe help me? They aren't evil. Besides, we stopped Sal and Vek, which is what Kolahn wanted, wasn't it?* Hasefi was still bothered by the fact Kolahn had told Vek that he was going to return to her and wondered if that was why he was avoiding her.

I can't just lie around anymore, she thought. *I need to talk to him.* A pang tightened her chest. *Even if I need to find a new home afterwards.* Hasefi focused on the entrance, determined to wait until her friend returned. But sleep soon overtook her and she found herself slipping into a dream.

She was walking along the mountaintop where the fire had burned everything into soft gray dust. There weren't any signs of trees or life, but there was something ahead that caught her attention.

Before she even started towards it, she knew what lay ahead were the corpses of the wolves the mountain lion had killed along with those she had sent herself to wherever wolves without ancestors went.

I did this, she thought. *But I had no choice. I couldn't let them kill Kolahn.* Hasefi whirled around without quite knowing why, but when she did, her eyes landed on Sefonis.

"Sefonis," she gasped. "I'm dreaming, aren't I?"

"Aye," he told her.

"But...are you really here?"

"I am, wee lass."

Hasefi let out a long sigh and sat down. Sefonis came to sit beside her, pressing his armor-clad flank to her bare one.

"I was sort of expecting to see you sooner," she admitted.

"You needed to rest," he told her. "You endured quite a lot—more than any lynx could hope to survive." Silence floated between them for a few heartbeats before Sefonis spoke again. "You're not as wee as you once were."

"I'm still not full grown," she pointed out.

"That's not what I meant."

Hasefi lifted her gaze and studied her uncle's expression. "Why did you help me?" she asked after a few heartbeats.

"You asked for us. We answered," he told her.

Hasefi shook her head. "But why? Those wolves...they...they killed you, but...I just did the same thing to them. Doesn't that make me evil?"

"Does it?"

Hasefi hung her head. "I let them die. I knew what would become of them by bringing a mountain lion. But I did it anyways. I am evil." She slumped to the ground. "I don't deserve to be a Highchief."

"Do you know why those wolves attacked us in the first place?" Sefonis asked gently.

"I heard them talking...Sal just wanted to take out a big target to prepare for whatever plan they had."

"And why did you attack them?"

"I...wanted revenge," she murmured guiltily.

Sefonis's gaze was only affectionate as he peered down at her. "Are you sure there wasn't something else?"

"Well...I was afraid they'd kill Kolahn," she admitted. "But that doesn't change anything."

"Doesn't it?"

Hasefi gave him a questioning look.

"Sal attacked us for the sake of attacking us," Sefonis said. "You attacked them to save your friend. Not only that, but you risked your life by doing something no creature could expect to survive. I think you're more of a Highchief than you realize."

Hasefi lifted her head, feeling faintly hopeful. "You think so?" she asked.

Sefonis blinked affectionately and let out a soft purr. "I know so."

Hasefi stretched her neck so she could touch his cheek with her nose, breathing in his comforting scent.

"Thank you," she whispered. When she drew away, she tilted her head and gave him a questioning look. "So is this what ancestors do?" she asked. To her surprise, Sefonis's gaze darkened.

"No," he said, his lips lifting in the beginning of a snarl. "They would prefer to lay back and watch."

Hasefi blinked. "So how are you here?"

The look Hasefi's uncle gave her was filled with a sort of desperate affection that made her wonder if perhaps her tribe had still suffered even after their spirits left their bodies.

"We refused them," Sefonis replied.

"The ancestors?" she asked with disbelief and he nodded. "How?"

"With immense difficulty," he sighed. "Which is why we were so distant."

Hasefi's ears perked up.

"I was…angry. The others, they were already there before me, so I saw all of their faces when my spirit was separated from my body. And all I felt was *hate*. But not for the wolves that killed us—sure, I wanted revenge, every murdered creature does. But my blame was somewhere else."

"The ones who were supposed to protect us," Hasefi whispered.

Sefonis nodded slowly. "They came to us, but I was so overwhelmed. I fought them, which I suppose is something they deal with from time to time, because they were pretty quick to subdue me." A gleam entered his eye. "But they surely didn't expect the entire tribe to refuse them."

"Really?" Hasefi gasped. "You all…?"

Sefonis nodded again. "They tried to…put us away until our minds cleared. But they were foolish to think clarity would make us easier to deal with." The gleam turned into a triumphant glow. "We clawed our way out of their territory until we could finally be with you again." The glow faded, darkening with pain.

"I can't imagine that was easy," Hasefi murmured.

Sefonis lowered his head. "We fought and fought. When infection entered your blood and you were dying, I grew desperate. We all did." A flicker of pride crossed his face, but it was met with anguish. "The tribe let me get to you, covering my escape. But then...one of the Wanderers killed...." Sefonis trailed off and his head hung lower.

"Who?" Hasefi demanded.

"Hykalof," he said, his voice hardly audible. A pang swept through Hasefi and she doubled over as if she were going to be sick. She had spent more of her life without her tribe, but the short time she had been with them, Hykalof was one of the few lynxes she was close with. The fully armored lynx entered her head, along with all the little memories she'd had with him. She even saw what he was like with his unnerving helmet removed. He was tall, his head rising over the heads of all the other lynxes in the tribe. But his face was startlingly handsome when he had revealed it to her, though such a thought hadn't crossed her mind then. His fur was a golden brown with black spots lining it in a neat pattern. A black stripe ran along the middle of each ear before they turned black at the tips. His eyes were golden and she remembered the protective gleam that always shone in them.

"Hykalof," she echoed, dismayed at the pain she felt. "I thought I already mourned your deaths."

"There is more beyond the world in which you exist," Sefonis told her, giving her cheek a comforting nuzzle. "But there are connections between our worlds everywhere—and you're ours."

"What does that mean?" Hasefi asked, daring to let herself hope.

"We've broken free of the restraints the Wanderers have put on those in their territory. We roam free. And our focus is you, wee lass. We will follow you anywhere and everywhere. And we will heed every command."

"What we did," Hasefi breathed. "That was…like I was gifted."

"The energy of a creature is powerful," he agreed. "And it wears away as anything does. But we don't have our bodies to help regenerate what energy we use."

Hasefi looked at him with dismay. "So if you do too much, you'd die?"

"More like cease to exist," he told her.

Hasefi shook her head. "Then I won't ask anything of you," she decided.

There was faint amusement in Sefonis's eyes, then he looked around. Hasefi followed his gaze and was amazed to find they were surrounded by others.

"You're here," she whispered. "You're all here." She let her gaze linger on each one until it reached a fully armored lynx. His armor was like Hykalof's, but his did not bear the same spikes Hykalof's had. The lynx bowed his head as if seeing her thoughts and acknowledging the absence of the champion.

"Gelinaf," Hasefi murmured, recalling his name. *He's a…keeper,* she thought, memories returning to her as if her tribe unlocked the part of her mind that had lost them. *He's the only keeper. Which means….* "You're the only one who could take his place as…."

"Keeper Overlord," Sefonis offered.

Hasefi nodded, moving to stand in front of the black-clad lynx.

"Perhaps," Gelinaf admitted. "But I am no champion."

Hasefi glanced towards Sefonis before responding. "If what my uncle says is true, then you managed to get away from the control of our ancestors," she pointed out. "I really don't think another keeper has done that before." Hasefi wasn't able to glimpse any sort of reaction from the other lynx other than his head lowering slightly. "If you really are all here, then I'm going to need an Overlord, aren't I?"

The keeper nodded.

Hasefi looked to Sefonis again. "I'm not sure if there's any sort of ritual for this but, well..." Hasefi hesitated, clearing her throat. "I name you Keeper Overlord Gelinaf in honor of Keeper Overlord Hykalof." As she watched, Kilarsa stepped beside the Keeper, her eyes beginning to glow. Gelinaf's armor slowly transformed until it was identical to what Hykalof's had been.

Hasefi felt warmth spread through her and she gave the new champion a happy look. The lynx pawed off his helmet, revealing his faint gray and white fur. He blinked at her with narrow green eyes and bowed his head low.

"It is an honor, my Highchief."

Without really meaning to, Hasefi leaned forward and touched her nose to his cheek. He lifted his head just enough so their gazes met and she saw the protective expression he shared with Hykalof melt into affection. Then he nodded and straightened and Hasefi stepped back.

"I started to forget you," she admitted, meeting the gazes of her tribemates. "No matter what I did I forgot names and faces even though you were everything to me." Her gaze lingered on a lynx in plated armor like her uncle's only without the black design and fur. Her name had been one of the ones she'd forgotten first, but now, as she met the other lynx's green eyes, she remembered her name as if she'd known it for the last seven moons. *Refarmi.* "But when Kolahn found me, he helped me and gave me new strength to use for my mission. Even if...it failed."

"It was destined to fail," Kilarsa admitted, her eyes now alight with grief. "In fact, the ancestors had planned for you to die the same day we did."

Surprise rippled through Hasefi, but she remained quiet as the gifted continued.

"It seems their prophecy for you was a cruel one."

A ripple of anger went through Hasefi. "Well, we showed them how much 'power' their little words have," she growled and she heard chuckles from some of the other lynxes.

"So, what now, Highchief?" Dahsefer asked.

Hasefi met the hooded lynx's gaze as she thought, processing the idea that her tribe was with now with her. "I think...I'd like to figure out what's going on with Kolahn," she decided, speaking slowly. She forced herself to meet her tribe's eyes despite being afraid of their reactions.

"An interesting wolf," Tenarli, a lynx with thick green and brown armor and a hood spoke. Her muzzle was covered, but she used her paw to swiftly remove the piece muffling her words. "I don't think I've seen one like him."

"But his fur is black," Lelisi pointed out.

Hasefi recognized her as the first lynx she had watched die and she was overjoyed to be able to put that memory aside now that new ones could be made.

"Perhaps there's more to these new wolves than we thought," Sefonis said. His gaze moved to Hasefi. "He saved your life more than once and protected you better than we ever could."

Hasefi started to shake her head, but her uncle continued.

"He is a friend to us, whether he knows it or not." He ended with a wink and Hasefi narrowed her eyes.

"He didn't believe me before when I said you were helping me back in the high mountains," she pointed out. "I can't imagine he'd believe me now."

"Either way, there is a more pressing matter to attend to," Dahsefer pointed out and she gave him a questioning look. "You two haven't spoken since the battle. It is time to change that."

"He thinks I'm evil," she pointed out. "He's angry with me. But he's too afraid to confront me about it."

"And that's going to stop you?" Kilarsa asked.

Hasefi raised her head slightly. "Well, no. I suppose not."

"I didn't think so," the gifted lynx purred.

"So you want me to talk to him?"

"It's not about what we want," Sefonis pointed out. "All we want is for you to be happy. So it's up to you to decide what does that for you. And we'll follow."

Hasefi saw all of her tribemates nodding and she felt touched by the utter loyalty they had shown to her.

"Thank you," she murmured.

Her uncle stepped forward and touched his nose to her cheek. She closed her eyes for a moment, relishing the touch. Then her eyes opened and she was awake.

We're still here, Sefonis told her when she glanced around the empty cave she was lying in. *All you need to do is ask.*

"Okay," she murmured. She could feel that something was different, as if something inside her had shifted. She felt strengthened even though her legs shook when she stood and pain still throbbed where wounds had yet to heal. It was the same strength she had lost almost eight moons ago until Kolahn had found her in that pit. The strength that came from knowing she wasn't alone.

Hasefi? Kilarsa's voice entered her mind.

What is it? she responded with her own thoughts. The magic-user didn't respond and Hasefi wondered if she had to speak aloud for her tribe to hear. Then she felt a shift in her as if something important was about to be said.

You never asked us where we came from.

Surprise went through Hasefi and she sat down. *Where we came from?* she thought. *But...I thought there was nowhere to go—I thought our home was gone.*

The rising sun wasn't leading you to where we had come from, Kilarsa explained. *It was leading us somewhere new. Or so we had thought.*

So...there's still somewhere out there for me to go? Hasefi thought, this time to herself. Her old thoughts of meeting her mother and father entered her head, but the desire that had once been with it was no longer as strong. *It's okay,* she told Kilarsa after thinking for a while. *Right now I'm worried about Kolahn. But...could I ask one thing?*

Anything.

Am I the last lynx? She felt amusement from the gifted lynx which sent relief through Hasefi.

No, Hasefi. You are far from it. And if you ever want to find them, all you need to do is ask.

Hasefi nodded, wondering if that was something she would end up doing soon if Kolahn decided it was time for them to part.

It's time to face him, she thought.

It was difficult to stay awake, but she did anything to keep her eyes from closing. She tried pacing when she grew tired, but it only made her more exhausted having to fight the stiffness in her muscles and the pain movement caused. Instead, she alternated between standing and sitting, her gaze focused on the entrance where she could glimpse the grassy clearing and part of the pool just to the right.

Finally, a shape moved into the cave and Hasefi perked up, relieved the waiting was over.

"Kolahn."

The figure stopped.

"I didn't mean to wake you," he replied softly.

"You didn't."

Kolahn started moving back towards the entrance, so Hasefi started to push herself up.

"Don't waste your strength," he growled.

"Don't make me waste it."

Kolahn hesitated again, but said nothing.

"Are you just going to stand in silence?"

"There's nothing to say."

"That's not true and you know it." Hasefi took a step towards him before deciding to lean against the cave wall. "Talk to me, Kolahn, or would you rather spend the rest of our lives in silence?"

The wolf sat down, his shoulders sagging and his head low.

Hasefi stifled a sigh. "I don't regret what I did," she told him and he flashed a shocked look at her. "I'd do it again."

"Revenge only leads to darkness, Sefi. What do you think I've been trying to avoid all these moons?"

"I didn't do it for revenge," she explained. "I did it to protect you."

Kolahn's dismay only worsened. "You did it because of me," he whispered. "I made you this way."

"No, Kolahn. Sal was the one who showed me evil. But it was my choice to do what I did."

"But…you're no better than him."

"Maybe not," she admitted. "But if I ever have to choose between a pack of wolves who took everything from me once and the everything I have now, I know I won't hesitate to choose the latter."

Kolahn shook his head. "How did you do it? How did you bring a mountain lion?"

Hasefi hesitated until she came to a decision in her head. "My tribe helped me."

Kolahn continued to shake his head. "Ancestors don't just help us. That's why we have gifted."

"They're not my ancestors," she corrected him. "They are my tribe. Even in death. Besides, you said your ancestors guided you with the falling moon even though you think they abandoned you."

Kolahn's mouth opened, but no sound came out.

"I'm not asking for forgiveness," she told him. "I'm not even asking you to let me stay. I just want you to know I would do anything before I let you die. Do you think I would do that if I thought you were evil, too?"

Kolahn was silent, his gaze on his paws for a long while before he finally looked up at her. "Do you really think I'd cast you out?" he asked quietly.

"Well, you haven't talked to me in half a moon," she pointed out. "I sort of thought you were waiting until I left."

Kolahn shook his head. "I wouldn't do that to you," he assured her. "But I just want you to promise me one thing."

"What?"

"Don't risk your life like that again for me. Please."

"You know I can't promise that," she snorted softly.

"If you die because of me, I'll never forgive myself."

"Yeah and if you die, I'll never forgive *myself*. Would you make that promise if I asked it of you?"

He was silent.

"Yeah, that's what I thought." She waited for him to say something, but the wolf remained quiet. "Are we okay?"

"We both have darkness inside us," the wolf murmured. "It comes from different places, but it is the same. I just don't want you to suffer the way I did—*do*. I don't want you to be afraid of hurting those around you."

"I'm not. And you shouldn't be, either, because we both use our darkness to help those we care about. I don't think darkness is the same thing as evil."

Kolahn's ears perked up and he gave Hasefi a surprised look.

"What?" she asked.

"Darkness isn't the same thing as evil'," he echoed. "Maybe you're right."

"I am. Now, will you stay with me?"

The wolf turned and sat in front of her his head bowed and his eyes looking up at her apologetically. "I'm sorry," he told her.

"It's okay, you silly furball. Why don't we sit under the stars and enjoy the fact we don't have to worry about scary wolves or fires or empty prophecies anymore?"

"Well, I wouldn't be so sure we're completely safe...." he murmured.

Hasefi frowned. "Why not?"

"There were others," Kolahn explained. "Vek had another group—I don't know where because I stayed with Sal's, but there were more. More than what Sal had, I think."

"Fallen stars," Hasefi sighed. "I was really hoping that would be the last of them."

"They still suffered a big loss," Kolahn pointed out. "I think...I think we'll be okay tonight."

Hasefi let out a small purr and Kolahn helped her to her paws. Then they left the cave and settled just outside, watching the stars above them. When Hasefi lowered her gaze to Kolahn, she could see he was still bothered.

"Is everything okay?" she asked him.

"The time that I was there...I never thought...." Kolahn trailed off and Hasefi waited patiently for her friend to find the words he needed. "Life there was horrible. And I don't mean for me. Those wolves fought for everything—food, a decent place to sleep. Not because they were forced to, though. It was because they wanted to. Even the pups would fight the adults. There was no compassion there."

"They probably didn't have the chance to learn it," Hasefi pointed out. "If Resahn was the first black wolf, then his care is all they know, right? If they spent their lives being shunned for their fur and the actions of a dead wolf, they would know nothing but cold and violence."

"But why am I different?" Kolahn asked.

Hasefi cocked her head in thought. "Maybe because you found me before you found them."

Kolahn didn't seem convinced by her answer, but he didn't argue.

"I think it's more important that you *are* different rather than *why* you're different."

"Maybe," he sighed. "Can you promise me something?"

"Is it different than before?"

"Promise you won't let me turn evil."

Hasefi gave him a sympathetic look and reached her good paw towards him. "I promise."

Kolahn reached out his paw and laid it across hers. When he withdrew, he continued talking about his time with the other wolves.

"Sal and Vek were the leaders. Vek was the mind and Sal was the muscle of the Pack. The other wolves didn't really have any roles...any form of rank was just based on who was stronger."

"Vek," Hasefi murmured. "He had red eyes. I've never seen that before."

Kolahn looked at Hasefi with surprise. "You saw Vek?"

Hasefi nodded. "I was there when he exposed you."

Kolahn's eyes stretched wide.

"You...told them I was waiting for you."

"Sal didn't trust me at all," Kolahn explained, glancing away. "I had to make it as realistic as possible. Every time they were on to me, all I could think of was giving them a piece of what they wanted. I was actually heading out before Vek called out to me."

Hasefi relaxed slightly.

"Did you think I would turn against you?"

"You're a convincing liar," she admitted.

"When you give part of the truth, adding in a bit of false information is easy."

Hasefi nodded. Her thoughts shifted, returning to Kolahn's words about how Vek still had others out there.

How long will it be until Vek decides to do something? she wondered. *He'll definitely come after us...but how much time did I give us by destroying Sal's camp?*

Even if he has more wolves to spare, Sefonis's voice filled her head, offering comfort. *He'll be hesitant to risk having what happened to Sal happen to him and the remainder of his wolves.*

Hasefi nodded slightly and returned her gaze to Kolahn, seeing the faintly disturbed look on his face as he watched the trees.

"Did they make you do anything when you were there?" she asked warily.

Kolahn shrugged. "Not really. When I went to the valley, a patrol brought me to Sal. I fed them some empty words and they led me to Vek. Like I said, I told Sal about you to try and gain some trust, so they had me leading a hunt for you." Kolahn narrowed his eyes. "There was talk about some plan they had, but I never found out what it was."

"Yeah, I heard Vek and Sal talking about it. Actually, that reminds me. Sal said something to me that I didn't really think about until now. He said that they would have dominated all the wolves and lynxes if it weren't for me."

Kolahn's eyes widened and he looked towards the stream. "Are they planning to take the Great River?" he asked. "What if they want to fight the Clan?"

"Maybe for revenge?" Hasefi suggested.

Kolahn's eyes widened further with horror. "I need to warn them."

"What? Warn the Clan?" Hasefi asked.

"Yes. They need to know about the Pack."

"Why? They lost a lot of numbers. Whatever they're planning to do won't be happening anytime soon."

"But it'll still happen when they recover."

Hasefi's whiskers twitched with agreement. "Well, I think we'll be the first ones he comes after, so we need to worry about that, first. Besides, why would you want to warn the Clan? They cast you out and told you it was death to return."

"That doesn't mean they deserve to suffer the likes of the Pack," Kolahn pointed out.

"Is it worth risking your life for, though?"

"I am loyal to my clan," he insisted. "I would give my life for them."

Hasefi shook her head. "They wouldn't do the same for you," she tried to reason.

Kolahn lifted his head. "You said the same thing about yourself when I first met you."

Hasefi winced. "Okay. Well…what exactly do you plan to do?"

"I'll talk to the Lord and Lady. I'll tell them what we did and about the Pack's plan."

"Okay and what about me?" Hasefi asked and the wolf hesitated. "Do you expect me to stay here?"

"I…" the wolf trailed off and looked helplessly at the grass between his paws. "I don't know."

"I won't stop you," she told him. "I don't want you to go. But if you insist, then I want to come."

"It's too dangerous for a lynx to be on Clan territory," he said quickly.

"More dangerous than it is for you?"

Kolahn hesitated.

"I think we should just think about recovering from all this, first," Hasefi stated. "Like I said before, it'll take time before Vek can face an entire clan and we need to worry about protecting ourselves, too."

"Do you think they'll stop us before we can warn them?" Kolahn asked quietly.

"I believe they'll try."

Chapter Twenty

The following days were much easier to handle as Hasefi continued to heal. Her leg didn't show any signs of infection, but she knew it would look even more mangled than it already did. She was hardly bothered, though, knowing it would no longer slow her down when she was truly in need.

It took her some getting used to having her tribe in her head. Their presences were always there and she often heard their voices. At one point, she had to tell them to quiet because she couldn't understand Kolahn when he was describing his hunt that day. So, they moved to the back of her mind to give her more room.

Hasefi noticed that Kolahn was still upset, though. She assumed it was the threat of the Pack on his former clan, yet he never said anything about it. But she was hesitant to press, since these were the first days they'd had where they weren't running to or from something.

When almost a moon had passed since the battle, Hasefi was able to leave the cave on her own and walk through the forest. She relished the feeling of wind in her fur and grass beneath her paws.

I've been confined to dark stuffy caves a lot these last couple moons because of injuries. I hope I get to leave that behind. At least for a little bit. She looked up from where she was peering at herself in the pool and watched as two birds flew over, chirping happily at each other. Hasefi let out a content purr and resumed studying herself.

She still found it strange being able to see how she looked to others. The scar on her face still made her just as scary as the first time she saw it, but there was something else she noticed when she met her own gaze.

There's no sign of the scared kit I saw the first time I looked at my reflection, she thought.

Rustling to her left caused her to look up. Kolahn emerged from the treeline, carrying a hare in his jaws. Hasefi hummed with contentment and joined him as he laid it on the ground.

"Hungry?" he asked.

"For hare? Always." Hasefi crouched and took a bite. Kolahn settled into the grass and she did the same. He was silent and Hasefi gave him a sympathetic look. She was about to let herself slip into silence, but then she urged herself to speak. "You're still afraid Vek will come to us."

"It's only a matter of time. And...I think he'll have something planned for the both of us. We both wronged him one way or another."

"Well, he hasn't come yet and I think he would check here before anywhere else. Maybe he gave up?"

"There's no way. He could be assembling an army."

"Maybe. But Vek isn't rage-driven like the others. He'll think about a plan of attack."

"Exactly," Kolahn argued. "We might not have a chance to fight back."

"We can always fight back," Hasefi assured him. "And Vek wouldn't just kill us off quickly. He'd take his time."

"Is that supposed to comfort me?"

"All I'm saying is we shouldn't be afraid anymore. We've won against them once—we can do it again."

Kolahn didn't look at all convinced, but Hasefi didn't know what else to say. He seemed disinclined to believe anything she said about her tribe helping her, so she didn't know how to explain that they'd be there—that they had always been there.

Kolahn didn't pursue the topic further and neither did she, hoping that the wolf would begin to relax.

However, when the sun left the valley bathed in the fading rays of dusk, Hasefi found she had become too restless to sleep. She wasn't sure why, but she just felt too awake to rest. She thought about going out to collect herbs or explore, but she decided Kolahn would be upset if she left the cave alone in the dark. So she forced herself to lay on the ledge she had made hers, twitching until sleep came.

It felt like moons, but sleep did eventually come, though it wasn't exactly pleasant. So when Hasefi was woken by a voice, she had to stifle an irritated hiss as she glared around in the darkness.

She was alone.

Kolahn? Her gaze turned towards the entrance and she ducked against the wall. The voice that had woken her wasn't one she recognized.

"…a lynx over us? You deserve to suffer just as much as she does!"

Hasefi's ears flattened and she felt her tribe stir.

"You're the ones who started this by attacking her tribe in the first place." Kolahn's soft growl floated into the cave.

"Yeah, some tribe that was. It had, what, maybe a dozen lynxes?" a second unfamiliar voice scoffed. "They barely put up a fight."

I'd like to change your mind on that, Sefonis growled.

You and me both, Tenarli added.

"You know not many creatures can stand against wolves like us," Kolahn pointed out.

"And yet *she* can. She brought a *mountain lion* into our camp, for shadow's sake!" the first snapped. "She's gifted."

"There's no star on her chest," Kolahn replied, causing a ripple of surprise to move through Hasefi. *I didn't think he'd know about that.*

"Don't be dumb. She can hide it. Are you sure you even know what kind of monster you're hiding in there?"

They think I'm a monster? Hasefi felt amusement flicker through her and she straightened.

"Let us kill her while she sleeps."

"Do you really think I can sleep through your irritating barking?"

Two yellow gazes snapped towards Hasefi as she left the cave and stood beside Kolahn. A gasp stuck itself in her throat as she took in the two wolves that stood before her.

One was missing an ear and the gray flesh around where the base of the ear would have been was twisted and furless all the way down to the wolf's jaw. On the other side of his mouth, his lower lip had been torn, revealing the large teeth within.

The second wolf had torn ears and an ugly scar across her muzzle. Half of her tail was missing and, to Hasefi's utter shock, the wolf's underbelly was mangled with claws and bites like something had tried to dig into her belly.

"How are you alive?" she couldn't help but whisper.

"We don't die that easily, little kitty," the wolf with the missing ear growled.

How many other wolves are still alive? Could Sal be...? Hasefi dismissed the thought immediately and returned the wolves' loathing gazes.

"Did Vek send you to try and finish us off? Because we don't die so easily, either," she growled.

"Vek can be dead for all we care. The coward," the second wolf growled.

"Wow, you really respect your leader," Hasefi snorted. The second wolf stepped towards Hasefi, her gaze blazing.

"Vek only managed to keep the Pack together because he promised we would be able to overrun the Clan and teach those arrogant gray-furs that they made a mistake by casting us out. But Vek's promise proved empty when you did *this* to us. Now all I want is to shred you piece by piece so you can feel what I did when that mountain lion tore into me!" The mangled wolf looked ready to charge, but Kolahn stepped in front of Hasefi.

"Why don't we just stop this bloodshed? Vek had you leading miserable lives, but you don't have to keep living like that. You can find a place just like this to claim and live your days without worrying about the Clan or anything else."

"A home would be nice," the first wolf growled, his eyes glinting menacingly. "This right here looks perfect."

"Sorry. Cave's only big enough for two," Hasefi growled, moving out from behind Kolahn.

"Then all we have to do is go through you two and we already came here for that," he snarled.

Hasefi snorted. "Save your strength and leave," she told them.

"What, afraid of a little fight?" the second mocked. "You sure seemed to enjoy it when you had a mountain lion to hide behind."

"Unlike you twisted mange-furs, I don't enjoy tearing apart other creatures. I have some decency to me."

"No, you just let another creature do it for you."

"I'm tired of all this talk!" the second wolf lunged towards Kolahn, sinking her teeth into his shoulder. Kolahn let out a yelp and tried to jerk free. Hasefi swiped at the wolf's face, but the other one shoved her off her paws.

Hasefi barely managed to avoid the wolf's jaws as they clamped down where her throat had been just a heartbeat before. With a snarl, she landed a hard blow to the wolf's cheek where blood began to seep through his fur. She could feel strength entering her body, but she silently commanded her tribemates not to offer her more than was necessary.

"Just die!" the wolf barked, jumping on top of her. Hasefi was pushed into the ground with enough force the air in her chest rushed out. She couldn't catch her breath with her face buried in the wolf's thick fur and she clawed desperately, curling her claws until they caught on flesh.

When the wolf moved off of her to get a better grip, she rolled to her paws and swiped at his underbelly.

An agonized howl took her attention and she watched as the wolf fighting Kolahn buried her teeth into his throat. Hasefi launched herself towards them, latching onto the wolf's flank and raking her hind claws into her flesh until she stumbled off of Kolahn.

Teeth grabbed her scruff and she was ripped off of the wolf. She was shaken violently until her senses were scrambled and she was too dazed to move when the wolf dropped her.

"There's nothing for you to hide behind now," one of the wolves sneered in Hasefi's ear. "You're just a little lynx-kit."

I don't agree. She tried to get her paws under her, but the wolf slammed her head back into the ground, making her vision spark.

"Sefi," she heard Kolahn's voice, but it seemed faint.

"Shut up, you weak little pup." The wolf's retort was followed by a faint vibration that rippled through the ground. Hasefi moved a paw so her pad touched the ground, feeling the weak movements underneath. *Why is the ground shaking?* she thought, her mind still trying to gather itself after the blow to her head.

Kolahn let out a yelp and Hasefi started to get up again. A paw forced her down and she twisted so she could sink her teeth into it. The wolf let out a frustrated bark and she felt teeth clamp down on her broken foreleg. Hasefi cried out as the wolf pulled and her shoulder cracked.

"Del."

The wolf let go of her and looked towards the other one. "What?" he barked, blood dripping from his mouth.

"The ground is shaking."

Hasefi realized the ground beneath her was vibrating more noticeably now. The wolf standing over her, Del, glared at her.

"What are you doing?" he snapped.

"It seems you two aren't the only ones that tremble at the sight of me," she mocked. Del growled in her face and Hasefi flinched as saliva and blood sprayed her cheek. She reached up and curled her claws into the twisted flesh under the wolf's missing ear and he let out a half-pained, half-furious snarl. He backed off of her until she could slam her hind paws under his chin and send him staggering away.

Hasefi was able to get her paws under her, her legs shaking as the earth continued to vibrate. She backed away from the wolves and looked around to see if she could find an answer.

This doesn't feel new to me, she thought. *Have I felt the earth shake before?* Her gaze moved towards the cliff face behind Del as he stalked towards her. A faint cloud of dust seemed to hang over the top. Hasefi's eyes widened as realization spread through her.

"Landslide!" the wolf with Kolahn barked as dirt and rocks began to pour over the edge. Del took one look and turned tail to flee. Hasefi's gaze moved to the top of the cliff where a figure in gray armor reflecting the sunlight stood.

Sefonis.... she thought with awe.

He was facing away from her, but he soon turned towards her. She couldn't see his face beneath his helmet, but he started moving back and forth.

Hasefi frowned. *What's he doing?*

Hasefi, you need to get out of there! Kilarsa's voice roared through her mind. *It's the ancestors! They've summoned this landslide. I think they're trying to finish what they started!*

As the gifted lynx spoke, Hasefi watched Sefonis contort his body so his back was arched and his legs stuck out straight in a stance of pure terror. He vanished as a tree trunk took his place, falling over the cliff and landing near where Kolahn and the other wolf were. Reality hit her as a large rock came down soon after, killing the other wolf before she even slumped to the ground. Fear surged through Hasefi.

"Kolahn!" she cried, forcing her paws into action and running towards the wolf. Rocks and dirt spilled around them and Hasefi flinched as her pelt was bruised and cut. "Kolahn get up!" The wolf was trying to scrabble to his paws and Hasefi used her shoulder to help him. "To the cave! We'll be safe there."

"Sefi...we can't—" Kolahn's voice cut into weak coughing and she shoved him towards the cave. She could hear her tribe in her head, but she thrust aside their voices as she focused on getting her and Kolahn out of the landslide's path. A wave of dirt poured over them and Hasefi was knocked to the ground. She thrashed her legs until her head met air and clawed her way out, choking on dirt and stumbling against debris that cut into her. She found Kolahn half buried and got a hold of his scruff, dragging him towards the cave.

A heavy weight slammed the spot between her shoulders and she crumpled to the ground. For a moment, she couldn't see or breathe and thought she had been killed, but then Kolahn's limp form getting buried came into view and she pushed herself up again.

She pulled Kolahn far into the cave away from the landslide piling up outside. Hasefi slumped to the ground, her entire body in pain. She watched as the landslide filled the entrance to the cave, growing thicker and carrying more trees and large boulders. The commotion filling her mind began to clear and she was able to make out some of the voices that were urging her into action.

Hasefi! She heard her name from various tribemates, but it was Farsalim's, another gifted lynx that used his talents as a healer, that was the loudest. *If the entrance is blocked, you could run out of air.*

Hasefi frowned, too dazed to try and understand what he was saying. *That doesn't make sense.*

He's right, Dahsefer added, his normally smooth tone elevated with fear. *There is a certain substance in the air that allows creatures to breathe. If there's no way for it to flow, you'll run out and suffocate.*

Hasefi still didn't understand, but the panic in their voices stirred her and she tried to get her paws under her. *I need help,* she thought. *I'm not....* She went limp, shuddering with pain and panting with exhaustion. Dust filled her mouth and she coughed against it.

Hasefi, you need to fight.

She wasn't sure who spoke, but even as a desperate surge of strength filled her legs, she felt her mind slip away until she fell into darkness where no voice could reach her.

"Sefi. Wake up, please. Sefi."

Hasefi's eyes opened, but only darkness met her. For a brief heartbeat, she thought she might have been blind. But her experience in caves during her time in the high mountains alone kicked in and she realized she was just in a closed off chamber. *Where am I?* she thought. *The last thing I remember was going to our cave. Did Kolahn move us?*

"Sefi?"

"I'm here," she rasped.

Kolahn responded with weak coughing and Hasefi tried to move towards him. However, the moment her paws even twitched, pain rippled through her and she let out a low moan.

By the stars, everything hurts. *I don't even think I was in this much pain after I was swept away in that avalanche moons ago.* She relaxed, giving herself time to catch her breath.

"We need to get out of here," she heard Kolahn say, his voice barely a whisper.

"Where are we?" she asked, her breathing still difficult.

"We're in the cave. But the landslide blocked it. We're running out of air."

"Running out...?" Hasefi closed her eyes, understanding what Kolahn was trying to say. She recalled the words her tribe had said to her before she passed out and realization set in. *Sunblind kit!* she scolded herself. *I should have known we'd be caved in.*

The ground was still and Hasefi assumed the landslide had stopped. She prayed that it had stopped not long after the cave was blocked.

This time, as Hasefi rose to her paws, she didn't let the throbbing and stinging pains in her pelt stop her from getting up. She limped towards where she figured the entrance was and found herself climbing up dirt and rocks.

"I'll get us out," she gasped towards Kolahn. Hasefi stretched her paws as far as they would go and began pulling away debris from the entrance of the cave. She removed countless pawfuls, but each was only refilled by more dirt and rocks. She quickly began to tire, but she forced herself to keep digging, even when her claws were twisted and bloody.

I have to get us out of here, she thought. *We can't die in here! Sefonis!* To her dismay, her uncle didn't respond, nor did any of her tribemates. *I need help. Please!*

Her next pawful sent dirt running under her paws and she slipped down the pile. Dust filled her nose and mouth and she coughed, but it only became harder to breathe.

We're dying.

Hasefi moved her head towards Kolahn, trying to hear his breaths, but she couldn't hear anything over her own.

I have to keep digging. She pushed herself to her paws again and dragged herself up the pile. *Kilarsa said the ancestors sent this landslide. Are they trying to finish me off? Why do they want me dead in the first place? What did I ever do to them?* Hasefi's anger quickly changed to worry. *Is that why my tribe isn't here? Did the ancestors do something? Sefonis was up there...was he trying to stop it? Did something happen to him?* Despair crept into her and she crouched as it threatened to overwhelm her. *They tried to warn me so Kolahn and I could escape, but I might have killed us by using the cave.* Hasefi latched onto a bigger rock and pulled on it, but it didn't move. *Please,* she begged. *I can't have killed us.* The rock moved, but it fell into her chest, crushing the breath from her and shoving her back down where it rolled over her head, scattering her vision into random lights like stars. She lay, dazed, while her thoughts slowly came together in grim realization and her vision formed a dull outline of her bloodied paws.

I've killed us, she thought. *I'm sorry, Sefonis.* Her eyes began to flicker closed, but a voice pushed them open again.

Your paws, Hasefi. She frowned, unable to identify the faint voice and not understanding what was so important about her paws. She thought perhaps she had actually just imagined the voice, but then she understood.

I can see my paws. Her eyes slid up to where a tiny gap at the top of the pile choking the cave entrance shone a tiny shred of white moonlight upon the ground in front of her. Some loose dirt poured over it and Hasefi scrambled to her paws.

"No!" she choked, coughing as she clawed her way towards the hole. She stuck a paw through it as small rocks and debris poured over it, hitting her in the face. When it stopped, Hasefi began to dig again, careful to keep a paw through the hole so it wouldn't disappear again.

Before long, her legs gave out once more and she tumbled back into the cave. The hole was big enough for her to stick her head through and she decided it would be enough for now.

"Kolahn," she sighed with relief. "Kolahn, look."

The wolf made no response and she pulled herself towards the faint outline of his bulk. She gave his cheek a weak nudge with her nose, but the wolf still didn't react.

"Kolahn?" she whispered, fighting the dread that had begun to flutter in her chest. "We're free. Come over so you can breathe better." She nosed his cheek again, a little harder this time. "Kolahn, come on." She shuffled closer to him, barely noticing the blood that soaked her fur as she pressed against him. "Wake up, Kolahn." She licked his cheek, then his ears, urging him to move.

He's okay, her mind insisted. *He's just asleep. He has to be. He* has *to be.* She continued to lick his face even after her stomach twisted at the taste of blood. She could hear the voices of her tribe returning, but emotion distorted their words.

"Just open your eyes," she whimpered. "Please, you can't leave me now. We beat those two mange-furs and we escaped the landslide my ancestors sent for me. They didn't get us. They didn't take you away. Right? They didn't take you away."

Did I take you away?

A burst of defiance went through her and she got up, grabbing a mouthful of Kolahn's scruff. *I'm going to get you out. I won't let you die!*

Hasefi tugged, but she could barely roll the wolf onto his side as her broken claws scraped agonizingly on the ground and her legs shook with lack of strength. She let go and slumped beside him with a long whimper, staring at his relaxed face.

"I can't lose you," she told him. "I can't. Why does it have to be you? Why can't it be me?" She buried her face in the back of his neck, emotion overwhelming her. *Why can't it be me?* Hasefi went limp, feeling numbness creep into her heart the same way it had when she knew her tribe would no longer be able to follow the rising sun.

You have to save him, please, she thought to her tribe. *There has to be something you can do.* The voices had quieted and none of them responded to her. *Please! Dahsefer, can't you heal him?* Heartbeats passed before the gifted lynx responded.

I can no longer use my gift in your world, he admitted sadly. Hasefi wanted to snap at him, but she forced her desperate anger aside.

Sefonis? she asked. *Please, there has to be something we can do.* Her uncle didn't respond to her words. *Sefonis, why won't you talk to me?* She waited, but there was only silence. Hasefi pressed harder against Kolahn as if she could somehow force some of her own life into him.

I'm sorry, Kolahn. I'm so, so sorry.

Chapter Twenty-One

Hasefi stared at her surroundings with a heavy heart. She had managed to make the hole to the cave bigger so she could squeeze through, but she had barely stepped out when she caught sight of her surroundings.

It was the fifth sunrise since the landslide had come, the third since she'd seen the result, but Hasefi was still shocked by the devastation that lay before her.

The waterfall no longer poured water into the valley and the pool was piled with dead plants, earth, and rocks. The stream was drying up. When she followed it for a bit, she found small, muddy puddles lying still in the debris-choked path that had once carried fresh water through it. The water was undrinkable now.

The clearing was also filled with dirt and rocks and logs which had pushed over and even uprooted some of the trees on the rim of the clearing. The pile continued on into the forest just a few pawsteps away from where the stream suddenly dropped a wolf-height down.

What happens now? she wondered. *I have no idea what to do.*

The sky above was filled with dull gray clouds, making the ruined valley look even more miserable. *I could search for my tribe's origin,* she thought. *But....*

She looked behind her into the cave, but there was nothing in the faint light that reached in. With a breath, she climbed through the hole until her gaze landed on a large bulk lying on the ground.

"Sorry for not being as good of a caretaker as you've been," she murmured.

The wolf stirred, turning his head until he could look at her. "Don't be ridiculous," he told her. "You're all I need."

A purr rose in Hasefi's throat and she padded closer to him so she could nose his cheek affectionately. "How are you feeling?" she asked him.

"Everything hurts," he replied. "Breathing hurts. But I think I'm getting better," he added. Hasefi lowered her head so she could inspect the wound in his throat. She was still caught off-guard by how terrible it was, despite his quick healing—she guessed a normal wolf probably would have died to such a wound.

"Nice catch, by the way," Kolahn rasped.

Hasefi followed the wolf's gaze to the limp deer tucked away under the ledge. She shrugged. "It was old," she admitted. "And it was my fourth try."

"We'll be eating tonight because of you."

Hasefi gave another shrug.

Kolahn began getting to his paws and Hasefi jumped forwards. "Woah, slow down, you big furball. You may heal fast, but that doesn't mean you can just open up your wound again."

"I'm getting restless," he protested. "Besides, you can't hide what the landslide did forever."

Hasefi lowered her gaze guiltily. After a heartbeat, she shifted so he could use her to balance himself as he stood. Then she led him carefully up the pile in the entrance and out into the open.

When Kolahn stepped out into the light, he moved away from Hasefi and limped forwards a few steps before stopping. Hasefi watched him, her heart breaking as his head moved slowly, scanning the devastation before him.

After a while, the wolf starting moving again, following the stream. Hasefi got up to do the same, staying a few paces back. Kolahn said nothing as he walked, not even asking for help when he reached the steep drop.

I have no idea what he's feeling, she thought. *His home has been taken. He's had this for almost as long as I've been alive. I can't imagine what that's like.* Kolahn stopped when he reached a part of the stream where some murky water remained, with rocks sticking out and pieces of wood floating about.

During Hasefi's brief scout ahead, she saw that the stream had carried much of its torment along its path, showing the rest of the valley what had happened to it. But without the waterfall to feed it, the water quickly weakened until it grew still as if it, too, was mourning the destruction that had occurred.

Poor Sefonis, she thought with a quiet sigh. Not long after Hasefi had discovered the consequences of her ancestors' actions, Kilarsa had explained that Sefonis had been devastated by what they had tried to do and blamed himself for it. He'd also been terribly drained by his attempt to face the ancestors, leaving Hasefi and the other tribemates in order to risk himself to stop the ancestors. He'd barely managed to make his way back to Hasefi and the tribe and was too close to what counted as death in their realm to be able to reach out to her.

Fortunately, the gifted lynx explained she and the others like her could manipulate the tribe's energies in order to strengthen him. So now Hasefi knew her uncle was choosing not to talk to her.

I don't blame you, she thought, hoping he could hear. *It's not your fault they came after me. It's not your fault that I got hurt. That we got hurt.* She looked again to the wolf as he stared into the opaque water. His face was twisted with misery and she felt her heart crack yet again.

"I'm so sorry," she whispered after coming up beside Kolahn. He didn't respond and she retreated into silence again.

Eventually, the wolf continued walking. Hasefi slowly followed until he stopped in a part of the forest that was almost untouched by the landslide and the water was less littered. He stepped into it and knelt, letting out a sigh as the water drew away blood and dirt from his fur.

Hasefi waited as he washed, relying mostly on the water since his movements were limited. When he finished, he stepped back onto the rocky shore and joined her on the grassy patch she was sitting on.

They watched in silence as the sun sank, casting a golden glow through the trees. It wasn't until it disappeared behind a mountain that the wolf finally spoke.

"Thank you," he rasped, moving his dull gaze to her. "For being here."

"I'll always be here," she told him.

"I know. And...this was supposed to be your home, too. I'm sorry."

Hasefi shook her head at his words. "I've spent little time in this valley," she pointed out. "And, like I said before, home isn't a place for me. It's a feeling."

The wolf lowered his head. "But it still hurts," he whispered.

Hasefi shifted closer and pressed her nose to his cheek. "I know. But you'll get through it, okay? We'll get through this. Together. And..." she moved back, holding his gaze with a meaningful look. "Maybe we can find somewhere that's far away from all this danger. You mentioned the mountains flatten out eventually, right?"

The wolf nodded.

"Maybe we could see what kinds of places are out there."

The wolf gave the ground an unhappy look.

"Or we could stay in the mountains and find somewhere here. Stars, I would even go into the high mountains again if you wanted. Point is, we'll find somewhere, okay? Together." To her dismay, he still seemed unfazed by her words. Not knowing what else to do, she pressed her flank against his. He rested his chin on her head and she gave him a comforting purr.

"Thank you, Sefi," he told her. Then he drew away, not quite meeting her gaze. "But I can't go anywhere until I warn my clan."

"Okay. So we warn your clan."

Kolahn shook his head. "Not we, Sefi. Me. I have to do this alone—"

"Did you forget what happened the last time I let you go alone on some mission?" she cried with exasperation. He stepped back in surprise and she lowered her voice. "I'm not letting you go anywhere alone again."

"Sefi, this is different."

"How?"

"These are good wolves."

Hasefi snorted.

"They don't kill for the sake of it. If I say I have important information, they'll hear me out."

"How can you be so sure?"

"Because I know them. I lived with them. Please."

Hasefi shook her head. "If you're not wanting me to come because it's 'too dangerous', then it doesn't make sense. It's likely even more dangerous for you because trespassing is practically guaranteed death. But for me, I'm sure I wouldn't get more than a warning, right? What would they do to me that's worse than what they'd do to you?"

Kolahn didn't answer.

"You helped me follow the rising sun, let me help you with this."

"No," he told her firmly. "The Clan is closed off. They don't like other creatures."

"You didn't seem all that concerned when you told me to go to them if you didn't return after infiltrating the pack." Hasefi could see frustration in the wolf's eyes, but she refused to relent.

"If you could warn your tribe, would you pass the chance?"

"Not if they cast me out and threatened to kill me if I came back! They made their choice! I won't stop you from going, but I won't let you go alone." Kolahn turned away and Hasefi half-expected him to run off. "You have to understand, Kolahn," she continued, her tone soft. "I thought I lost you. In Sal's camp and then here. The way I felt…it was like I had lost my tribe again. I *can't* go through that again, okay?"

Kolahn was silent.

"I'm sorry, but you have to understand."

The wolf's mouth parted and he looked like he was going to argue, but then something passed through his eyes and he let out a long sigh. "Okay," he whispered.

"Now, before you say we should leave right away, remember that we have time before the Pack recovers. And even if there's still some angry wolves who want to flay us left, you still have to rest, fast healing or not." To her surprise, Kolahn merely nodded. "Wow, I thought I was going to have to fight you about that, too."

"You're right," he told her. "We can't keep going like this. We need to take advantage of what time we have so we aren't caught off-guard by anything else." He lifted his head and met her eye. "How about we settle down for a meal?"

"Sounds like a plan," Hasefi purred. They returned to what remained of the clearing and Hasefi climbed through the debris until she could squeeze into the cave. She dragged out the deer she had caught earlier and brought it to Kolahn where he waited in a relatively flat space she had cleared out a couple sunrises ago.

"You know," Hasefi started as she swallowed a mouthful. "You're a better wolf than the ones that cast you out."

Kolahn didn't respond.

"I just don't understand why any creature would do that to one of their own. And yet…you still want to help them. I'm not saying they deserve to suffer the Pack's wrath, but why? They left you because they just assumed you'd be like the others. Why help them?"

"To prove I'm not."

Hasefi opened her mouth, but she had no response. Instead, she gave a single nod. "Okay," she said. "How about we leave the sunrise before the full moon?"

Kolahn simply nodded.

"Right. Until then, you focus on getting better, okay?"

They finished eating and Kolahn moved into the cave to rest. Hasefi lingered outside even though she could feel exhaustion urging her to follow her friend into the cave. Pushing it aside, she sat beside the smothered pool and watched the stars appear in the sky. It wasn't until a quiet voice entered her head that her attention shifted.

I'm sorry.

For what? she asked her uncle.

I never meant for this to happen.

I know.

There was silence for a time, but Hasefi was content to wait.

I should have known they would try to harm you when we came, he told her. *I wanted to prove to them they had no control over us. But…I forgot what they could do in your world and.... I should've known. I should've known this would have put you in danger.*

Well, making a landslide isn't that *impressive, really.* Hasefi could feel confusion coming from her uncle. *I've done something like that before. Only I did it with a bit more snow.* There was a flicker of amusement from Sefonis and her whiskers twitched with delight. *And besides, if it's true they wanted me to die with you, then I'm sure they would've come after me anyways. That they still will.*

I suppose you've got a point.

Any idea why they're after me?

I wish I did, but I'm as confused about it as you are, Sefonis admitted.

I figured as much.

Silence fell, but Hasefi could feel that her uncle was feeling better than he had been.

You know, you already make a great Highchief, he told her.

You keep saying that, she told him with an amused twitch of her whiskers.

It's the truth. I'm just saddened by the fact you won't get the chance to be one.

Not a normal one, you mean, she pointed out. *I still have my tribe. You're still my champion. We may not be able to grow like we could've, but we are a tribe. We could even exist forever.*

Now Sefonis let out a full laugh. *If any creatures could pull that off, it would be us,* he agreed. *Now, you should get some rest, wee lass. You have your own wounds to recover from.*

Hasefi made no effort to argue, fully aware of the ache deep in her bones and the soreness of the cuts and bruises along her pelt. This time, she decided to relent to the heavy exhaustion pulling at her.

"Goodnight," she murmured to her uncle.

Goodnight, wee lass.

Chapter Twenty-Two

Hasefi woke up to sunlight peeking through the entrance of the cave. She was surprised to see it was so late into the day. *How long did I sleep?* she wondered, in no hurry to get up. *It was the best sleep of my life, but I didn't think I was that tired.* She lifted her head and found the cave empty. *Where's Kolahn?*

"Kolahn?" she asked, but there was no response. *He's probably just outside.*

Hasefi pushed herself up and hopped off of her ledge. She climbed out of the cave and peered around the clearing, trying to spot Kolahn's pelt against the debris that surrounded her. She found no sign of the wolf.

Maybe he's trying to hunt? Or he went down to the stream again? Hasefi trotted into the forest, her gaze scanning everything as she searched for Kolahn. After following the stream for a bit and seeing no sign of him, she stopped.

"Kolahn?" she tried again. "Kolahn, are you here?" A terrifying thought came to mind and she ran back to the cave. *What if Vek came back for him?* When she was back in the clearing, she opened her mouth to taste for scents. But the only ones she could find were his, her own, and that of stale deer. *If more wolves came here, I would've been woken up one way or another*, she reasoned. *So, Kolahn must have gone out at some point. But where?*

Hasefi brought her nose to the ground to better detect his scent. *It goes in the opposite direction of the deer, so he must not be hunting. Where has he gone? His scent isn't fresh, either.* Hasefi was about to follow it when another scent caught her attention. She opened her mouth again, barely able to taste what had stopped her. She frowned until a thought came to mind. She ran to the cave until she skidded to a halt in front of the bones that had been pushed aside to be buried next time they went out. She inhaled deeply, trying to smell past the stale scent of prey.

Chamomile, Dahsefer murmured suddenly.

What is that? Hasefi asked him.

An herb. I used it to help soothe restless lynxes so they'd sleep better.

Hasefi let out a growl and backed away from the bones. "How in the stars did he manage to trick me into eating herbs?" She glared at the entrance. "That sorry furball went off to find his clan." Hasefi raced back outside and followed the direction of his scent. It took a twisting path through the trees until eventually meeting up farther down the stream where she lost it.

He told me to follow the stream to find the Clan, she remembered. *Hopefully there isn't some other, quicker way he knows about.* Hasefi let out a frustrated snarl as she hurried along the dried streambed. *I swear by the stars I'm going to cuff his ears until they're numb when I find him. How can he care so much about a clan that cast him out? They exiled him because of his fur! Because they assumed it made him evil! Why would he want to help them so bad?*

To prove I'm not. The wolf's words echoed in her head and she let out a sigh.

You don't have to prove anything, Kolahn. Not to them. Hasefi hurried faster, hoping that the wolf's wounds would slow him down enough for her to make up for the time he had gained. *You're only going to get yourself killed.*

She tried calling out to him a few times, but there was no response. She soon entered a part of the valley she hadn't been to and grew wary that Kolahn may not be the only wolf around. *I have no idea how far away the Clan is, but hopefully it's near enough that none of the Pack is lurking around.* Nevertheless, she decided to be as silent as she could be.

He's right, you know, Sefonis's gentle voice entered her head.

About what?

The Clan won't do anything to him if they believe he has information.

How can you be so sure? Hasefi asked him, but Sefonis was silent. *I still have to go after him.*

I wasn't saying you shouldn't, Sefonis told her. *Just keep a clear head —you can't let your fear blind you.*

I know, she sighed inwardly.

When the sun began to rest behind the distant mountains, Hasefi came to the end of the forest. At her paws was a huge drop where the forest continued below.

Where in all the stars did he go? Hasefi swung her head side to side, but she found no sign of her companion. Her gaze returned to the land below and she let herself examine it.

It was unlike anything she had seen before. A large, relatively flat section seemed to have been carved into the mountains she was in, continuing to her right in the direction of the high mountains. Almost directly in the middle of the cliffs on that side, a huge waterfall poured into the forest below, spraying mist in all directions that sparkled in the dying golden light. The bottom of the fall was hidden by the trees, but Hasefi could see where a large path was cut between them and glimpses of the rapidly moving water could be seen in thinner parts of the trees.

I think that would be a river, right?

Indeed, Sefonis answered her question even though she had asked it absently.

To her left, the forest eventually faded out and the ground remained flat, allowing her to see forever. Ahead of her, the ground was similar, but it eventually sank down and she could barely make out the tops of dark trees.

Starlight, how much bigger could the world be? It looks like it goes on forever!

Hasefi pulled her attention away, looking around again for Kolahn. She tried to catch his scent, but there was nothing to indicate he had even been there.

Where could he have gone? Hasefi looked to the stream beside her and saw that, when it had been full, it would have spilled over the side. The fall wasn't as high as the side where the giant waterfall fell, but it would still have been bigger than the one by their cave.

She peered down, realizing there was an opening in the trees below. The ground fell away from the trees, creating a large rocky ravine that stretched from the side of the cliff towards the river. To her surprise, she could see movement below.

Is that it? she wondered. *Is that the Clan?* She tried to make sense of the shapes, but all she could see was light glinting off what she assumed was armor. *It must be. But how in all the stars do I get down there?*

Kolahn must know of a way, Sefonis offered.

Hasefi tried picking up his scent again.

If he didn't want you to follow, he likely used what little water is left to hide his scent. Hasefi glanced towards a still puddle in the streambed a few pawsteps from the edge.

"Clever wolf," Hasefi growled, looking around again. "But you've forgotten two things. I've been following your trail for moons. I know how you move." Something dark caught her eye and she trotted away from the water to peer at a bush with broad leaves. "And second, you're still hurt. You may heal fast, Kolahn, but you still bleed." She found more blood a few paces away and knew that the wolf had left the stream behind.

She followed his trail until she found scarlet spots leading to a narrow ledge jutting out of the cliffside. To her dismay, she could smell Kolahn's fear-scent and knew that he had somehow climbed down.

"He definitely went this way," she mumbled nervously. "Oh, Kolahn, you brave, foolish furball." She peered over the edge, hoping to glimpse the path down, but movement caught her eye instead. Shock rippled through her as she saw a black shape slink through the shadows below.

There you are! With a quick breath, Hasefi stepped onto the path and began following it down.

She wanted to hurry, but the ledge was almost too narrow for her to put two paws together. When a breeze swept by, she pressed herself against the cliffside, hoping she wouldn't be knocked off the precarious ledge. *How did Kolahn make it down there? This path would be way too small for him, wouldn't it?* Her broken leg was tucked tightly against her chest to keep from tripping over it, hoping each step she took wouldn't be her last. Every time her claws slipped or pieces of rock broke off and fell to the far off ground below, her heart leaped and she waited to feel herself plummet to her death. But, somehow, she managed to make it to the end of the path.

Unfortunately, that was only half way down the cliff.

I came down the wrong way, she thought frantically. *But Kolahn* must *have come this way! I can still smell his scent and I'm sure that was him I saw down there. Where did he go from here?* Hasefi tried to glance up, but she couldn't do so without risking her balance. *I can't even try to go back. I'm stuck!*

Be calm, Hasefi, her uncle soothed.

Hasefi opened her mouth to draw in deeper breaths until her heart wasn't pounding so hard. She crouched as best she could and tried to peer over the edge. Her vision blurred and her legs felt weak, so she quickly pressed against the rocky wall again and closed her eyes.

There has to be a way. Kolahn got down, so can I. She opened her eyes and forced herself to look down again. Her claws scraped painfully against the rock as she held on with all her strength. Then her eyes caught something that caused a breath of relief to escape her mouth.

"Thank the stars," she gasped. A ledge a little wider than what she was clinging to stuck out a few pawsteps behind where she was. Very carefully, Hasefi backed up, feeling each paw before she dared put weight on it. It seemed to take an eternity before the ledge was below her, but she knew moving back was the easy part.

Now I have to drop down. Hasefi drew in a shaky breath. *I can't hang down—my broken leg won't support me.*

We can lend you strength—

Not yet, Hasefi interrupted Sefonis. *I can't waste your energy.* She took in a deep breath. *I'm going to have to drop down all at once.* She crouched as low as she could get, staring at the spot she intended to land until her eyes ached.

I have to move now! she told herself. *Kolahn will reach the Clan at any moment. I don't know what will happen if he does, but I can't risk another heartbeat.* Holding her breath, Hasefi pushed off of where she was crouching. Her paws aimed for the ledge, her claws curling out to grab any crevice they might catch on. She felt three of her paws hit ground, but her good foreleg missed and she almost went tumbling down the side of the cliff. But her bad leg caught the side of the ledge and she rolled over before it could give out. A huge breath left her jaws and she lay limply against the rock wall for a moment, waiting for her body to stop shaking.

I think this is more terrifying than being chased by a mountain lion, she thought.

Without a doubt, Dahsefer murmured and she was surprised to find he was almost as scared as she was.

When her breaths came somewhat normally and her legs allowed her to put weight on them, Hasefi turned herself and began descending the rest of the way down. It was much easier since the ledge gradually grew wider and her steps more confident. Regardless, the moment her paws touched the grass below, a huge wave of relief passed through her.

I hope I never have to do that again, she thought as she crouched, relishing the solid ground beneath her paws. She quickly pushed herself back up when she remembered why she had endured the terrifying descent in the first place.

A burst of strength sent her flying across the grass and into the forest. The trees quickly thinned out as she came to the edge of the ravine.

He must already be down there, she thought with dismay. A large fern grew along the side and Hasefi used it for cover as she peered down into the ravine.

She could now make out strange looking wolves—creatures that had fur like her own, but were shaped like Kolahn, if smaller. Most of them wore armor that was surprisingly similar to what her tribe wore. Some bore the same kind of silver plate her uncle had while others were dressed in all black. She could tell the armor was more like that of the hunters in her tribe because it was dull and more flexible. She also spotted a couple wolves wearing soft golden armor with bands wrapping beneath their ears. *Those must be gifted wolves,* Hasefi thought, finding their robes similar to that of her guardians' and healers'.

Her eye caught one wolf in particular that stood out. Its fur was white as the snow in the high mountains with armor of the same color. It was this wolf along with several others that stood before the only black-furred wolf in the ravine. Hasefi angled her ears forwards, hoping to understand the voices floating towards her.

"You know the punishment for returning here," the white-furred wolf spoke, her voice clear with authority yet with a particular gentleness that was foreign to Hasefi. *Kolahn said her name was Eilwyn, right?*

"I know," Kolahn responded, his voice quieter and harder to make out. "But I am willing to risk my life for the sake of my clan." Even from this distance, Hasefi could hear the pain in his voice, both physical and not, and it made her wince.

"This isn't your clan, you corrupt spawn," one of the wolves wearing heavy silver sneered. Hasefi noticed a black mark on the chest of his armor.

"Kowvis, please," Eilwyn sighed before bringing her attention back to Hasefi's friend. "Why have you returned, Kolahn?"

"To warn you," he replied. "The wolves you have exiled have banded together and call themselves the Pack of the Greater Wolf. Their leader, Vek, plans to take revenge on the Clan."

Hasefi noticed that wolves were creeping out of various caves in the rock walls to watch what was happening. *No better than ravenous scavengers too cowardly to fight their prey so they wait for it to die on its own.*

"When you say Vek..." a wolf in soft black armor spoke, her voice almost too soft for Hasefi to pick up. "Do you mean Vekhil?"

"Maybe," Kolahn admitted. "When I was with them, they called me Kol."

"You were with them?" the wolf called Kowvis snapped before turning on the white one. "Not that we had any reason to trust this excuse for a wolf, but he's only proving that we can't!"

"Silence, Kowvis, or I will treat you like the pup you are acting as and send you to your den."

The wolf backed away and sat, his head low. Hasefi felt a sliver of satisfaction, but it was quickly wiped when she remembered that it was Eilwyn who had convinced Kolahn he was evil.

"It's interesting that he comes now," a wolf with soft golden armor spoke. Unlike the others with his armor that Hasefi had noticed, this wolf had a hood. *The Seer Alpha,* she thought, recalling Kolahn's words from what felt like a lifetime ago. "We were warned by the Watchers of what might follow when our stream dried up."

Eilwyn turned to him, but was silent.

"Maybe his warning has some merit," the Seer Alpha mused.

"Or he's the reason they warned us," Kowvis growled. Eilwyn snapped her gaze towards him and he ducked his head. Then she looked to Kolahn again.

"There is no way we can trust your word," she told him and Hasefi thought she could hear regret in the white wolf's voice. "Even if we could, you know the consequences of returning here."

"I know. But if I let that—"

"Lady Eilwyn!" A voice caused all the wolves to look to the left. Another wolf in black armor hurriedly approached the group from the entrance of the ravine.

"What is it?" Eilwyn demanded. "Make it quick."

"The Knight Emperor is here. He comes alone."

Hasefi could almost feel the tension that reverberated through the ravine. *Knight Emperor?* she thought with confusion. *Sefonis, that's what you are.*

Hasefi—

"Tell him he must wait," the Lady's voice rang out, now hard with anger. "More important matters than his kind accusing ours of stealing prey has come to my attention."

"No, Lady, we are beyond waiting." The voice made Hasefi's heart skip a beat, which then seemed to stop altogether as she watched another figure come into view. It was smaller than the wolves around it and it wore silver armor with black design and had a tuft of black fur on the helmet.

Sefonis?

Hasefi, wait—

Barely noticing her tribe trying to catch her attention, Hasefi ran down the side of the ravine until she reached the entrance. She burst through and halted behind the lynx that could only be her uncle, shock rooting her to the spot as she stared at him.

Alarm and anger burst through the clearing and wolves in black immediately surrounded the two of them, quickly joined by ones in heavy silver. Eilwyn came to the forefront, her strange blue eyes glittering with icy fury.

"What is the meaning of this, Emperor?" she demanded.

"You foolish kit!" the lynx spat, ignoring the white wolf as he turned towards Hasefi. "How did you follow me all the way here?

You—" he cut himself off and retreated a step. "Wait, I haven't seen you before."

"Your voice," Hasefi gasped, her own barely a whisper as she realized her foolishness. "You sound like Sefonis and…you look like him, but…you're not him." She realized she had trapped herself amidst the wolves and had little chance of finding a way to save Kolahn without asking her tribe for help. She glanced around, but the lynx before her moved close until she could see his pale green eyes through his helmet.

"Look at that, they can't even keep their kits in check," Kowvis mocked. "No wonder prey keeps escaping them."

"Sefonis," the lynx echoed, making no reaction to the wolf's words. "What does that name mean to you?" he demanded.

"Sefonis was my uncle," Hasefi explained. "I thought…y

ou were him." Disappointment flooded through her, but she was also filled with confusion. "Who are you?"

"Who are *you?*"

"I'm Hasefi."

The lynx took a sudden step back, then lifted his helmet, revealing his pale brown face. "How is this possible?" he whispered.

"What?" Hasefi asked, puzzled by the wonder glittering in his eyes.

"Sefonis is my brother."

Shock rippled through Hasefi and she stared at the lynx with realization. Her mouth wouldn't work, but it didn't have to. The lynx spoke the words running through her mind.

"Hasefi, I'm your father."

www.ingramcontent.com/pod-product-compliance
Lightning Source LLC
Chambersburg PA
CBHW060653190726
48289CB00002B/393